SHE KNEW SHE DIDN'T NEED A MAN— BUT *WANTING* ONE WAS SOMETHING VERY DIFFERENT.

After years of working in Washington for the woman's suffrage movement, Katie Jones returns to her native Idaho, where women have the right to vote, but seldom exercise it. Her arrival back home—with unpopular beliefs and the courage to voice them—throws the entire town into an uproar, inspiring some and angering many more.

Ben Rafferty, her oldest and dearest friend, proves to be her most ardent supporter . . . and possibly her downfall. For seeing Ben again sparks feelings in Katie completely at odds with her notions of women's independence—emotions her mind fervently resists, but which have her heart voting an enthusiastic "yes!"

Books by Robin Lee Hatcher

Liberty Blue
Chances Are
Kiss Me, Katie

Published by HarperPaperbacks

Harper
Monogram

Kiss Me, Katie

⋈ ROBIN LEE HATCHER ⋈

HarperPaperbacks
A Division of HarperCollinsPublishers

📚 **HarperPaperbacks**
A Division of HarperCollins*Publishers*
10 East 53rd Street, New York, N.Y. 10022-5299

———

This is a work of fiction. The characters, incidents, and
dialogues are products of the author's imagination and are not to
be construed as real. Any resemblance to actual events or
persons, living or dead, is entirely coincidental.

ISBN 0-06-108388-7

HarperCollins®, 📚®, HarperPaperbacks™,
and HarperMonogram® are trademarks of
HarperCollins*Publishers* Inc.

Cover and stepback illustrations by Jim Griffin

First printing: November 1996

Printed in the United States of America

Visit HarperPaperbacks on the World Wide Web at
http://www.harpercollins.com/paperbacks

❖ 10 9 8 7 6 5 4 3 2 1

In memory of my grandmother,
Madge Ruth Ashmore Johnson,
1880–1963
A masterful storyteller,
A farmer's wife,
A mother to four daughters—my wonderful mom
among them—
And a candidate for public office in Idaho so long
ago.
I think you would have liked Katie, Grandma.

ACKNOWLEDGMENTS

My deepest appreciation to Penny at the Idaho Secretary of State's Office; Tomas Jaehn of the Idaho Historical Library; and Mike Reynoldson, of the Idaho Republican Party, who provided information I couldn't find anywhere else.

My thanks also to my many readers who asked for one more book about Homestead, Idaho. I'm so glad you encouraged me to return so I could tell Katie's story. I hope you find her "scrumptious!"

Give me a kiss, and to that kiss a score;
Then to that twenty, add a hundred more:
A thousand to that hundred: so kiss on,
To make that thousand up a million.
Treble that million, and when that is done,
Let's kiss afresh, as when we first begun.
                    —From "To Anthea: Ah, My Anthea!"
                              by Robert Herrick

Kiss Me, Katie

Prologue

The Homestead Weekly Herald, *Homestead, Idaho
Friday Morning, May 19, 1916*

LOCAL WOMAN RETURNS TO HOMESTEAD

The Homestead Herald *has recently learned that Miss Katherine L. Jones, daughter of Mr. and Mrs. Yancy Jones of the Lazy L Ranch, is returning to Homestead after residing in the East for several years. Miss Jones was born and raised in Long Bow Valley and is a 1913 graduate of Vassar College in Poughkeepsie, New York.*

A welcome home potluck is being planned for Friday, May 26, at the Homestead Community Church. All members of the community are invited.

1

The wind tugged at Katie's hat, and mud splattered her duster as her motorcar bumped and rocked its way toward Homestead. She thought of a few choice words—in two different languages, thanks to her years at college—to describe the despicable conditions of the road between Idaho's capital city and Katie's hometown.

Not that she hadn't been warned about attempting such a trip.

"You ain't meanin' t'take that 'mobile up thataway, are you?" the old man at the hotel had asked her last night. "That road's not fit for those confounded contraptions. If'n you had a lick o' sense, you'd wait and take the train, young lady."

It certainly would have been easier to heed the man's advice, she thought as the automobile hit another rut, but she hadn't wanted to wait until Friday. The Susan B, as Katie had fondly named the intrepid—and often cantankerous—Model T Ford, had come too far, had climbed too many hills in reverse, to be left behind now.

The motorcar wasn't about to be undone by a few more deep ruts or other adverse road conditions.

Nor was Katie herself.

She thought of her father as she tightened her grip on the steering wheel. Yancy Jones wasn't going to be any too pleased when he found out his daughter had motored, unaccompanied by a male escort, across the country in her own automobile. For the past several weeks she'd been a participant in the "Suffrage Special," as it had become known in the newspapers. The mission of these gifted speakers and leaders of the suffrage movement, who were touring the West by motorcar, was to call upon women voters to help form a new political party dedicated to the passage of a national woman's suffrage amendment.

Of course, Katie had left out those "small" details when she'd written her parents about her return to Homestead. Her father was somewhat old-fashioned. Although he tried to be tolerant of his free-thinking daughter, he didn't care for many of Katie's "newfangled notions," as he put it. He would have found the idea—that his twenty-four-year-old daughter could make such a lengthy and difficult journey without the presence of a mature male to protect her—both incredulous and highly objectionable.

The front tire hit a large hole, sending the Susan B jouncing toward the side of the road and the sharp drop-off to the river below. Katie felt her hair slipping free of its pins as her hat slid sideways on her head. The end of her scarf flew up into her face, blinding her. Quickly she braked, bringing the motorcar to an abrupt halt.

Katie let out an exasperated sigh as she tried to right her touring hat, but all she succeeded in doing was loosening the remainder of her hairpins, causing her hair to tumble into her face.

"Oh, bother," she muttered in frustration. She removed the straw bonnet and shoved back the mass of hair. "I've a good mind to cut it all off." Men wore their hair short so they didn't have to be concerned with such nonsense. Maybe she *would* cut it once she got to Homestead. Nothing like a fast hairstyle to get folks talking.

With a quick twist and the jab of a few hairpins, Katie secured her hair atop her head once more, then set her hat back in place. A quick glance at the sun hovering above the canyon rim told her she'd best hurry if she wanted to reach town before dark. Although the Susan B was equipped with headlamps, it would still be dangerous to negotiate this winding river canyon after nightfall. And Katie certainly didn't warm to the idea of spending the night on the road, sleeping in the motorcar.

Besides, she was excited about getting home. It had been three years since her parents had come back east for her graduation from Vassar College, and she hadn't seen her brothers, Sammy and Ricky, in seven years. They would be young men by this time instead of the boys of ten and nine she'd left behind.

And then there was Ben Rafferty. Dearest, best, beloved Benjie. It would be grand to see him again. He was the only one who hadn't tried to dissuade her from remaining in the East, working for the National American Woman Suffrage Association. His letters while she was at school and then in Washington had been filled with encouragement. He'd always told her to pursue her dreams, no matter what stood in the way.

And that was exactly what she'd done.

She'd had dreams for Ben, too, and frankly she'd been puzzled when he'd returned to Homestead after his graduation. He could have had a marvelous career in any number of cities around the country. He could have made a name for himself, become a famous man of letters. Instead he'd gone to work for the *Homestead Herald* and then had purchased the newspaper when Mr. Bonnell, the owner, died.

But wasn't it lucky for her that he had? she thought as she pressed her foot on the accelerator and proceeded along the bumpy road, her mind churning with all she had to accomplish now that she was coming home.

Home. She was surprised how good the word made her feel. Of course, it wouldn't be the same town she'd left behind. So much must have changed. Some of the older folks had died. Some of the younger people had moved away. Most of her schoolmates had married and already had children.

What will they think of me? she wondered. But she knew the answer to that question. They would think her as strange as they always had. Katie had never fit in well. She'd always been different.

"Too headstrong for your own good," her father had told her more than once.

"Just like me," her mother had added with a chuckle. "I knew what I wanted and went after it. That's how I got your father to marry me."

Katie grinned at the memory. Yes, it was good to be coming home. Until recently she hadn't realized how much she was needed in Idaho. Not until Inez Milholland, the spirited suffragette lawyer, had explained to Katie the good she could do.

"Miss Jones," Inez had said a few months ago, "you come from one of the few enfranchised states in our Union. But are the women of Idaho exercising their right to participate in their government? I fear not in the numbers they should. We must find a way to see they do so, for all our sakes. It is women for women now and shall be until the fight is won. We shall stand shoulder to shoulder for the greatest principle the world has known, the right of self-government. Victory is in sight, Miss Jones. We must not let it slip away for lack of attention."

Katie felt a shiver of excitement roll up her spine as she recalled Milholland's words. She must not fail the women who were working so tirelessly in support of a federal suffrage amendment. She must do her part. She *would* do her part.

Her attention returned to the road as the mountains suddenly parted and she beheld her first glimpse in seven years of Long Bow Valley and, in the distance, Homestead.

Katie was home.

Ben frowned as he read over his editorial for the third time. Boring, he thought. The words were as dry as dust, pure and simple. With a sigh he dropped the papers onto his desk, then leaned back in his swivel chair and rubbed his eyes with his knuckles. He wondered if he was ever going to get it right.

Staring at the ceiling, he allowed his thoughts to drift once again to Katie Jones. Only three more days and she would be here. Damn if it wasn't about time, too.

His mother had feared Katie had been gone so long they wouldn't even recognize her. But Ben knew that was impossible. He would always know Katie, no matter how long she stayed away. Even now he could imagine her as clearly as if it were only yesterday he'd bade her good-bye at the train station as he'd left to attend school in the East. Yesterday instead of eleven long years.

He remembered the little girl with the thick black braids reaching to her waist and the enormous brown eyes that had always seemed too big for her face. He remembered the tomboy, often dressed the same as he was, in shirt and trousers, scabs on her knees, scrapes on her hands. He remembered the girl who could swing a baseball bat as hard as any boy in Homestead and who was absolutely fearless as she raced her horse alongside the train. He remembered her in a hundred different ways, and all of them made him smile.

Katie Jones was unforgettable.

Grinning, he got up and walked to the large plate-glass window. Main Street was quiet, as usual. Just the way he liked it. But even he had to admit he missed the way Katie could liven up a town. Nobody else had ever been so full of ideas or mischief. She'd gotten him in plenty of hot water when they were kids, but he'd always forgiven her. He couldn't help but forgive Katie anything.

Yes, he thought, it was going to be great having Katie home again. But she wouldn't be home until Friday's train pulled into the station, and in the meantime he had an article to write for the next edition of the paper. Reluctantly he returned to his desk.

As he sat down, he stared at the editorial awaiting him. It hadn't changed in the last few minutes while he'd been daydreaming. It was still boring, boring, boring. He picked up his pen, swearing silently that he was going to finish this tonight, even if he had to sit there until the wee hours of the night.

Maybe if he added a paragraph right here, and then—

"You're working late, Mr. Rafferty."

He glanced up, surprised someone had entered without him knowing it. The hinge was badly in need of oiling and creaked abominably whenever the door opened.

The woman in the doorway smiled softly. "Haven't you a welcome for an old friend?"

Ben stood abruptly. He knew his expression bordered on the ridiculous, but he couldn't seem to stop himself from staring in disbelief.

"Have I changed so much?"

Had Katie changed? *Yes!* When had she become a woman? A beautiful woman? And despite the flecks of mud on her cheeks and clothes, she *was* beautiful. She hadn't been beautiful before, had she? Ben didn't think so. She'd just been Katie.

A frown replaced her smile. "Well, for pity sake, say *something.*"

He moved out from behind his desk, stepping toward her, studying her face for some sign of the gawky school-girl he'd remembered. Her eyes were the same luminous dark brown, but they no longer seemed too big for her face. Her complexion was smooth, her skin the color of honey. She was still tiny, a good foot shorter than he was, but she was noticeably more curvaceous than the girl he'd left behind. The braids were gone, he suspected, but he couldn't be certain because of the broad-brimmed hat and scarf she wore.

"Have I *really* changed so much?" she asked again.

"I can't believe it's you."

Her dazzling smile returned. "It's me all right, Benjie." Then, without warning, she threw herself into his arms and kissed him on the cheek as she hugged him tightly. Her laughter warmed the office like a fresh ray of sunshine. "Oh, Benjie, it's so good to see you."

Suddenly he laughed with her, all else forgotten. "It's good to see you, too, Katie." He set her back from him, his hands still on her upper arms. "How did you get here? You're not expected until Friday."

"I arrived in Boise City yesterday and decided to drive up. My motorcar is out front."

"You *drove?*"

"All the way from Washington. I've been following the 'Suffrage Special' on its tour of the West in the Susan B."

"The Susan B?"

Katie took hold of his hand and drew him toward the door. "She's my Ford Touring Car. I named her for Susan B. Anthony, of course. Come take a look at her."

This was Katie all right, he thought as he followed her out onto the sidewalk. Leave it to her to be the first valley resident to own an automobile. Leave it to her to motor clear across the country, and to heck with the convention that said a woman didn't do such things.

"There she is," Katie said proudly, waving an arm toward the Model T Ford parked in front of the *Homestead Herald* office. "Isn't she scrumptious?"

He lifted an eyebrow but echoed, "Scrumptious."

Katie squeezed his fingers as she turned toward him. "Will you drive out with me to the Lazy L? I'm sure Papa will loan you a horse to get back to town, and I'd love to talk with you awhile. It's been so very long since we've seen one another, and I want to catch up on all the news. Letters just aren't the same as hearing things firsthand."

"Don't want to face your father alone, huh?"

She lifted her chin defiantly. "That's not it at all."

"No?"

"No."

"No?"

Katie pursed her lips for a moment, then broke into a smile. "All right. Maybe that is it. A little. But *just* a little." She stepped closer, and he caught a whiff of rosewater. "Honestly, Benjie, I do want to talk with you."

When he was twelve and Katie just shy of eleven, Ben had kissed her. They'd been up on the ridge near Tin Horn Pass, and she'd said she didn't know what made grown folks want to get married, but maybe it had something to do with kissing since her father was always kissing her mother. She'd wondered what all the fuss was about, so they'd decided to find out. Afterward they'd decided kissing wasn't anything special. Certainly nothing they'd ever cared to try with each other again.

That had been a long time ago, and Ben had kissed more than a few girls since then. Now he found himself wondering if Katie had discovered, as he had, that kissing wasn't so bad after all.

"Say you will, Benjie," she prompted. "Please?"

Memories of Katie saying those very same words rushed over him—*Say you will, Benjie. Please?*—and he knew it was useless to argue with her. She would get her way before she was through. It had always been so between them.

He nodded. "Let me get my hat and lock up."

While Ben was inside, Katie let her gaze wander the length and breadth of Main Street. She was surprised by the welling up of emotions inside her at the sight of her hometown. She hadn't thought she wanted to return to Homestead, to leave her friends and the intense activities of Washington for the quiet sameness of Idaho. Yet now that she was here, she was glad.

She heard the door close, and she glanced at Ben as he stepped up beside her.

Homestead might not have changed much, she thought, but the same couldn't be said for Ben Rafferty. He'd grown tall, and his shoulders were amazingly broad beneath the cut of his suit coat. The angles of his face had sharpened, matured. The boyish good looks had more than fulfilled their promise in the man he'd become. The color of his hair—which brushed his collar, begging to be trimmed—had darkened to a rich shade of gold, and she thought it a shame when he placed his hat on his head, hiding it from view.

"Ready?" he asked, glancing down and meeting her gaze.

She felt a sudden embarrassment, as if she'd been caught doing something inappropriate.

"Katie?"

She saw a teasing good humor in his dark blue eyes, and her embarrassment vanished. This was Benjie. This was her dearest friend in the world. He had grown up, just as had she. It was only natural she would notice the changes in him, as he had in her.

"I'm ready," she answered.

Ben took hold of her arm. "Mind if I do the driving?" he asked as he guided her toward the passenger door.

She cast a dubious look in his direction.

"I *know* how to drive, Katie. I went to college, too."

It was on the tip of her tongue to tell him she never allowed anyone else to drive her motorcar, but his next words caused her to swallow the argument unspoken.

"You wouldn't withhold the pleasure from me, would you?" He ran his fingers along the side of the door. "It's been a long time since I've had such an opportunity."

"Of course you may drive her, Benjie. Anytime you wish."

Grinning like a schoolboy, Ben reached inside the automobile and pulled the latch, then opened the door with a flourish and assisted Katie onto the running board and into the Susan B. When she was settled and the door once again closed, he went around to the driver's side, reached in, and set the levers. He whistled a tuneless melody as he walked to the front of the motorcar and gave the engine crank a hefty turn. Without a trace of her sometimes temperamental behavior, the automobile sprang quickly to life.

Straightening, Ben shot Katie a look of pure joy before returning to the driver's side, where he vaulted over the stationary door and settled onto the seat behind the wheel. A few minutes later the two of them were well on their way to the Lazy L Ranch.

Ben had forgotten just how much he enjoyed sitting

behind the wheel of an automobile. Homestead had a way of making one forget there was a whole other world beyond this valley and the surrounding mountains. Maybe it was good to remind himself of that fact every so often.

Overhead, dusk splashed the smattering of clouds with shades of pink, announcing the coming of night.

"The headlamps are electric," Katie said softly.

Her voice drew Ben's gaze in her direction. She was holding on to her hat with one hand while the fingers of her other hand fiddled with a button on her duster. He wondered if she was nervous about going home.

Hoping to distract her, he asked, "It hasn't changed much, has it?"

She looked at him. "Homestead?" She shook her head. "No. Not much."

"Surprised?"

This time she smiled. "No. Not really." She took a quick breath, then said, "Tell me about the newspaper."

"Nothing much to tell. It's still a weekly. I do everything but the typesetting. Harvey Trent does that. Harv's the best typesetter west of the Mississippi. He used to work for the *Idaho Daily Statesman,* but I lured him away." He chuckled to himself, remembering how hard it had been to convince the man to move to Homestead. Ben had succeeded only after Harvey started sparking Esther Potter, the proprietress of Zoe's Restaurant.

"Do you write all the articles and columns?"

"Yes."

"It must be a great deal of work. Week after week. Maybe you should hire a columnist to help you."

"A columnist?" He had a niggling suspicion.

Katie met his gaze and flashed him another smile. "Don't you think a woman's column would be of interest to your readers?" Before he had a chance to respond to her question, she continued, "Of *course* it would be of interest. Women read your newspaper, too. Don't you think they would enjoy a column from a woman's perspective?"

"And just who would write this column?" As if he didn't know.

She twisted on the car seat, then leaned forward, touching his arm. "Oh, Benjie, there is so much they need to hear about. Do you know how fortunate the women of Idaho are, to be able to vote? But so many just waste that right. It's a right that should be exercised, but they throw it away, leaving it up to men to decide what happens in our country. If only we could make them see—"

"*We?*" He allowed the automobile to roll to a stop.

Katie's eyes danced with excitement. "Yes. *We.* Don't you see how much good we could do? You own the newspaper, and I have so much to share about my work. I've met some of the most distinguished and gifted women in the country. Even now they're calling upon women voters of the enfranchised states to—"

"Hold up a minute, Katie."

Her expression sobered.

Ben searched his mind for the right words. It wasn't that he didn't support suffrage for women. He did. A woman's vote was as valid as any man's.

But he wasn't certain Homestead—or the rest of Idaho, for that matter—was ready for Katie's firebrand variety of women's concerns. Katie never did anything halfway. He didn't need a fortune-teller to know she would stir up a hornet's nest in no time.

And there he'd be, smack dab in the middle of it.

Her fingers tightened on his arm. "Benjie, you mustn't disappoint me." Her voice was low and earnest. Her gaze never wavered from his. "I need your help."

He looked away, staring off toward Tin Horn Pass and the darkening skyline. "Katie—"

"You know I wouldn't ask if this weren't important to me."

A woman's column. Perhaps it wasn't a bad idea. The *Homestead Herald* did lack some sort of sparkle. Katie would no doubt give it that.

"I received very high marks in composition while at Vassar College, Mr. Rafferty, and I'll be happy to provide references related to my work experience and performance, should you require them."

He glanced back at her, but the light had grown too dim to tell if she were teasing him or not.

"Benjie." Her voice had lowered still further. "Papa has opposed so many of the things I've wanted to do. I need someone to support me in this."

That was it, then. There was no point in trying to fight it any longer. "Do you have a title for this proposed column of yours?" he asked as he placed his hand over hers.

Katie leaned forward and kissed his cheek. "As a matter of fact, I do," she answered a moment later. "I plan to call it 'Unshackled.'"

"'Unshackled?'"

"Isn't it wonderful? Penny—you remember me writing you all about Penelope Rudyard?—she thought of it. Penny said women must be unshackled from the restraints that have bound them for centuries, but before they can break free they must first realize they're in bondage. That's what my column will do. Help women see the truth. Do you like it? Don't you think it will catch women's attention?"

"Oh, Lord," Ben whispered to himself. To Katie he said, "I'm going to have to give it some thought. I'll let you know my decision."

*   *   *

Yancy Jones leaned against the stall gate and watched the newborn filly struggle to rise. His boys, Sam and Rick, stood on either side of him, just as they'd done at many animal birthings through the years.

"She's a fine one," Sam said, drawing his father's gaze to the right. "'Course, Shadow always produces good foals. Best brood mare we've got on the place."

Yancy's oldest son was a lot like Yancy himself. Sam didn't talk to fill a silence. He spoke when he had something to say or he was quiet. Just as it should be. The boy didn't hold with fancy things like telephones and automobiles, and he didn't have an urge to see anything but what was right here. He was most comfortable on the back of a horse, surrounded by cattle. He had one interest: the Lazy L Ranch.

"Say, Pa. What did you decide about that barn dance over in Rock Creek on Saturday night?" Rick interjected. "Are we going?"

Yancy turned his head to the left and looked at his younger son. Unlike his brother, Rick showed little interest in the ranch these days. His attention was centered entirely on fillies of the human variety. It didn't take a genius to read the lust in the sixteen-year-old's eyes whenever girls were around. If the boy didn't get himself in a world of trouble before he was grown, Yancy would be surprised.

"Can't go," Sam answered. "Katie gets home on Friday."

"Well, maybe she'd like to go to the dance," Rick argued.

"She'll be too tired, dummy."

"You don't know that, stupid."

"Boys," Yancy interrupted sternly. "That's enough."

The silence was sullen as his sons glared at one

another. Eventually both turned to look at the filly and her dam, leaving Yancy to his own thoughts.

Katie gets home on Friday.

Just her name could tie Yancy's heart in a knot. His Katie. His little girl. He'd longed for the day she would return home, yet he dreaded it now that it was about to happen.

Yancy didn't understand his firstborn child at all. Katie confused him. She angered him. She frustrated him. Katie, with her wild ideas of what the world should be like. Katie, the modern woman. Katie, with her causes. Katie, his little tomboy. Katie . . .

The dog started a racket out in the yard, interrupting Yancy's troubled musings.

"Sam, go see what's botherin' Josie."

"Sure, Pa."

Yancy raked his fingers through his graying hair, then set his hat back in place. He was just about to open the gate and step into the stall when Sam's voice stopped him.

"Pa, it's an automobile! And it's headin' our way!"

Rick was off in a flash, running to join his brother. Yancy hesitated a moment, then followed, muttering a few private thoughts about how unwelcome automobiles were in Homestead.

Katie's heart raced as the Susan B puttered slowly along the road toward the Lazy L, the way lighted by the electric headlamps. The ranch house stood at the end of the road, a black silhouette against an even darker backdrop of mountains. Golden light spilled through the windows, looking warm and inviting.

She felt a tumble of nerves as she leaned forward on her seat. Odd. This was her home, yet she suddenly felt like a stranger. She'd left this place a girl and had come back a woman. Would everything at the ranch have changed as much as she? But Homestead was still the same. Could the Lazy L be so very different?

As if he'd read her mind, Ben said, "Everyone's missed you, Katie. They'll all be glad to have you home."

Will they? she wondered, but she didn't voice her worries aloud.

Actually she was concerned only about one person: her papa. It had been such a very long time since he'd approved of anything she'd done.

She straightened on the car seat and folded her hands in her lap. She wasn't responsible for her father's feelings or actions. She was responsible only for her own. She was doing what was right for her. She was doing what was right for the cause. If her father couldn't see that—

She swallowed hard as she saw two male figures run into the light from the house. They were joined a moment later by a third man. Once again Katie leaned forward, straining to see more clearly. Could Sammy and Ricky have grown so tall, or were those some of the ranch hands? Were they men she would know, or had her papa hired new cowboys to work the place? Was one of them Papa himself? Then a woman—it had to be her mother—stepped onto the porch, and Katie's heart skipped a beat in anticipation.

As the motorcar rolled into the yard, Katie heard a shout. "It's Katie!"

The car stopped, and everyone rushed forward.

The next few minutes were a blur of hugs and kisses and exclamations. Her brothers had, indeed, grown tall—so tall, her feet left the ground when they hugged her. Her mother smelled of lemon verbena, just as Katie remembered. And her father . . .

Yancy cupped the side of her face with one work-roughened palm. "I reckon I'm as pleased as a flea in a doghouse t'have you home, Katie Lark. 'Bout time, too." Then he hugged her tightly.

I love you, Papa, she thought, but her throat was too tight to say it.

"Where'd you get the automobile, Ben?" Rick asked.

"It belongs to Katie."

She felt her father stiffen. Then Yancy stepped back from her. "Yours?"

She nodded, holding herself as straight and tall as possible. "Yes." She drew a deep breath, then added, "I drove it up from Boise City this morning."

Rick whistled. "You *drove* it up? All by yourself?"

She never let her gaze waver from her father's. "It's not such an amazing thing. Driving an automobile is really quite simple. Even for a woman."

An all-too-familiar expression settled on Yancy's face, and Katie knew now was not the time to tell him she'd motored all the way out from Washington in that very same automobile.

Her mother placed an arm around Katie's back. "Let's not stand out in the night air any longer." Lark drew her daughter toward the house. "Katie has had a long trip and a tiring day. Ben, would you like some coffee?"

"No, thank you, Mrs. Jones. If I can borrow a horse, I'll be getting back to town. I've still got some work to do at the newspaper."

Katie stopped and glanced over her shoulder. "Thank you for driving me out, Benjie."

"I was glad to do it." He winked at her, then added softly, "It's good to have you home, Katie."

She felt a warm glow of happiness as she smiled at her lifelong friend. "Thanks, Benjie."

Nobody but Ben Rafferty had ever understood how hurt Katie was by any disapproval from her father.

There'd often been times she'd wished she were different, when she'd wanted so much to be what she thought her father wanted her to be. But she was who she was, and Ben, at least, accepted her just that way.

"Stop in at the newspaper when you're settled," he told her.

"I will."

Yancy set off toward the barn. "Come on, Ben. I'll get you that horse."

Katie watched as Ben followed her father across the yard, disappearing into the shadows of night. She'd missed him. All these years, no matter what she'd been doing or where she'd been living or who her other friends were, she'd always missed Benjie. He'd been her rock throughout her childhood. No matter who else had criticized her, Benjie had been there to restore her faith in herself and in her dreams. She'd disappointed her father many times during her almost twenty-five years, but Ben had never seemed disappointed by anything she'd said or done.

Katie had returned to Homestead on a mission. She had important work to do in Idaho. She'd come because the National American Woman Suffrage Association needed her here, just as they needed dedicated workers in all the enfranchised states. But she wondered if she would have had the courage to return if Ben Rafferty hadn't been here, too.

Her mother's arm tightened around her shoulders. "Come inside, dear. It's turning cold."

Katie glanced at Lark, and her niggling doubts dissipated. "It's good to be home, Mother," she whispered. "So very good to be home."

2

Katie awakened to the song of a robin outside her open window. Smiling contentedly, she snuggled deeper beneath the warm quilt, reluctant to get up just yet. Slowly she became aware of other sounds besides those of the bird.

The bark of a dog. Josie was her name. Just a year old and as yet without manners or the good sense not to bark so early in the morning.

Men's voices. Laughter, good-humored and low. The sort of laughter peculiar to men when they think there's no woman within hearing distance.

The snort and stomping of horses as they milled in the corral.

The strident bawling of a calf, probably lost from its mother.

A screen door slamming closed.

The creak of a loose board on the front porch.

Katie opened one eye. Morning sunlight slipped between the curtain and the window casing, bright and promising, a reminder that she was wasting time abed.

With a sigh of resignation she pushed aside the sheet and quilt and sat up on the bed, then drew her knees to her chest beneath her nightgown as she gazed about the room. This had been her bedroom for most of her life, and trappings of girlhood were everywhere. Dolls, never played with, lined a shelf along one wall. Dresses that were now too youthful in style filled the wardrobe. A jump rope, frayed at one end. A black satin pouch, filled with her favorite marbles. A baseball and bat.

For some reason, these things were both familiar and foreign to her. It seemed to Katie that the girl who had lived in this room years ago had been someone other than herself.

A light rapping sounded. "Katie?" came a muffled voice from the other side of the door.

"Grandma?"

Katie hopped out of bed and hurried across the room. She yanked open the door before her, and there stood Addie Rider, Katie's maternal grandmother. Addie opened her arms, and Katie moved into them, just as she'd done countless times as a girl.

"Oh, Grandma, it's so good to see you."

After a tight hug, Addie held Katie at arm's length and inspected her with that schoolteacher's gaze of hers. Finally she gave an approving nod. "It's mighty good to see you, too, my darling girl."

Katie took her grandmother by the hand and pulled her into the bedroom. "Come and sit. You look absolutely scrumptious, Grandma. I've missed you so much. It's been weeks since I got your last letter. How's Grandpa Will?"

"Your grandfather is fine. His back bothers him more than he cares to admit, but Will's always been the stubborn sort." Her faded green eyes twinkled, and Katie could tell her grandmother was looking back through time. Then Addie gave her head a shake. "But it's not your grandfather I've come to talk about. Let me have another look at you."

Obediently Katie stepped back and turned slowly, her arms held out at her sides.

Her grandmother clucked her tongue. "I do declare, Katherine Jones. You became a woman while you were away." She sat on the edge of the bed, then patted the mattress. "Now, sit and let's talk. I've missed our chats."

"So have I. More than you know."

"I hear you've brought an automobile back with you."

"Yes, and Papa wasn't any too pleased about it."

"No, Yancy wouldn't be. You know how protective he is."

"*Over*protective, you mean."

Addie chuckled. "It's only because he loves you."

"I know."

And Katie *did* know her father loved her. If only he could approve of her, too. *That* she was certain he did not.

"I suppose all the men in this family tend to be overprotective," her grandmother continued. "Perhaps it's one of the things that attracts us to them, even when it makes us crazy at the same time. Your grandpa always was trying to take care of me, as if I didn't have a mind of my own. And it was the same with your mother and father, although in a different way." She paused thoughtfully, then added, "It'll be interesting to see what sort of man you choose to marry, Katie Lark."

"But I don't plan to marry."

Her grandmother raised an eyebrow.

"Truly, I don't. For centuries, women have been subject to the whims and demands of men. We are on the verge of gaining the right to vote throughout this country, but the work won't stop there. We must have women willing to sacrifice for the cause of freedom for all, just as Miss Anthony did. That's what I've dedicated myself to. It's my calling."

"My!" Addie placed the palm of one hand on her chest, as if shocked by Katie's emphatic and impassioned declaration.

Katie leaned forward. "You of all people should understand, Grandma. You came out here all by yourself, a schoolteacher facing a brand-new challenge. You lived in your own small cabin, and you earned your own way. You didn't marry just because it was expected of you."

"No, Katie, I didn't. I married your grandfather because I fell in love with him."

"Well, love is a fine reason for women to marry, I suppose. But marriage just isn't for me, so I simply won't fall in love."

"Were it only that easy," her grandmother said softly. After a moment she added, "Speaking of marriage, you must have heard Ben is courting the Lutheran minister's daughter."

Katie felt an odd twinge in her chest. "No, I hadn't heard. He didn't tell me."

"Well, it's nothing official, of course, but everyone expects he'll ask Miss Orson to marry him before the summer's out."

"Benjie married . . ." She let the words drift into silence, disquieted by the sense of loneliness that swept over her. It shouldn't surprise her, shouldn't matter to her. But for some reason, it did.

After a few moments Addie asked, "So what do you intend to do now that you're back?"

Katie straightened and met her grandmother's gaze. "You won't believe it. I'm going to write a column for the *Herald.*" Excitement returned. "I talked to Benjie about it yesterday, and he agreed that I could. A column for women. Not about how to make an apple pie or starch a shirt properly or any of those old things. My column's going to be about woman's suffrage and how politics are as important to us as to men."

Addie chuckled as she gave her head a slow shake. "Oh, dear. Does your father know about this?"

"Not yet. And you mustn't tell him. Promise me, Grandma, that you won't say a word. I want him to be surprised, to read it with an open mind."

"Oh, I wouldn't think of spoiling the surprise."

Katie tilted her chin. "This is something I mean to do, Grandma. I don't care if Papa likes it or not."

"I can't guess what he'll think." Addie leaned forward and kissed Katie's cheek. "And I reckon you'll do it no matter what, just like you say. You're as stubborn as any of the men in this family. And then some."

Ben leaned against the awning support in front of the hardware store. "Headed for the dress shop again?" he asked his sister as she and her fiancé came toward him on the sidewalk. "Matthew, are you certain you can afford such a wife? Sophia's likely to drive you to the poorhouse."

Sophia gave him a dark glance, but Matthew Jacobs merely agreed in good humor. "It's true. My income from the Book Shoppe is meager." He patted Sophia's hand where it rested in the crook of his arm, turning a doting gaze upon her. "But every bride should have new dresses with which to begin her married life, and we're thankful your father has been so generous. I'll have little enough means with which to spoil Sophia after we're married. I guess I should have had greater ambitions than to be a small-town shopkeeper."

"I'll have everything I desire, Matthew," Sophia told him sweetly, "as long as I have you."

Ben rolled his eyes but kept silent. It was useless to tease these two lovebirds. They would just go on billing and cooing as they'd been doing for months. Thank goodness the wedding was a mere two weeks away. He wasn't certain how much more of it he could take. Still, there were moments when he envied the two, when he wondered what it might be like to be so in love that one forgot all else.

Suddenly a passing carriage horse reared in its traces. Its shrill whinny split the air. As the horse bolted, the driver, Norman Henderson, shouted a curse that caused Sophia to blush bright red. Ben turned to see what had caused the commotion, and there came the Susan B down Main Street—puttering, popping, and choking—and drawing the attention of all within sight.

He should have known it was Katie causing the furor.

"My stars," Sophia whispered. "Is that *Katie?*"

Ben grinned. "It is indeed."

"She's driving an automobile," Matthew said incredulously.

Ben's smile broadened. "That she is."

Katie brought the Model T to a stop in front of the three of them. "Hello," she called out, her face aglow, her expression only moderately sheepish. "It seems I've upset Mr. Henderson's horse."

"*And* Mr. Henderson." Ben stepped off the sidewalk and offered his hand to help her out of the motorcar.

Her dark brown eyes twinkled as she slid across the seat toward him. "I suppose I should apologize to him," she whispered without the slightest note of remorse.

Years ago, Ben and Katie, with the encouragement of the three Henderson brothers, had set off firecrackers underneath the farmer's porch in the middle of the night.

Norman Henderson had raced out of the house in his striped nightshirt and nightcap, waving his shotgun and cussing a blue streak. Luckily for them all, he'd never found out who was to blame. Otherwise they'd have all faced a tanning they wouldn't have forgotten.

As Katie placed her hand in Ben's and disembarked from the motorcar, Ben wondered if she remembered that episode, too. But the memory was quickly forgotten when he saw what she was wearing—bright pink cycling bloomers!

Katie released his hand and stepped onto the sidewalk, obviously unmindful of everyone's stares.

And Ben, for one, couldn't stop staring. The Turkish-style trousers extended to just below her knees, and the white stockings she wore did little to hide her shapely calves from view. He could be wrong, but he thought they were probably the first pair of adult female legs ever purposely revealed on Homestead's Main Street. Certainly they were the prettiest it had ever been Ben's good fortune to look upon.

Katie gave Ben's sister an enthusiastic hug. "Sophia, it's so good to see you. I heard you're getting married." She turned toward Matthew. "May I offer my congratulations, Matthew. You're getting a wonderful bride."

Matthew Jacobs mumbled a greeting while Sophia continued to stare in wide-eyed silence. With a curtness bordering on rude, Matthew nodded, bade both Katie and Ben good day, then led his intended down the sidewalk.

After the couple disappeared into Madeline's Dress Shop, Katie looked at Ben. "I've written my first column," she announced. "I hope you like it." She held out several sheets of paper that were covered in neat script.

"I wasn't expecting anything this soon," he said, taking the papers from her.

"No point in dallying, Mr. Rafferty. I take my obligation to the newspaper and to the people of this valley quite seriously."

He lifted one eyebrow. "Ever think of writing a fashion column?"

Katie laughed as she glanced down at her attire. "Do you suppose your sister is ordering an identical outfit this very moment? I noticed she couldn't seem to take her eyes off mine. And Matthew was obviously overwhelmed."

"Katie, you're the limit."

"So I've been told. Quite often, in fact."

Ben loved the way her brown eyes sparkled when she laughed. He loved the gentle bow of her mouth when she smiled. He'd always thought women looked ridiculous in cycling bloomers, and the color would have been unsuitable on anyone else. But Katie looked wonderful, bloomers and all. Her hair was tied back at the nape with a pink satin ribbon. Wisps had pulled free to curl around her face, giving her a wild, abandoned look. Had she always had such an adorable, heart-shaped face and turned-up nose and—

"Well?" she prompted. "Are you going to read it?"

"Read what?"

"My column." She frowned, tilting her head to one side. "Benjie, are you all right?"

To be honest, he wasn't sure. He was feeling mighty peculiar at the moment. As if the lunch he'd eaten at Zoe's Restaurant weren't sitting too well.

Katie leaned forward, still frowning. "Benjie?" Her black hair smelled of rosewater and gleamed with blue highlights in the midday sun.

He blinked and gave his head a quick shake. "I'm all right." Then he held up the papers between them. "I'll go and read these right now." He took a step backward, but the faint scent of roses lingered in his nostrils and the odd feeling remained in his midsection.

He muttered a sudden farewell, then turned and strode quickly along the sidewalk toward the offices of the *Homestead Herald*.

Maybe he wasn't all right, he thought grimly. Maybe the roast beef had been bad. Or perhaps it was due to too little sleep last night. Or maybe it was Katie's bright pink bloomers.

Lord! Didn't she have *any* common sense? Didn't she know how folks in Homestead would react? An automobile *and* bloomers! Why, she would be lucky if she weren't drummed right out of town, Katie and her injudicious clothes and outrageous ideas.

He heard the Susan B come to life and stopped, glancing behind him in time to see Katie slide across the seat, then back the automobile into the middle of the street and drive away.

He swore softly. He didn't want others looking down their noses at Katie. He wanted them to see her as he did—like a forest sprite, free and wild, full of life and laughter. He supposed it would be up to him to save her from herself, just as he'd done time and again through the years.

His irritation vanished as quickly as it had come, and he smiled ruefully. Come to think of it, he'd rather missed saving Katie Jones from herself. He'd certainly had no greater challenge. Not even owning the newspaper provided the same sorts of tests and trials Katie did.

Madeline Percy stared out the window of her dress shop, her wrinkled face flushed with indignation. "Well, I never," she puffed. "When Reverend Percy hears of this . . ." She shook her head, then turned toward her customers. "Matthew, I expect your father and my husband shall both have a few words to say from their pulpits about the devil's work come Sunday."

"I should think so," Matthew replied.

Sophia wanted to protest. Katie Jones had always been different from other girls in Homestead, but she wasn't bad. She was simply . . . not ordinary. Naturally Sophia couldn't approve of the other woman's choice of apparel, but she couldn't help being fascinated by it, either. Still, she kept her thoughts to herself. She didn't want to disagree with Matthew.

Madeline stepped behind the counter and reached toward a large box on the shelf. "Her father should lock her in her room until she learns some modest behavior. But I suppose we shouldn't any of us be surprised. That girl was always a strange one, and going off to attend college has only made it worse. If you ask me, women have no business in college. They can get all the education they need at home. That's where they belong until they find a husband." She clucked her tongue. "Thank heaven for levelheaded young men such as you, Matthew Jacobs. At least we can rest assured that you would never allow your wife to wear such inappropriate clothing."

"No, indeed I wouldn't."

Sophia felt a flash of irritation but again kept silent. She and Matthew never disagreed on anything. They never argued. Not ever.

"Now here is what a respectable young woman wears in public," the dressmaker said as she pushed aside the tissue paper and lifted the dress from the box.

Sophia hated the unadorned white dress upon sight, despite the fact that it was in the height of fashion this season.

"Step into the back, dear, and try it on," Madeline said as she held it out to Sophia.

Sophia thought of Katie in her pink bloomers and suddenly wished she had the courage to wear something just like them. But she knew she wouldn't dare. She wouldn't do anything to displease Matthew. She wouldn't ever risk making him angry with her. It would have been unthinkable.

Still, as she walked into the back room and closed the curtain, she couldn't help wondering what it must have been like for Katie to go to college, then live and work in Washington, D.C. Sophia had visited her grandparents in San Francisco a few times through the years, but she could scarcely imagine living in such a metropolis. The idea both frightened and intrigued her.

"Thank the good Lord I need never worry about my Sophia being anything other than an obedient, God-fearing wife," she heard Matthew say. "The Raffertys have brought her up properly."

Sophia paused to stare at her reflection in the cheval glass. *Matthew's obedient wife.* Was that who she saw before her?

Yesterday she would have considered her fiancé's confidence in her a compliment. Even this morning that would have been true. But now? Now it left her feeling strangely uneasy.

His obedient wife.

Wasn't that what she was supposed to be? What she wanted to be? Wasn't that what was expected of all women when they married?

Of course it was.

Then why did Matthew's words make her think of a faithful hunting dog, doing its master's bidding? Why did she suddenly want to toss this dress in his face and order a pair of cycling bloomers?

She gave her head a swift shake, driving off the unsettling thoughts. With her wedding only two weeks away, she wasn't about to let anything spoil her happiness. Not even her own unexpected misgivings.

Nestled in a grove of trees to the west of town, the Rafferty residence stood tall and stately, the most elegant house in all of Homestead, as befitted the town's wealthiest family. But it was also a home filled with love and warmth, and Katie had many fond memories tied to it.

"We've missed you, Katherine," Rose Rafferty said as she refilled Katie's coffee cup.

"I've missed all of you, too, Mrs. Rafferty. But I suppose Benjie hasn't gotten in nearly as much mischief since I've been away."

Rose chuckled as she settled onto the chair across from Katie. "No, he hasn't. In fact, he's become quite the serious businessman." Her smile faded. "Actually, I think his work consumes him. Far too much. He seems to live in his office. I realize the newspaper means a great deal to him, but still . . ." Rose's words drifted into silence.

Katie frowned. "I always thought Benjie would go to work for one of the large newspapers in the East."

She remembered the times Ben had read stories to her about places like Chicago and Boston and New York City or even Paris and London and Rome. It had always seemed to her that it was Ben who was destined to see other places and then to write about them. She'd never known anyone as quick to grasp things as Ben Rafferty. With his intelligence and golden good looks, she'd been certain he would make a name for himself in the newspaper world.

"I'm glad he chose to return." Rose leaned forward and patted Katie's hand. "I've seen how hard it's been on your mother, having you so far away from home for so long. When the time comes for my children to marry and start their families, I want them all to be close to me."

There was that curious feeling in Katie's chest again. "Do you expect Ben to marry soon?"

"I don't know. For several months he's been keeping steady company with Charlotte Orson, but he hasn't said a word to me about his feelings. He can be quite close-mouthed sometimes, you know."

"She must be new to Homestead. Charlotte, I mean."

Rose nodded. "I'd forgotten you haven't met. You've been away a long time, Katherine. Charlotte and her father—Mr. Orson is the reverend of the Lutheran church over on South Street—they moved here nearly four years ago. She's a lovely young woman. I'm sure you'll like her when you meet her."

For some inexplicable reason, Katie was even more sure she *wouldn't* like Miss Orson.

Unexpectedly Rose frowned and wagged her finger at Katie. "I suppose you know you spoiled your mother's surprise by arriving the way you did."

"Yes, I know. Sammy said Mother arranged for the town band to greet me at the depot. I don't know whether to be disappointed or not. Does Mr. Leonhardt still play the tuba?" She could almost hear the off-key *oom-pa-pa*, could almost see the red, puffed-out cheeks of Mr. Leonhardt.

Ben's mother smiled, sharing the memory with Katie. "He does, and you'll still have the pleasure of listening to him. The ladies of the Morning Glory Circle are going ahead with our potluck supper in your honor, surprise or no, and the band is going to be there."

Katie let out an exaggerated groan and covered her ears with the palms of her hands.

Rose laughed. "Fanny McLeod promised to make some of her wonderful huckleberry pies."

"Mmm." Katie lowered her hands and rolled her eyes in ecstasy as she savored her favorite dessert in her imagination. "It's been years since I've tasted huckleberry pie."

"And no one makes them like Fanny."

"No indeed." She grinned. "I guess I can stand Mr. Leonhardt's tuba in exchange for some of Mrs. McLeod's huckleberry pie."

"I thought you'd say that, Katherine. Some things never change."

3

The next afternoon, Ben drove out to see Katie. As his buggy horse trotted along the road, he rested his forearms on his thighs, the reins looped through his fingers. His gaze swept over the gently rolling valley toward the mountains in the east. He couldn't see the house or outbuildings belonging to Yancy Jones, but he could see plenty of Lazy L cattle. He'd always liked the sight of the sluggish bovines grazing in pastures of knee-high grasses. It was just one of many things he'd missed when he was away from Homestead.

Ben had quickly discovered, during his school years back east, that this was where he belonged. Things were changing fast everywhere else. Even now many European countries were at war, and Ben suspected the United States wouldn't be able to avoid participation much longer. But here in Long Bow Valley, life continued as it had for decades.

He grinned, remembering Katie as he'd seen her yesterday, standing beside her automobile in her pink bloomers. Maybe everything wasn't the same as it had always been. And maybe some change wasn't bad.

He glanced at the folder on the seat beside him. In it was Katie's column. He'd been pleasantly surprised by what she'd written. It wasn't a firebrand diatribe on the national suffrage situation, as he'd been expecting. It was a story about pursuing one's dreams, and it was warm, witty, and well crafted. He'd had to do little editing, which he knew would please Katie. Harvey Trent was busy typesetting the article at this very moment for tomorrow's edition of the paper.

Ben's horse and buggy crested a small rise, and the Lazy L came into view. The two-story white clapboard house had been added on to several times over the years as the Jones family grew and their fortunes improved. The additions had given the home an odd shape, but the place had always appealed to Ben. Perhaps it was because it wasn't fancy or pretentious. It had a lived-in look that somehow defined the word "home."

As if she'd been expecting him, Katie stepped onto the front porch. She lifted her arm and waved, then hurried down the steps into the sunshine. She wore a black-and-white shirtwaist, an attractive dress that accentuated her feminine curves. Her head was uncovered; her black hair—long and lush and gleaming with bluish highlights in the sun—was captured by a ribbon at the nape.

Ben found himself wondering once again at the changes time had wrought in Katie Jones. He also wondered at the way those changes made him feel.

"You must have known I was thinking about you," she called as he entered the yard.

"Were you?" He drew his horse to a halt.

She smiled. "You know I was. And you know why."

He grinned in return. "I guess I do at that."

"Well?"

"Well . . ."

She walked to the side of the buggy and touched his thigh. "Tell me. What did you think?"

"It's good, Katie. You've got a real talent."

She beamed. "Do you really think so?"

"Yes."

"Oh, Benjie, you can't know how much your opinion means to me. You've always been so wonderful with words."

Had he? Then why was he feeling at such a loss for them at the moment? He couldn't seem to focus on anything except Katie's fingers on his trousers, warming the skin beneath. The touch left him feeling strangely disoriented.

"Come inside. Mother made lemonade before she went over to Grandma and Grandpa's."

"I could use a drink," he mumbled. "It's a bit warm for this time of year."

"I suppose it is, but I'm ready for summer." Katie led the way toward the house, talking all the while. "It was a harsh winter in Washington. The building where I worked was terribly drafty, and the house Penny and I share is sometimes even worse. Then, of course, there was the trip out here. Most of the time, I love the Susan B, but when it's cold—" She ended her sentence with a laugh.

Following after her, Ben tried his best to concentrate on what she was saying rather than noticing the gentle sway of her hips or the way her skirts caressed her ankles as she walked.

He suddenly found himself comparing Katie to Charlotte. Where Katie Jones was petite and shapely, Charlotte Orson was tall and willowy. Where Katie's coloring was dark, Charlotte's was pale. Where Katie's personality was outgoing and vibrant, Charlotte's was quiet and contained. Katie's energy sometimes created a drain on those around her; Charlotte's presence brought peace. Katie seemed to pull against society at every turn; Charlotte lived easily within the boundaries of her world.

"I haven't told anyone except Grandma Addie about my column," Katie said, drawing him abruptly from his reverie. "Will it be in tomorrow's paper?" She stopped just inside the kitchen and glanced over her shoulder, not waiting for his reply before asking her next question. "Do you think Papa will be pleased, Benjie?"

"I don't see why he wouldn't be." His throat felt dry.

Her brown eyes darkened with worry. "There isn't much I do that *does* please him. He already hates the Susan B."

Katie seemed suddenly fragile and easily bruised, so unlike the girl Ben remembered. "You've always been too sensitive when it came to your dad," he said gently as he reached out and briefly touched her sleeve. "The automobile is new to him. He'll get used to it. And you're *not* a disappointment, Katie."

"Not to you, maybe, but you've always understood me better than anyone. You've never made me feel . . . different."

But you are different, Katie. Maybe that's what I love about you most.

Love? The notion caught him by surprise, almost stopped his heart.

But why should it? He *did* love her. He always had. And she loved him. In her letters, she called him her "beloved Benjie." Love was only one of the words that described his friendship with Katie. There were so many more—trust, laughter, camaraderie, loyalty. She was closer to him than his own sister was, understood him better than anyone else he knew. He hoped the same was still true for her.

Katie smiled, chasing the worry and vulnerability from her eyes. "Sit down, Benjie, and let me get you your lemonade. And then you can tell me how truly wonderful and exceptional my first column for the *Herald* really is."

Ben laughed. His tension eased. It wasn't so strange that he should love Katie. Who wouldn't?

Addie Rider looked at her daughter, sitting across the table from her in the large kitchen of the Rider home, staring down into her coffee cup. Lark Jones was a handsome woman who looked much younger than her forty-three years. Her dark hair had yet to reveal even a touch of gray, and there was a soft curve in the corners of her mouth that bespoke a lifetime of contentment and happiness.

Looking up, Lark caught Addie watching her. "It's good to have Katie home again," she said, as if needing to explain her pensiveness.

"When I saw her, I couldn't believe how much she'd changed. I suppose I wanted her to stay the girl of seventeen we saw off to college, but she's all grown up." Addie chuckled. "She reminds me a great deal of you when you were that age."

"I was never as independent as Katie."

"How can you say that? If you hadn't been, you'd never be married to Yancy today." Addie leaned against the spindle-backed chair as she shook her gray head. "Remember the night you told me you were in love with him?"

"I remember."

They both smiled.

"I didn't think I'd ever forgive Papa for punching Yancy over a kiss," Lark added.

"And I didn't think he'd ever relent and let the two of

you marry. If it weren't for your stubborn independence, he wouldn't have."

Lark's expression sobered. "I wish Katie would fall in love and settle down. I don't want her leaving again. And she's so caught up in this cause of hers, I think she's forgotten about what's really important in life. Home and family and love."

"You're wrong about that, my dear." Addie rose from her chair and went to the large black stove to retrieve the speckled coffeepot. She carried it to the table and refilled both cups with the strong, dark brew. "Katie has a good head on her shoulders. You and Yancy raised her well. When she finds the right man, she'll want all the right things with him. You'll see."

"Sometimes I think we allowed too much. She was always pulling so hard against what she was expected to be. Maybe we shouldn't have allowed her to go away to college. Maybe—"

"Lark Rider Jones!" Addie exclaimed as she set the coffeepot back on the stove with a clunk. She turned a disapproving gaze on her daughter. "You stop that nonsense right this instant. You and Yancy have been wonderful parents to your children. Katie has a heart big as the sky. She's working hard for something she believes in, something that will help other women. She knows right from wrong. Why would you want her to be any different?"

Lark stared back at her mother, her expression changing slowly to chagrin. "I wouldn't change her. You know that." She sighed softly. "I just want her to be happy. I don't want her to miss out on what her father and I have had."

Addie rounded the table and put an arm around Lark. "She'll have to find her own way to it, my dear. All you can do is stand by and be supportive. That's all any parent gets to do when their children grow up. And it's hard on all of us."

Blanche Coleson kept a close eye on her pupils as they filed out of the small schoolhouse at the end of each day. Personal experience had taught her that to lower her guard was to leave herself open to all kinds of practical jokes. Especially from the older boys.

Miserable heathens that they were.

She ran her fingertips over her hair, checking for any truant strands. There weren't any. She hadn't expected there to be. Blanche Coleson allowed no disorder in her very orderly life.

When the door closed behind the last departing student, Blanche let out a long sigh, then rose from her chair and set about cleaning the blackboards. Afterward she wrote the next day's math problems on the side blackboard and the next day's language questions on the blackboard behind her desk. When all was in readiness, she claimed her handbag and lunch pail, put her straw hat on her head, and left the school.

The town of Homestead provided its schoolteacher with two rooms above Yardley's Drugstore as part of her wages, and that was where Blanche went at the close of each school day. Her walk home took her past Berchtwald's Watch Shop, Long Bow Billiards Saloon, and Carson's Barber Shop. Occasionally she would stop in at Berchtwald's and allow the old German to verify the accuracy of her watch, but never did she so much as turn her head in the direction of the billiards saloon. Such a place was suitable only for the lowest forms of humanity. Which meant, of course, that it was a suitable place for men.

Main Street bustled with activity this time of day. At least for Homestead it was bustling.

Across the street, Sophia Rafferty hurried along the sidewalk toward the Book Shoppe, no doubt so she and Mr. Jacobs could stand behind one of those tall shelves and kiss. Scandalous! And he a minister's son who should know better. Disgusting!

Several men loitered outside the hardware store, making Blanche thankful her lodgings were on this side of the street. There was little she hated as much as having to walk past a group of idle males and feel their gazes on her. It positively made her skin crawl.

Vincent Michaels, the town's lawyer, drew his buggy to a halt outside the sheriff's office. Blanche wondered on whose behalf he was making his call, then thought with some disgust that if the sheriff and lawyer were doing their jobs properly, she wouldn't have to be concerned about men who loitered outside the hardware store.

She had nearly reached the outside staircase leading up to her two-room apartment when Rose Rafferty came out of the drugstore, stopping her progress.

"Good afternoon, Miss Coleson," Rose greeted her. "Is school out so soon?"

Blanche checked the watch pinned to her bodice. "The same time as always. Precisely four o'clock."

The other woman chuckled, acting as if Blanche had said something amusing. Then she shook her head. "Sometimes I swear the days get shorter every year. Don't you find it so?"

"Twenty-four hours have always been twenty-four hours, Mrs. Rafferty. Now, if you'll excuse me . . ." Blanche turned toward the side stairway once again.

"We will see you tomorrow evening at the potluck supper for Katie, won't we?"

She paused and glanced over her shoulder. "I'll be there, Mrs. Rafferty. I've been looking forward to making Miss Jones's acquaintance for quite some time."

Rose bade her farewell then, and Blanche was at last able to retreat to the privacy of her rooms. As she removed her hat and set it on the small table near the door, she found herself thinking about Katie Jones. It was no exaggeration to say she was looking forward to meeting her. She'd heard the young woman had been working for the National American Woman Suffrage Association in the nation's capital for some time. It was even said Miss Jones personally knew such women as Inez Milholland, Lucy Burns, and Alice Paul. Blanche would give almost anything to be able to say the same about herself. Of course, if she'd been born to a privileged family, she too might have attended Vassar and traveled the country and met such dignitaries from the suffrage movement instead of being stuck in some backwater Idaho village like Homestead, teaching school to a group of ungrateful brats.

But then, life often wasn't fair to women. Blanche Coleson had always found it so. And she despised all men because of it.

The day had taken on a special glow for Katie as she'd sat in the kitchen, reminiscing with Ben. She'd found herself thinking again how much he'd changed. He was taller and even more handsome than the teenager she'd remembered. But he was the same, too. His dark blue eyes revealed his enthusiasm and intelligence. His smile came slowly but was real and honest. And he could still spin a story like no one else Katie knew.

She'd soon been wrapped up in the lives of the people of Homestead, some old friends and some strangers to her. The one name that hadn't come up that afternoon was Charlotte Orson. Katie had been curiously glad of that, and she'd prudently avoided asking Ben about the Lutheran minister or his family—especially the reverend's daughter.

It caught her by surprise when her father and brothers traipsed into the kitchen, brushing off the dust of a day's labors. Somehow an entire afternoon had slipped away, and she hadn't begun to prepare supper as she'd promised her mother.

"It's my fault, Mr. Jones," Ben volunteered in a valiant attempt to shoulder the blame. "I've been monopolizing Katie's time." He rose from his chair. "I've just hired her to write a column for the newspaper."

"A column?" Yancy's glance shifted from Ben to Katie.

She nodded.

Her father watched her in silence for what seemed an eternity, then gave a slow nod.

A spark of joy ignited in Katie's chest in response to his tacit approval. She'd been so certain he wouldn't condone her new endeavor. Of course, he hadn't seen the title of her column yet, nor did he know what she intended to write about next. Still, it was a step in the right direction.

"Listen," Ben interjected, "since it's my fault your supper isn't ready, why don't we all go into town to eat? My treat."

"All right!" Sam and Rick exclaimed in unison.

"I don't reckon that's necessary," Yancy began.

"I insist, Mr. Jones."

"Come on, Pa," Rick urged.

"It'd be a nice treat for Ma," Sam added. "She's been workin' mighty hard on tomorrow night's doin's for Katie's homecomin'."

Yancy looked from one young person to the next, then

admitted his defeat. "Looks like I'm outnumbered. Guess we'll accept your invitation, Ben. Soon as Lark gets home, we'll come into town."

Rick let out a whoop. "Can we ride in Katie's motorcar?"

"No." The single word brooked no argument and spoke volumes about Yancy's sentiments toward the Susan B. "We'll take the surrey, as usual."

Katie wanted to kick her brother for mentioning her automobile. There had been a moment, however brief, when she'd felt she and her father were taking a step toward mending the invisible breach between them. Judging by the expression on his face, that moment was lost.

Why can't I ever seem to please you, Papa?

"Katie," Ben said softly, "I'd like you to come back to town with me. I'll show you around my office and introduce you to Harvey Trent. We can meet your family at the restaurant later."

She looked at him, grateful for his understanding. "I'd like that, Benjie. Thank you." She glanced back at her father. "Do you mind, Papa?"

"No. Go on ahead," he said gruffly.

Katie turned toward the kitchen door. "I'll just be a moment while I get my hat." Then she hurried from the room.

A short while later, she was seated in Ben's buggy, the horse pulling them away from the Lazy L. Katie stared ahead with unseeing eyes, lost in thought. She was remembering all those times, as a little girl, when she'd sat on her papa's lap and he'd hugged her and told her how special she was.

Why couldn't he still think she was special? When had she become such a disappointment to him?

It was Ben who broke the lengthy silence. "It will get better, Katie."

"Do you think so?"

"Yes."

She glanced at the man beside her. "I'm not going to change, Benjie."

"No one's asking you to."

"Papa is."

"I think you're wrong, Katie. Give it some time. You've only been home a couple of days."

She let out a long sigh. "He always makes me feel that I've failed him in some way. I can't be what he wants me to be."

"And what do you think that is?"

She gave a helpless shrug. "Something I'm not." She added with a weak smile, "Something I don't even want to be."

4

The Homestead Weekly Herald, *Homestead, Idaho*
Friday Morning, May 26, 1916
KATIE JONES TO PEN WEEKLY COLUMN FOR
WOMEN;
"KATIE'S CORNER" DEBUTS ON PAGE THREE OF
THIS WEEK'S HERALD

The Homestead Herald *is pleased to announce the debut of a new column of interest to our women readers. The column will be written by Miss Katherine L. Jones, daughter of Yancy and Lark Jones of the Lazy L Ranch. Miss Jones, a graduate of Vassar College, has recently returned to Homestead after several years in the East, where she was active in the work for passage of a national woman's suffrage amendment.*

In addition, articles of specific interest to our women readers will now be found in the "Women's News Department" on page three of every edition of the Herald.

The door to the *Homestead Herald* flew open, crashing against the wall. Ben jumped up from his desk, but not before Katie entered the office, waving a copy of the newspaper in her right hand.

"'Katie's Corner'?" She spat out the words as if they were poison. "You called my column *'Katie's Corner'?*" She slammed the door closed, then marched toward him, fury in every step.

He grinned. He wasn't surprised to see her. In truth, he'd been wondering what had taken her so long to get there. "I thought it had a nice ring."

"How could you do it, Ben Rafferty?" She dropped the paper onto his desk. Her eyes flashed with anger as she rested her fists on her hips. "It sounds like a column about canning peaches or quilt making or something. Exactly what it *won't* be, and you know it."

He considered letting her fuss and fume a little longer. He was enjoying the way she looked, her cheeks infused with indignant color, her mouth set in a stubborn line. It reminded him of the time she'd punched Elmer Henderson after he'd shoved Esther Leonhardt into a mud puddle. Katie, about eight years old at the time, hadn't thought twice about attacking the much larger boy.

Come to think of it, she looked mad enough to start punching again. Only Ben would be the target this time.

"Think about it a moment, Katie. You'll catch more flies with honey than with vinegar."

She raised her eyebrows skeptically.

"If you put a heading like 'Unshackled' on your column, you'll lose some of the very readers you want. They'll think it too radical. You might even have some husbands refusing to allow their wives to read it."

"What right has any man to refuse his wife to read anything she wants to read?"

Ben leaned forward, placing his knuckles on his desktop. "Probably none, but a lot of them would do it anyway."

"All the same—"

He cut her off. "All the same, you know I'm right."

She dropped her gaze to the newspaper on his desk. Her shoulders slumped as her anger dissipated. "But 'Katie's Corner'?" she said with just a hint of a questioning whine. "It's so . . . so *bland.*"

"But the column won't be bland, and that's what matters."

Katie considered his comment in silence.

"What did your father think of it?" he asked, knowing he was striking the winning blow.

A gentle smile curved the corners of her mouth. "He said it was very good. I think he was proud of me."

Ben felt an odd tightness in his chest. *I'm proud of you, too, Katie.*

Her sudden laughter caught him by surprise. "You should have been a politician, Mr. Rafferty. You maneuvered me quite expertly." Her eyes sparkled with mischief. "You won't manage it so easily in the future, I promise you."

For some unknown reason, Ben once again recalled the time he'd kissed Katie up at Tin Horn Pass.

As if reading his mind, Katie took hold of his hand. "I was planning to saddle one of the horses and ride up to the pass today. Come with me."

He glanced down at the stack of papers on his desk.

"You can spare an afternoon," she added before he could voice an excuse.

He couldn't refuse. He didn't want to. But before he could voice his acquiescence, the door opened again, this time slowly, accompanied by its usual squeak.

And there, in the opening, stood Charlotte.

Her gaze flicked from Ben to Katie to Ben again. Uncertainty filled her pale blue eyes.

Ben felt an odd combination of irritation and guilt as

he pulled his hand from Katie's and stepped around his desk, then crossed to the door. "Come in, Miss Orson. There's someone I'd like you to meet." He gently took hold of her elbow and drew her into the office. "Miss Orson, this is Katie Jones. Katie, Charlotte Orson."

Charlotte's smile was as gentle and sweet as her voice. "I'm so pleased to meet you, Miss Jones. I've been hearing stories about you ever since I arrived in Homestead. Ben's always telling my father and me about what trouble the two of you got into as children."

Ben wasn't sure what he saw in Katie's eyes. Vulnerability? Irritation? Whatever it was, she hid it a split second later.

Katie held out her hand. "I'm sure none of those stories have painted me in a particularly flattering light, Miss Orson. I hope they won't influence you adversely."

"On the contrary," Charlotte answered with an airy laugh, "I am predisposed to like you very much."

Charlotte's smile remained even after the handshake ended. "Your column in today's paper was wonderful. That's what I came to tell Mr. Rafferty."

"Thank you."

"I know everyone will be talking about it at the potluck tonight." Charlotte turned to look at Ben. "I would never have the courage needed to write for a newspaper. Would I, Mr. Rafferty? I'm much too shy."

Ben could think of nothing to do except nod in agreement.

"Well," she continued, "I didn't mean to disturb you. You two were probably discussing Miss Jones's next column, and here I am intruding on your business."

"Not at all," Katie interrupted quickly. "I was just leaving." She glanced at Ben. "I'll see you tonight." Then she was gone.

Ben walked over to the large window that looked out onto Main Street and watched Katie start the Susan B with a quick crank, then hike up her skirts and climb into the motorcar. As she drove away, his thoughts drifted to a day eleven years before.

The August sun beat down unmercifully upon the platform of the Homestead train depot. Ben felt the sweat trickling down his spine, but he didn't know if it was from the heat or from nerves.

"You're certain you have everything?" his mother asked again.

"I'm sure."

"You didn't forget to pack your—"

"Rose," Ben's father interrupted, "stop fussing over the boy." Michael Rafferty placed his hand on Ben's shoulder. "You'll do fine."

Ben wished he thought so. He'd been waiting for this day for what seemed an eternity. Now that it was here, he wasn't so sure he wanted to leave Homestead. Higher education didn't seem quite so appealing when it meant leaving all one knew.

Katie took hold of Ben's hand and drew him away from the two families—the Raffertys and the Joneses—who had come to see Ben off. When they reached the corner of the depot, she stopped and reached into the pocket of her dress—something she usually wore only to church and to school. "I want you to have this." She held out her favorite marble. "Maybe it'll bring you luck."

"You don't have to do that, Katie."

"I want to." Her dark eyes filled with tears. "I'm gonna miss you, Benjie," she whispered.

He gave one of her long braids a quick tug. "I'm going to miss you, too. But I won't be gone so long. You'll see."

"It's not fair, you going off to school and me being stuck here. I want to go with you."

"Reddington Academy is just for boys. And after that I'll be at Harvard. Girls aren't allowed there."

She stuck out her chin. "That's not fair, either."

Ben didn't know what to say to make Katie feel better. How could he make her understand this was just the way things were?

"What if you don't ever come back?" she asked softly.

"Ah, I'll be back, Katie. Don't you worry about that. I gotta come back to see you, don't I?"

Charlotte touched Ben's forearm. "I can see why you've missed her."

He blinked and looked at the woman beside him. He'd forgotten she was there.

What was the matter with him? he wondered. It wasn't like him to spend time woolgathering.

Charlotte smiled her sweet smile. "I'll see you at six?"

"Six? Oh, yes. I'll be at your home at six o'clock."

Her complexion pinkened just before she rose on tiptoe and placed a kiss on his cheek. "Good day, Mr. . . . Good day, Benjamin." Then she lowered her eyes and excused herself, rushing out of the office with quick, silent footsteps.

And Ben was left once again thinking how different Charlotte and Katie were—and uncertain why it mattered to him.

Katie's column was the subject of conversation in many kitchens and places of work that day. Everyone seemed to be surprised that the irrepressible Miss Jones had written such a warm and gentle piece, although there were many who were relieved by it.

"I'd say your brother put her in her proper place,"

Matthew Jacobs told his fiancée when they met for lunch at the hotel's restaurant.

Sophia felt a stab of disappointment. "Do you think so?"

"Of course. Ben couldn't let her write anything fanatical for the *Herald*. The men of Homestead wouldn't stand for it."

"The men of Homestead," she repeated beneath her breath.

"What that young woman needs is someone to take her in hand," Matthew added. "A husband is just what she needs. Although who in his right mind would want to marry Katie Jones, I can't imagine."

Sophia straightened on her chair. "Matthew, what an unkind thing to say."

"It's nothing but the truth. Katie isn't exactly wifely material."

She felt hot. *And I am, no doubt!*

"The good Lord alone knows what sort of disreputable behavior she's practiced while in the East," he continued, oblivious of Sophia's anger.

"A college education is not a sin, Matthew Jacobs."

He looked surprised. "I didn't say it was."

"No, but you implied as much."

"Did I?" He shook his head. "You must have misunderstood me, my dear. It isn't a sin, although I do believe it to be a waste of time and money. What will Katie do with all that learning once she's married?"

"What if she doesn't marry? You just said no man in his right mind would want to be her husband."

"No indeed, but it would be better for her if she would marry. She needs someone to remind her of her proper place." He shook his head slowly. "I'm glad you've had better sense than to befriend her as your brother has. And I'm more than a little surprised he's continued that friendship, considering how things are between him and Miss Orson."

Sophia pushed away her plate, her appetite lost. "Why shouldn't Ben continue to be friends with Katie? They've been close since they were babies in the nursery."

"Isn't it obvious?"

"No, Matthew, it isn't. Please explain it to me."

He sighed deeply. "Your brother has an important standing in this community. The Raffertys have always been one of the town's most influential families, and now Ben owns the newspaper. He has the ear of many, and his opinions are known far beyond this valley. He has a responsibility to the citizens of Homestead. Renewing a childhood friendship with that disreputable young woman would be betraying his responsibility."

"Katie isn't bad, Matthew. She's merely high-spirited."

"Be that as it may, I want you to keep away from her. I won't have your reputation tarnished by her crazy antics."

"Am I allowed to speak to her at the potluck supper tonight?"

But Matthew didn't seem to notice the sarcasm so evident in her terse question. "Well, of course, my dear. We needn't be rude."

Had he always spoken to her like this? Sophia wondered as she stared at her fiancé across the table. Had he always treated her like a dense child?

She felt more than a little unsettled by those questions.

It had been years since Katie had donned a pair of boy's trousers, sat astride a horse, and galloped across open fields as if racing the wind itself. She'd forgotten just how good it could feel.

Katie had enjoyed many sorts of freedoms while in

Washington, but riding like this hadn't been one of them. There'd been little time to pursue personal pleasures. The intensity of their work had been all-consuming for the women of NAWSA, Katie first among them.

As she reached the top of the pass, she reined in her mount, then twisted in the saddle to look at the scene below. Freshly turned earth and spring green pastures checkerboarded the land. Pony Creek, like a blue ribbon, wriggled and wound its way toward the mouth of the mountains at the opposite end of the bow-shaped valley. In the center was Homestead, small and neat, a tidy and safe community, tucked away from the hurry and bustle of the rest of the world.

If Ben were with her, he would have said this was why he'd returned. She could almost hear him saying it. "This is where I belong, Katie."

She wished she could say she belonged here, too, but she couldn't. She didn't know where she belonged. If there was such a place, she hadn't found it yet.

She gave her head a sudden shake. What a preposterous thought! She knew exactly where she belonged. Wherever the cause needed her most, that's where. She belonged right where she was, doing the work she was doing. And it was high time she gave more thought to what she'd come back to Homestead to accomplish.

Katie dismounted and started walking along the ridge, leading the small bay mare by the reins.

Her first column for the *Herald* was a success, judging by her father's reaction as well as Miss Charlotte Orson's. She had tried to prove women could have whatever they wanted, if they would but pursue it. She'd wanted to let them see that dreams could come true, if only one knew what to dream.

Her next column would need to be more specific. It had to have more punch, more grit, more reality than hope. But Ben was right about catching more flies with honey than with vinegar. She must learn to be subtle.

She smiled. Subtlety had never been one of her virtues. *Charlotte Orson is probably subtlety personified.*

Katie's thought brought her to an abrupt halt. She glanced over her shoulder at the mare, as if the horse had voiced the comment.

"Who wants to be subtle?" she asked aloud.

The animal stared at her in unblinking silence.

"Do you suppose he's going to marry her?"

More silence.

"Well," she said as she turned and began walking once again, "I shouldn't be surprised if he does. She's terribly pretty."

She pictured Ben and Charlotte as they'd looked standing side by side in the newspaper office, both of them blond haired—his the shade of a gold piece, hers as pale as wheat at harvesttime—and both of them blue eyed. They would no doubt produce beautiful, fair-haired children.

She kicked a rock out of her path, feeling suddenly irritated with Ben Rafferty—and not because he'd named her column "Katie's Corner." No, she was angry for something even she couldn't define.

And she had the feeling it would be best if she didn't even try.

The ladies of the Morning Glory Circle had done themselves proud. The Homestead Community Church had never looked as festive as it did for the potluck supper that night. Dried flower arrangements decorated each of the tables, thanks to the talents of Miss Maud Leonhardt. Lacy tablecloths, courtesy of Leslie Blake, covered the rough wood tables. Rose Rafferty had provided her silver tea service and elegant china for the occasion.

Nearly the entire population of Homestead and the surrounding valley had turned out to welcome Katie home. The hall buzzed with voices as men grouped together to discuss farming and politics and women busied themselves laying out the dishes of food while keeping an eye on their respective offspring.

Ben was standing with Reverend Orson; Albert Tobias, Homestead's mayor; and the three Henderson brothers— Isaac, Elmer, and Andrew—when the Jones family arrived. He saw Katie pause just inside the doorway. Her gaze swept the room, not pausing until she found him.

Ben smiled.

She smiled back.

"My daughter was quite right," Obadiah Orson said. "Miss Jones is an attractive young woman. Not at all what I'd expected after the tales I've heard."

Charlotte appeared at Ben's side, as if summoned by her father's comment. After sharing a glance, she moved past the small gathering of men, smiling warmly as she walked toward Katie.

"Hello again, Miss Jones. Everyone's been awaiting your arrival. Good evening, Mr. and Mrs. Jones." Then, as naturally as if it were her own home, Charlotte took on the role of hostess, drawing Katie into the church hall and introducing her to one and all.

Charlotte's warmth and her kindness to others were just two of the traits that had drawn Ben to her. She was patient with old folk and children alike. She never uttered a cross word. In fact, he couldn't recall ever seeing a frown crease her forehead. She was the picture of serenity.

So different from Katie.

As his gaze shifted to that night's honored guest, he remembered the way Katie had stormed into his office that morning, her eyes sparking with fury, her cheeks flushed. Katie did everything with passion. He wondered if she ever knew a moment of serenity.

Isaac Henderson let out a low whistle. "I never thought she'd grow up t'be so pretty." He elbowed Andrew in the ribs. "Did you?"

"You kiddin'?" the youngest Henderson brother answered. "I can't hardly remember her wearin' a dress, let alone cleanin' up so nice. What about you, Elmer?"

Elmer chuckled. "And t'think she gave me a shiner. Come on, boys. Let's get reacquainted."

The urge to pass out a few shiners himself almost overwhelmed Ben.

He stared at Katie in her dark blue tubular skirt wrapped with filmy scarves, noticed how the outfit accentuated the curve of her hips and thighs, and again he remembered the rough-and-tumble tomboy with her unruly black hair.

Why hadn't he expected Katie to grow up? Why was he so surprised by the changes in her? And why was he so bothered by them?

Albert Tobias shook his head and grinned. "Haven't seen those Henderson brothers so excited since their pa brought home that prize bull last year. You wait and see. There's going to be a lot of traffic goin' back and forth to the Jones place this summer."

"I do believe you're right, Albert," the reverend answered. "I do believe you're right."

Ben was prone to agree, and the idea left him feeling more irritated by the second.

Katie couldn't remember ever enjoying herself as much as she did that night. Being welcomed home. Feeling awash with acceptance. Hearing she'd been missed by so many people. She'd almost forgotten what it was like to be known so well by so many. Here in Homestead she wasn't lost in the masses. She was one of the community.

Over the course of the evening she stuffed herself on the good home cooking provided by the ladies of the Morning Glory Circle—which Katie was invited to join as soon as she was more settled. She cooed over new babies and marveled at the handsome toddlers of her former classmates. She listened to Homestead's band play and managed not to wince when Mr. Leonhardt's tuba hit its usual sour notes.

And she observed Ben with Charlotte.

She wondered why he'd never written to her about Charlotte. He'd never so much as mentioned her name, even though, according to others, they'd been keeping company for some time now. Katie had thought Ben shared everything with her in his letters, yet it was clear she'd been wrong. There were some things he'd chosen not to share. Charlotte was one of them.

Katie wanted to dislike the woman. Perhaps it was because the minister's daughter was everything Katie's father had ever wanted Katie to be.

And apparently Charlotte was everything Ben wanted, too. Throughout the evening they were nearly always together. They sat beside each other as they ate supper. Charlotte's hand was often within the crook of Ben's arm as they visited with people of the community. There was a rightness about the look of them as a couple.

Yes, Katie wanted to dislike Charlotte Orson. But it seemed it was impossible *not* to like her.

Especially if she made Ben happy.

5

Katie chewed on the end of the pencil while glaring at the white sheet of paper on the desk. Her second column was not going well. She kept thinking about Ben's advice. How on earth did she couch the unpleasant truth about the conditions of women in honeyed terms to keep it from sticking in the craws of the newspaper's readers?

She dropped the pencil onto the desk, then rose from her chair and began pacing her bedroom, hands clasped behind her back. The voices of so many women rang in her head, those softer voices of the National American Woman Suffrage Association and the more strident tones of the Congressional Union for Woman Suffrage. How did she make those words palatable to the readers of the *Homestead Herald*?

She stopped abruptly. Palatable? Was that her job? To make woman's suffrage *palatable* to the readers of her column or to any of the men and women of Long Bow Valley?

Most assuredly not! Her job was to tell the truth.

She returned to her desk and began to write with new enthusiasm. She lost all track of time as her pencil skimmed across the paper. The words seemed inspired, flowing onto the pages with little effort.

"Katie? I'm sorry to bother you, dear. Do you have a moment?"

The sudden interruption caused the rest of an unfinished sentence to vanish into thin air. With a sound of impatience, Katie dropped the pencil onto the desk and turned to look at her mother.

"You have a caller," Lark explained.

"Who is it?" Katie did her best not to sound irritated.

Her mother motioned toward the stairway. "It's Sophia Rafferty. I told her you would be right down."

Katie glanced dolefully at the paper on her desk. Just when she was getting the words right, too, she thought. But curiosity overruled the temptation to send back her regrets. She and Sophia were nearly the same age, and they'd gone through school together. But the two had never been close friends. Katie had been far too much of a tomboy for that. Thus a visit from Sophia was completely unexpected.

Subduing a sigh, Katie rose and followed her mother downstairs.

"Here she is, Sophia," Lark announced as they entered the front parlor together.

Sophia turned from the window where she'd been gazing out at the fenced pastures.

"Hello, Sophia," Katie said. "This is a pleasant surprise." She realized as she said the words that they were true. It was pleasant. After the way Sophia had looked at her in town three days before, she hadn't expected any overtures of friendship.

"Hello, Katie. I hope I'm not intruding."

"Not at all," she lied in response.

Sophia had the same smile as her elder brother. It came slowly, moving from the corners of her mouth up to the pretty blue of her eyes.

"Why don't the two of you sit down and get reacquainted," Lark suggested, "while I make some tea. It won't take me but a minute or two."

Sophia seemed relieved by Lark's disappearance into the hall. She sat on the edge of the sofa, her hands folded primly in her lap, while Katie took the matching overstuffed chair nearby.

"The potluck last night was lovely," her guest said after a few moments of silence.

"Yes."

"There was such a crowd, I didn't have a chance to really talk with you."

"No, it was difficult to spend much time with anyone."

"Katie . . ." Sophia let the word drift into silence, then drew a deep breath and began again. "Katie, I'd like to ask you about your work."

"My work?" Nothing could have surprised Katie more.

Sophia nodded.

"I'm not quite sure—"

"Matthew says an education for a woman is a waste of time and money. That it will do you no good once you're married."

Anger flared, hot and instant, in her chest. "Oh, he does, does he? Thanks goodness I have no intentions of marrying. I would hate for those years at Vassar to be squandered."

"Oh, dear." Sophia began twisting a handkerchief in her hands. "Please don't misunderstand me, Katie. I've spent so many years wanting nothing more than to marry Matthew and"—she blushed—"have his children.

Sometimes I despaired he would ever propose." She paused, and her gaze moved to the window. "But there are times when . . ."

Katie thought it best to remain silent until Sophia chose to continue. She hadn't long to wait.

"It's just I would like to understand more about . . . about why you're doing . . . why you want to risk so much criticism for . . . I mean, women in Idaho already have the vote." The last words rushed out, as if she feared she would never be able to get them out unless she hurried.

Excitement flared inside Katie. Would Sophia be her first convert? How perfect if it was to be Ben's sister who shared Katie's work. How absolutely perfect.

She leaned forward and touched the back of Sophia's hand. "I'd love to tell you about it. It's so important for the women of this community to become more involved in helping their sisters throughout the country have the same privileges we enjoy."

It was well-known that Will Rider and Yancy Jones raised the finest horses in the entire state. It was equally well-known there'd been a time when the two men hadn't spoken to each other. In fact, Will had knocked Yancy to the ground the night he'd found out the young cowpoke was sparking his adopted daughter, Lark. But those ill feelings had long since been forgotten, and it wasn't unusual for the two men to be seen together, leaning on a fence rail, staring at mares and foals grazing in a pasture.

Much as they were doing today.

Yancy pushed his Stetson back off his forehead and squinted up at the midday sun. "We don't get some rain soon, we're gonna be drier'n jerked buffalo in an empty water barrel." He glanced at the man standing nearby. "Hottest spring I remember in these parts."

"It's been mighty warm all right," Will answered with a nod of agreement.

At seventy Will Rider still stood straighter than most men half his age, despite the constant ache in his back. His hair, once the same tawny shade of a lion's mane, had turned completely white, and his vision wasn't as keen as it once was. But Yancy didn't figure he'd ever known a better man—or a wiser one—than his father-in-law. Didn't reckon he ever would. That was one reason he'd ridden over to the Rocking R that afternoon. He needed some advice.

As if reading Yancy's mind, Will said, "I'm anxious to get a look at that automobile of Katie's. Didn't think I'd live long enough to see one of our own motorin' about in one of those contraptions."

"Guess we shoulda known it'd be Katie." Yancy shook his head. "I don't understand her, Will. Try as I might, I don't understand her. I never have."

"Ever think you might be tryin' to understand who she isn't instead of who she is?"

Yancy thought on it a moment, then answered, "Not sure I know what you mean."

"You remember how, when she was little, she was always bringin' home strays, injured things that needed tendin'?"

"I remember. But what's that got to do with what she's doin' now?"

"Addie's always sayin' Katie's got a big heart in that little body o' hers." Will removed his weather-beaten hat and tapped it against his thigh. "A heart as big as the western sky. Big enough she wants t'go out and make things right for the whole world. Or at least the world o' females."

Yancy frowned.

"Back when Addie came to Homestead, there wasn't hardly anything an unmarried woman could do to support herself except teach school or be a nurse. Things haven't changed much in all these years. Katie's understood that from the time she was just a mite. She wants to see things change." Will turned a hard look on his son-in-law. "You afraid of lettin' that happen?"

"No," he answered quickly—then wondered if he was telling the truth. Maybe he wasn't. Maybe he didn't want things to change. Maybe he thought they were changing too fast already.

"Lark was a timid little thing when she came to live with me," Will continued thoughtfully, his gaze back on the horses. "But Katie . . . she's never known a timid day in her life. She's never been satisfied to sit and watch life happen. She's gotta be in there, right in the thick of it." He paused, then added, "And she doesn't want anything more from you except for you to love her enough to let her be who she is."

Yancy wanted to say that's what he'd done. He'd always loved her, just never understood her. But the more he thought on Will's words, the more he began to wonder if the older man wasn't right. He let out a deep sigh. "I'm afraid for her, Will. It ain't easy t'be the one who's different."

"I reckon she knows that already. You and Lark have raised up a fine, intelligent young woman. She can handle what comes."

Yancy stared off across the valley. "I sure hope you're right," he said, adding silently, 'Cause I sure don't want t'see her hurtin'. Not my Katie.

Sophia Rafferty hadn't been gone from the Lazy L more than fifteen minutes when more visitors arrived.

This time it was Lark's sister, Naomi Murray, and her nine-month-old son, Donald.

After placing the baby on the floor near her feet, Naomi sat on the sofa, saying, "There was such a crowd at the supper last night, I scarcely had a chance to say hello, Katie. And I'm dying to hear all about your experiences back east. Lord knows, nothing very exciting ever happens around here." She grinned. "Except for the mischief three children can make, that is." She glanced down at her youngest child, watching as he crawled toward Katie. "Especially Donnie there. He never stops."

"I can't believe I've got three cousins." Katie leaned forward to smile at the baby.

"It'll be four come December."

"Naomi!" Lark cried, jumping up from her chair and rushing to hug her sister. "Why didn't you tell me?"

"I didn't know for sure. You know how I—" She stopped as color brightened her cheeks. She glanced quickly at her niece, then away before lowering her voice and saying, "Well, you know how things are for me, Lark. I thought I was just . . . late with my . . ." Her blush intensified. "But I saw Dr. Tom this morning, and he said it's certain."

Katie could have told the two older women that she understood a good deal more about a woman's reproductive system than they thought and that they didn't have to couch their words in euphemisms and whispers. But she realized it would only make them more uncomfortable. They would certainly think her fast, perhaps worse. After all, these things weren't discussed in polite society and should never be understood by an unmarried woman of twenty-four.

To give her aunt a moment to recover from her embarrassment, Katie lifted Donnie into her arms. She cooed at him, then nuzzled his neck beneath his ear. The baby laughed gleefully.

Unexpectedly Katie felt a poignant tug in her chest. Her aunt Naomi was only seven years older than she was, but she already had three children, with a fourth on the way. Katie suddenly wondered what it might be like to give birth, to hold a baby that had grown inside her own body for nine months, to nurse a baby at her breast. It was a totally new and unexpected feeling, and Katie wasn't the least sure it was one she welcomed.

Ben had always enjoyed coming into the newspaper office on Saturdays. It was Harvey Trent's day off, and the building was completely silent. Ben could work without interruption, catching up on reading other newspapers, seeing what more he could do to improve the *Herald*. This was a time when he came up with ideas for new articles or better layouts or new ways to advertise. He could usually get lots done on a Saturday.

But today he found himself unable to concentrate. His thoughts kept drifting.

Mostly to Katie.

Last night at the potluck supper, she'd looked as pretty as anything he'd ever seen. She'd been surrounded by the young men of the valley, particularly the three Henderson boys. Only they weren't boys, they were men, and they hadn't been looking at Katie as though she were just one of the gang, either.

Not that it should matter to him. Katie was her own woman. And she would certainly be bright enough to steer clear of the Hendersons. Oh, not that they were a bad lot. Actually he rather liked the three brothers. But they wouldn't be right for Katie. No indeed. They wouldn't be right at all.

He gave his head a shake. What was he worried about? Katie had no intention of marrying. She'd told him so herself. She wasn't interested in marriage or a husband. She had her cause to fight for.

But what if she changed her mind? What if one of the Hendersons was able to woo her, win her? What then?

It would be disastrous, that's what!

Maybe someone should warn the Henderson boys. Maybe *he* should warn them—for Katie's sake.

Restless, Ben rose from his desk chair and walked to the window. Across the street, Leslie Blake was sweeping the newly paved sidewalk in front of the mercantile. At the corner of Barber and Main, Frank Murray, Homestead's sheriff, was talking to his wife, Naomi. Dr. Tom McLeod drove his buggy past the newspaper office, probably on his way to make a call on a patient out in the valley. Several children raced down Barber Street, Sigmund Leonhardt's ugly yellow dog following after them.

Just a typical day in Homestead, the kind of day Ben had always liked best.

He wondered what Katie was doing right now.

As if in answer, just then he saw the Susan B roll into town, accompanied by its usual coughing and putting, breaking the silence of the peaceful day.

Ben grinned.

Katie must have seen him standing near the window. She steered the motorcar over to the front of the newspaper and braked. She smiled and waved, then got out. A moment later she entered his office.

"Are you working on a Saturday, Mr. Rafferty?" she asked, her voice scolding. "Shame on you. On a beautiful, sunshiny day like today? Even a newspaperman needs to have fun."

In the back of his mind he remembered Charlotte saying much the same thing to him not long ago. He'd paid her no heed when she'd tried to tempt him from his work.

Katie's words had a different effect on him.

"We've had visitors all day at home, and I needed some time away," she continued. "I decided to go for a drive. Why don't you come along?"

"Well, I . . ."

Her eyes sparkled. "It's as hot as midsummer. I thought I might go out to the old swimming hole."

When they were kids, they'd spent many a summer day at the swimming hole at the north end of the valley, stripped down to their underwear, their horses grazing contentedly. Ben had hung a rope to the limb of a tall tree, and they'd swung out over the clear water of the pond and dropped into the cold, backed-up waters of Pony Creek.

He wondered what Katie would look like in wet underwear these days, then found it all too easy to imagine her that way, her nipples, hardened by the cold, pressing against the nearly translucent fabric of a cotton chemise.

Good Lord!

He turned abruptly and crossed to his desk with long, determined strides. "I've got work to do." His voice cracked, making him sound thirteen again.

"Oh, come on, Benjie. I've got my bathing costume in the Susan B, and we can stop and get yours on our way out of town. It will be fun. No one else will be there. The water's too cold for most folks."

"Too cold for me these days." He met her gaze. "I'm not a young boy anymore."

She laughed. "What's that got to do with it?"

Everything, he wanted to tell her. It's got everything to do with it.

Especially when he looked at her and saw anything but his childhood friend and swimming buddy. Especially when she watched him with those luminous, guileless eyes of hers.

"Come on, Benjie. We haven't had hardly a moment alone since I got back. You can spare me a few hours."

Guilt warred with temptation in him. It was almost sick, thinking about Katie the way he'd just done. She was like his sister. Hell, she was closer to him than his sister.

Besides, it was Charlotte he ought to be fantasizing about. Charlotte Orson was the young woman everyone expected him to marry. Didn't he expect it, too? But even if he tried, he couldn't imagine Charlotte in wet undergarments, her body shivering from the cold.

"All right," he said. "I'll go." But he was going to be sorry. He knew it as surely as he knew his own name.

Two hours later they lay on a blanket, warming themselves in the sun. Katie couldn't remember a more perfect afternoon than this one. It was like being a child again. She and Ben had swung out from the old rope and plunged into the icy pool below, just as they'd done when they were kids. They'd splashed each other in a water war, their shouts and laughter rising above the noise. They'd raced each other to one end of the pond and back again. And finally, shivering, their lips turned blue, they'd dropped onto the blanket and waited for the sun to drive away the chill from their bones.

Perfect. A perfect day.

Katie rolled onto her side, her head supported by the heel of her hand, her elbow resting on the ground. Ben's eyes were closed, his face turned up to the sun.

His mother had told her Ben worked too hard, and Katie believed it. She'd noticed the tightness that appeared occasionally around his eyes and mouth, but it was gone for the moment. He looked so much more like the boy she remembered from her childhood.

"It's good to see you relax, Benjie."

He opened his eyes, and Katie felt a strange drop in her stomach, like when she'd let go of the rope and fallen into the icy water. Her insides went all aquiver and her breathing came hard.

She sat up and stared at the pond, not understanding the wave of emotions rushing through her. A moment later Ben did the same.

"Why did you come back to Homestead, Benjie? I always thought you would go to work for one of the big papers. Why did you come back here instead?"

"I never wanted to live anywhere but here."

"But I thought—"

"Your dreams always took you away from here, Katie. Mine always brought me back."

She heard a warm contentment in his voice, a contentment she'd never known and couldn't understand.

He tossed a pebble into the water. "I like the quiet sameness of each day. I like knowing by name everyone who walks into my office. I like being part of a place where people care about one another, where they care about the ordinary, everyday kinds of things."

"But you could have been famous. You could have—"

"That sort of success wasn't worth what I would've had to give up, Katie. I want to put down roots here in Homestead, same as my parents did. I want a home, a wife, children. All the normal things, I guess. I suppose that doesn't sound like much to you, but it does to me."

Silence fell around them, as if anticipating Katie's next question.

"Are you going to marry Charlotte?" Her chest felt tight. She didn't dare look at Ben, but she wasn't sure why. She didn't understand much of anything at the moment.

"I've often thought I would," he answered after a long while. "She's a lovely woman."

"Yes, she is."

"Charlotte likes you."

"I get the feeling she likes everyone." Saint Charlotte, she thought to herself.

"What about you, Katie? Is there anyone special, any-one—"

She jumped to her feet. "I've already told you I don't intend to get married." She walked to the water's edge.

"That could change if you met the right man."

"I don't *want* it to change." She turned to look at him. "I don't want to meet the right man, Benjie. My work is too important to me." Her throat hurt, making it difficult to speak. "This is the way it has to be."

She watched as Ben rose from the blanket, keenly aware he was no longer the boy she used to swim with, cognizant of how tall he'd become, of the breadth of his wide shoulders, the cut of his strong jaw, the set of his fine mouth. He drew near to her with just two strides of his long legs, and her awareness of the changes in him intensified.

It wasn't until he'd gathered her in his arms and pulled her head against his chest that she realized she was crying.

"It's okay, Katie. Nobody's asking you to change. Especially not me."

But he was. In some strange, indefinable way, Ben Rafferty had silently asked her to be someone and some-thing different from who and what she was. She'd felt it in her heart, seen it in his eyes. She wasn't sure what it meant or why it hurt her so much. She only knew their friendship had just been altered.

Katie rarely felt fear, but at this moment she *was* afraid. She felt as if she were standing on a precipice, ready to topple over the edge, and the bottom was too far away to see.

Ben's hand gently stroked her head. "I think it's time we started back to town. I . . . I'm having supper tonight at Charlotte's and I need to clean up."

She fought a new wave of tears, hot and burning in her throat, but she swallowed them back as she slowly withdrew from his embrace. "Of course," she said, wiping her eyes with the backs of her hands. "I didn't realize it had grown so late."

"You go on and change. I'll stand watch here by the Susan B."

Her throat was too thick to speak, so she simply nodded, then went to gather her clothes so she could dress and then drive Ben back to town . . .

And back to Charlotte.

6

A shiver of excitement traced Katie's spine as she entered the Homestead Community Church the following Tuesday evening. She'd been asked to speak to the women of the Morning Glory Circle about her experiences in Washington, D.C. She knew this was her first—and, perhaps, most important—opportunity to share with the women of Homestead the significance of the suffrage movement.

For three days now she'd been wrestling with a strange malaise, a feeling that nothing was going to go right, a depression of her mind and a disquiet of her heart. But now she was herself again. Her sense of purpose and direction had returned with a new and greater assurance.

She smiled at the group of women seated before her. "Thank you all for coming tonight and for asking me to be here with you." Her gaze scanned the crowd.

In the first row were Katie's mother and grandmother. Their eyes shone with pride, love, and support. Beside them were Sophia Rafferty and her mother, along with

Charlotte Orson. Sophia leaned slightly forward on her chair, as if afraid she might miss some word of importance. Charlotte's demeanor was much more reserved. The new schoolmarm, Blanche Coleson—dressed all in black, not so much as a hair out of place—sat in the second row next to the three Barber sisters: Leslie Blake, Annalee Leonhardt, and Rachel Henderson. Fanny McLeod, the doctor's wife, sat behind Blanche in the third row. Even Madeline Percy, although now a member of the First Methodist Church since becoming the Methodist minister's wife, had come to hear Katie speak. And there were others, many more than she had dared hope to expect.

"I must tell you before I begin that I'm rather nervous. I have not done a great deal of public speaking."

"You'll do just fine," Priscilla Jacobs stated with a nod of encouragement.

Katie smiled without conviction, drew a deep breath, and then began. "As most of you are aware, I've been living and working in Washington, D.C., ever since my graduation from Vassar College. During the past three years, I've had the rare opportunity to meet many dedicated people who are working hard so that all women have equal opportunities in this great country of ours."

Images of the women she'd worked with flashed in her mind, each of them smiling, as if to say "You're doing fine, Katie."

"For centuries, women have been at the center of the home. We have believed in the sanctity of marriage. We have raised our children to be moral and upright citizens. We have sought to help others through our Christian work. In such organizations as the Woman's Christian Temperance Union, women have sought to broaden the sense of social responsibility in men, not only in the home but in the larger community."

"That's true," Leslie Blake whispered to her two sisters, but loud enough for everyone to hear. "Mother worked with the WCTU before we came to Homestead."

"Much has been accomplished in the past fifty years since the end of the Civil War. Improvements have been realized in laws that govern property rights for married and single women, legal guardianship of minor children, and rights of contract. But we have a long way to go to reach true equality. We do not yet have the same rights under the law as men. We are still often at the mercy of others, solely because of our sex, rather than being able to make decisions for ourselves."

Katie seemed to have everyone's full attention, and knowing it made her pulse race with excitement.

"Even now," she continued, "the 'Suffrage Special' is finishing its tour of the enfranchised states. Suffrage leaders are calling upon women voters to meet in Chicago on June fifth to form a new party of women voters. Those of us currently entrusted with the right to vote must continue to use every means at our disposal until the right to vote is granted to all women."

Katie noticed a few furtive glances exchanged but ignored them.

"The current Democratic administration refuses to support woman's suffrage, and our strategy must continue to be that of holding the party in power responsible. It is up to those of us who have the right to vote to see that the Democrats are not reelected to office at any level."

This time there was some noticeable shifting on chairs. Katie could almost feel members of her audience pulling back from her emotionally. Her tone strengthened with new urgency. She couldn't let them slip away. She had to convince them of the truth in what she said.

"Tonight I am asking that you exercise your right to

vote in the coming elections. I ask you to consider your votes carefully, both in the primaries and in November. I ask that you do *not* reelect Governor Alexander because of his party affiliation if for no other reason. I ask that you speak to your husbands and encourage them to do likewise. We must refuse to uphold any party that has ignored the claims of women."

Madeline Percy rose from her chair. "I cannot believe we have been invited to this church—to this holy place of worship—to listen to such rubbish. Miss Jones, the glory of womanhood has been her purity, her superiority to men in the possession of a higher moral sense and standard. Would you have us risk this precious certainty for a doubtful good?"

"Is it your wish, Mrs. Percy, to be dominated by ignorance or selfishness or by both?" Katie challenged, undeterred. "Why otherwise would you oppose the movement that would enfranchise all women?"

"Well, I never!" Madeline's pointed chin thrust upward, and her eyes flashed with indignation. She whirled, pushing her way past Sarah Wesley as she marched out of the church.

Katie swept her gaze over the remaining women in the room. Their expressions were varied, from horrified to confused to exultant. Hoping to soothe those who had been affronted, she softened her tone. "Susan B. Anthony once wrote that sometimes those women who oppose their own freedom have been so thoroughly trained to let men do all the thinking, they have really come to believe it is unwomanly to think and express an opinion themselves concerning a public question. They conscientiously and earnestly believe it is somehow more creditable to beg a man to vote than it is to show one's appreciation of the dignity of a vote by using the ballot oneself. They forget, too, but for the suffrage movement, they would not have the privilege of coming before men in public to criticize and to ask that we, those of us who fight for suffrage for all, not be given the things for which we pray."

A frown creased Lark's forehead, but Addie Rider continued to smile, as if delighted by every word Katie uttered. Sophia Rafferty looked, at turns, both confused and inspired. Blanche Coleson's face was flushed, and she was nodding in agreement. Charlotte Orson remained serene, her expression revealing none of her thoughts.

Katie drew another deep breath, then said, "The politicians in Washington are currently consumed by the problem of neutrality toward the European war. They say they cannot allow anything such as suffrage for women to interfere with these concerns. These politicians—all men, I might remind you—believe it is their business to keep the United States of America out of the carnage in Europe. But when, I ask you, have men shown themselves adept at keeping nations out of war? Woman's suffrage is not unimportant, nor should it be shuffled aside. Women must pursue this right, no matter what other issues arise. We have voices. We must raise them."

Blanche Coleson jumped to her feet and began to applaud. "Bravo, Miss Jones! Bravo!" The light of holy fervor burned in her eyes.

Some women, however, were not in agreement with the old maid schoolmarm. They quickly gathered their belongings and slipped from the room, no doubt wishing they had followed Madeline Percy when she'd first stormed out. But the majority remained. They came forward to congratulate Katie, to tell her they had enjoyed her speech, to say she'd done an admirable job, and to ask questions about the association.

By this time the nervousness she'd felt earlier had

completely disappeared. Katie was in her element. She didn't mind that some of her audience had rejected what she'd said. She'd known better than to expect all to embrace her cause. But more had stayed to ask questions than she'd dared hope for, and she delighted in telling them what she'd learned from the wonderful leaders of the cause.

She could scarcely wait to send a letter to Penelope Rudyard, detailing tonight's triumph. Her friend would be proud of her as would all the others in NAWSA's offices. There was still much to be done, as Katie had told the women here tonight, but she'd made a start.

It wasn't until she and her mother, having watched Grandma Addie ride away with Grandpa Will, were climbing into the Susan B for the drive home that Katie realized Charlotte Orson had not remained to talk to her after her speech was over. She had been one of the women to leave, an obvious show of disapproval.

Ben's future wife was not interested in woman's suffrage.

For some reason, that knowledge took some of the glow off the evening.

As Ben reached for his suit coat, a knock rattled the window in the newspaper office's door. He turned and was surprised to find Charlotte standing on the other side.

He hurried to open the door for her. "I was just on my way over to the church. Why didn't you wait for me there?"

"I did wait for a while. But when you didn't arrive, I thought I would come here." There was an almost imperceptible quaver in her voice.

Ben glanced at the clock on the wall. He hadn't forgotten the time. In fact, he was early. He hadn't been supposed to meet her for another ten minutes.

"The meeting didn't last as long as we'd expected," she said in answer to his unspoken question.

He put his hands on her upper arms. "Charlotte, is something wrong?"

She shook her head without meeting his gaze.

"Charlotte?"

She looked up. "I'm afraid Miss Jones has made herself rather unpopular with certain members of our community. Oh, Benjamin, you really must tell her to be more circumspect."

"What's happened?" he asked, feeling some alarm.

"She has no idea how outrageous she sounds, spouting those progressive ideologies. She can only cause trouble, making women unhappy with their lot in life."

Ben felt a rush of relief. So Katie was being Katie. He smiled, imagining what she must have said, how her eyes must have sparkled with enthusiasm.

"Benjamin, are you listening to me?"

He focused his gaze on the woman before him. "Of course."

"Miss Jones is your friend. You must caution her before she gets hurt. There are some who can be cruel under the guise of righteous indignation. You know whom I mean. They will make things very unpleasant for her."

How like Charlotte to disagree with Katie but want to protect her at the same time. He should love her for that alone.

But he *didn't* love her.

The realization shook him. He'd courted Charlotte with marriage in mind. She was pretty. She was intelligent. She was kind and thoughtful and easy to be with. Everyone thought they were well suited. He'd fully intended to fall in love with her.

But he hadn't.

Why not?

And then he thought of Katie in her bathing costume, her dark hair stringing down her back, swinging on the old rope over the pond. He pictured her letting go, falling with a shriek and a great splash. It was as though that splash rippled through him, this time carrying a startling realization with it.

He loved Katie Jones.

And *not* just like any childhood friend.

Perhaps he'd known it, that day by the water, that day when she'd told him she would never marry, that day when he'd held her against him and she'd cried. Or perhaps he'd known it the day he'd called on her at the Lazy L, the day he'd convinced himself everyone was as fond of Katie as he was. Or perhaps he'd known it the very moment she'd arrived back in Homestead, when she'd stood before him, a woman instead of a tomboy in pigtails.

But he hadn't wanted to face it then, and he didn't want to face it now. Because nothing else had changed. Katie still had no intention of sharing her life with a man, of marrying and settling down and having a family. That wasn't what Katie wanted.

And what did *he* want? The very things Katie didn't want—marriage, children, a home and family.

"Benjamin?" Charlotte's fingers alighted on his forearm. "You *will* talk to Miss Jones, won't you? You will caution her about the things she says?"

"Yes," he answered absentmindedly, "I'll talk to Katie."

"Thank you. I knew I could count on you." Her smile was warm. "Are you finished with your work for the evening? Are you ready to walk me home?"

Impulsively he reached for Charlotte, drew her to

him. He saw the look of surprise in her eyes as she realized he was about to kiss her for the first time. Not a chaste kiss on the cheek such as they'd exchanged once or twice before, but the kiss a man shared with a woman.

Their lips met. The kiss was tender, sweet, brief. Too brief, perhaps, to cause the reaction he wanted to feel. The reaction he *didn't* feel.

"Benjamin," she whispered as he lifted his mouth from hers. Her cheeks were flushed, making her look as sweet and innocent as her kiss had been.

Ben pushed away a sudden sense of guilt. He'd believed before that he would grow to love Charlotte, given time. There was no reason to stop believing it would happen. And passion would be a natural result of that love. It wasn't important that he felt no passion now. He needed only to be patient. Passion would follow love as surely as summer followed spring. As soon as he learned to love Charlotte, all would be right.

As for Katie, time would take care of her, too. The two of them had been friends all their lives. They would go on being friends. This . . . *feeling* he had for her would pass, and what would remain in its wake would be the affection of old friends. A friendship that had withstood the test of time.

"Charlotte," he said, offering his arm to her, "allow me to see you home."

The large plate-glass window of the newspaper office, combined with the golden glow of lamplight, provided an easy view of the kissing couple for anyone who happened along Main Street. Certainly both Katie and her mother saw them as the motorcar rolled past the *Homestead Herald* on their way out of town.

"Well, it shouldn't be long now," Lark commented.

"What shouldn't be long?"

"Before we hear the announcement of their engagement. Ben and Charlotte's. Not that we all haven't been expecting it. They've always seemed so well suited."

"Have they?"

Lark glanced toward her, and Katie was glad for the shelter of night. She didn't know what she was feeling at the moment, but whatever it was, she didn't want her mother to see it.

"You should be happy for Ben," Lark chastised gently.

"I am."

"Charlotte will make him a perfect wife."

"I'm sure."

"Katie . . ." Lark paused a moment, then continued, "Did you and Ben have a quarrel?"

"No, Mother, we haven't quarreled."

An unwelcome memory flooded her mind. The memory of Ben's arms around her, his hand stroking her head. The clean, manly scent of him lingered yet in her nostrils. The gentle tone of his voice wafted still in her ears.

Ben would marry Charlotte before long. Everyone had expected it. Even Ben. Tonight Katie had seen evidence that confirmed the expectations of one and all. She should be glad for Ben. She should be glad for Charlotte. They were perfect for each other. Ben wanted to be married, and Charlotte would make him a wonderful wife. It was as clear as anything that this was the right choice for Katie's dear, dear friend.

Then why didn't she feel happy for him?

She wasn't so naive that she didn't recognize envy when she felt it. But *why* was she envious? She didn't *want* to marry. She'd made that decision long ago. It wasn't that she didn't believe in the institution of marriage. She had grown up surrounded by good examples of what marriage could and should be like. But . . .

Lark's fingers alighted on Katie's arm. "What's troubling you, dear?"

"I don't know." She glanced toward her mother, then back at the road. "Maybe I just realized Benjie and I aren't children any longer."

Lark laughed softly. "No, indeed you're not."

"Will she really make him happy, Mother?" Sadness pierced Katie's heart as she asked the question, not certain what she wanted the answer to be.

"Yes, Katie, I believe Charlotte will make him happy."

She released a shallow sigh. "Then I'm glad for them both. Honest and truly, I am."

Steadfastly Katie refused to allow the memory of Ben's arms around her to linger.

7

Ben was on his way to the office the following morning when he noticed a small group of men standing in front of Childers Livery.

"Well, I'll be hanged if I'll have my wife listenin' to such claptrap," Norman Henderson shouted, loudly enough to be heard nearly a block away. "Yancy Jones ought t'have enough backbone to make that gal of his stay at home and mind her tongue. Her and her fast ways."

So, it had begun already, Ben thought. Then he walked across the dusty street to join the others.

Seeing his approach, Norman pointed an accusing finger in his direction. "Ben Rafferty, you're as much at fault as that father of hers."

"At fault for what, Norm?" he asked, pretending innocence.

"What possessed you t'let Katie Jones write for your newspaper?"

"Because she has the necessary skills and education to do it and do it well. And because—as owner, editor, and publisher—I thought the paper ought to have just such a column."

"We don't need her puttin' her highfalutin eastern ideas in your paper for our women to read. Gives 'em notions to want things they weren't meant to have."

Ben raised an eyebrow. "Are you afraid of what *your* wife might learn, Norm? Are you afraid she'll start thinking for herself?"

The farmer turned as red as a beet, and his eyes nearly bulged out of their sockets.

"Listen, Ben," Leroy Smith, the town's banker, interrupted before Norman could explode. "I'm not saying women shouldn't have the right to vote. They've had it in Idaho for the last twenty years, and it hasn't done this state any harm." He adjusted his glasses on the bridge of his nose. "But when Miss Jones begins telling folks to vote the governor out of office because his party isn't supporting something she wants . . . "

Oh, Katie, you are stirring up a hornet's nest, aren't you?

Leroy Smith's father-in-law, the Reverend Simon Jacobs, cleared his throat. "Seems to me she's done nothing except speak her mind regarding a public official. That's done in every election. It's a time-honored tradition."

"What else could you say, Reverend?" Norman asked gruffly. "She was invited to speak in *your* church last night. And I still want to hear what Rafferty means to do about that gall-blamed column."

Ben skewered the farmer with an intense gaze but held his anger in check. "I don't intend to do anything except publish it. Miss Jones hasn't abused her position with the *Herald,* nor has she jeopardized the integrity of the paper by what she's written. As a citizen of this town and of this state, she has a right to express her opinions."

"What she needs is a good thrashin'," the other man growled.

One quick stride brought Ben almost nose to nose with Norman Henderson. When he spoke, he measured his words with care. "I think not."

"Gentlemen, please," Reverend Jacobs said softly. He placed his arms between Ben and Norman and eased them apart. "We accomplish nothing by fighting among ourselves."

"We don't need her kind of thinkin' 'round here," Norman muttered, not one to give up easily.

Ben itched to punch the older man square between the eyes.

"Let's all be about our work now," the reverend encouraged before Ben could follow through on his impulse.

For a moment no one moved. The air, totally motionless, seemed thick. Then the men began to disperse, heading off to their places of business or to their farms and homes. Finally only Ben and Reverend Jacobs remained.

Ben let out a long breath of air, not realizing he'd been holding it until that moment. "Sorry, Reverend."

"Quite all right, young man. I must confess I, too, was losing my temper."

"You?"

Reverend Jacobs chuckled. "I'm no saint, Benjamin. Just a minister trying to tend to his flock." He tapped his chin with his index finger, his expression thoughtful. "You might warn Katie about the attitude of these men, my son Matthew included."

That was the second time in less than twenty-four hours Ben had been asked to talk to Katie, but he didn't particularly want to oblige either Charlotte or the reverend. He wasn't prepared to face Katie just yet, not while the realization of his feelings for her was still so fresh in his mind.

And in his heart.

The reverend gave his head a slow shake. "My wife

doesn't agree with Matthew. Mrs. Jacobs was quite taken by what Katie had to say last night, and I suspect others were, too. I don't believe Mr. Henderson or Matthew or any of the others realize what they're up against."

"No, they don't."

"I daresay Homestead is going to be changed by the return of Miss Jones."

Once again Ben remembered Katie as she'd looked at the swimming hole. Definitely not a tomboy anymore. Yes, Homestead would be changed by her return, and Ben's whole world was changing right with it.

"Well, I must be on my way. I promised to make a call out at the Evans farm first thing this morning. Mr. Childers should have my buggy ready to go by this time. Good day to you, Benjamin." With that, the reverend turned and disappeared through the open doorway of the livery.

Wednesday, May 31, 1916
My dear Penny,
Last night I spoke to the women of the Morning Glory Circle, explaining the importance of woman's suffrage and how very much their votes are needed in this year's elections. My speech met with some resistance, but overall, I would say it was a success.

Mrs. Percy, wife of the Methodist minister, walked out in the middle of my presentation. I am afraid there was an exchange of words between us, and my attitude was not very Christian. But everyone else remained to hear me through, despite my lapse in judgment. Although some were obviously affronted by the notion of women thinking and acting for themselves, independently of their husbands or fathers, most were at least willing to listen and consider what I had to say and not reject everything straightaway.

Upon my return to Homestead, my dear friend

*Benjamin Rafferty agreed to allow me to write the col-
umn for the newspaper. He's given it a highly objectionable heading which I shall not repeat to you herein.
(Your title, dear Penny, was by far superior.) My first
entry appeared in last week's edition of the <u>Herald</u>. It
was a pleasant little piece, written with great care in
order to appeal to one and all. I must have succeeded
because my father liked it exceedingly well.*

*Since I was much too excited after my speaking
engagement to sleep, I finished my second column early
this morning, long before the rising of the sun. I was not
so restrained this time as I was with my first endeavor. I
suppose I must prepare myself for even more objections
than those which my speech aroused. But when haven't
we encountered resistance and objections to the truth we
share with others?*

*I realize, dearest Penny, that this letter shall be posted
and arrive in Washington before you return from the
convention in Chicago. I am quite envious of you and
the thousands of women who will be there, and I sometimes wonder at my decision to return to Homestead
before rather than after such a momentous and historic
event. However, my work is begun, and I cannot leave it,
so I will be content with my choice.*

*I must close now and deliver my column to my editor.
I wouldn't want Mr. Rafferty to be upset with his new
columnist.*

Give my regards to one and all.

Your devoted friend,

Katherine Lark Jones

*Post Script. It appears my dear Benjie will be getting
married soon. The woman's name is Charlotte Orson.
She is truly lovely, and I am certain they shall be quite
happy together.*

*   *   *

Sophia's hands paused above the bread dough. "Mother?"

"Hmm."

She glanced over her shoulder toward the table where Rose Rafferty was rolling out pie crusts. "Has Father ever made you feel that . . . that you hadn't the right to think for yourself?"

Her mother looked up. "What a question!"

"I know you and Father love each other, and you think he's just about perfect in every way. But do you ever wish . . ." She let her voice trail off into silence, uncertain what it was she wanted to ask.

Rose got up from her chair and walked over to her daughter's side. A frown knit her dark brows. "Has this something to do with Katie's talk last night?"

Sophia shook her head, then sighed. "Not really. It has more to do with Matthew."

Her mother touched her shoulder in gentle encouragement but said nothing. She simply waited until Sophia was ready to continue.

Tears welled in her eyes as she stared down at the lump of bread dough. "I'm not sure I can be the sort of wife he expects me to be," she whispered, her throat tight.

"And what is that?"

"Obedient."

"Ahh." Rose placed her arm around Sophia's back. "I see."

"Don't mistake me," she rushed to add. "I think Matthew is wonderful in so many ways. But sometimes . . . I don't know. Sometimes it seems he doesn't listen to me or care what I think or feel. As if . . . as if whatever I have to say couldn't possibly be of any importance because"—she paused to take a quick breath, then finished—"because I'm a woman."

"I see," her mother repeated.

Sophia moved away from the counter, away from her mother's protective arm. Restlessly she paced the circumference of the kitchen. "I was so happy when Matthew proposed. But what if I was wrong about marrying him? What if I don't . . . love him enough?"

"Sophia, come and sit down."

She paused in her pacing to glance at her mother.

Rose pointed at a chair near the table. "Sit down, dear. We need to talk."

With her shoulders suddenly slumped, Sophia did as her mother instructed.

Once they were both seated, Rose leaned forward, reaching across the table with both arms. She took hold of her daughter's hands and gave them a light squeeze. "Sophia, marriage isn't easy under the best of circumstances. Even when two people love each other and want only the very best for each other, it's difficult. It takes listening and compromise and understanding and patience." She smiled gently. "Goodness knows, it's a miracle when the right people find one another. I know it was a miracle I found your father. I tried hard enough to run away from my feelings for him."

For as long as she could remember, Sophia had witnessed that tender expression steal across her mother's face whenever she talked about Michael Rafferty. It had always been Sophia's dream to marry and have children and to talk about her husband with that same sort of rapt countenance. But lately it seemed all she felt for Matthew was irritation.

Rose's grip tightened. "I wonder if I haven't given you the impression things have simply always been perfect for your parents. If so, I can assure you that isn't true. Your father and I have had disagreements—plenty of them— throughout our marriage. But our love and respect for each other as individuals always helped us solve our dif-

ferences. And we solved them by talking them though."
Her eyes narrowed. "Have you told Matthew what it is
you're feeling? Have you tried talking to him?"

She shook her head.

"Well then, you must do so at once." She released her
daughter's hands and sat back on her chair. "Your wedding is less than a week away."

"But I don't know what to say to him," Sophia
protested in a whisper.

"You'll think of something."

"What if . . . what if nothing changes after we've
talked? Or what if I'm wrong, and then he decides not to
marry me and I lose him?"

"Better to find out now, before you're married rather
than after and it's too late to change things."

Sophia knew her mother was right, but fear made it
difficult to follow the advice. Not a fear that nothing
would change. Fear that *everything* would change.

She'd had a crush on Matthew Jacobs ever since she
was a girl in braids and short skirts. She'd decided he
was the man she wanted to marry when she was sixteen
and he was twenty-three. She'd nearly given up hope of
his ever proposing, especially as one year after another
slipped away. She'd begun to believe she was destined to
be an old maid.

Then, last winter, the day a gently falling snow had
turned the valley into a wonderland of white, he'd
appeared on her front porch and made all her dreams
come true with just three little words: Sophia, marry me.

Was she prepared to risk the future she'd dreamed of
by causing an argument? They'd never disagreed on anything before Katie's return to Homestead. Was this the
right time to begin arguing, just days before their wedding? What if he was right about Katie? What if Katie's
views were nonsense and she was being led astray by

them? What if she was merely feeling prewedding jitters and nothing more?

As if in answer to her unspoken questions, she heard Katie's words echoing in her head. *"The real problem with marriage is that women throw away every plan and purpose for their own lives to conform to the plan and purpose of the man's life. Men seem to want wives with intelligence, and then, after they are married, they want to keep these same women meek and submissive and merely a willing reflection of their husbands. But when women no longer are willing to do so, when women insist upon being seen as an equal partner whose intelligence and feelings are viewed with respect, then all people shall benefit."*

Sophia lifted her gaze to look at her mother. "You're right, Mother. I really must speak to him."

"Yes, dear. You really must." Rose offered a smile of encouragement. "It will be all right. You'll see. No matter what you decide to do, it will be for the best."

"I hope so, Mother," she whispered. "I do hope so."

Katie sat on the running board of the Susan B, her chin cupped in her hands, elbows resting on her thighs, while steam rose from the automobile's radiator. Of all the times for the flivver to overheat, this was not the best. Her column was due in to the paper this afternoon.

Why, oh why, had she waited until the last minute to get it finished? She'd started it last Saturday. Why had she allowed other things to interfere with its completion until last night?

"We must not allow other demands on our lives to impede our work," Alice Paul had told her once. "We must remain focused on our goal at all times, even when the demands of families—be they parents or husbands or children—would draw us away."

The rattle of harness and clip-clop of a horse's hooves intruded on her memory. She straightened and looked down the road. Coming toward her in his buggy was Ben.

She felt an odd shortness of breath, as if she were as overheated as the Model T.

"Problems?" Ben called to her as he drew closer.

He was going to marry Charlotte. Everyone knew it. Katie knew it. She'd seen them kissing only last night.

She stood up. "The Susan B overheated. I'll be able to get her started again in a little bit."

He stopped the buggy, then looped the reins and climbed out. "Does this happen often?"

It was easy to see why Charlotte would love Ben, would want to marry him. He was easily the most handsome man in all of Long Bow Valley.

Katie watched as he stepped over to the front of the motorcar and lifted the hood. He leaned forward and stared at the machinery. "You're sure you don't have some other problem?"

Her heart twisted. "Like what?"

"With the engine." He glanced up, meeting her gaze. "Not that I'd know. I'm no mechanic."

He was going to marry Charlotte, and he was going to be very happy, and Katie was going to be thrilled for him. When his children were born, they would call her Auntie Katie, and perhaps she would take care of them on occasion. She would hold them as she had Naomi's baby, and they would giggle and coo, and she would love them. When they were older, she would tell them stories about their father when he was a boy, and Ben would do the same about her.

"Katie?"

She blinked. "What? Oh . . . no, there's nothing wrong with the engine. The Susan B just likes to overheat every now and again. It's part of her charm." She turned and reached into the car. "I was bringing you my column."

Ben closed the hood. "And I was on my way out to see you."

Her heart thudded. "You were?"

"Yes." He paused. "Charlotte asked me to speak to you."

"Charlotte." *Oh, Benjie, I do so want you to be happy. Really I do.*

"Your talk last night has upset some folk."

Katie nodded, reminded suddenly of what must be of paramount importance to her. She held out the carefully penned papers. "If so, then this shall no doubt upset them further."

"Are you sure this is what you want to do, Katie?" he asked as he took the document from her.

"I'm sure."

His voice softened. "Are you?" he repeated.

She wanted to be angry with him. She wanted to upbraid him for speaking to her as if she were a school-girl, questioning her actions. But it wasn't anger she felt. It was confusion.

He drew a step closer as he perused the column she'd finished that morning. The sun glinted off his golden hair, cast a broad-shouldered shadow on the dusty road near her feet. He had such strong arms, yet when he had cradled Charlotte in those same strong arms last night, they had appeared gentle.

"Katie?"

Looking up, she felt a shortness of breath. "Don't worry about me, Benjie." She forced a smile. "I know what I'm doing."

But at the moment, she had to wonder if that were true.

8

The Homestead Weekly Herald, *Homestead, Idaho*
Friday Morning, June 2, 1916
KATIE'S CORNER:
CURRENT LAW SAYS WOMEN'S JUDGMENT
UNSOUND

In 1896, when I was but four years old, the governing body of the state of Idaho saw fit to enfranchise women. Ever since, the vote has belonged to each of us as a right of our citizenship in this state. Yet many—dare I say most—women of Idaho do not exercise that right of citizenship.

Why not? I must ask.

What a glorious thing it is to vote! Susan B. Anthony once said the law granting such a right implies that your judgment is sound and your opinion worthy to be counted. Yet most women live where the law says their judgment is unsound and their opinions unworthy.

Without the right to vote, the blessings of liberty are

*forever withheld from women and their female posterity.
The time is now for Idaho women in all walks of life,
married and single, old and young, to step forward and
be counted in support of the national suffrage amendment. . . .*

---

*WOMEN'S NEWS DEPARTMENT:
BE GRATEFUL IF YOU ARE HANDED A LEMON
A lemon has many uses as a cleanser of the body,
mind, and white goods, so be grateful if you are handed
one. The juice from a half a lemon in half a glass of
water before breakfast will correct the most torpid liver
and prevent bilious troubles. For hoarseness, a lemon
and sugar . . .*

That Friday's edition of the *Homestead Herald* incited
more arguments than any edition since the paper was
founded.

At the Lazy L Ranch, Yancy Jones found himself in
hot water with Lark when he suggested their daughter
might want to give up writing for the newspaper. How in
Sam Billy heck, he inquired, was she going to get some
fella's spurs all in a tangle if she kept on actin' like she
didn't have enough sense to teach a hen to cluck? His
wife responded by saying maybe their daughter wanted
more out of life than to just tangle some idiot's spurs. At
which point each quit speaking to the other, Yancy riding out to check fences and Lark yanking weeds from her
garden with more than the usual vengeance.

At the Henderson farm, Norman made it clear he
would not tolerate his wife—and the mother of his three
grown sons—attending any future meetings of the
Morning Glory Circle where Katie Jones might be speaking. Nor, he added, was he to see her reading the propa-
ganda included in *that woman's* column. Rachel

Henderson agreed meekly, but he found his next meal charred almost beyond recognition.

When George Blake commented that Katie's progressive notions wouldn't hold with the womenfolk of Long Bow Valley—since they knew their proper place—Leslie Blake wanted to know if he thought her vote was wasted just because she was female. His reply regarding women and the ballot box, spoken with a laugh and meant as a joke, guaranteed he would be sleeping on the sofa for at least the next week.

While eating his breakfast at Zoe's Restaurant that morning, Phillip Carson made a ribald comment about fast young women who didn't know their place was to be either wives or schoolteachers, whereupon Blanche Coleson, who was seated at the next table, rose from her chair and dumped her meal of fried eggs and sausage over the top of his head.

After a fistfight broke out behind Childers Livery between Sam Jones and Andrew Henderson, the mayor and the sheriff paid a joint call on the editor of the *Homestead Herald*.

"Listen, Benjamin," Albert Tobias, the mayor, pleaded, "I'm asking you to stop publishing that column. For the sake of the community, if for no other reason."

Sheriff Frank Murray—who was married to Lark's sister, Naomi, and was, therefore, well-acquainted with the entire family—rested his knuckles on the top of Ben's desk. "No one knows better than I do how pigheaded that niece of mine can be. The whole lot of Rider women are all headstrong and opinionated." He rapped the desk four times, in rhythm with his words. "But by heaven, Ben, this is letting them go too far. You're the one who hired Katie, and you've got to fire her. Cancel that dadburn tripe before we've got every wife in the valley knocking her husband over the head with an iron skillet."

Ben couldn't help himself. He laughed.

The mayor puffed up like a bantam rooster. "This is *not* a laughing matter."

Ben rubbed his hand over his face, fighting for control. He knew it wasn't funny. The suffrage issue had divided many people down through the years, and his quiet little hometown wasn't likely to be any different. But as editor he also knew the matter to be newsworthy. He didn't ask everyone to agree with what was in the newspaper, only that they read and consider it.

For that matter, he wasn't sure *he* agreed with everything Katie had said in today's column. But he did believe in the freedom of speech, and he wasn't about to allow anyone to silence her just because they didn't want to hear any opinion different from their own.

Ben rose from his chair, his serious demeanor restored. "Gentlemen, I know this isn't a joking matter, and I apologize for my laughter. I also regret anything printed in the *Herald* should cause fights to break out amongst our citizens." He gave each of them a pointed look. "But the readers of my newspaper will be kept apprised of matters of interest in our country and our world. The passage of a national suffrage amendment is just such a matter." His voice deepened. "And there is no one else in Long Bow Valley more qualified to write about it than our own Miss Jones."

Frank took a step backward. "Dang if you don't believe that nonsense, too."

What Ben really believed was that he loved Katie. Loved her too much to let folks stop her from doing whatever would make her happy, whatever she cared about so passionately.

He wanted to shield her, too, from the anger her words had stirred to life, but she wouldn't let him. Although she hadn't said it aloud, she'd made it clear, the day he'd come upon her and the overheated Susan B, that she wouldn't have him protecting her. She was determined to do this, to convince the people of this valley and probably the entire state to use their ballots to help all women get the vote.

And, come to think of it, didn't all women *deserve* that right?

He met Frank's inquisitive gaze. "Yes, by dang, I guess I do believe that nonsense."

Yancy fought with the fence post as if it were a grizzly bear. Not that it needed that much wrestling to get it standing straight again. He just needed to work out his frustration, and this seemed the best way. He hadn't felt so exasperated in a coon's age. He couldn't figure out why Lark was so riled with him. All he'd said was it'd be better for Katie to find herself a husband than to go stirrin' up trouble, the way her column and her speechifyin' was bound to do.

He caught his glove on the barbed wire and tore it when he gave an ill-thought tug. He let out a string of curse words as would sizzle bacon, not because of the ruined glove but because he and Lark rarely disagreed about anything, and it always left him in a foul mood when they did.

Besides, all he wanted was for his little girl to be happy. He couldn't help it if he believed she'd be happier once she was married. Maybe because the same had been true of him. It wasn't until he'd met Lark that he'd known what real happiness was. Nothing he'd ever done had amounted to a hill of beans until he'd had Lark in his life.

He swore again as he returned to his horse and swung into the saddle.

Hell, this didn't have nothin' to do with women and the vote, far as he was concerned. This had to do with Katie findin' a contentment in her heart. Was he the only one who saw something was missin' in her smile, in her laugh, in her eyes? He knew she believed in this suffrage business. He did, too, for that matter. He wouldn't have done well in the Rider family if he didn't, as strong willed and hardheaded as the women tended to be. But there was more to life than social causes. That's all he wanted Katie to realize. He wanted her to find something closer to the heart than just ideals. Ideals were a good thing, and the world was a better place because of people who fought to make them come to pass. But Yancy wanted Katie to experience love, with all its joys and sorrows.

With that thought in mind, Yancy turned his horse toward home. He might have to let Katie work things out for herself over time, but he couldn't let his wife go on stewin' in anger. He had some fence mendin' to do with her, and he reckoned he'd better get to it sooner rather than later.

Katie was horrified when her oldest brother walked into the kitchen just before noon, sporting a black eye, a swollen nose, and various other cuts and bruises.

"This ain't nothin'," Sam said as he gingerly washed the dried blood from the corner of his nose. "Wait 'til you hear what Miss Coleson did to old Mr. Carson at the restaurant."

Despite Sam's jocular way of telling a story, Katie's horror didn't lessen when she heard the details of both his fight with the youngest Henderson brother and the altercation between the schoolmarm and the barber.

"Oh, dear . . ." She sighed and covered her face with

her hands. "Benjie warned me. I knew some folks would disagree with what I had to say, but I never thought it would come to fisticuffs." She looked at Sam through parted fingers, needing reassurance that he wasn't badly hurt.

"You needed someone to stand up for you." He gently fingered the swollen corner of his mouth. "I couldn't have Andrew sayin' things about my own sister. Not the sorts o' things he was sayin'."

Her voice dropped to a whisper as she lowered her hands. "Like what?"

"Ain't important."

"Like what, Sam?"

Her brother just shook his head, a stubborn look turning his face to stone. It was that same look all the Jones men got when they were through talking and nothing anyone did could drag another word out of them.

But she didn't need him to say anything more. She could guess what Andrew Henderson had said. Or at least come close to it. She'd heard enough insults slung at the women who participated in suffrage parades or who spoke at assemblies and conventions. Her imagination was fertile enough to fill in her brother's silence with any number of comments that might have incited Sam to feel obligated to fight on her behalf.

She rose from her chair and crossed the kitchen. Even though Sam was seven years younger than his sister, he stood a good ten inches taller, and Katie had to reach high up to touch his cheek with her fingertips.

"Thank you for defending my honor, Sammy. I should have realized what my work would do to all of you. I'm sorry. Truly sorry."

"Ahh, it's all right, sis. I don't reckon I minded. I never have cared much for Andy anyhow." He tried to smile, but the swollen left corner of his mouth wouldn't oblige.

Katie felt like hitting somebody herself. It shouldn't have to be like this. Why couldn't they all see that? Why were the hopes and dreams and desires of women thought to be unimportant, secondary—even to the women themselves?

Then she felt a shiver of exhilaration. Why was she upset? This could be a good thing, all this fighting and dissension. She could use it to further the cause. It would make some women, normally content to allow their husbands to do all the thinking and planning, realize they had some rights, too. This was not the time to pull back and apologize. This was the time to organize, to take action.

Katie turned away from her brother and hurried across the kitchen.

"Where're you off to?" Sam called after her.

"To town," she answered. "I need to pay a few calls."

It took Katie only a matter of minutes to gather her handbag, a pencil and notebook, and her hat. Then she was down the stairs and out the front door, hurrying toward the Susan B.

"No acting up today," she told the automobile as she set the spark and throttle levers. "We have important work to do." She walked to the front of the motorcar, where she seized the crank with her right hand and slipped her left forefinger through the choke wire.

Katie was small, but she was strong. Starting the Susan B for the past year had seen to that. It took only two revolutions of the crank before the engine roared to life. Quickly she jumped onto the running board and adjusted the levers again. The Susan B coughed, sputtered, then settled into her normal putting and chugging noises.

"Atta girl," Katie murmured as she slid across the imitation leather seat and took hold of the steering wheel.

She unblocked the hand brake and pressed down on the first gear pedal, and they were off, Katie's thoughts moving even faster than the Model T's twenty-two miles per hour.

She would pay a visit to Sophia Rafferty first. Sophia was well liked in Homestead. Unlike Katie, who had always been viewed as a bit strange, Sophia was a model of Homestead society's vision of proper young womanhood. If Sophia continued to show interest in woman's suffrage, it would strengthen the cause in Long Bow Valley.

Then, Katie decided, as soon as school let out she would stop in to see Blanche Coleson. Katie wasn't sure how she felt about the unmarried schoolmarm. Something in Blanche's manner made Katie nervous, but she couldn't quite put her finger on it. However, her feelings were secondary. Blanche was obviously a staunch supporter of the cause, and that was what Katie needed now.

Finally she supposed she should drop by the paper. She didn't have to be told there were people already pressuring Ben to cancel her column; she just knew. She also knew he wouldn't do it. Ben had too much integrity, was too good a newspaperman, to give in to such demands. Still, this was exactly what he'd been expecting to happen. This was what he'd hoped to protect her from. She had to let him know she was holding up just fine.

I wonder what Charlotte has had to say about it.

She frowned, and her hands tightened on the steering wheel. She should make a special effort to win Miss Orson's support. Did she want her own dear Benjie married to a mealy-mouthed Milquetoast sort?

Her frown deepened. That wasn't fair. She didn't know if Charlotte was mealy-mouthed or a Milquetoast.

In fact, she'd liked her almost from the moment they'd met. Despite herself, she'd liked her.

And who wouldn't? Ben certainly did.

She recalled the way the two of them had looked, standing near the plate-glass window of the newspaper office, lamplight spilling over them as they'd kissed.

Katie had never been kissed like that, with a man's arms wound around her, her head bent back, her body close to his. Of course, she'd had only a few gentlemen callers and so hadn't had many opportunities. Nonetheless, those kisses she'd received had been hurried and furtive and had left her uninterested in pursuing more of them.

But maybe, if she'd been kissed the way Ben had kissed Charlotte . . .

She felt a curious tightness in her stomach. Something she couldn't quite define. Something she'd never felt before. Something she was certain she would be better off not to feel.

The small chimes above the Book Shoppe's doorway jingled as Sophia entered.

"Be right with you," Matthew said from somewhere behind a bookshelf.

Sophia waited nervously for him to appear. It had taken her two full days to work up her courage, and it was all she could do to stand her ground.

As he stepped out from behind the bookshelves and saw her, Matthew's face lit up with a smile. "Sophia. What a pleasant surprise." He strode forward and placed a chaste kiss on her cheek. "I assumed you'd be much too involved with last minute plans for the wedding to come see me today. Only four days more and you'll be mine."

You'll be mine. . . . Why should those words bother her so much? Wasn't being his what she'd always wanted?

"I . . . I needed to . . . to see you," she stammered. She drew a deep breath, trying to steady her nerves. "Matthew, we need to talk."

His fingers closed gently around her upper arms. "Is something wrong?" he asked with genuine concern.

"No." She shook her head. "No. I mean, I don't *think* anything's wrong. But we . . . I think we need to talk, Matthew."

"All right."

Cupping her right elbow in the palm of his left hand, he guided her toward a bench beneath the west side window. She settled onto it, smoothing her skirts as she did so. Then her fiancé sat beside her. Words whirled in her head as she sought the right one with which to begin. But none seemed right.

"What is it?" Matthew prompted after a lengthy silence, with just a hint of impatience.

She looked up. "Did you read Katie's column this morning?" She almost hoped he hadn't.

His expression hardened. "I did, and I'm of the firm opinion that your brother needs to put an end to it."

"Why do you think that, Matthew?"

"Because it's simply more of her nonsense, that's why. Katie always has been a peculiar one, but she's infecting the whole town with her odd views now. Good Lord above, you've no idea how angry folks are. It's nonsense, all of it."

"Why is it nonsense? *I* voted in the last election. Did you think that was nonsense? Was it wrong of me?"

He raised an eyebrow. "Of course it wasn't wrong, my dear girl. As you'll recall, we discussed each of the candidates, and I explained why you should vote as you did."

Sophia clenched her hands in her lap. "Are you so certain I voted as you wished?"

He looked confused.

She rushed on. "You really don't believe I'm intelligent enough to judge a candidate for myself, do you? You don't think I could cast a vote without asking you first."

"Sophia, you've changed the subject. But if it's politics you wish to discuss, I can only say women shouldn't concern themselves with it. It's a man's business. It always has been, and that's how it should remain."

She felt coiled as tight as a spring. "And what is a *woman's* business, Matthew?" Her voice was barely above a whisper. "Can you tell me that?"

"Why, the home, of course, and the children when they come." He looked so genuinely bemused by her questions that it might have been funny. It might have been. . . .

But it wasn't.

Sophia rose from the bench and stepped away from it. She heard Matthew rise as well, but she didn't look behind her. "I'm going to help Katie with her suffrage work, if she'll let me. I think you should know that."

"Help her! Great Scot, Sophia! Have you entirely lost your senses?"

"No, I haven't. I may have just found them."

He took a quick step forward, stopping behind her, placing his hands on her shoulders. "My dear, you're going to be far too busy making your home comfortable for your new husband to be gadding about with Katie Jones."

Anger flared with a suddenness that shook her. "Not if I choose to give time to her work instead." She stared at the shop door, wishing he wasn't holding on to her shoulders, wishing she could leave now before anything worse happened.

"Think what it is you're saying, Sophia. You'll be ostracized. Half the town is already angry with Katie. Do you want them angry with you, too?"

"It's mostly the men who are angry, isn't it?"

"Does it matter?" he half shouted.

She turned to face him. "Not to me, it doesn't. I'm going to do it whether they're angry or not. I don't care what any of them think."

"Sophia, I *forbid* it."

She'd feared it would come to this. Deep down in her heart, she'd known it would come to this. And it was deep down in her heart where she hurt, now that it had happened.

She drew a breath and let it out on a sigh. "You can't forbid me, Matthew. I can do what I please."

"As your husband—"

"Don't say it," she interrupted quickly as she took a step backward.

"I will not have my wife—"

"Matthew"—her voice quavered slightly—"I've loved you for a long, long time." She drew another quick breath, and her voice steadied, strengthened. "But I'm not a little girl with fairy-tale dreams any longer. I'm a woman. I can think for myself. I don't need anyone to hold my hand and tell me what I should or shouldn't do."

"Of course you—"

"I want to be your wife, Matthew. But not if it means I cease to be a person who matters."

"That's the sort of idiotic blather you've been getting from Katie."

"It's not blather! And it's not from Katie." She pointed at her chest. "This is me talking, Matthew. Me. Sophia. The woman you're supposed to care about and listen to. The woman whose thoughts and feelings should matter to you more than anything else."

"Why are you acting so crazy? Have I said I didn't care?"

The anger drained out of her. Calmly she answered, "I'm not acting crazy. I am trying to tell you how I feel. I'm trying to tell you what's important to me. But you don't hear me, do you?" She shook her head. "Either that or you don't care. Which is it, Matthew?"

"Sophia, you're just tired. Getting ready for a wedding is hard on everyone. Why don't you go home and have a nap? You'll see things more clearly when you wake up."

Her heart was breaking, shattering along with her dreams. "I see things quite clearly right now." She removed her engagement ring and set it on the counter. "I'm very sorry, Matthew, but I cannot marry you after all."

Before he could voice another protest, she turned and fled the Book Shoppe.

9

Just as the Susan B was rolling up to the Rafferty house, Katie saw Sophia walking toward her from the direction of town. She slid across the seats and disembarked, waiting beside the automobile for Ben's sister to arrive. Then she saw her dab at her eyes with a handkerchief.

"Sophia?"

She stopped and looked up.

Katie hurried forward. "What's wrong?"

She shook her head.

"What happened?"

Sophia offered a weak smile, accompanied by a shrug of her shoulders. "I just broke my engagement to Matthew."

"Oh, no," Katie whispered, her fingers covering her mouth, her eyes wide. Suddenly her stomach felt like lead. "It's because of my column, isn't it?"

"No," Sophia answered forcefully.

"I never thought—"

"It's not because of your column, Katie. It's because we weren't suited for each other. That's all."

But Katie found her protest hard to believe. She remembered too well how lovesick Sophia had been at the age of sixteen. Back then Katie had been eager for college and new adventures, but Sophia had wanted only Matthew. Katie remembered the letters from home that had said what a perfect couple these two were. She couldn't believe that everyone—including Sophia and Matthew themselves—had been wrong.

Sophia touched Katie's forearm. "This has nothing to do with you." She smiled again, and this time the expression didn't appear as forced. "It really is for the best. I realized earlier this week that Matthew needs a different sort of wife than I can ever be."

"But you've loved him so very much."

"Yes." The word was spoken softly—and with great finality.

"Oh, Sophia," she whispered, unable to think of anything else to say.

Ben's sister glanced toward the house. "I must go in and tell Mother."

"Of course. I'll come back another time."

Looking at Katie, Sophia said, "I know this is going to hurt for a while, but it *is* for the best. For both of us. We wouldn't have done well together. I would have made him unhappy in the end. And I would have been unhappy, too." Again she smiled gently. Again she touched Katie's arm. "Don't worry about me, and don't you dare blame yourself. This would have happened with or without your column."

Katie watched Sophia walk across the yard, climb the steps, and enter the front door of the Rafferty home. She hoped with all her heart that Sophia was telling the truth. But even if this was for the best, even if Katie shouldered no responsibility for it, she knew others would blame her.

Mentally she wrestled with her confusion as she turned and moved toward the Susan B.

Katie believed, without a shred of doubt, in what she'd written, just as she believed in the truth of what she'd said during her speech to the ladies of the church circle and what she'd said to Sophia last Saturday. But still, if this breakup was her fault . . .

By rote she went through the motions of starting the Susan B, then climbed into the automobile and drove to the school. She parked on West Street and stared at the white building as memories washed over her.

Years ago Katie had envied Sophia, who'd been so sure of what she wanted while Katie had still been searching. Sophia had known she wanted to marry Matthew, to settle down in Homestead and have a family. Katie, on the other hand, had felt a pull on her heart to go beyond this valley, to see more, to learn more, to do more—not knowing what "more" could be, knowing only that she had to find out.

It was while at Vassar that she'd first heard Inez Milholland speak on the suffrage issue. That night, for the first time in her life, she had felt a rightness, a sense of belonging, of not being out of step with the rest of the world. All the pieces of her puzzled existence had seemed to fall into place.

The old schoolhouse came back into focus, along with her conviction that she had a mission to accomplish in Idaho. Would she have said anything different, done anything different, if she'd known Matthew and Sophia might break their engagement over it? The answer was clearly "no." And thus she could only continue as she'd begun.

The doors of the school opened, and children—from six

to sixteen—ran out, filling the air with shouts and laughter. They scattered in different directions, some of them on foot, some of them on horseback. The Susan B drew many a gaze, and three of the older boys mustered the courage to follow her brother toward the automobile.

Rick jerked his head toward those behind him. "You don't mind if my friends have a look, do you, Katie? I told 'em you wouldn't."

"No." She grinned at him. "I don't mind." She got out and walked to the front of the motorcar.

She recognized all three of the boys. Shane Rafferty she'd known as long as she'd known her own brother. He and Rick had been friends since childhood, just like Ben and Katie. Kirby Evans lived on a farm out in the valley. Even though Kirby had been only eight years old when Katie had left Homestead, she recognized him now because he was the spitting image of his father, Ralph. The last boy, Clarence Yardley, was the druggist's son. She'd met Clarence and his father, Lee, at the potluck supper the previous Friday.

Katie greeted them each by name as they surrounded the automobile.

"How fast does it go?" Shane asked as he lifted the hood to stare at the engine.

"I've heard the Touring Car can go as fast as forty miles an hour, but I've never had the courage to test it for myself."

"What's keepin' it runnin'?" Kirby inquired. "Pa said you're bound t'run out o' fuel sooner or later and then you'll just have t'let it sit and rust. He says a horse'll never run out o' power as long as there's grass t'eat."

She laughed. "I'm afraid your pa will be disappointed. I've had gasoline sent up from Boise City on the train. There's not going to be any lack of fuel for the Susan B."

Clarence leaned over the door to check the interior. "Is it hard t'learn to drive?"

"Not really."

Struck with inspiration, Rick turned wide eyes on his sister. "You reckon you could teach us, Katie?"

The others all turned to look at her, too.

"Sorry, boys. I'm the only one who drives the Susan B." She watched disappointment wash over them, and she couldn't help but respond to it. "Tell you what. You come out to the Lazy L sometime, and I'll show you how everything works. I won't let you actually drive, but I can teach you about starting her and what each of the pedals do and so forth."

There was some excited shoving among the four boys.

"We'll be there, Miss Jones," Kirby promised. "How 'bout tomorrow?"

"Yeah. How 'bout tomorrow?" the others all chimed in.

She considered it a moment, then relented. "All right. When you're done with your chores and if your folks say it's all right, then I'll do it."

"Swell!" they chorused.

Katie looked at her brother. "I've got some errands to do in town. Do you want to wait for a ride home?"

"Naw," Rick answered. "I've got my horse over at the Raffertys' place."

After that, the boys bade her good-bye and dispersed in pairs, Kirby and Clarence headed toward town, Shane and Rick walking along the road in the opposite direction. Katie watched them go, then turned toward the schoolhouse just as the door opened and Blanche Coleson stepped onto the landing.

The schoolmarm's eyes lit up when she saw Katie. "Miss Jones," she called, "how fortuitous. I was just thinking about paying you a call." She turned and quickly locked the door, then descended the steps and closed the distance between them.

Katie had the urge to draw back and wondered again at the way Blanche Coleson made her feel.

As for Blanche, she was experiencing true elation, something akin to religious fervor, like nothing she'd felt in years. Although Katie Jones was over fifteen years her junior, Blanche believed she had found a kindred spirit in the younger woman. Here was someone who understood the superiority of the female, someone who understood why it was better not to marry, better not to chain oneself to a man for any reason, especially when to do so meant being subjected to unspeakable acts that didn't bear consideration.

She shivered with disgust at the mere thought of it.

"Your column this morning was truly inspired, Miss Jones. I feared this school day would never end so I could send my students home. I did so want to tell you in person my reaction to your column. I have not felt this way since I heard Miss Anthony herself speak many years ago."

"Thank you." Katie's smile was fleeting. "However, I'm afraid my ideas have caused a bit of trouble in town."

"Of course they have. They should. You have sounded the call of liberty to the women of this valley, Miss Jones. You should be proud of yourself."

"Thank you," she repeated. "I only wrote what I believe to be true."

Blanche nodded. "Of course. And we must do more, Miss Jones. We carry the torch of truth, you and I. We must help the misguided see. I can be of real help to you. What will we be doing next?"

"I haven't decided."

"I'm sure we can come up with something if we just put our heads together."

Katie murmured a soft word of agreement as she pulled open the door to her motorcar.

Blanche reached to stop her, grabbing hold of Katie's free hand. "You're not going, are you? We haven't had a chance to talk."

"I'm afraid I *must* go, Miss Coleson." Katie eased her hand free.

She felt intense disappointment but tried to hide it. "Please. You must call me Blanche." She took one step backward. "I will look forward to hearing from you soon. And in the meantime, I'll be thinking of ways we might do even more for the cause."

Katie nodded, then hurriedly started her automobile and drove away from the school.

Well, Blanche thought as she walked slowly away, it was clear Katie Jones didn't appreciate what she was offering to do. She would have to be more forceful in the future. She'd waited too long for this. Too long.

Ben left the newspaper early for a change. He didn't want to see or talk to one more person. He'd lost count of how many men had come into the office during the day, all of them with the same purpose—to put an end to Katie's column. Reverend Percy's visit had been the last straw. The minister had railed against Katie, saying that what she was doing was a sin against God and nature. Ben had nearly thrown him out of his office.

What was the matter with all of them? he wondered as he followed the sidewalk down Main Street, his hat brim pulled low. He purposely avoided looking about for fear he would make eye contact and then have to stop and listen to another diatribe against Katie and her outlandish ideas.

But they weren't outlandish. In between interruptions

Ben had read over the column again, just to make sure, and he'd discovered the same sense of pride in what Katie had written. He'd been able to hear her voice in the turn of every phrase. Her earnest belief in the cause of woman's suffrage was clear, and because of it she'd forced Ben to take an honest look at himself and his own beliefs.

Why couldn't others see it as clearly as he did?

He had passed both the Book Shoppe and the office of Vincent Michaels, attorney-at-law, when he heard his name called.

Not another one, he thought wearily as he turned to see who had hailed him. It was Matthew. While waiting for his future brother-in-law to catch up to him, Ben removed his hat and raked his fingers through his hair, unmindful of the impatience clearly visible in the gesture.

When Matthew stopped in front of Ben, he was breathing as hard as if he'd walked a mile instead of the length of a few storefronts. "Ben," he huffed, "you've got to talk some sense into your sister."

He was taken entirely off guard. He'd been expecting another complaint about Katie. "Sophia? What's she done?"

"What's she done? She's called off the wedding!"

"Good Lord."

Matthew waved his hand in the air. "She's got a bee in her bonnet about that stupid suffragette business."

Ah, there it was. Katie. Just as he'd expected.

"Ben, she doesn't realize how this is going to look to people. I've never seen her behaving this way. She's always been the model of gentility and common sense. This isn't like her." He shook his head. "Not like her at all."

"I don't know. If she isn't ready to get married—"

"She doesn't know what she's doing. You've got to talk to her." Matthew jabbed his finger at Ben's chest. "You printed that dad-blamed nonsense in your paper. Now you've got to make things right."

Come to think of it, Ben never had warmed up to Matthew Jacobs. He was small minded and judgmental. Maybe not a bad person, but certainly intolerant of those who didn't see things his own way.

Ben took a step backward, then set his hat on his head. "I'll talk to Sophia," he promised vaguely.

"Good. And what about that column? Is this the last of it we'll see?"

Come to think of it, he didn't like Matthew at all. And he was liking him less by the minute.

"Miss Jones will continue to write for the *Homestead Herald* as long as she wishes. Her ideas are thought provoking, which is exactly what I want. To make people think when they read my paper." He saw Matthew's face redden with anger. "Good day to you," he said quickly. Then he turned and strode away before he could tell his sister's former fiancé just exactly how he felt about the broken engagement.

It was with a sense of relief, a few moments later, that Ben stepped through the wide double doorway of the Rafferty Hotel. He was looking forward to a peaceful evening in the suite of rooms he kept on the top floor. As short-tempered as he was feeling, he was afraid the next person to say something about Katie was going to get a taste of his knuckles.

Then he saw Katie herself rise from the satin-tufted sofa in the hotel lobby, and he immediately forgot his desire not to talk to another living soul. Instead he felt a sudden pleasure. "What are you doing here, Katie?" he asked as he moved toward her.

"I wanted to see you."

"Why didn't you come to the paper?"

"I was trying to escape Miss Coleson. The hotel seemed a good place." Katie wrinkled her nose. "She's rather . . . *odd*, isn't she?"

Ben chuckled. "Yes, I think that would describe her."

She acted as though he hadn't spoken. "Besides, I needed a moment of quiet to think." A frown knitted her brows, and she pursed her mouth as she dragged in a breath.

"Trouble?"

"I saw Sophia a little while ago."

"Oh. *That.*"

"You know? About her and Matthew?"

"I know." And he couldn't be more pleased, Ben considered adding but didn't.

"This is more difficult than I thought."

"What is?"

She swept at a wisp of hair, fluttering along the side of her face. "Everything."

"Come on." He took hold of her arm and guided her toward the hotel dining room. "You look like you could use some cheering up."

Uncharacteristically she said nothing as she allowed him to steer her toward a corner table.

Ben pulled out a chair. "Sit," he commanded.

She did.

"Okay, spill. What exactly is upsetting you, Katie?"

She looked up, and he was struck afresh by all the things that made her beautiful and special, both inside and out. He had an unspoken understanding with Charlotte, but it was Katie he wanted to kiss, Katie he wanted to hold, Katie he wanted. If he thought she might ever . . .

"It's very different here from the way it was in Washington," she said softly. "It doesn't change how I feel about things, but I don't want to hurt the people I care about. My father is upset with me, and he and Mother are barely speaking to each other today. And I never meant for my words to cause problems between Sophia and Matthew."

He covered one of her hands with one of his. "You're not at fault."

"But I—"

"It's *not* your fault."

She gave him a weak smile. "You're sweet to me, Benjie. You always have been."

He didn't want to be sweet. He wanted to be selfish. He wanted to make her love him as he loved her. But Katie saw a childhood friend when she looked at him, not the man he'd become. She saw someone akin to a brother, not a lover. She wanted a life dedicated to a social cause. He wanted a wife and children and a quiet home life.

"It isn't only that," she said, interrupting his disturbing train of thought. "Miss Coleson is eager to help me organize, and Sophia says she wants to help, too. But I can't seem to think of what to do next." Her voice lowered. "I feel so confused lately. It's not like me."

He wanted to erase her confusion. He wanted to make her smile. Really smile, the way only Katie could. He would do anything to make it happen. "I have an idea," he said, giving her hand a squeeze.

It was crazy. He shouldn't do this. He should keep quiet. He didn't want or need any more complications. He wanted peace and tranquillity. That was what he'd returned to Homestead to find. Whatever Katie did, he would find himself smack dab in the middle of it. He would regret getting himself more deeply involved with her schemes and causes. He knew it as surely as he knew his own name.

But he didn't heed the small voice of reason in his head. "Why not invite the candidates to come to Homestead? We'll have a debate or a rally of some sort."

Her entire countenance brightened. "A rally?"

He got his wish. She smiled. And before he knew it, he was making another suggestion. "Maybe you should have an Idaho version of the 'Suffrage Special.' You could take the Susan B around Idaho and hold meetings to encourage women to vote."

"Oh, Ben, what a scrumptious idea!"

Scrumptious. A good word to describe Katie.

"I knew I could count on you." She rose from her chair, leaned across the table, and kissed his cheek.

And Ben had to remind himself once again that they were only friends and that was all Katie wanted them to be.

10

On Saturday Homestead fairly buzzed with the news of the broken engagement, and people debated—in homes, in businesses, and on the street—what part "Katie's Corner" had played in the breakup.

From his pulpit on Sunday, Reverend Simon Jacobs reminded the congregation of the Homestead Community Church that marriage was a serious and sacred act into which no one should enter in haste or with doubts. He added that while he would have loved to call Sophia Rafferty his daughter-in-law, he would not criticize her for making a difficult decision. He reminded all those listening to him to heed God's instructions to judge not, lest they be judged.

For his part, Reverend Charles Percy railed against the fast and immoral practices of modern women. And everyone in the First Methodist Church understood precisely whom he meant. He encouraged his flock to be mindful of a woman's proper role in life, first as daughter and later as wife, and he cautioned against those who would forget said roles. It was such forgetfulness, he warned, that had caused trouble for two of Homestead's respected young people. Reverend Percy asked all his devout parishioners to be in prayer for the young woman, that she might see the error of her thinking and make herself right with her intended.

Charlotte's father, Reverend Obadiah Orson, made no reference to either the broken engagement or to Katie's newspaper column. Seated beside Charlotte in the first pew of the King of Glory Lutheran Church, Ben was relieved by the omission. He was tired of hearing about both. It wouldn't be until later in the day that he would learn such was not the case in the two other churches of the town.

Although the chasm between the two sides of the suffrage amendment issue continued to widen as the week progressed—George Blake still slept on the sofa and Phillip Carson shot hateful glances at Blanche Coleson whenever he saw her—Katie was too enthusiastically involved in her work to give it much notice. She sent letters to both state and national candidates in Idaho, inviting them to participate in an election rally. She requested literature from NAWSA's offices in Washington. She pored over the writings of Susan B. Anthony and others, promising herself she would be the best-informed speaker at the assembly. She met with her suffrage committee—made up of Sophia, Blanche, and their newest member, Leslie Blake—and mapped out an itinerary for the route of the "Idaho Special," to be undertaken during August and September. And she wrote her next column for the *Homestead Herald*, blissfully preparing to add more fuel to the already hot fires of disagreement.

Every day she drove her automobile into Homestead, where she met with Ben in his office. He encouraged her, bolstered her, and advised her, and those visits were her favorite part of the day. Ben was the best friend anyone had ever had. She was convinced of it.

It was on Friday morning, the day Katie's third column appeared in the *Herald*, that Charlotte Orson paid a visit to the Lazy L Ranch.

"You have caused quite a stir in town," Charlotte said as she settled onto the sofa in the front parlor. "Benjamin is enjoying it, although he would profess his preference for peace and quiet."

Katie nodded her agreement, remembering all the ideas Ben had come up with during their meetings in his office and acknowledging to herself that the real credit for whatever success she might have in the next few months would be due to him.

"I understand Benjamin is assisting you with the rally you've planned," Charlotte went on.

"Yes, he is. I had no idea Ben knew so many people in the government. He's been a great help to me."

Charlotte leaned forward, her expression earnest. "Miss Jones, I know how fond you are of Benjamin." She smiled briefly. "I am, too."

She loves him, Katie thought. She's going to make him the perfect wife. Something tightened in her chest.

"Miss Jones." Charlotte shook her head. "May I call you Katie?"

"Of course."

"Katie, I wonder if you're aware that some of the businessmen in town are refusing to advertise in the *Herald* as long as the newspaper publishes your column."

Katie caught her breath. "But that isn't fair."

"No, it isn't."

"Are you positive? I've met with Ben every day this week, and he's never mentioned it."

"He wouldn't. He says the paper is in good financial condition and can handle a reduction in revenue. He says he won't have editorial decisions made by"—she allowed another little smile—"bigots and ignoramuses."

Katie found no reason to smile. "Why didn't he tell me what was happening?" *Why would he tell you and not me?* was what she really wanted to ask.

"Because he doesn't want to hurt or worry you." Charlotte's tone was gentle. "Because he cares for you a great deal."

A yearning for something undefined twisted Katie's heart. "I don't want Benjie to be hurt, either," she whispered.

"Of course you don't. That's why I felt free to come and speak to you." Charlotte hesitated a moment. A look of indecision crossed her face before she continued, "Because we both love Benjamin, I hope we can become good friends, you and I. Between the two of us, perhaps we can be sure he doesn't act unwisely. The *Herald* means more to him than he might ever admit. And he's much too proud to borrow money from his father to save it, if it should come to that."

Because we both love Benjamin. A lump formed in Katie's throat as Charlotte's words echoed in her mind. *Because we both love Ben.* She looked down at her hands, folded tightly in her lap.

"Miss Jones? Katie?"

She glanced up.

"You *will* help me, won't you? Sometimes, Benjamin . . . sometimes his deep affection for you affects his better judgment. He has an important position in Homestead. People look up to him. They depend upon him. He's trusted by so many. He mustn't jeopardize that position." Her blue eyes appeared misty. "Not even for friendship." Another pause. Another brief, halfhearted smile. "Not even for you, Katie."

We both love Ben.

In that one terrible moment, she realized the significance of those words. They both loved Ben. *Katie* loved Ben. Not just as his friend. Not the way Charlotte meant.

Or was it *exactly* the way Charlotte meant?

Katie looked into the other woman's eyes and saw the truth. Charlotte had understood Katie's feelings even before she had understood them herself.

And there was another truth to be seen in those pretty blue eyes. Charlotte was afraid. Afraid of what Katie would do with her newfound understanding. Afraid that she would lose Ben to Katie. Charlotte had come here to plead for Katie not to take Ben away from her.

As if she could have done so if she'd wished to.

It might have been amusing if it weren't so very tragic.

Katie rose from her chair and walked over to the parlor window, where she stared out at the sweep of land that curved west and north, framed by tall, pine-covered mountains. But she didn't see what lay before her. Instead she saw Ben—and she wondered why she hadn't realized before the depth of what she felt for him.

And if she had, would it have made any difference? To either of them? No.

"I suppose I don't need to write another column," she said at last. "Perhaps I've accomplished what I set out to accomplish with it."

"Thank you."

"Ben will have to report on the rally." Katie glanced over her shoulder. "It will mean nothing if it doesn't appear in the papers. It will be a newsworthy event."

Charlotte blinked away tears. "Of course he'll report on it. Benjamin is an excellent journalist."

"I'll be terribly busy over the remainder of the summer. My work is of paramount importance to me. It always has been. I won't be able to see much of Ben." She felt as if she'd been kicked in the chest by a horse.

Charlotte rose from the sofa. "He'll miss you."

But he'll have you, Katie thought, and tried not to be made miserable by it.

"I must go now."

"I'll see you to the door." She led the way out of the parlor.

Once there, Charlotte paused in the open doorway. "I wish you much success in all your endeavors."

"That's very kind of you," she replied woodenly, eager for Charlotte to be gone, wanting to be alone so she could sort out her thoughts and feelings.

"Good day, Katie." She paused, then added softly, "Thank you."

"Good day."

She watched as Charlotte walked to the waiting surrey and climbed in. Automatically she lifted her hand to wave farewell when Charlotte glanced back her way.

Please make him happy, she thought as the horse pulled the surrey out of the yard.

Please.

Ben looked at the clock and wondered again where Katie was. It was well past the hour she usually dropped in at the newspaper.

He got up from his chair and paced to the window. He heard the bleak wail of a train whistle. The weekly Union Pacific, up from Boise City, was on time today. But where was Katie?

He would have thought she'd be certain to come in today, what with her latest column in the newspaper. He would have thought she'd want to learn people's reaction to it, to the election rally she was proposing. He could ring her on the telephone, of course, but he didn't want to simply *talk* to her. He wanted to *see* her.

Seeing Katie had become a vital part of his day. Like breathing.

He raked his fingers through his hair as he faced a hard truth. He wasn't ever going to fall in love with Charlotte. He couldn't. He already loved Katie too much, and time and determination weren't going to change that.

He had to break things off with Charlotte. There would be more talk in town, more unpleasant gossip, just as there'd been about Sophia and Matthew. Some would blame Katie, just as they had before. Another Rafferty romance ruined by her modern thinking, they would say.

But Katie couldn't help it if her enthusiasm was contagious to those around her. And she couldn't help being the woman he'd fallen in love with—hook, line, and sinker.

Which brought him back to Charlotte.

He had his usual supper engagement with her tonight. For the past several months, on almost every Friday, he had taken her to eat at the hotel restaurant. He would have to tell her tonight. It wouldn't be fair of him not to.

He remembered the night he'd kissed her right in front of this very same window. He'd known then he didn't love her, that he loved Katie. But he'd kissed her anyway. Made her think there was more between them than there was. Had been making her think so for a long time. She deserved better. None of this was her fault. Charlotte was lovely and warm and gentle and . . .

"Hell," he muttered as he reached for his hat. "I should go tell her right now."

But before he could move toward the door, it opened and a couple of strangers came through the opening. The man and woman were both handsomely dressed, although a bit wrinkled from travel, the young woman in a green shirtwaist of fine lawn, the fellow in a white linen suit and straw hat.

The woman—attractive enough, in an ordinary sort of way—took another step forward and held out her hand. "How do you do, Mr. Rafferty?"

"I'm sorry. Do I know—"

"I'm Katie's friend, Penelope Rudyard, and I would have known you anywhere from Katie's description." She tossed a smile over her shoulder. "That's my brother, Geoffrey. We've come all the way from Chicago as a surprise for Katie. We thought to hire someone to take us to her home, but then I remembered you would be the logical person to help us find her. And so here we are. Can you help us?"

"Penny," her brother interrupted, "it looks as if Mr. Rafferty was about to go out. Perhaps we're intruding."

"No, it's all right," Ben said quickly, glad for the opportunity to postpone the less pleasant duty of breaking off with Charlotte, even more glad for an excuse to see Katie. "I'd be delighted to take you out to the Lazy L." He motioned toward a pair of wooden chairs. "Make yourselves comfortable while I go over to the livery for my buggy. I'll be back for you shortly."

While Blanche Coleson and Leslie Blake stared down at the sketches on the dining room table, Sophia studied Katie. There was something wrong with their fearless leader today. Katie was distracted. There was a decided lack of energy in her voice and in her movements. Sophia hoped she wasn't ill. This fledgling group of suffragettes badly needed Katie's leadership or they would flounder.

Katie rose from her chair and stepped over to the window, where she leaned her shoulder against the casement. Her index finger fiddled with the gold locket she wore around her neck as she stared outside with a glazed sort of look. Her shoulders lifted and fell with a deep sigh.

"There are several large shade trees behind the hotel," Blanche said in her precise, no-nonsense tone of voice. "It will be the perfect place to hold the rally."

Leslie nodded. "We can hire someone to build a platform." She pointed to the sketch. "We can place benches here. What do you think, Katie?"

"Yes, that will be fine," she answered without pulling her gaze from what lay beyond the glass.

Sophia got up from her chair and went over to stand beside Katie. She heard Leslie and Blanche resume their discussion, the two older women seemingly oblivious of Katie's strange mood.

"Katie." She placed her hand on her friend's shoulder. "Are you feeling all right?"

"What?" Katie blinked, glanced quickly at Sophia, then away again. "Oh, yes. I'm fine."

Sophia frowned, more convinced now than ever that something was wrong. "You *would* tell me if something was troubling you, wouldn't you?" she asked softly, so the other women wouldn't hear.

"Hmm."

"Katie?" Her fingers tightened. "You're not upset because of your mother, are you?"

"Mother?"

"Because she's not here today? Has she changed her mind about working with us? Are your parents still arguing?"

Katie shook her head as she resumed twisting her necklace, flipping the locket over her finger again and again. "No, they seem to have settled their differences. Mother will be here next time. Today she's trying to convince Grandpa Will to see a doctor in Boise City next week about his back. That's what Dr. Tom wants him to do."

"Are you worried about your grandfather, then?"

"A little, I suppose. But Grandma Addie thinks he'll be all right if he just follows the doctor's orders." She released a dry chuckle. "She says he needs to remember he's seventy, not twenty."

Sophia still wasn't satisfied. "Well, *something* is bothering you, Katie Jones, and I wish you'd tell me what it is."

"Would you two quit whispering over there," Blanche interrupted, "and come participate in this discussion? We have a great deal to accomplish in very little time."

Katie straightened away from the casement. "Yes, we do, don't we?" She offered a cheerless smile to Sophia. "Our work is important, and I mustn't forget that. It's the reason I came back to Homestead, after all." Then she returned to the table and sat down again.

And Sophia was more convinced than ever that something was amiss.

Over the next half hour Katie did her best to concentrate on the plans the committee was making. She knew Sophia was watching her and wondering what was wrong. It would be utterly awful were Ben's sister to guess the truth. Nearly as bad as it would be for Ben himself to discover it.

How had she allowed this to happen? His friendship meant the world to her. Now she feared losing it forever. Despite Charlotte saying she hoped the two of them would become friends, Katie knew it was never to be. How could it, when she would be jealous of Charlotte for what she had?

But Katie didn't want marriage. She never had. She was different from Ben in that way. Marriage was a wonderful institution for some, but not for her. Her work had to come first.

And Ben was going to marry Charlotte.

"Katie?"

She looked up.

Sophia was frowning at her. "There's someone at the door. Would you like me to answer it?"

"No." She rose from her chair. "I'll get it."

As she walked toward the front entrance, she scolded herself silently. She had to put Ben out of her mind. She had to remain focused on what was important.

She pulled open the door and felt her heart skitter. "Benjie," she whispered.

He grinned like the Cheshire cat in Lewis Carroll's *Alice's Adventures in Wonderland.* "Look who I've brought to see you." He motioned with his arm as he stepped to one side.

Nothing could have astonished Katie more than having Penelope Rudyard step into view.

"Penny!" she cried. "Oh, what a perfectly scrumptious surprise!"

Laughing, the two women hugged each other. Then Katie saw Penelope's brother, waiting quietly behind her.

"Geoffrey? You came, too?"

"I wasn't about to let Penny have all the fun of surprising you," he replied.

"I'm so glad you didn't. Come in. Come in, both of you. I want you to meet the ladies who are helping me with our work here." She drew Penelope into the house. "And we want to hear everything that happened at the convention in Chicago."

It would be all right now, she thought as she led the way into the dining room. With Penelope here to help her, she would be able to put aside her feelings for Ben. This was going to make all the difference in the world.

Purposely she avoided glancing toward Ben to see if the words rang true.

*   *   *

Lark Jones insisted Penelope and her brother stay at the Lazy L. "It isn't anything fancy," she told them, "but it's got enough bedrooms. Besides, Katie's not about to let you leave until you've told her everything she wants to hear. Mark my words. You'll be up half the night, talking."

And that was exactly what Katie, Penelope, and Geoffrey did. Katie asked her friends question after question about the convention in Chicago. She could close her eyes and imagine the thousands of women— and a sprinkling of men—who had gathered there to demand the right to vote for all.

"Oh, Penny, I wish I'd gone with you. I could have come home afterward."

"But look at what you've accomplished in such a short time," her friend replied. "You're much further along than even I expected. You've formed a committee, and you're planning a rally, and you've been writing a column for the newspaper."

Katie felt a little skip in her heart. "I may not write another column."

"Why ever not?" Geoffrey inquired. "I've read your latest. It's a truly excellent piece. Had we known what a fine writer you are, we would have put you to work on the association's literature."

She shook her head, even though she was warmed by his praise. "But all I did was use the words of other women who have fought for suffrage for decades."

"Don't be so modest." Penelope patted Katie's hand with her fingertips. "You have a real gift. Your writing is easy to understand and it's written with passion, which makes it interesting. Even those who violently disagree cannot help but keep reading."

"Thank you," she whispered.

"Surely your Mr. Rafferty doesn't want you to stop, does he?"

Another little skip, this one painful. *My Mr. Rafferty . . .*

Only he wasn't hers.

He belonged to Charlotte.

Geoffrey stifled a yawn. "I'm afraid the days are catching up with me." He rose from the overstuffed chair. "If you ladies will excuse me, I'm going to retire for the night." He stepped over to where Katie was seated, leaned down and kissed her cheek, then kissed his sister in the same fashion. "Good night, you two."

"Good night, Geoffrey," they returned in unison.

Once he'd disappeared through the parlor doorway, Katie stood. "You must be tired as well. Come on. I'll see you to your room."

Arm in arm they climbed the stairs to the second floor. They didn't speak, both of them comfortable in their silence.

Penelope and Katie had become fast friends at Vassar, quickly learning they had the same dedication to the suffrage cause. They'd shared a room their last two years at college, and it was then the idea was conceived for the two of them to go to work for the association.

Penelope and Geoffrey were from a wealthy and prominent family in Massachusetts. Eugenia Rudyard, a widow, was a leader in the suffrage cause in her own state. It was she who had paid the rent on the apartment in Washington where the two young women lived. Without Mrs. Rudyard's generosity Katie would have been forced to return to Idaho. She couldn't have asked her father for financial help.

Still, Katie had tried to insist she should be making her own way. Mrs. Rudyard had waved away her words with an aristocratic flip of her wrist. "Don't be silly, Katie dear. We need young, enthusiastic workers such as yourself. I am able to do this and much more. You and Penny make a wonderful team. The two of you must use your wages for other than necessities. I'll see to those."

With the memory still drifting in her thoughts, Katie asked, "How's your mother? It's been ages since I last saw her."

"Oh, you know Mother. She's positively brewing over with ideas after the convention. I daresay President Wilson had best watch his step."

Laughing softly, Katie stopped before the entrance to the guest bedroom.

Penelope stepped into the open doorway, then turned to look at Katie. "Is something wrong? You don't seem yourself."

She forced herself to smile. "I don't know what you mean. Nothing's wrong."

Her friend leaned forward and kissed her cheek, just as Geoffrey had done not long before. "You would tell me if there were, wouldn't you?"

The question was almost identical to the one Sophia had asked that afternoon, but Katie was no more inclined to answer honestly now than she'd been before. "Of course I would. Now get some rest. We'll have plenty of time to talk tomorrow."

Penelope hesitated, looking as if she would say something more. Then she nodded and closed the door.

Thoughts of Ben tried to intrude again, beckoned by Penelope's question, but Katie pushed them aside as she made her way to her own room. Things would be different now that Penelope and Geoffrey were here, she reassured herself. Her friends would help keep her focused on her work, on what was important.

Everything would be all right now.

* * *

Ben grew tired of tossing and turning. It seemed sleep was bound and determined to elude him. With a sound of exasperation, he tossed aside the rumpled bedsheet and got up. He strode over to the window of his bedchamber, looking out on the sleepy street below. Even the billiard saloon was darkened at this wee hour of the morning.

Those fortunate folks with untroubled consciences were fast asleep in their beds. Only Ben was awake.

And he knew why.

He'd canceled his supper engagement with Charlotte last night. Upon his return to town, he'd gone straight to the parsonage and told her he was feeling a bit under the weather and thought he'd best get some rest.

Coward!

He should have told her the truth. He should have broken off with her right then. He could have gotten it over with. It would have been better than letting it drag on.

And then there was the matter of his raging jealousy. Oh, yes, he recognized the demon that was tormenting him. He'd recognized it the moment it raised its ugly head at the Lazy L Ranch. The moment Katie had hugged Geoffrey Rudyard and Geoffrey had kissed her cheek and called her his dear Katie. The moment he'd learned Geoffrey had lived next door to Penelope and Katie for the past three years.

Katie hadn't mentioned Geoffrey in her letters. At least not by name. Only as Penelope's brother and then only occasionally. Why? Was there more between them than she'd wanted Ben to know? Was Geoffrey, perhaps, her lover?

Ben leaned his forehead against the cool window glass and closed his eyes, calling himself all kinds of a fool.

Geoffrey Rudyard, an attorney, was rich, handsome,

cosmopolitan. More important, he was as deeply involved in the suffrage movement as his mother and sister, not to mention Katie herself. Why wouldn't Katie be swept off her feet by such a man?

He reminded himself that Katie didn't want to get married. But a lover . . . Would she take a lover?

He swore softly as he gazed once again down at the quiet, moonlight-bathed street. He'd chosen to rent these rooms from his father's hotel partially because of the view of the town. He was fond of Homestead and the people who lived here. He'd spent all the time he ever wanted to spend in big cities. They weren't for him. This was what he wanted. This quiet. This peace. This was what he'd always wanted.

What if it wasn't what Katie wanted? What then?

But none of that was of any real importance to him. Only one thing mattered.

He had to win Katie's love. The rest would take care of itself.

11

Obadiah Orson spent every Saturday morning in the church, practicing his sermon and praying for his small but faithful congregation. Charlotte always rose early to prepare him a good breakfast, and this morning was no different.

Except, he thought, she looked a little pale today.

"Daughter, are you ill?"

She glanced up as she set a plate of scrambled eggs on the kitchen table. "No, Father. Why do you ask?"

"I'm not certain. You just don't look yourself."

She pushed a vagrant lock of golden hair back from her forehead. "I didn't sleep well last night. That's all."

"Do you have something on your heart that's keeping you awake?"

Charlotte's gaze dropped away. "No."

Obadiah knew his daughter well. She was unfailingly honest with him, but this was one time he suspected she was, at the very least, withholding the truth. "Perhaps we should pray about it," he suggested gently.

Turning back toward the stove, she shook her head. She remained silent as she lifted the last of the sizzling bacon out of the skillet and onto a plate.

The reverend waited patiently. He knew she wouldn't disappoint him.

Finally Charlotte glanced over her shoulder. "You could pray for God's will to be done, Father. I know what I want, but I think it would be better if I simply asked for God's will to be done."

"I see."

She brought the rest of the food to the table, then sat down opposite him. Immediately she bowed her head. Obadiah had the distinct impression it was to avoid his watchful eyes more than to prepare for the food's blessing.

"Dear Heavenly Father," he began, "we thank you . . ."

Charlotte whispered the familiar prayer along with him, and he couldn't help but hear the note of pain therein. A particular kind of pain. That was when he knew what was troubling his daughter. That was when he recognized the sound of a broken heart.

The blessing over, the reverend began to eat. Silently he searched for the right words to say but had to settle for, "I hope Benjamin's illness isn't serious."

His daughter glanced up, her eyes wide and stricken. "His illness?"

"You did say he was under the weather last night."

"Oh. Yes." She looked back at her plate. "I'm sure it's nothing serious, Father."

It's over between them. The thought saddened him greatly. Charlotte loved the young man. It had been obvious for some time now. In truth, Obadiah had wondered what was taking Benjamin Rafferty so long to propose. Now, it seemed, he never would.

The reverend finished his breakfast in silence, his

heart aching for his only child. He wished there were a way to ease the pain she felt, but he knew only time and God's mercy would make a difference.

Finally he rose from the table. "I'd best get over to the church."

"Yes." She kept her gaze fixed on her plate.

"I'll do as you asked, daughter. I'll pray for God's will to be done."

"Thank you," she whispered.

He walked to the door, then glanced back at her. She appeared so small and helpless, and he wanted to do nothing so much as cradle her in his arms and comfort her, just as he'd done when she was a little girl. Only he knew she wouldn't welcome his comfort now. Not just yet.

"Charlotte."

"Yes."

"'And we know that all things work together for good to them that love God, to them who are the called according to His purpose.'"

"I know, Father."

"You know the words with your intellect, my dear, but do you believe them in your heart?"

Her honesty returned. "No," she replied bleakly, her voice breaking.

Another familiar verse from the Bible came to mind— "Lord, I believe; help thou mine unbelief"—and Obadiah knew it would be the first prayer he would say for his daughter.

Silently he turned once again and left the parsonage, his footsteps heavy.

Walking along East Street, Ben saw Obadiah Orson making his way toward the King of Glory Lutheran Church. His head was bent forward, his eyes downcast, his hands clasped behind his back. He was a man obviously deep in thought.

Ben stopped on the boardwalk and waited. He didn't want the reverend to look up and see him. What he meant to do this morning was hard enough without facing Charlotte's father, too. He wouldn't be able to avoid it forever, but he'd just as soon avoid it for now.

He watched as Obadiah climbed the steps to the back of the small white church with its tall steeple. The older man slipped a key into the lock and opened the door without ever glancing around him. A moment later he disappeared into the dark interior.

Ben let out a sigh of relief as he continued along the sidewalk, passing the church on his way to the parsonage. Once there he paused a second time, looking at the house and wishing he were anywhere else but here. Still, he knew it was the honorable thing to do. He couldn't put it off another day.

With the fateful strides of a man on his way to the gallows, Ben moved up the walk. He didn't allow himself another hesitation; he immediately rapped on the door.

It opened in a matter of moments. Guilt tightened in his chest as he looked down at Charlotte. He'd never seen her appear so wan. Nor had he ever seen her in her dressing gown, her head still covered with a nightcap. Loose strands of hair curled around her face, not unbecomingly, but somehow quite sad in appearance.

"Benjamin," she whispered, her eyes wide. Nervously she smoothed the front of her dressing gown. "I wasn't expecting you. I look a sight."

"We need to talk."

Her shoulders drooped and her hand stilled. "I know." She stepped back from the opening. "Come in."

This was going to be more difficult than he'd imagined—and imagining it had been bad enough.

He followed Charlotte inside, closing the front door behind him. She led the way into the small sitting room near the front of the house. Quickly, as if her legs wouldn't support her, she sank onto a wooden rocker. When she looked up at him a moment later, Ben hated himself.

He chose a spindle-backed chair opposite her and sat down. He clenched his hands together, resting his forearms on his thighs as he leaned forward. "Charlotte—"

"I know why you've come, Benjamin." Tears swam before eyes of blue.

"I never meant to hurt you."

"I know."

"It's just that we—"

"We don't love one another," she finished for him in a whisper. She tried to smile but was unsuccessful.

Ben raked his fingers through his hair, wishing he did love Charlotte, wishing he could propose marriage. Charlotte Orson represented everything he'd ever wanted in a wife. She would be caring and kind. She would be a loving mother to their children. She would be supportive of his work. She would never want for more than Ben was able to provide because it was not in her nature to do so.

Only the good Lord himself knew what sort of wife Katie Jones would make—and that was only if Ben could convince her to marry him.

"Benjamin?"

Charlotte's gentle voice drew him abruptly from his private thoughts.

She attempted another smile, this one slightly more successful than the last. "There were no promises between us."

"I never intended to mislead you, Charlotte."

"You didn't. You're an honest man. It's one of the things I've admired about you."

He felt like swearing. Instead he said, "I'm sorry."

Holding herself erect, her chin tilted bravely, Charlotte rose from the rocker. "We shall always be friends, Benjamin, and you shall always be welcome in our home." The dismissal was gentle, but a dismissal nonetheless.

Ben followed her lead, rising to his feet. She'd called him honest, but there was still more to be said before he would feel it. He reached out before she could turn away, grasping her wrist and holding her in place.

"It's a difficult thing, to be unable to express myself. I've always been a man of words, and now, it seems, there aren't any. I wish . . ." He wished he could love her. He wished his life were going the way he'd always planned. He wished he didn't feel like a cad. "I wish things had turned out differently for us."

"So do I." She eased her wrist from his hand. "But I imagine you and Miss Jones will be very happy. I hope so. I'll pray it will be so."

Were they so obvious, his feelings for Katie? Had others seen what he'd just discovered only a matter of days ago?

Before Ben could say anything else to her, Charlotte turned and retraced her steps to the front door, opening it for him without glancing behind her to see if he followed. It wasn't until he paused before her that she raised her gaze one more time.

She held out her hand to him. "I truly do wish you every happiness," she whispered as he took her proffered hand.

"Charlotte—"

She shook her head. "Please, Benjamin. Just go."

He knew she was right. There were no words that would make the situation better. He'd said what he'd come to say. It was time for him to go.

With a brief nod and a slight squeeze of his fingers, he released her hand, then turned and departed the parsonage.

With Katie behind the wheel and Penelope seated beside her, Geoffrey gave the Susan B's engine crank a hard turn, releasing it just in time to avoid the sudden kick for which the Model T's crank was infamous. "Why didn't you buy a Buick or a Cadillac or a Stutz?" he grumbled as he rounded the side of the car and hopped into the rear seat. "A friend of mine broke his arm on a blasted machine like this one."

"Don't criticize the Susan B." Katie patted the wheel as if the automobile were a favored child. "She's perfect."

Penelope looked over her shoulder at her brother and said in a stage whisper, "Besides, this was all Katie could afford at the time."

Although secretly enjoying herself, Katie shot a dour look at her friend, sniffing indignantly. "The Susan B is worth every cent of the four hundred and forty dollars I paid for her and then some."

The Rudyard siblings laughed heartily.

Katie stepped down on the left pedal, and the motorcar jumped forward, jolting her passengers.

Once he'd caught himself, Geoffrey reached forward and placed his hand on Katie's shoulder. "My dear girl, in case you haven't noticed, this flivver rattles and shakes. It frequently overheats. It's damned difficult, when not impossible, to start on cold mornings. It needs a running start to mount hills, and unless you're backing up said hill in reverse, the fuel line goes dry and the car stops altogether." He laughed again. "Penny, help me. What am I forgetting?"

"You're forgetting the one advantage," his sister answered. "There's no need for a speedometer."

"Ah, yes. One can always tell how fast it's going without buying a speedometer. When it's running five miles an hour, the fender rattles; twelve miles an hour, your teeth rattle; and at fifteen miles an hour, the transmission drops out."

Again, brother and sister laughed.

Katie feigned anger. Everything they'd said was close to the truth, of course, but wild horses couldn't have dragged that admission out of her. "I'll have you know the transmission has never dropped out of the Susan B, and I drive her quite regularly at a greater speed than fifteen miles an hour. Need I remind you this Touring Car carried all of us across this country as we followed the 'Special'? And she did it without any serious mishaps."

Penelope leaned toward her. "Oh, Katie, we're merely teasing. You needn't get your feelings hurt. We'll apologize, won't we, Geoffrey?"

"Absolutely. We beg your forgiveness, my dear Katie." He thumped the car seat. "Frightfully sorry, Susan B. Do forgive us."

Katie grinned, letting them know she wasn't upset. In truth, she was more than a little thankful for the banter. It kept her thoughts from drifting in unwelcome directions.

"You'll pay for forcing that apology, of course," Geoffrey warned, then said, "So tell us how long it will take to reach your grandparents' farm."

"It's a ranch, not a farm," she corrected him. "Grandpa Will was the first person to arrive in Long Bow Valley. He built the Rocking R Ranch from nothing, eventually raising the finest horses within five hundred miles in any direction. The U.S. Calvary still purchases livestock from him, although not as many as they did before the turn of the century."

Penelope gazed about her. "I've never seen so much wide-open space as I've seen these past few months. The mountains. The rivers. It's all quite spectacular."

Katie agreed with Penelope. The West was spectacular, and few places more so than this valley. A sense of pride washed over her as she saw it afresh through the eyes of her friends.

"You belong here," Penelope added softly, her gaze now locked on Katie.

She couldn't help it. She thought of Ben. "Do I?"

"Yes, I think you do."

Katie wondered how long she would stay here, belonging or not. She didn't think she could bear to see Ben and Charlotte together, married, having a family. Besides, she'd never intended to remain in Idaho after the November elections. She'd always meant to return to Washington and continue her work there. It was good to come home for a short while, but she couldn't stay. Not while there was still so much to accomplish.

She hoped Ben and Charlotte wouldn't decide to marry before she left Homestead.

"Tell us more about your committee," Penelope said, intruding on Katie's thoughts.

She was glad for the distraction. As the Susan B continued along the dusty country road, she told her friends about her first two weeks in Homestead and how each woman had come to be a part of the local suffrage committee. But she avoided mentioning Ben, leaving out the many times she'd sat in his office, talking and laughing, or the afternoon they'd gone swimming in the pond, or the night she'd seen him kissing Charlotte.

Which meant there was much that went unsaid.

"Do you suppose Miss Rafferty is still in love with her former fiancé?" Geoffrey inquired when Katie fell silent. "Is it possible they might reconcile?"

Something in his voice caused her to glance quickly over her shoulder, then back at the road.

"I would hate to see your committee lose one of its members," he added, as if in explanation. "There's too much work for all of you as it is."

Yes, there was too much work. Plenty enough to keep Katie's mind occupied, to keep her from thinking unwanted thoughts about Ben.

At least she could hope and pray that would be the case.

A short while later Katie drove the automobile into the yard of the Rocking R. Her grandmother came out onto the porch, allowing the screened door to slam closed behind her. Her wrinkled face was wreathed in a smile as she waved a greeting.

Katie felt better just looking at her.

"Hello, Grandma!" she called as the Susan B came to a halt.

"Hello. Come in, all of you."

Katie and her friends got out of the motorcar and joined her grandmother on the porch. After the introductions were made all around, Addie invited everyone into the house.

"I've just pulled a cherry pie out of the oven," she said. "Could I interest anyone in a piece?"

"You could me," Geoffrey answered quickly.

Penelope laughed. "My brother is always interested in food, Mrs. Rider."

"Good. I like a man with an appetite." Addie linked her arm with Katie's and took them into the house.

From the moment of their arrival, Addie suspected something was troubling her granddaughter, and as the afternoon progressed she was all the more sure of it. Oh, Katie laughed and teased along with her two friends, and she talked with the usual amount of enthusiasm about her work and what the committee was planning to do next. But underneath it all, Katie was worrying about something.

At first Addie wondered if Katie's worries concerned Geoffrey Rudyard. The young man was handsome, intelligent, and certainly well mannered. In fact, Addie almost hoped it did have something to do with him. But the longer she observed the threesome, the more convinced she was that Katie's only feeling for Geoffrey was friendship.

Yet a sixth sense told her Katie's problems were those of a troubled heart. Perhaps a broken one.

Mentally she pictured the available young men of Homestead. One by one she discarded them as unsuitable for her granddaughter. Until she thought of Ben Rafferty.

Lord, have mercy!

She remembered the morning she'd visited Katie, just after her return to Homestead. Katie had said she wasn't ever going to fall in love, and Addie had responded that it just wasn't that easy. Now it appeared Katie had found out that truth for herself. She had fallen in love after all, but with a man who was courting someone else.

Addie felt her own heart breaking for her granddaughter. She remembered, as if she were still a young lady in her twenties, what it had been like to love Will and think they would never marry because of his inability to tell her he loved her. She remembered how she'd suffered for her daughter when Will had stubbornly refused to let Lark see Yancy because he didn't think the cowboy was good enough for his daughter.

But this was worse. And Addie could do nothing to fix it for Katie.

* * *

Ben heard the soft ripple of whispers as he entered the Homestead Community Church the next morning, walking behind his parents, his sister's hand in the crook of his arm. He knew folks were wondering why he wasn't over at the King of Glory Lutheran Church with Charlotte. He knew Sophia and his parents were wondering, too, although they'd refrained from asking him for an explanation.

As his family slipped into their usual pew, Ben glanced across the aisle and up one row. Katie was there, seated between Lark Jones on her right and Penelope Rudyard on her left. Her black hair was swept up onto her head, topped by a straw bonnet with a gay yellow ribbon. Her neck was long and delicate, the skin soft gold, the color of honey. He thought about kissing the spot just below her earlobe—imagining she might taste as sweet as honey, too—and decided right then and there that she looked far too fetching for her own good.

Katie leaned left and said something to Penelope, causing them both to smile. As she straightened, Katie's gaze caught with his. Her lingering smile vanished in an instant, and her eyes widened.

Luminous, beguiling eyes of brown. Had they always been as beautiful as they were now? Was it possible he could see more in them than simple surprise? Or was that merely wishful thinking on his part?

She faced forward again, breaking the tenuous connection between them.

The morning's worship service began with a hymn, accompanied by Priscilla Jacobs on the organ. The congregation's voices melded together, but Ben heard each and every perfect note of Katie's sweet voice, no matter how softly she sang, no matter how loudly the organ played.

With the last "Amen" still echoing in the church, Geoffrey leaned around his sister to say something to Katie. Ben clenched his jaw, wishing he were somewhere other than church. The thoughts whipping through his head were anything but suitable for a house of prayer.

He heard little of Reverend Jacobs's sermon that morning. He was too busy debating with himself what his course of action should be to win Katie's love. Her love as a woman, not a friend.

I've got to get her away from all these people, he thought. But under what circumstances would she allow herself to be taken from her work or her guests? It wasn't going to be easy, wooing and winning Katie. Not when she was so determined not to be wooed or won. Not when she looked at him and saw only a childhood friend and not a man.

But Ben was going to change her mind. No matter what it took. No matter how long it took.

As for Katie, she didn't hear that morning's sermon, either. She couldn't. Not with her heart hammering so loudly in her chest, the blood pounding in her ears. It was silly that Ben's nearness should cause such an internal commotion. She should have been able to control her rampaging feelings, but she couldn't seem to do so.

When the service was over and Priscilla Jacobs began playing a soft hymn on the church organ, Katie tried desperately to compose herself, then rose from the pew and turned toward the aisle. He was there, standing almost within arm's reach.

"Good morning, Katie."

She drew a quick breath before answering, "Good morning." She searched for something more to say. Anything. "I was surprised to see you here." She felt a flush warm her cheeks; her words sounded like an accusation of heathenism or something. She tried again. "I understand you usually attend services with Charlotte at her father's church."

A short step brought him closer. "I wanted to come here this morning." He offered his arm. "May I walk you to your automobile?"

Katie glanced at Penelope, then at Geoffrey, and finally back at Ben. In the end she realized she couldn't avoid placing her fingers in the crook of his elbow. She longed to touch him too much to ignore the impulse.

She should have urged him to offer his other arm to Penelope, but she didn't. She wanted him to herself, if only for a few moments.

"I missed seeing you yesterday," Ben said as they walked slowly toward the back of the church.

I've missed you, too. "I took Penny and Geoffrey to see my grandparents."

He looked down at her and smiled. "I imagine your grandmother charmed them as she does everyone. There's no one quite like Addie Rider."

Her heart did a thousand flip-flops in the space of a few seconds. *Why did I have to fall in love with you?* she wondered. *Why?*

"Katie, I know you have many demands upon your time, but I'd like to steal you away tomorrow. Do you think you can leave your guests to their own devices for a day?"

Steal me away? Her breathing nearly stopped.

"I'd like us to drive up to the logging camps. We should tell those folks about the election rally that's coming to Homestead. Besides, I've heard there are a couple of women loggers in one of the camps up there. They might make a good subject for one of your columns."

Disappointment washed over Katie. Her column. Of course that was what he wanted to talk to her about. What else?

Seemingly oblivious of her inner turmoil, Ben continued, "We ought to be able to make the trip all in one day if we take your motorcar. That is, if you wouldn't mind taking the Susan B up that rough trail."

A day with Ben. Just to themselves. Just the two of them. She shouldn't. She'd promised Charlotte, although not in exact words, that she would stay away from him. She'd planned to quit writing the column in order to avoid him.

But why should she? Why should she avoid him or quit writing for the newspaper? Benjie was her dearest friend in the world. Simply because he loved another woman and planned to marry her didn't mean Katie should have to lose that friendship.

Did it?

No. No, it didn't.

"How about it, Katie?" Ben asked as the two of them stepped through the church doorway and into the bright June sunlight. "Are you game?"

Her decision was made. "Yes, I'm game. It sounds like a perfect story for my column. Let's do it."

"Good. I'll ride out to the Lazy L first thing in the morning."

"I'll be ready."

I'll always be ready to see you, Ben. That was one more reason for her to finish her work and go away. Because she'd always want to be with him, even when he would be with Charlotte.

Katie shoved away the unwelcome thoughts. She refused to allow anything to spoil their plans for tomorrow. Perhaps on Tuesday she would be forced to face reality, but tomorrow was for her and Ben.

12

Katie was up at the crack of dawn after a long night of troublesome dreams and restless wakefulness. Whether she was sleeping or not, Ben had remained in her thoughts. A much different Ben from the boy who had been her companion throughout childhood. A tall, strong, and handsome Ben with a devastating grin and masculine appeal. Just thinking about him made her wonder about things—*intimate* things—she'd never considered before.

She knew she ought not to think about him that way. He would soon marry another woman. He would soon share another woman's home and bed. Besides, Katie was bound to her life's work. Single womanhood was what she had pledged for herself. It was what she wanted, what she'd wanted for many years.

Staring at her reflection in the mirror while she brushed the tangles from her hair, Katie recalled the words of Miss Anthony.

There is not one woman left who may be relied on; all

*have "first to please their husband," after which there is
but little time or energy left to spend in any other direction. I am not complaining or despairing, but facts are
stern realities.*

Yes, facts were "stern realities." If Katie were to give
her heart and soul to the betterment of all women, if she
were to be relied upon, she could not become fettered by
selfish desires. She could not indulge her secret fantasies
about Benjamin Rafferty.

But just once, her traitorous heart asked, wouldn't it
be wonderful to experience love? Wouldn't it be wonderful to experience it with Ben?

With a groan, she dropped the hairbrush and covered
her face with her hands. She had to stop this at once.
How could she meet Ben this morning with such thoughts
roiling in her head? How could she look at him and
remember they were friends and nothing more?

Her breath caught as an even more horrible thought
replaced all others. She lowered her hands enough to
uncover her eyes and look once again in the mirror.

Madeline Percy thought Katie was without good
upbringing or good sense. Probably she also thought
Katie fast, corrupt, and immoral. The opinions of women
like Mrs. Percy had never bothered Katie before because
she'd known they had no basis in fact. But this morning
she had to wonder: Would she allow Ben liberties should
he wish to take them?

She watched as heat flooded her cheeks with color. A
strange longing flared someplace deep inside, a longing
to be kissed and caressed, to know what the union
between a man and woman was all about.

"Oh, Benjie," she whispered, knowing the answer to
her unspoken questions, knowing she would allow him
any liberties, no matter how wrong society might view
them, no matter how wrong she might view them.

She remembered the day she and Ben had gone swimming at the pond. She remembered the way he'd held her in his arms as she'd cried. She'd felt the shift in their friendship that day, only she hadn't known it was she who had shifted, she who had changed.

When she'd made the choice never to marry, she'd thought it would be an easy decision to keep. She would be as dedicated to the cause as Susan B. Anthony, her greatest inspiration. She would simply not fall in love, and therefore there would be no temptation to wed.

"What a fool I was," she said aloud as she turned away from the mirror. "What an unmitigated fool."

She drew a deep breath and pressed her lips together, then walked across the room to her wardrobe. She selected a brown skirt and cream-colored blouse, unconsciously seeking to look as prim, proper, and spinsterish as possible.

What are you going to do now, Katie? she asked herself as she shed her dressing gown. She tossed the robe over the back of a chair, then reached for her undergarments.

She couldn't leave Homestead. Not now. Not with things progressing so well with the work she'd come home to do. The political rally was only a couple of weeks away. Several candidates had already consented to attend; many others were expected to do so. Besides, she had made a promise to the leaders of the association that she would do her part here in Idaho. This election year was critical if they were going to see the passage of the suffrage amendment.

So that was settled. She couldn't leave Homestead. Not until after the elections in November.

Katie donned a camisole and knickers of crepe de chine, the edges decorated with ribbons and lace. Then she sat on the side of her bed and drew on a pair of beige stockings, her thoughts continuing to churn.

Since she was to remain in Homestead for the time being, she would have to deal with her attraction to Ben on an intellectual level. She could no longer act like a schoolgirl when she was with him. She could no longer throw herself into his arms with joyful abandon and kiss his cheek, nor could she let him hold and comfort her when she was feeling down.

Another treasonous thought snuck past her defenses, whispering, Could I make him forget Charlotte?

She swore aloud, a string of unladylike oaths that would have horrified her mother and had her father dragging her off to the woodshed for punishment in a hurry.

She reached for the blouse and slipped her arms into the sleeves, then buttoned the front closing with clumsy-feeling fingers.

What kind of friend was she, to even consider hurting Ben that way? He wanted a home, marriage, family. He wanted all the things Charlotte was willing to give him and Katie was not. Would she destroy his happiness with another woman for a few moments of selfish pleasure—which was all she would be able to give him?

No, she must make certain such a thing never happened. She must make sure Ben never learned what she felt in her heart. She must never allow Ben to be hurt because of her own selfishness.

Even so, the Judas in her head couldn't help wondering if it would be as pleasurable as she imagined, were she to be joined with Ben in an act of passion.

Blanche Coleson awoke at her usual time. It didn't matter that school was in recess for the remainder of summer. Especially not this year. Other summers she'd found herself with little to occupy her time. She had filled the hours with needlework and other mundane chores. But this year was different. This year she was accomplishing something of real value.

She drew a robe over her nightgown and cinched a belt around her waist, then walked from her bedroom into the living area of her apartment. She crossed to the small kitchen area and reached for the coffee grinder while her mind ticked off the things she had to do today.

First on her schedule was the writing of several letters to the wives of some public officials down in the capital city. Katie Jones thought it a poor idea, to rile up the wives against their husbands, but Blanche didn't care what Katie thought. Not anymore.

She had been delighted at first to find a kindred spirit right here in Homestead. Only Katie Jones didn't believe precisely as Blanche did. While the young woman was passionate about gaining the right to vote for all women, she still didn't understand the truly disgusting nature of men. *All* men. Miss Jones continued her friendship with Ben Rafferty, telling him the committee's plans, involving him in the rally. And now there was that Mr. Rudyard visiting from the East, pretending to be a great supporter of the cause.

Blanche snorted in disbelief. No man truly wanted women to enjoy the same freedoms as men. Why would they when the subjugation of females was so beneficial to their creature comforts?

But did Katie understand that? It seemed not.

To make matters worse, everyone treated Katie as if she were a saint or something. Blanche was growing increasingly tired of the attention everyone paid to Katie's thoughts and opinions. Sophia Rafferty didn't do a thing without first checking with her former schoolmate. And Leslie Blake wasn't much better. She hung on every word falling from Katie's mouth.

If they had any sense, they would have appointed

Blanche the first president of the Homestead Woman's Suffrage Committee. Anyone could see Katie was incapable of proper leadership. She was too young, too inexperienced. She needed a good dose of Blanche's common sense and life experiences.

Blanche poured water from the pitcher into the coffeepot, thinking how unfair life had been to her. The only child of an aging dirt farmer and his homely, mousy, timid wife, Blanche had always possessed a great deal of intelligence but little else. Throughout her life she had been overlooked for those with beauty or wealth or both. She hadn't had the opportunity to travel, to attend a fine college, to see much beyond the small towns where she was forced to teach the children of ignorant men like her father.

Oh, what she might have done had she had Katie Jones's opportunities!

Feeling more irritable by the moment, Blanche set the pot on the stove, then stoked the fire before returning to her bedroom to complete her morning ablutions. Then she was going to write those letters. She was going to prove to Miss Jones and the others that she knew what was best.

Ben had offered to drive the Susan B before they'd started out from the Lazy L, but Katie had been adamant about being the one behind the wheel. Ben wasn't sorry. It gave him the freedom to watch her while she had to concentrate on the rough road they were following into the mountains. He'd taken full advantage of the opportunity.

She looked utterly fetching in her brown outfit. On any other woman it would have looked plain and dowdy, but on Katie, it seemed perfect. *She* was perfect, from the dark wisps of hair curling near her temples to the tip of her buttonlike nose, from the length of her delicate throat to the gentle swell of her breasts beneath her blouse, from the top of her straw bonnet to the tips of her sturdy brown boots.

It was a pleasure just to look at her.

The question now was, how did he go about telling her what he felt without scaring her away? He wasn't sure what the answer was, but he knew he wouldn't get anywhere by allowing this silence to stretch out any longer. He decided to start with something simple.

"It's a beautiful day for a drive, isn't it?"

The Susan B backfired, drowning out Katie's monosyllabic reply.

He slid a little to his left. "You're sure you don't want me to drive?"

"I'm sure."

It would be easy to slip his arm around her shoulders, but they were likely to end up in a ravine if he did. Katie seemed to be wound tight as a spring today. He wondered why. She'd seemed to like the idea of this little trip yesterday.

Katie, I love you.

He wished he could say it just like that, but he couldn't.

Katie, I'm no longer courting Charlotte.

That would be a good start. Let her know he had no obligations to anyone else.

But Katie didn't give him a chance to say what was on his mind. "Ben, if I asked you something personal, would you answer me honestly?"

It seemed an odd question. Maybe she already knew about Charlotte. "I always try to be honest. What is it you want to know, Katie?"

"Is it true the newspaper has lost advertisers because

of my column?" She glanced at him, then back at the road.

Disappointment didn't prevent him from answering, "Yes, it's true."

"What does that mean to the paper? Is it going to hurt you?"

"Hurt me?"

She frowned. "You know. Will it cause a financial hardship? Is the paper in danger because of me?"

If it was possible, he loved her even more because of her concern. "No, Katie, the *Herald* isn't in any danger because of you."

"But—"

"And even if it were, I wouldn't do anything differently." He leaned toward her. "You need to understand something. I'm a journalist because I believe in the freedom of speech, in people's right to know, every bit as much as you believe in suffrage for all women. I'm not going to have a group of advertisers tell me what's news and what isn't. Nor will I let them tell me who can write for my paper just because they disagree with the point of view expressed in a column."

"But if our friendship is influencing you—"

"Katie, I'd want you to write that column even if we'd never met before."

He saw a shadow of doubt cross her face and knew now was his chance to say something of a more personal nature.

"Katie, I'd like to tell you something. About Miss Orson and me. You see, we—"

He was interrupted by a loud pop, followed by a jerk of the automobile toward the sudden drop-off at the side of the road. He grabbed hold of the door as Katie braked to an abrupt halt. A cloud of dust flew up around them, making them both cough and sneeze.

Even after the air cleared, Katie continued to grip the steering wheel, her knuckles white. "Dear me," she whispered at last, her voice quavering. She glanced over at him. "I think I was going a bit too fast. We nearly went over the edge."

"But we didn't." He opened the door. "I'll have a look." He got out of the motorcar. A quick check located the problem. The left front tire was flat.

"The tire?" Katie asked, still seated behind the wheel.

"Yes." He began rolling up his shirtsleeve.

"This isn't a very auspicious beginning. Perhaps we should go back to Homestead."

"Don't be ridiculous." He wasn't about to let her get away from him today. Not until he'd said what he needed to say. "It won't take but a few minutes to change it."

And then maybe he'd find the right moment to begin wooing Katie.

But things didn't work out quite as Ben had hoped. After the incident with the flat tire, the Susan B overheated twice and the fuel line ran dry on three different inclines. When it wasn't the automobile causing problems, it was Katie who stopped Ben from speaking his mind. Whenever he tried to bring up his feelings, she quickly changed the subject. The only topics she seemed inclined to discuss were her suffrage committee, what she hoped they could accomplish in the fall elections, her eagerness to return to Washington, and how important her life's work was to her.

By the time they were on their return journey, Ben was feeling more than a little discouraged. Perhaps he was hoping for something that could never be. Perhaps it would be easier to rope the moon than to win Katie's love.

*   *   *

Katie was never more glad of anything than she was to
see the lights of Homestead twinkling in the distance as
the Susan B rolled down out of the mountains just as
dusk turned into darkness.

The interview with the two women loggers had gone
well, and she knew it would make an interesting story for
her column. But the day itself had been a tremendous
strain. Try as she might, she hadn't been able to relax,
not even for a moment. She'd been too afraid Ben might
see the longing in her eyes, and then everything would be
ruined between them.

It had been a mistake to come with him today. More
than once she'd feared she would dissolve into tears,
especially when he'd started to tell her about Charlotte.
And if he'd put his arms around her and tried to comfort
her, she would have done something foolish. She knew
she would have.

Just as a full moon began to ascend from behind the
eastern mountain range, the Susan B coughed, sputtered,
and died. The electric lights dimmed, then went dark.

"What now?" Ben asked.

"I don't know," she answered, feeling again the threat
of tears.

"I'll see if I can get her started." He opened the car
door and got out.

As he walked to the front of the automobile, moonlight silvered his usually golden hair. The light fell upon
his face, revealing the strong angles and lines Katie knew
so well.

Was it possible to love him even more tonight than
she had this morning?

"Ready?" he asked, just the sound of his voice causing
her pulse to miss a beat.

With shaking fingers she set the levers. "Ready."

He gave the crank a hard turn. Nothing. He tried

again. Still nothing. A third try brought the same results.

Ben rounded the car to the driver's side. "I don't think she's going to start. Looks like we'll have to leave her here until morning."

Katie nodded, barely thinking about the automobile as she stared at Ben in the moonlight.

"I'll bring Edgar Childers out here in the morning, and we'll tow her back to town." He leaned forward slightly. "At least it's a nice night for a walk."

She found it hard to breathe. He was so very close. She couldn't seem to look away from his mouth.

"Katie?"

She drew back, realizing just where her thoughts had been leading. "I'm ready." She slid across the seat and got out. "Let's go."

She set off at a brisk walk, leaving it to Ben to catch up with her.

"Katie." His fingers closed around her upper arm. Gently he pulled her to a halt, then turned her to face him. "What's wrong?"

"Nothing." *Everything.*

He lifted her chin with his index finger. "Come on. We've always been open with each other. You can tell me."

"There's nothing to tell." *I can't tell you this.*

The earth went suddenly still, the night sounds fading away. A cool evening breeze caressed Katie's cheek, contrasting the warmth of Ben's finger on her skin.

She wasn't sure how it happened.

He leaned down. She stretched up.

He cradled her face. She clasped her hands behind his neck.

His mouth grazed hers. She released a tiny sigh through parted lips.

It lasted forever.

It happened in an instant.

It was more wonderful than she'd dared imagine.

It was more devastating than she'd ever feared.

Katie stepped back from him. His fingers slid across her cheeks until they lost contact. The night turned suddenly cold. "We shouldn't have done that," she whispered in a shaky voice.

"Why not?"

There was an ache in her chest that made each breath come hard. "You know why not."

"Didn't you want me to kiss you?" His voice softened. "Didn't you like my kisses?"

He wasn't being fair. He had to know good and well what the answer was. He couldn't have helped feeling her response.

"Katie," he began, "about Charlotte. You must think—"

"Stop!" She clenched her hands together. "Benjie, we've been friends too long. Don't spoil everything."

"Does it have to spoil things? Can't we be friends and even more to each other?"

No! her mind shouted.

Yes! her heart countered.

Katie covered her face with her hands. "I don't know. I don't know anything anymore."

A long silence fell between them while Katie wrestled with what her mind told her had to be done and what her heart told her she wanted to do. There was Charlotte. There was her work. There were promises and obligations and commitments.

He was her dearest friend. Would she risk that friendship to become his lover?

"Katie, if you'd just let me explain—"

She turned her back to Ben, unable to look at him and

think straight. "I don't want to talk about it tonight. I can't. Please." Her voice broke. "Please don't ask me to."

His fingers touched her shoulder, but she pulled away from him. She heard him sigh.

"All right, Katie. We won't talk about it now." He stepped up beside her. "Come on. We'd better start walking. I don't want your folks to get worried about where you are."

Side by side they walked toward Homestead, not speaking, not touching. Just two people walking in the moonlight, wondering what the next day would bring.

13

For the remainder of the week Katie took refuge from her confused emotions in her work and with her friends. She didn't go into town, not even to retrieve the Susan B; she had Geoffrey bring back the repaired automobile.

And not once did Ben make any attempt to see her. She wasn't sure if not seeing him made things better or worse. She only knew she despised herself for what she had allowed to happen, for what she had discovered about herself. And for what she'd discovered about Ben. How could he kiss her the way he had when he was planning to marry Charlotte? How could he have betrayed his future bride *and* his friendship with Katie?

Even so, Katie longed to see him, longed to be with him, longed for more of his kisses.

That Friday the Homestead Woman's Suffrage Committee met at Katie's house to go over the final plans for the rally. An undercurrent of expectation charged the air in the dining room as the members of the committee—including Lark Jones and the Rudyards—gathered around the table.

There was good news to share at the start of the meeting. The majority of incumbents running for reelection had accepted the invitation to attend the rally, and one hundred percent of their opponents had agreed to be there as well. Although the official time period for declaring for office had yet to begin, it looked as if this would be a hotly contested election year.

"Katie, you should be proud of what you've accomplished," Geoffrey said, and everyone around the table concurred.

She smiled, although there was no real feeling behind it. It was hard to be praised by her friends when she was feeling less than praiseworthy.

Sophia leaned forward. "I have something of interest to share. A reporter from the *Idaho Statesman* is coming to Homestead to cover the rally. My brother told me about it this morning when he stopped by the house."

Katie's heart skittered at the mention of Ben.

"He says Katie's second column was picked up and reprinted in several other newspapers in Idaho. It's created quite a stir, just as it did here in Homestead."

Did he ask about me? Katie wondered.

"He says we can expect lots of folks to come to Homestead next week to hear what the candidates are going to say, not just on national suffrage but on plenty of other issues of concern, too. He says they'll definitely want to know where everyone stands on the war in Europe." Sophia dropped her gaze to the table, her manner suddenly subdued. "Ben says we won't be able to stay out of the war much longer."

Blanche Coleson harrumphed, then added, "There would be no wars if such things were decided by women." She slanted an accusatory glare toward Geoffrey.

Rather than arguing with her, he shrugged and said, "Unfortunately, we don't see any women sitting in Congress, where such things are decided."

"Katie will be the minimum age in September," Penelope interjected. "Maybe she should run for office."

Silence fell around the table. All heads turned in Katie's direction. It took her a moment to register what had been said, since her thoughts had been lingering on Ben. But once she realized why they were looking at her, she quickly scoffed at the suggestion. "That's a preposterous idea!"

"Is it?" Geoffrey asked.

"Of course it is. Utterly preposterous."

"You know more about politics and the way government works than most candidates, Katie," Penelope countered. "You've been living in Washington for three years. And what you don't know, my mother could tell you."

Blanche's expression was so brittle, it looked as if she would crack. "Since it's obvious Miss Jones has no intention of running for political office, I suggest we turn our attention back to the real matter at hand."

Katie quickly agreed. After all, the last thing she ever intended to do was run for political office. The idea was positively absurd.

For the second Friday in a row, the weekly train from Boise brought a surprise visitor to Homestead. And just as the Rudyards had done the previous week, this visitor made his way to the offices of the *Homestead Herald*. When Ben returned from the mercantile, he found Uriah Cobbs sitting at his desk, smoking his pipe and reading that morning's edition of the paper.

Uriah—a short, wiry man of fifty with a receding hairline and wire-rimmed spectacles—looked up as the door opened. "Nice work, Rafferty," he said, pipe still clenched between his teeth. "This little burg is lucky to have you."

"Thanks." He pushed the door closed behind him. "I'm surprised to see you. I wasn't expecting you till next week."

Uriah stood. "Thought I'd better get a jump on the competition. When do I get to meet this Miss Jones?"

Ben had always considered Uriah one of the best newspaper reporters in the business. He also considered him a pompous ass. Uriah Cobbs would be fair in his reporting, but Katie would be subjected to plenty of cutting questions and snide remarks in the meantime. Ben wished he could get the first without the latter.

"Well?" Uriah prompted.

"Let's get you a room at the hotel first. Then I'll give her a jingle on the telephone to see when she can drive into town to meet with you."

The reporter grabbed his satchel. "Whatever you say, Rafferty. You can tell me about the little lady on our way."

Ben didn't know what he wanted to tell Uriah about Katie. He wasn't even sure what he would say to her when he called. He'd spent the last four days trying to figure out what his next step should be. He wasn't giving up on winning Katie's love. In fact, after the kiss they'd shared, he was fairly sure she was well on her way to caring for him as more than just a friend. But he also knew she was determined not to give in to those emotions.

Getting Uriah Cobbs to cover the rally was Ben's way of showing his support for the work Katie was doing. He hoped she would be appropriately grateful for the help, grateful enough to give him a chance in a more personal area of her life. He believed that once he won her love, all would be well. Of course, marriage to Katie wouldn't be easy or smooth sailing. She wasn't going to give up her independent ways overnight. But they would be happy. And life would never be dull. Of that he was certain.

As the two men left the newspaper office, Ben gave a brief sketch of Katie's childhood, leaving out most of her more outrageous escapades. Of his feelings for Katie he said nothing, other than that they and their families had been friends for many years.

He didn't say he hoped they would join the two families by having children of their own one day. He would have to convince Katie of that first.

After the meeting adjourned, Katie went to the door with those who were leaving. Blanche and Leslie said quick good-byes, then walked toward the Blake carriage, but Sophia hung back for a moment.

"Katie, do you think you might speak to Ben? Mother and I are worried about him."

"Worried? Why?"

"Ever since he and Charlotte broke off, he's been spending even more hours at the newspaper. He doesn't look as though he's slept all week."

A knot formed in her stomach. "Ben and Charlotte aren't seeing one another?"

"I thought you knew."

"No," she whispered. "No, I didn't know."

"Well, it was quite a surprise to everyone, especially coming on the heels of my broken engagement. I guess I needn't tell you, the town gossips are having a field day. The scandalous Raffertys, that's what they're calling us."

This is my fault, Katie thought as she turned her gaze in the direction of Homestead. This is all my fault.

The jangle of the telephone sounded from inside the

house. Blanche called for Sophia to get into the carriage so they could be on their way. A fly buzzed against the parlor windowpane, as if trying to gain entry to the house. Buzz. Click. Buzz. Click. Buzz.

But all Katie was conscious of was her own echoing thought: This is my fault.

Sophia's fingers closed around Katie's wrist. "I'll see you in church Sunday. If you have a chance, please talk to Ben. Maybe there's something you can do to help. He won't discuss the matter with us." Then she hurried off the porch and out to the carriage.

Ben and Charlotte weren't seeing each other. He'd broken off with her, no doubt out of guilt for the other night. Or perhaps Charlotte had guessed about Ben's faithlessness. Perhaps she'd sent him away.

"Oh, Ben. What have we done?" she whispered.

"Katie," her mother called from inside. "You're wanted on the telephone. It's Ben."

The knot in her stomach turned to lead. What would she say to him?

"Katie?"

"Coming, Mother." Squaring her shoulders, she opened the screened door and walked down the hall toward the telephone. Reluctantly she picked up the receiver and put it to her ear, then rose on tiptoe to speak into the mouthpiece. "Hello?"

"Katie, it's Ben. I was wondering if you could come into town this afternoon."

Cowardice overwhelmed her. "I just finished a committee meeting. I don't think I could get away—"

"Well then, maybe I could come out to the Lazy L?"

"Ben, this really isn't a good time. Perhaps—"

"It's important, Katie," he broke in again. "We've got a reporter here from Boise. Uriah Cobbs. He wants to interview you."

"Mr. Cobbs is here? In Homestead?"

"He's come to cover the rally." There was a pause on the other end of the line. Then Ben added, "This is a great opportunity. I think you should meet with him."

"Of course." But how could she face Ben? "Of course. I . . . I'll meet you and Mr. Cobbs in your office at about three o'clock."

"Good." Another pause. "Katie?" There was a slight change in the timbre of his voice. "We need to talk. About the other night."

"Yes," she whispered.

"I'll tell Uriah you'll be in my office at three."

She hesitated a moment before responding, "Three o'clock. I'll be there." She hung up the receiver without saying good-bye.

What was she to do? she wondered as she leaned her forehead against the wall. How could she ever make things right between them again?

"Katie?"

She straightened. Her father stood in the doorway to the kitchen, watching her. "Papa." Tears welled up in her eyes, and before she could give a thought to what she was doing, she was in his arms, her face pressed against his chest as she sobbed out her confusion and sorrow.

"What's the matter, kitten?" Yancy stroked her head with a work-worn hand.

The lump in her throat prevented her from answering.

Her sorrow hurt Yancy more than she would ever know. He'd always felt helpless around weepy females, and he felt even more helpless when the female was his little Katie.

"Here now," he murmured. "There, there. It'll be all right. You don't need t'cry. It'll be all right."

"No, it won't," she whispered against his shirt.

"'Course it will." He took hold of her arms and set her

back a step from him. "Now, tell me what's causin' all those tears."

She sniffed. "It's Ben. I . . . I think I've done something to hurt him. I didn't mean to, but—"

"Maybe it's just as well. Once you quit holdin' them meetings and writin' those columns, things'll get back to normal. Ben'll forgive you, and things'll be right between you two again."

She pressed her lips together as she wiped the tears from her cheeks. "I'm not stopping any of my meetings, Papa. It's not about that."

"Kitten—"

"I'm not stopping."

Yancy shook his head, feeling frustrated and weary.

"Why can't you understand how important this is to me?" she asked plaintively.

He looked at his daughter a long time before replying, "I don't reckon I know."

"Oh, Papa."

Yancy turned and walked to the back door, pushing it open so he could stare outside. "Your ma gave up a lot t'marry a no-account drifter like me. It was a mighty long time before she had anything close to the comforts she'd been used to at the Rocking R." He scratched his head. "I guess I'd like your life t'be easier than your ma's has been. I'd like t'see you happy 'fore I'm in my grave. And I don't think your fancy causes are gonna make you happy."

"You're a long way from your grave, Papa. And besides, isn't it my choice to make?"

He glanced over his shoulder. There was no trace of tears left in her eyes, and he was reminded anew that Katie was no longer a little girl. She was a grown woman with a mind of her own. And she was pretty much the woman he and her mother had raised her to be, a woman who wasn't afraid to face the world on her own terms.

Maybe Katie was right about him. She thought he was old-fashioned and set in his ways, and maybe he was. Maybe the times were changing faster than he realized.

"Isn't it my choice, Papa?" she asked again, softer this time.

"Yeah, I reckon it is, kitten. I reckon it is."

Uriah Cobbs was obviously surprised by Katie when he met her. No doubt, Ben thought, he'd been expecting a dried-up old spinster with her hair combed into a tight bun and a sour countenance, like someone who'd just sucked on a lemon. Instead Ben introduced him to a beautiful young woman with intelligent brown eyes and a lovely smile.

"We hadn't expected anyone to arrive so soon, Mr. Cobbs," Katie said as she settled onto a leather-upholstered chair. "We're honored you came."

"You've taken on quite a task for a little lady such as yourself, Miss Jones. Are you sure you're up to the work it will take to defeat both an incumbent governor and an incumbent president?"

Ben could see Katie bristle behind her composed facade.

"Nothing of true importance ever comes easily. Don't you agree, Mr. Cobbs?"

He wrote something on his notepad. "I suppose not. Tell me, why bring your campaign to Idaho, where women already enjoy the vote?"

"Because if we're to make certain all women share that right, it will be because women of the enfranchised states rise up in support of their sisters who are told, by lack of a right to vote, that they are unimportant, that their needs have no value, that they are less than their male counterparts."

"But why hold Governor Alexander responsible?"

"The governor is a Democrat, and his party has refused to support the cause of woman's suffrage. You've heard of the policy of holding the party in power responsible, Mr. Cobbs?" She paused long enough for the reporter to nod. "It is the Democratic Party that must be defeated in the November elections, not just Governor Alexander and President Wilson. Be assured that should Mr. Charles Hughes be elected president and should the Republicans not then support the amendment, we shall work just as vigorously to see to his party's defeat in the next election."

"I see." Uriah scribbled a few more notes with his pencil. "Why don't you tell me a little about yourself?"

Katie inclined her head and began to speak. As Ben listened along with Uriah Cobbs, he felt a welling up of pride in his chest. There was so much about Katie that he loved. It went far beyond her pretty face or enchanting figure. He loved her spirit, her nerve, her unwavering faithfulness to the things she believed in. He supposed it was some sort of miracle that the little tomboy had grown into this self-assured young woman. But it was no miracle that he loved her. How could he have helped it?

And love her, he did.

Ben hoped Uriah's interview wouldn't take much longer, because he wanted to talk to her privately. He wanted to let her know, if the kiss they'd shared the other night hadn't already told her so, that he cared for her as a man, not just as her friend.

Uriah rose suddenly from his chair. "I would be obliged if you'd show me around Homestead, Miss Jones. I'd like a better understanding of this place. I'd like to meet the people who live here." He offered her his elbow as he glanced at Ben. "You're welcome to join us, of course."

"Thanks," Ben muttered. It didn't make him feel any more charitable to know he'd have wanted the same thing if he were in Uriah's shoes. What was important to him now was to have Katie to himself, to perhaps steal another one of her sweet kisses, and then . . .

"I'll be happy to show you Homestead, Mr. Cobbs." Katie took hold of his proffered arm.

Ben had to keep from grinding his teeth in frustration as he reached for his hat, hanging on the coat rack. He set it on his head, then crossed to the door and held it open for Katie and Uriah as they passed by him.

They stopped first at the sheriff's office, where Uriah met both Sheriff Frank Murray and Vincent Michaels. Across the street at Barber Mercantile, the reporter was introduced to Leslie and George Blake, as well as Ophelia Turner, the postmistress; Annalee Leonhardt, Leslie's sister; and Fanny McLeod, wife of the town's doctor.

After introductions were completed, Uriah asked a few questions, innocuous questions that seemed no more than polite chitchat. But Ben could almost see the wheels turning in the other reporter's head as he formed his opinion of this little town in the central Idaho mountain country.

Zoe's Restaurant was their next stop, and it was there that fate stepped in to change the course of things.

Ben should have seen it coming but he didn't.

14

When Katie entered the restaurant with Uriah and Ben, she was surprised to find Geoffrey and Sophia sharing a table, deep in conversation. She'd known Geoffrey had left the ranch on horseback after their committee meeting had ended, but she hadn't expected to run into him here with Sophia.

After Katie introduced Uriah to her committee members, the reporter said, "You're from Massachusetts, Mr. Rudyard. Any relation to Mrs. Jonathon Rudyard?"

"My mother."

"Well, well." Uriah made a notation on his papers. "I had no idea Miss Jones's committee included anyone such as yourself."

Geoffrey cocked an eyebrow but said nothing.

"Do you plan to remain in Idaho long, Mr. Rudyard?"

Geoffrey glanced at Sophia, then back at Uriah. "My plans are open at this time. My sister and I will remain as long as Miss Jones needs or wants our assistance."

"If you're such a strong supporter of this woman's suffrage business"—Uriah's eyes narrowed—"why aren't you doing something back in Washington? For instance, why aren't you running for political office? It seems to me that's the only way to make real change. Or perhaps you haven't the gumption to stand behind your mother's convictions?"

Sophia gasped softly at the insult even as Katie opened her mouth to give Mr. Uriah Cobbs a piece of her mind.

But Geoffrey didn't appear offended by the remark. He merely responded with a bored smile and said, "I am not the least bit afraid to stand behind either my mother's or my own convictions, sir. But I should much rather see Miss Jones run for Congress than for me to do so. I am merely an attorney, and the government is filled to over-flowing with attorneys. Miss Jones, on the other hand, has a real understanding of the issues and concerns of women." He winked at Katie. "Being a woman herself, you understand." His expression sobered as he looked once more at the reporter. "In truth, Mr. Cobbs, Katie Jones is highly qualified to serve in office. We were just discussing it this morning, weren't we, Katie? That you should run for Congress."

"Miss Jones?" Uriah turned to Katie. "Surely Mr. Rudyard jests. Surely you aren't considering such a ridiculous stunt?"

That morning Katie had considered the idea just as ridiculous as Mr. Cobbs thought it. But looking at his mocking expression caused her temper to overheat as quickly as the Susan B on a summer day. "Do you think a woman incapable of filling such an office, Mr. Cobbs?"

He had the audacity to laugh. "As a matter of fact, Miss Jones, I do." Still chuckling, he gave his head a slow shake and looked once more at the notes he'd written on his pad. "But since it isn't likely any woman will ever sit in the United States Congress, I won't have to worry about such a catastrophe as that would be."

Katie balled her hands into fists. "I hope I shall prove you wrong come November."

Uriah glanced up. His eyebrows arched. "You don't mean—"

"That's exactly what I mean, Mr. Cobbs. I have every intention of declaring my candidacy for office. I'm going to run for the U.S. House of Representatives. And I'm going to *win*, too."

Geoffrey leapt to his feet. "Bravo, Katie!" he shouted, drawing the attention of the other customers in the restaurant and causing Esther Potter to scurry out from the kitchen to see what the commotion was all about.

"Katie, that's wonderful," Sophia joined in, reaching out to take hold of Katie's hand.

Katie glanced toward Ben to see what his reaction might be, but it was impossible to read the expression on his face. Perhaps he thought she'd just lost her mind. If so, he could be right, but there was no taking back her declaration now, not with Uriah Cobbs writing furiously on his notepad.

"And do you plan to make this announcement public at the rally?" the reporter queried.

It was Ben who answered the question for her. "Yes, she does." His smile was mercurial, there and then gone, but it shored up her courage nonetheless.

Uriah turned a dubious look upon Ben. "Don't tell me *you* support this idiotic stunt?"

"Not only do I support it," he answered, "but I intend to manage Miss Jones's campaign. If she'll have me."

"Benjie," she whispered softly, her heart ratta-tatting in her chest.

Uriah Cobbs spun on his heel and headed for the door. "Excuse me, folks. I've got to call this in to my editor. He's never going to believe it. Not in a million years. A woman running for the U.S. House. Unbelievable!" He was out the door in a flash.

Katie's knees suddenly went weak. She grabbed for the nearest chair and sank onto it. "What have I done?" She looked from one friend to another.

"You've done what you were meant to do," Geoffrey answered. "By Jove, this is a stroke of brilliance. A woman running for Congress when most women can't even cast a vote at the ballot box. It will get the attention of people across the nation. Katie, my girl, it's wonderful." He leaned down and kissed her soundly on the cheek. "Wait until Mother hears."

Katie's stomach felt as if she were at sea in the middle of a violent storm. She looked at Ben again. "What do you think?" She paused, then added, "Really."

He drew her up from her chair. "Come on. We're going to talk in private." He didn't bother to look at Geoffrey or Sophia. He didn't make any excuses. He simply escorted Katie out of the restaurant and down the street.

She dreaded what was coming. Ben was going to read her the riot act, and she would deserve everything he said. She'd done some crazy things in her life, but this was certainly the craziest one yet.

She expected him to take her to the newspaper, only he turned on Barber Street and headed straight out of town, not stopping until they'd reached a tiny copse of trees along the banks of Pony Creek. Then, one hand on each of her arms, he turned her to face him.

She had a hard time thinking about the scolding she deserved or Uriah Cobbs or running for office when she was standing so close to Ben, looking up at his mouth and remembering the way his lips had felt, pressed against hers. She seemed to recall there was something else that should be troubling her, too, something she'd known they needed to discuss, but she couldn't recall it, either.

Ben's fingers tightened. "Before we discuss your campaign, Katie, we need to come to an understanding."

Charlotte. It was Charlotte she needed to talk to him about.

"The other night—" he began.

"Ben, I—" she said at the same time.

Then, just as had happened before, she was somehow in his arms, kissing him. The world slowed on its axis. The creek's gurgle turned into a melody of love, joined by the songbirds in the trees. Katie's heart pounded as loudly as jungle drums.

The kiss ended. Ben nuzzled her hair as one hand stroked her back. Then he whispered, "Katie," and the sound of her name was as sweet as any confection she'd ever tasted.

But she mustn't indulge in that sweetness, she told herself. She had to try to make things right, not make them worse.

She drew away from him. "Sophia told me that you and Charlotte . . . that the two of you . . ." She turned away, her gaze locked on the fast-running stream. "I don't know why this is happening, Ben. I never meant to come between you and Charlotte. You're my dearest friend. I never meant for you to be hurt, to ruin your plans. I never meant—"

"If I'd loved Charlotte, you couldn't have come between us." He drew up close to her back, leaned down to whisper in her ear. "It's you I love, Katie."

Her eyes widened. She held her breath. She couldn't have heard him right. She couldn't have.

She turned slowly. "What did you say?"

"I said I love you."

She shook her head. It couldn't be true. She'd been so certain he loved Charlotte. He'd said he was going to marry her. He'd said . . .

"I love you, Katherine Lark Jones," he said one more time, as if to make certain she understood him.

Then he kissed her again, thoroughly, wonderfully, deeply kissed her until the feel of his mouth upon hers was the only reality left in her topsy-turvy world.

Ben delighted in the feel of Katie's breasts against his chest as he drew her closer, savored the taste of her mouth as his tongue teased her lips until they parted. And he wondered at how this had all come about. It certainly wasn't the way he had intended to declare his love and devotion.

Finally, feeling the hot pulsing of desire fogging his brain and hardening his body, he broke the kiss and moved slightly back from her. When he spoke, his voice was deepened by emotion. "I love you, Katie. I want to marry you."

She gasped and lifted a hand to cover her just kissed mouth. Eyes wide, she stared at him as if he'd sprouted a second head.

Damn! He'd known he shouldn't move this fast.

"Come over here," he suggested gently, guiding her toward a large boulder beside the creek. "Sit down. You're shaking like a leaf."

A nervous laugh escaped her as she sank onto the rock.

It was too late for him to take back his proposal, so he pressed forward. "Will you marry me, Katie?"

"Ben, I don't know what to say. I'm totally confused." She rubbed her forehead. "I just told Mr. Cobbs I was running for office, and you said you were going to manage my campaign, and now you're asking me to marry you." She drew a deep breath as she lowered her hand. "How could I possibly marry you if I'm going off to Washington as a congresswoman?"

He could have told her he agreed with Uriah. He didn't think a woman would ever be elected to a national political office. But discretion held his tongue. He was trying to win Katie's love, not make her angry with him.

"And there's my work," she continued, as much to herself as to him, it seemed. "I never intended to stay here in Homestead."

"But you're doing the work you came here to do, aren't you? You're doing it here, not in Washington."

Confusion swirled in the brown depths of her eyes. "But that was temporary."

Ben wanted to take her back in his arms. He wanted to persuade her with kisses and caresses. He wanted to make her feel what he was feeling—love, desire, tenderness, passion. But something held him back. Something told him not to push any further.

"Did you mean what you said, Ben? Will you help me run for office?"

"If it's what you truly want to do." Secretly he hoped she would say it wasn't what she wanted. He should have known better.

She worried her lower lip while staring off into space. Then, looking at Ben once more, she squared her shoulders and tilted her chin. "Yes, I think it *is* what I want to do. I know I said I was going to run because I was angered by Mr. Cobbs's comments, but now that I've thought about it, I realize Geoffrey is right. This isn't such a crazy idea. I do know what's needed. I could do this job, Ben." Her eyes narrowed slightly. "Don't *you* think I could?"

About this he could be honest. "Yes, Katie, I know you could do it." What he didn't add was that he didn't *want* her to do it.

She rose to her feet. "And you'll help me win the election?"

As had been true throughout his life, it was impossible for him to deny Katie anything. He found it no less impossible at this particular moment. "I'll do whatever I can," he promised. Then he took hold of her arms once again. "And what about us?"

She stared up at him for the longest time, and he was positive he saw the love he longed for her to proclaim. But she didn't admit to it. "I can't marry you, Ben."

But you will marry me, Katie. I don't know what it will take to convince you, but you will marry me.

Quite some time later Katie drove home, her thoughts churning, her emotions in a continuing state of confusion. So much had happened that day, she could scarcely assimilate it all.

By the time she and Ben had returned to the restaurant, word of her candidacy had spread throughout Homestead. Those who had not come to Zoe's to congratulate Katie on her decision stood in the doorways of the shops and businesses and stared at her with looks of horror or derision or a combination of the two. She knew it was just an inkling of what the next few months would be like.

She refused even to think what her father's reaction to her latest endeavor might be. She had enough to ponder—her candidacy for the U.S. House, Ben's proclamation of love, his proposal of marriage.

Ben's proposal of marriage.

Nothing could have shocked her more than the moment he'd said he wanted to marry her. Not even what she'd done in the restaurant had surprised her as much as that.

Ben loved her.

He wanted to marry her.

Katie braked to a halt, then closed her eyes and leaned her forehead against the steering wheel.

She didn't want to be married. She wanted her work. She wanted to return to Washington. She silently repeated the words like a litany, until she wondered if they were true or if she were trying to convince herself they were true.

She loved Ben. She couldn't deny it. She loved him with everything within her. And she desired his kisses with a longing that bordered on desperation.

But marriage?

She couldn't turn her back on everything she'd believed, everything she'd been saying for years. Like Susan B. Anthony, Katie knew that marriage could only be a complication to the work she wanted to do.

Wouldn't it?

Not all suffragettes remained single throughout their lives. Inez Milholland—whom Katie held in such high esteem—was married. It was possible to do both.

Or was it?

But that didn't matter now. She'd told Ben she couldn't marry him. And she couldn't, not in good faith. Marriage to Ben would distract her. Look how he distracted her already, and he wasn't even her husband. Besides, she'd made promises to others that she had to fulfill. There was no room in her life for that sort of commitment. No, marriage to Ben would be a big mistake.

Wouldn't it?

Katie drew in a ragged breath and straightened. She stared down the road toward the ranch.

It would be better if she left things as they were, she told herself. Ben would help her in the election, as he had always helped her in the past. He was her dearest and most beloved friend. It was better that they be friends alone. Better for everyone.

Now, if she could only believe those words were true.

15

The Homestead Weekly Herald, *Homestead, Idaho*
Friday Morning, June 23, 1916
LOCAL WOMAN ANNOUNCES INTENTION TO RUN FOR U.S. HOUSE OF REPRESENTATIVES ON THE REPUBLICAN TICKET

This last week, Katherine L. Jones, daughter of Yancy and Lark Jones, declared her intention to seek the office of United States Congresswoman from Idaho. Her announcement has caused considerable interest from politicians, constituents, and the press, especially as it comes in conjunction with the election rally being held in our town this Saturday, June 24, behind the Rafferty Hotel on Main Street.

Local businessmen have reported a significant increase in business as visitors arrive in Homestead in advance of the rally . . .

The week following Katie's decision to run for Congress was a complete blur of activity. Ben participated in daily meetings with the Homestead Woman's Suffrage Committee. He and Geoffrey began mapping out a strategy for Katie's primary campaign, beginning with a trip to Boise to officially file for office in the second week following the rally.

Surprisingly, Katie's father's reaction to her decision to run for political office was milder than she'd expected. He didn't tell her it was one more reckless action in a lifetime full of reckless actions, even though she thought he would have been right to say so. Instead Yancy gave her a sad smile and said, "I hope you know what it is you're doin', kitten."

"I hope so, too, Papa."

Her mother was more enthusiastic. "You've never been afraid to try new things, Katie. You've always been ready to spread your wings and fly." She gave her daughter a hug. "Go on and fly, darling."

"I'll try, Mother."

"And, Katie, remember this. You're your father's only little girl. You're not a disappointment to him. He's just afraid of losing you to this bold new world of yours."

By the next Friday, when Katie's name first appeared in the *Herald* as a candidate for office, every available room in Homestead—at the hotel, at the boardinghouse, and every private room anyone was willing to rent out—had been filled by reporters, candidates for office, and interested citizens from other cities and towns. The two restaurants in Homestead were doing a booming business, as were the other small shops. Folks gathered on street corners, in the billiard saloon, the barber shop, the drugstore, and in homes to discuss Katie Jones and her candidacy for the United States House of Representatives. Everyone had an opinion, and most of them spoke those opinions quite freely. New divisions arose between husbands and wives, between neighbors, between old friends. Women who hadn't objected to the suffrage issue expressed shock at one of their own running for national political office. Others saw a new hope because of one young woman's courage. Men who'd thought Katie's suffrage talk unnecessary but harmless suddenly saw what her candidacy could mean for their futures and quickly ridiculed her. Others, though smaller in number, expressed support for her actions and offered to help however they could.

Katie hadn't had a single good night's sleep all week. She'd slaved over a new speech for the rally because everything had changed after her declaration for office. She appreciated, more than she could say, the encouragement she'd received from Ben and Geoffrey, Sophia and Penelope, her mother and Leslie Blake. Blanche Coleson was the only member of the committee who hadn't seemed enthusiastic about what Katie was doing, but Katie never asked her why. She hadn't wanted any more doubts to wrestle with. Her own were quite sufficient.

On the Saturday of the rally, Katie drove the Susan B into Homestead, the Rudyards and both of her brothers riding along with her. Her parents followed in the surrey, the ranch hands on horseback.

A platform had been erected behind the Rafferty Hotel, and people milled around it, waiting for the rally to start, the air alive with a cacophony of voices. Wagons, buggies, and automobiles filled the open field south of the Homestead Community Church.

As Katie parked the Susan B, she shot a nervous glance toward Penelope, but her throat was too dry to speak.

Her friend patted her hand. "You're going to be wonderful, Katie. Just wait and see. I promise it's true."

"Penny's right," Geoffrey joined in from the backseat. "You were born for this moment."

Sam leaned forward. "Yeah. And if Andy Henderson says anything more about you, I'll black his other eye."

Katie groaned. "Don't tell me you've been in another fight because of me?" She glanced over her shoulder at her brother.

Sam shrugged, not bothering to deny it.

"What have I done?" Katie mumbled to herself as she turned her gaze toward the platform.

That was when she saw Ben, striding toward the Susan B. He wore a smile, and she knew it was meant just for her. A smile of encouragement and love. Her heart quickened at the sight of him. Ben stopped beside the car, placed his hands on the stationary door, and leaned in, bringing his face close to hers. Too close for Katie's comfort.

"You've just cost some folks a bit of spare change." His smile broadened. "They were laying odds you wouldn't show up for the rally."

Her back stiffened and her temper flared. "I hope you won a bundle, Benjie."

"I did."

"Good." She glanced at her passengers. "I believe it's time we got this rally started."

Everyone piled out of the automobile. Katie's brothers dashed off to join friends their own ages, leaving the others to cross the street toward the platform at a more sedate rate.

Ben took Katie's hand and slipped it into the crook of his arm, then covered her fingers with his opposite hand. "No matter what happens today or after, Katie, you can be proud of what you've accomplished." His voice lowered a notch. "*I'm* proud of you."

*   *   *

Two hours later, when it was finally Katie's turn to speak, Ben's words continued to warm her heart. She stepped up to the podium, feeling a strange calm settle over her. At the same time, a hush gripped the audience in the field below. All eyes were locked on Katie.

"My friends." She looked from face to face, recognizing the myriad emotions she found there—anger, anticipation, ridicule, hope. "Our republic has believed in no taxation without representation since its birth one hundred and forty years ago. In 1896, six years after gaining statehood, Idaho became the fourth state to extend full voting privileges to women, recognizing that native-born women should be at least as politically equal with native-born Chinese and Indian men. Most important, the people of Idaho affirmed that the ballot is a badge of equality for all classes."

She didn't need the notes for her speech. Every word was memorized, in her head and in her heart.

"In the two decades since this enfranchisement, Idaho women have been elected as the legislative chaplain, as the state superintendent of public instruction, to the Idaho Legislature, as county treasurers, and as deputy sheriffs, to name just a few offices. The Idaho Legislature has also—at the urging of women legislators and lobbyists—adopted acts prohibiting child labor, giving married women the same right to control and dispose of their property as married men, requiring saloons to close on Sundays, establishing a state library commission, providing a domestic science department at the university, and establishing an industrial reform school. These are all positive changes for the people of our state."

Were they listening or were her words falling on deaf ears? she wondered. Did they understand the importance of what she was saying?

"Now it is time to make a difference for our country. It

is time for all women in America to share the same rights as we have in Idaho."

Katie leaned forward, and fervor filled her voice. "Why am I running for office? many of you are asking. Wouldn't it be enough for me to simply work to elect men who support an amendment for woman's suffrage? No, that is not enough. It's time for a woman's voice to be heard in Congress. And I should like to feel that I have done something of consequence in my life. I should like to champion the causes that will better the lives of all women in this country, and to do so, I must be able to address the lawmakers of this land as an equal, as one of them."

"You belong at home!" a woman at the back of the crowd shouted.

Katie looked in the direction of the voice. Try as she might, she couldn't understand why all women didn't believe in the importance of suffrage. Knowing they didn't caused a pain in her heart and increased her determination to change their minds.

"It is not my intention to make a long speech today. You have heard many speeches. You have listened patiently to many candidates, some with vast experience in government. Certainly much more experience than I myself have."

"You've talked too long already!" a man jeered.

"Get a husband!" another yelled.

Katie ignored them both. "I will close with some words from a woman I have so greatly admired, Susan B. Anthony. When asked what message she had for the new century, Miss Anthony answered, 'We women must be up and doing. I can hardly sit still when I think of the great work waiting to be done. Above all, women must be in earnest, we must be thorough, and fit ourselves for every emergency; we must be trained, and carefully prepare ourselves for the place we wish to hold in the world. The twentieth century will see as great a change in the position and progress of woman in the world as has been accomplished in the previous century, but it will have ceased to cause comment, and will be accepted as a matter of course. There will be nothing in the realm of ethics in which woman will not have her own recognized place, and all political questions, and all the laws which govern us will have a feminine side, for woman and her influence, in making and shaping of affairs, will have to be reckoned with.'"

Again Katie paused and let her gaze sweep over the crowd. When she continued, it was with a strong, sure voice. "I want to be a part of what Miss Anthony foresaw for this nation and for its women. This is my promise to each one of you. Should I be elected to the House, I will represent the people of Idaho with integrity and a vision for a better future for all."

Her gaze met with Ben's. He'd spoken of his pride in her earlier. Now she could see it in his eyes. "Thank you," she ended, speaking to all but meaning it for Ben.

Then she picked up her notes and left the platform.

Sophia had been spellbound by every word Katie spoke. Never before had she heard anything so wonderful, so inspiring.

"Look at them, Sophia!" Geoffrey exclaimed as he hugged her shoulders. "Katie's won them over." Then he lifted his sister off the ground and kissed her cheek. "She did it, Penny. She really did it. By Jove, Katie's a marvel."

"We must send a telegram to Mother," Penelope said as she straightened her hat, which had been knocked slightly askew by her brother's enthusiasm. "She'll be waiting to hear. So will everyone."

"I'll go at once." Geoffrey took off toward South Street with long, purposeful strides.

Sophia watched him as he walked away and found herself wondering about the handsome lawyer. She'd liked both of the Rudyards from the first moment they'd met, but it was only now she wondered why Geoffrey had made woman's suffrage his cause, too.

As if she'd read Sophia's thoughts, Penelope said, "Our mother took us with her everywhere when we were young. Geoffrey and I saw the terrible squalor so many women and children are forced to live in because of unfair property laws. We saw what happens when a man decides to cast his wife aside. Geoffrey swore, while he was still just a boy, that he would help change things when he grew up. It's why he studied law. It's why he's helped work for the suffrage amendment."

"I don't think I ever thought of anything except what I wanted for myself," Sophia confessed. "I guess I've been terribly selfish."

"I don't think you've been selfish. Look what you've done, once you saw the need."

She shrugged. "I haven't really done anything."

"You're wrong, Sophia. Change doesn't happen because of one person doing one big thing. It happens when many people do their own small parts."

"I wish I could do more."

Penelope took hold of her hand. "Why don't you come back to Washington when this is over? I'm sure Katie would like to have another friend back there when she's elected. You could live with us and work for the association."

"Washington?" Sophia's eyes widened. Could she really do something so daring? "I don't know. I never—"

"You wouldn't be sorry. I can promise you that."

"I don't know," she said again, then added, "but I'll think about it, Penny."

* * *

Tears made Lark's vision blurry. She tried to blink them away, but more came in their place. Yancy's arm encircled her shoulders, and he squeezed tightly, pulling her up against his side.

"She's going away again," she whispered.

"So it appears," her husband answered, then kissed her temple as he handed her a handkerchief.

After wiping her eyes, she looked up and gave Yancy a weak smile. "I hadn't realized just how badly I wanted her to stay here until this minute. I got all caught up in the excitement of what we were doing and didn't think—" She stopped abruptly as tears welled up again.

"She may not get elected," he said, trying to comfort her.

"But she was so wonderful, wasn't she? I was so proud as I listened to her." She took hold of her husband's hand. "Yancy, can you believe we raised her? That she was ever our little girl?"

He gave a humorless chuckle. "Not hardly."

Her heart grew heavy again. "She's going to win." She pressed her face against his chest. "She'll be going away. Maybe for good."

"Lark?" His work-worn hand stroked her back. "I reckon nobody knows better'n you how I've felt about all this. I just couldn't help thinkin' she'd be better off t'marry and settle down. Like you and me." His voice lowered to a near whisper. "But maybe I was wrong. Maybe she won't ever be happy if she stays here. Maybe she doesn't want nor need the same things we did."

Lark couldn't have answered, not even to save her soul. She knew what Yancy was talking about. She'd seen the troubled look in their daughter's eyes all too often of late.

"We raised her up t'be her own woman," her husband continued. "She'll find her way, Lark."

She sniffed as she drew back from him. She forced a smile and said, "Of course she will. She's our daughter. Our Katie."

Blanche observed the commotion following the close of the rally from her spot near the rear entrance of the hotel. She watched as people crowded around Katie Jones, reporters asking questions and writing her answers on their notepads. Even some of the other politicians had gathered near her.

Ben Rafferty stayed close by her side, watching her with an adoring gaze. It was obvious what was going on there. Sinful. Shameful.

Disappointment washed afresh over Blanche. Katie was not at all what she'd expected her to be. Any suffragette worth her salt would do her utmost to avoid men. They were inferior, lustful, and evil, and a wise woman kept her distance from them all. If Katie was really concerned about the welfare of her own sex, she would have ended her association with Mr. Rafferty long ago. Instead Katie seemed to encourage it. Blanche suspected they were far more than friends.

She turned and slipped through the crowd unnoticed, making her way back to her apartment above Yardley's Drug Store.

Jealousy and envy ate at her soul. Katie Jones was young and pretty, and her family had money and prestige. If it weren't so, no one would have paid her any attention. Katie would have been as invisible as an old maid schoolmarm.

Bitterly Blanche thought of the letters she'd written two weeks before. Only one response, and that one from a woman who had called Blanche a few unkind names, then told her to mind her own business.

But Katie Jones? She had people gathered around her like a pack of jackals, hanging on every word she uttered as if each utterance were nectar from the gods.

Disgusting.

If those same supporters were to learn about Miss Jones's scandalous involvement with Mr. Rafferty, would they be so charitable to her? Would they think her such an inspiration, such a fine leader of the suffrage cause? Of course not.

Blanche paused at the stairway to her apartment, glancing back in the direction from which she'd come.

Perhaps someone ought to expose Katie Jones for what she was. Then maybe they would listen to Blanche, as they should have in the first place.

Ben waited patiently while Katie answered question after question. He understood people's desire to draw close to her. She'd always had a vivacious, infectious personality, but today everyone had seen much more than her charisma. They had seen her intelligence, her caring, her commitment to her beliefs.

He'd been proud of her before she'd given her speech. He'd been even more proud afterward. But he was also concerned. Listening to her, he'd realized for the first time it was not an impossibility for her to win the election.

And if she won, what would happen to the future he'd envisioned for them? She would, indeed, be going back to Washington, just as she'd said the night he'd proposed. Would she ever want to return to Homestead? Would she ever be willing to settle down in a quiet, small town, have a home, have a family?

His own wants and desires warred with Katie's dreams. He'd promised he would help her in her campaign. He would keep his promise. But he couldn't deny the secret hope within him that she would be defeated.

Because if she won, Ben was afraid everything that mattered most to him would be forever lost.

16

Uriah Cobbs, Katie decided, was a weasel of a man, sneaky, underhanded, and certainly not to be trusted. While the other reporters and all of the political candidates left Homestead in their automobiles and horse-drawn carriages in the day or two immediately following the rally, Uriah lingered—like a bad cough.

Twice he came out to the ranch to interview Katie, asking her the same questions time and again, doing his best to trip her up in some manner. If she went into town, he dogged her steps, pad and pencil in hand. When she went to church, he observed her from another pew. He talked to her girlhood friends and to her neighbors. Katie felt as if she couldn't keep a single private thought from the intrepid reporter.

In the meantime, the dining room at the Lazy L became the campaign headquarters for the Elect Katie Jones to Congress Committee. Morning, noon, and night, there was no escaping the ringing telephone or the onslaught of telegrams and letters or the plans that had to be made.

And although Ben came out to the ranch daily, there was never any time when they could be alone, just the two of them. Katie longed for a few minutes to be herself with him, to be able to laugh and tease, to go swimming with him at the pond or horseback riding with him up in the mountains.

Most of all, she wanted to step into Ben's arms and feel his heart beating near hers. The memory of his kisses filled her dreams, both waking and sleeping. Her subconscious teased her with the knowledge of his love. Charlotte was no longer a factor. Ben was free to love and be loved.

But even when they were briefly alone together, Ben didn't mention his proposal of marriage again. Not even once. He didn't try to change her mind about running for Congress. Nor did he list all the reasons she should marry him.

And it was oddly disturbing that she should want him to do so.

June rolled into July, with temperatures climbing once again. Rain was a thing of distant memories. Whenever anything moved in the valley, a cloud of dry, fine dust rose above it. Tempers grew short, even among friends.

Blanche Coleson no longer attended the committee meetings. She'd given no reason for her absence. She'd simply stated she no longer wished to participate. And because no one on the committee had ever felt particularly close to the schoolmarm, they didn't try to change her mind, especially since other volunteers had begun to show up at the ranch, offering their help.

Yancy Jones steered clear of all the political plotting and planning going on beneath his own roof, but Lark participated fully—often with tears in her eyes and sentimental comments about Katie as a child. Katie knew it was hard on both of her parents, the idea that she really wasn't going to stay in Homestead, that she was going back to Washington. And she was grateful for the love and support they showered upon her each day.

There was, however, no cause to rejoice about the chasm in Homestead between her supporters and those who thought she should be locked in her father's wood-shed until she came to her senses. Phillip Carson refused to shop at Barber Mercantile or to cut George Blake's hair now that he'd decided Katie had every right to run for office. Norman Henderson and his sons were now attending the First Methodist Church because of Reverend Simon Jacobs's refusal to speak against Katie from his pulpit; in her own small protest, Rachel Henderson continued to burn the meals she prepared for husband and sons. A group of boys threw eggs against the windows of the *Homestead Herald* one night, but they ran off before the sheriff could catch them. Katie suspected Frank Murray knew who the perpetrators were but didn't want to punish them.

On the Fourth of July the town held its annual celebra-tion, with a community picnic planned for the afternoon and a display of fireworks scheduled for the evening. By an unspoken agreement the opposing sides of the election and suffrage issues called a temporary truce so the towns-folk could celebrate the nation's independence without rancor.

As had happened the day of the rally, Katie drove her Touring Car into Homestead with the Rudyards and her brothers for passengers. But this time Ben wasn't waiting to greet Katie when she parked the automobile near the Homestead School. Today he was standing in the shade of a box elder tree . . .

With Charlotte Orson.

*　　*　　*

"Why didn't you tell me your father was ill?" Ben asked Charlotte as he took hold of her hand. "I had no idea."

"Neither did I. Father never said a word. If Dr. McLeod hadn't come to me and insisted Father take a rest . . ." She let her voice drift into a strained silence.

"Everyone will be sorry to see you and your father leave Homestead."

She made a brave attempt at smiling. "Perhaps it's for the best this way."

Ben knew she was referring to what had happened between the two of them. "I'm sorry, Charlotte."

"You needn't be, Benjamin. There is a reason for everything. I don't know when Father will be able to pastor another church, and with so much time on his hands, he'll need me to see that he follows the doctor's orders."

"But why California?"

"Father's always wanted to see the Pacific Ocean. This is his opportunity." Her voice lowered. "And he may not have many more opportunities if his heart—" She broke off abruptly, fighting tears.

"I'm sorry," he whispered again.

She pulled her hand free and turned her back toward him. He saw her wipe furtively at her tears with her fingertips. Then she drew in a long, deep breath before facing him once again. "What about you, Benjamin? Are you happy?"

"Katie's running for office changed some of my plans."

This time Charlotte's smile was more earnest. "She'll make a wonderful representative. I was most impressed at the rally."

"So was I."

"But?"

"But she doesn't want to discuss marriage because of her campaign."

It was Charlotte's turn to take hold of Ben's hand. "And even so, you're doing your best to help her win. You're a special man, Benjamin. But then, I always knew that about you."

He shrugged, uncomfortable with the compliment, especially knowing, down deep in his heart, that he wanted Katie to lose.

"I hope Miss Jones knows how lucky she is," Charlotte added. Then she changed the subject. "I understand you're driving down to the capital on Thursday."

"Yes. Katie's going to officially file for office. She'll be meeting with members of the press, and will probably talk to the suffrage leaders there."

"Then this will be my last opportunity to tell you goodbye. Father and I leave on Friday's train."

"So soon?"

She nodded.

"The community will miss you. Your father's congregation. Everyone."

"Thank you, Benjamin. We'll miss Homestead." She squeezed his hand one last time, then released it. "I'd better get back to Father. He shouldn't even be out in this heat, but I couldn't convince him to stay at home. Not today of all days." She walked away, headed toward the picnic tables set up near the banks of Pony Creek.

Ben watched her go, thinking what a special person Charlotte was and wondering again why he hadn't fallen in love with her. Odd, the twists and turns that happened in life. She'd asked him if he was happy, but he hadn't really answered her. Perhaps because "happy" wasn't the right word. He didn't know if Katie would ever agree to marry him, but he knew she was the only woman for him. He knew he'd done the right thing in ending his relationship with Charlotte and pursuing the woman who held his heart.

Loving Katie was worth the risk.

*   *   *

Katie's chest hurt, ached as if something inside had shattered in two. She pasted a smile on her face and went through the motions of greeting people, of making polite conversation. But all the while she kept envisioning Ben and Charlotte, standing so close together beneath that tree, holding hands.

It was for the best, she tried to tell herself. She hadn't been willing to marry him anyway. She wanted Ben to be happy, after all, and she was quite certain Charlotte would be able to make him happy. Yes, this was all for the best.

From the corner of her eye Katie saw Uriah Cobbs start toward her. Unable to bear the idea of answering one more of his intolerable questions or listening to another of his condescending comments, she quickly slipped into the crowd.

She made her way into the tall cottonwoods and underbrush growing along the banks of the creek. She followed a well-worn path, a path beaten into the earth by generations of children who'd come to play by the cool stream on hot summer days. As she walked, the trees seemed to close in behind her, shutting out the noise of the townsfolk as they shared food and enjoyed one another's company. She kept walking. And walking and walking and walking.

She was nearly to the lumber mill before she stopped her hasty retreat. With a great sigh she sank to the ground, her back against a tree trunk, her knees pulled up to her chest, and her arms wrapped around her legs. She pressed her face into the folds of her skirt.

Truth washed over her. She wasn't trying to escape Uriah or his interminable questions. She was trying to avoid seeing Ben and Charlotte. She realized she'd been waiting for them to come walking into the picnic, holding hands and smiling at one another. The couple everyone had known should marry, together again.

Why couldn't she just be glad for them? Was she so selfish, so small-minded, she would begrudge Ben his dream when she was so determined to achieve her own?

She didn't much care for the small voice inside her that said, *Yes,* in answer to her silent question.

"Mind some company?"

She raised her head as Ben stepped into view from between two trees. *Where's Charlotte?* she wanted to ask but couldn't. Her throat was too tight to speak, so she simply shook her head.

Ben chose another tree trunk to lean against, crossing one leg in front of the other and resting the toe of his shoe on the ground. He folded his arms over his chest. He'd removed his suit coat sometime earlier. His white shirt seemed rather startling amid the earthy tones of trees, grass, and soil that surrounded them. The brightness hurt Katie's eyes, so she turned away.

"Feels good to find some quiet, doesn't it?" he asked.

She nodded.

"Looks like those who oppose you are calling a truce for today. No speechifying. It'll be nice for a change."

"Yes," she whispered, not caring at the moment if everyone in Idaho opposed her.

"I've asked Childers to go over the Susan B tomorrow, make sure she's ready for the drive down to Boise. We shouldn't have any trouble."

Three days with Ben. A full day's drive down to the city. A day in the capital, registering her candidacy, talking to officials, meeting with other supporters of woman's suffrage. And then another long day's drive back to Homestead. Three days with Ben—and he'd be thinking about Charlotte.

"Katie." He stepped across the short distance separating them and sank to the ground beside her. "Why don't you tell me what's wrong? Is it Cobbs? Has he said something he shouldn't?"

Oh, Ben. Why do I have to feel this way?

He sighed. "All right. I won't press." He settled against the trunk beside her, so close she could feel the heat of his skin beneath his shirtsleeve. "Did you hear about Charlotte and her father?"

Katie's heart nearly stopped beating altogether. She wasn't ready for this.

"The reverend has been having trouble with his heart. He and Charlotte are leaving Homestead, moving out to California. Dr. Tom thinks it will do him good."

She turned her head to look at Ben. "They're leaving Homestead?"

"On the next train."

"Charlotte's leaving Homestead?" she repeated. She stared hard at him, trying to read what lay behind his eyes. "Will you miss her?"

When Ben realized what Katie was asking and why she was asking it, he had to work hard to suppress a grin. She was jealous. She must have seen him talking to Charlotte. She'd seen him and she'd jumped to the wrong conclusion. And she was jealous. Which meant she cared far more than she was willing to admit. Which meant she just might love him the way he loved her.

With a firm grasp he took hold of her shoulders, pulling her toward him, turning her until she lay across his lap, his left arm supporting her back while his right hand caressed her cheek.

She stared up at him with wide eyes. He could almost see the wheels turning in her head. She was thinking she should pull away from him, that she shouldn't let him hold her like this, that he belonged to Charlotte.

"Katie," he whispered, "didn't you believe me when I told you I love you? Charlotte is special, and I hope she finds a man who deserves her and who will make her happy. But that man's not me. Because I'm in love with you, and it's only you I want to be with."

He'd tried for so long—eighteen days, to be precise—not to pressure Katie. He hadn't told her he loved her. Hadn't asked her again to marry him. Hadn't kissed her. But there was a limit to his self-control, and he'd just reached it.

"Kiss me, Katie."

He drew her closer to him. The moment their mouths touched, he felt a hot surge of desire, and he knew kissing wasn't enough. He ached to do much more than merely taste the sweetness of her mouth and breathe in the delightful scent of her clean hair. He longed to run his hands over her firm body. He wanted to remove her blouse and corset, release her breasts from the fabric that bound them, let them spill into his hands while he ran his thumbs over the nipples until they hardened into peaks. He yearned to explore the feminine mysteries hidden beneath the layers of clothes, beneath her gown and petticoats and lacy undergarments. He craved the sound of her labored breathing as passion overtook her.

As if she'd heard his thoughts, she groaned softly. Then she wriggled, snuggling closer against him and causing his lust to burn even hotter.

He imagined her, lying there beside the stream, her dark hair fanned out across the grass. Sunlight, filtered through leafy tree limbs, would play across her skin, turning it to gold.

It was his turn to groan. He broke the kiss. "Marry me." It was a demand rather than a request.

Her cheeks were flushed, her gaze revealing the desire he'd ignited with his kisses. "I can't, Benjie."

He brought his face close to hers. "You're too stubborn for your own good."

"I know." Her smile was uncertain. "I've been told so quite often."

"Marry me."

"No." She freed herself from his embrace, rose to her feet, walked to the water's edge. With trembling fingers she straightened her blouse, then tried to tidy her hair.

Ben let his head fall back against the tree trunk. A deep sigh escaped him. "You win. But only for now. I'm not going to give up until you agree to become my wife."

She spun to face him, a spark of defiance replacing the look of love and longing that had been in her eyes only moments before. "Have the things you want changed, Ben? Don't you still want to live in Homestead and run your newspaper? Are you willing to live in Washington instead with a wife who leaves a rented house every day to go to work? What about children? Don't you want a wife who is prepared to give you children?" She gestured expansively, exhibiting her frustration. "Because *I'm* not. I'm not ready to be a wife. To you or anyone else. I cannot stop fighting and working until suffrage is a reality for all women. I can't and I won't."

He got up but didn't move toward her. "You know what I think, Katie?" His tone was serious, his voice deep. "I think you love me. I think you want to say yes. Only you're afraid. You don't want to trust me enough to support you in whatever you want to do. Marriage is about compromise. At least the good marriages are."

She crossed her arms over her chest, as if to stave off his words.

"No," he continued, finally answering her question, "I still want all those things you mentioned. I want to live in Homestead and have a home and a family. But I think we can find a way to have what we both want. I don't know how, but I think we can do it because we love each other."

"I'd only make you unhappy, Ben. I wouldn't make you or anyone else a good wife." She tried, unconvincingly, to smile. "I'm too stubborn. You said so yourself."

He couldn't stay away from her any longer. He couldn't bear the distance between them. He stepped forward, saw her lean slightly back, as if suddenly fearing his touch.

When he stopped a few feet away from her, he asked, "What makes a *good* wife? If I love you and you love me, doesn't that make it good?"

"Don't, Ben."

"You do love me, don't you?"

"Stop it." She covered her ears.

"Ah, Katie," he urged gently, "at least tell me you love me."

Tears welled in her eyes a split second before she turned and ran away from him, disappearing beyond the trees.

He wanted to chase after her, to catch her, hold her, kiss her, to force her to say the words he needed to hear. He wanted to, but he didn't.

Instead he simply said, "You can't run away from your feelings, Katie. And you can't run away from my love. Not today. Not ever. You'll see."

17

Yancy Jones hadn't had much book learning as a boy, but he'd been lucky in life. He was nothing but a saddle bum when he'd come to Long Bow Valley, and that was how he'd met Lark, working on her father's ranch. That she had loved him and been willing to marry him was still a source of some surprise. He knew he was mighty blessed by the riches of love he'd enjoyed all the years since.

Maybe that was why he recognized his daughter's misery for what it was.

The night before she was scheduled to leave for Boise, he sought her out, finding her in the barn's loft, sitting with her legs dangling out the open hay doors. Wordlessly he sat down beside her, and together they watched the sun sink behind the craggy mountain peaks. The clouds turned pink as shadows spilled across the valley floor. With dusk came a cooling breeze, a relief from the heat of the day.

"Nothin' quite so pretty as an Idaho sunset," Yancy commented after a long silence.

She didn't look at him. "No, there isn't. I missed them when I was away."

"I remember the first time I saw this valley, clear as if it was yesterday. Clearer, probably. Never planned to stay longer than a year or two. I'd never stayed any place much longer than that." He took hold of her hand, still staring at the fading colors of the sky. "I lit out on my own when I was younger'n Rick. Never knew what a home was. Never knew what a family was like. Took your ma t'teach me those things."

Katie laid her head on his shoulder.

"I reckon most fathers only want what's best for their children. Raise 'em up healthy and happy. Make sure they got an education and a portion o' common sense."

"I'm sorry I've disappointed you so often, Papa."

"Disappointed me?" He shook his head. "No, kitten, disappointed's not the right word. You're a puzzle t'me, that's true. I don't understand the way you think at times, and I don't reckon I ever will. But I've never been disappointed in who you are."

She straightened and looked at him.

Yancy squeezed her hand. "Your ma says you see things clearer than most folks, that you got a vision 'bout what things should be like. I think maybe she's right."

"Do you? Really?"

"Yep. You should know I'm mighty proud of you, Katie. I still don't know why you do some of the things you do, but I'm proud of you, all the same."

"Thank you, Papa."

"Kitten, you've bitten off a mighty big chew, runnin' for Congress an' all."

"I know."

"You sure this is what you want? You've had a small taste of what some folks, like the Hendersons or Mrs. Percy, will say about you. But it's gonna be worse when you get out away from Homestead. You got lots o' friends here. You got your brothers to fight for you and Ben and the Rudyards and others to help you with your plannin' and all. But when you get out there, it's gonna be different. It's gonna be harder."

"I know," she whispered. "But I've got to try."

"Well, if you're dead set on it, at least I know Ben'll do his best to protect you, any way he can."

She blinked quickly, then turned her head to stare out at the darkening valley once again.

Yancy felt at a loss. He was doing plenty of jabbering, but he didn't seem to be saying what needed to be said the most. He took a deep breath, then tried again. "Sometimes life makes us choose betwixt two things. Sometimes we want 'em both but can't have 'em. Times like those, choices can be mighty hard to make." He released her hand and got to his feet. "Times like those, kitten, it's most often better t'follow your heart instead of your head."

The air was filled with the sounds of night. Crickets chirped a familiar tune. A coyote howled from a faraway hill. A horse nickered in the corral beside the barn, another responded. A gentle breeze rustled the tree limbs, carrying the scent of pine with it.

Yancy stroked his hand over Katie's hair. "You'd best get yourself a good night's sleep. You'll have a long day tomorrow." He turned and strode toward the ladder.

"Papa?"

He glanced behind him.

"What if you don't know what your heart wants most?"

Yancy reckoned being a father was tougher than breaking the wildest of broncs. Knowing what was the right thing to do, the right thing to say, always seemed to escape him. He loved his daughter dang near more than anything. He wanted to shield her, to keep her from hurt and harm. But this was one time he knew he couldn't tell her what to do. This was something she was going to have to figure out for herself.

"Just keep listenin' to your heart, kitten. Just keep listenin'."

Just keep listenin' to your heart.

As Katie drove the Susan B into Homestead the following morning, her father's words repeated over and over again in her mind, just as they had throughout the night.

Just keep listenin'.

It had been much easier when she was in Washington. There, she'd been surrounded by women who had dedicated themselves, bodies and souls, to the cause of suffrage. She had also witnessed how difficult it was for those women who had husbands and children. No matter how committed they were to the cause, they were torn in different directions. Katie hadn't wanted the same sort of confusion for herself.

Yet that was precisely what was happening to her, married or not.

Eugenia Rudyard had once shown Katie a letter from Susan B. Anthony. "I am glad I chose not to marry," Miss Anthony had written, "because it will teach the young girls that to be true to principle, to live to an idea, even an unpopular one, that to live single—without any man's name—may be an honorable choice."

Katie had taken those words to heart. She had made them her own creed. Then why had she allowed herself to fall in love with Ben? How could she have been so reckless?

The memory of his kisses overtook her, flooding her with the heat of desire, making her body tingle with longing for more. If she married him, she would be able to experience it all. He wouldn't stop with mere kisses. He would touch her where she ached to be touched.

Katie brought the automobile to an abrupt halt, then squeezed her eyes shut. She mustn't think those things. She mustn't allow herself to indulge in them. She must remember the course she'd embarked upon.

Purposefully she recalled an article about Miss Anthony written by Ida Husted Harper: "Had Miss Anthony married, she would have been a devoted wife, an efficient mother, but the world would have missed its strongest reformer and womankind their greatest benefactor. It will be of far more value to posterity that she gave to all the qualities which in marriage would have been absorbed by the few."

"I don't want to be absorbed by you, Ben," Katie whispered. "And I would be because I love you too much."

There was the crux of the problem. She loved him too much. No matter what else she was doing, no matter what else was happening around her, Katie's thoughts turned constantly to Ben. She was already being absorbed by him. If they married, it could only become worse.

Suddenly she knew she'd made a grave mistake in allowing Ben to be the one to drive with her to Boise. He'd convinced her and everyone else that he was the logical person. He was managing her campaign, after all. Katie should have a man with her during the drive—which would take place during the daylight hours and so would not subject her to undue criticism. They would be able to make plans for her campaigning in the two months leading up to the primaries. His reasons were all valid.

But she should have insisted someone else accompany them. She never should have allowed herself to be alone with Ben for so many hours. How would she keep her thoughts from returning to forbidden things? How would she be able to keep herself from weakening in her resolve?

"God, help me," she prayed softly as she once again started the automobile down the road to Homestead.

Fifteen minutes later she'd nearly convinced herself she would be able to deal with Ben for the long hours ahead, that this would be a time to restore their friendship to its former lightness. Then the Susan B rolled into town. She saw Ben standing on the sidewalk in front of the *Homestead Herald*, and she knew she'd deluded herself.

These were going to be the worst hours of her life.

Water roiled and splashed over the rocky river bottom, sending up a fine spray to cool the occupants of the Susan B as the automobile followed the rough road south toward the capital city. Neither Ben nor Katie had said a word in hours, not since they'd stopped to eat their lunch. Silence seemed to be what she wanted most, and he had obliged her.

Now, as the automobile jounced and rocked over more ruts, nearly jerking the steering wheel from his tight grasp, Ben spared a quick glance toward Katie. She was seated as far to the right as she could get without hanging out the door. Her chin was tilted up, her mouth set in a firm line, her back stiff as a rod. She stared straight ahead with the resolve of a general perusing the battlefield.

Lord, she was stubborn!

And Lord, how he loved her.

Breaking the intolerable silence, he said, "We ought to be there in another hour or so."

She jumped, as if startled by gunfire.

Blast it all. Why didn't she just admit she loved him? Why couldn't she be sensible?

He tightened his grip on the wheel, determined to draw her into conversation, even if only a mundane one. "Good thing, too. It's been awhile since we ate lunch, and I'm getting hungry. The hotel's supposed to have a fine restaurant."

"It has been a long, hot day," she admitted with obvious reluctance.

Yes, it was hot. And that made Ben remember the way Katie looked in a bathing costume, the wet fabric clinging to her curves. "Too bad we can't take the time for a dip in the river to cool us off." Not too long ago he would have suggested they stop and do just that. And not too long ago she would have agreed. But he knew it would be useless to try now. She would only reject the idea.

Without warning, the Susan B sputtered and died. They rolled to a stop, the only sound that of the rushing water.

"What's wrong?" Katie asked.

"I don't know. I'll have a look."

Ben went over to the driver side of the motorcar while Katie slipped out the passenger door. Reaching back inside, Ben lifted the front seat and checked the fuel in the cylinder tank beneath it. There was more than enough to get them to the city.

For the next hour he checked everything he could think of. He knew a fair amount about automobiles, but he wasn't a mechanic, and he finally had to admit he was stumped.

"I don't know what else to try," he said as he turned toward Katie.

She had a smudge of grease on the tip of her nose and another, larger grease stain down the front of her bodice. Her hair had tumbled free of its pins and was falling about her shoulders like an ebony waterfall. She looked hot, tired, and far too lovely.

"I'll have to go for help." He glanced skyward. The sun had already moved pass the canyon rim, and shadows had grown long. "But I'll never make it tonight."

"Maybe she'll start again after it cools off," Katie suggested.

"Maybe." But he doubted it. "I think I should start walking. Cover as much ground as I can before dark. Will you be all right until I get back?"

"You think you're going to leave me here?"

"What else can I do?"

"I'm not staying here, Ben Rafferty. I'm going with you."

"But—"

"Ben, I've got to register tomorrow. Otherwise I'll have to wait until Monday, and neither you nor I wish to remain in Boise until then." She lifted her chin in that familiar stubborn pose. "I'm every bit as capable of walking that distance as you are."

Ben sighed inwardly. There was no point in arguing with her, and he knew it. "All right. But we'll spend the night here with the automobile. I'm not taking the chance of you getting hurt in the dark. We'll start out at first light. If we do, we ought to be able to make it to Boise by early tomorrow afternoon."

"Agreed." She turned away from him, but not before he saw a shadow of doubt pass over her face.

She didn't want to be alone with him for the night, and he knew why. She was feeling the same thing he was feeling. He was sure of it. He smiled. Maybe this was for the best. A night beneath the stars with Katie might be just what he needed to woo her.

It might also be the most difficult night of his life, being this close to her and not being able to take advantage of it.

* * *

While Ben gathered wood and built a small campfire, Katie took the blanket from the backseat and spread it on the ground for them to sit on. Then they dined on the few leftovers from lunch.

Surreptitiously Katie watched as Ben finished off the last piece of fried chicken. Firelight flickered across his face, a face she'd come to love looking at, just for the sake of looking. She loved the sharp cut of his jaw and the way his nose was shaped. She loved the deep set of his eyes, so blue by day but almost black tonight. She loved the tousled look of his golden hair and the almost straight line of his eyebrows.

Just keep listenin' to your heart, her father had told her. The only problem was, her heart was telling her the wrong thing.

She had obligations to fulfill.

She'd made commitments.

And she couldn't give Ben what he wanted.

She dropped her gaze to the campfire, watching as the inner coals began to turn white. But there wasn't enough heat to battle the cool night air rising off the river. She shivered, unsure if it was from the cold or because of her lonely thoughts.

"Here. You'd better put this on." Ben removed his suit coat and placed it around her shoulders. "As pretty as it is, that dress wasn't meant to keep you warm."

She touched the lapel of the jacket, feeling the lingering warmth from Ben's body. All day she had longed for his touch, an unrelenting longing that had nothing to do with logic. All day she'd pressed herself against the door of the Susan B, as far from him as she could get, trying to center her thoughts on something—*anything*—other than Ben. But it hadn't worked.

She placed her nose close to the fabric of his coat and breathed in the scent of him. It brought with it a flood of sensations to tempt her. She remembered the promise of his kisses and knew she wanted those promises fulfilled.

Never in her life had she felt this strange keening in her heart, a yearning for things forbidden. She'd never known a man's intimate caresses, but she knew they were what she wanted from Ben. She wanted him to touch her, to teach her, to let her feel and explore and experience.

Would it be so terrible to give in to her secret desires for just one night? She couldn't have forever with Ben, but she could have one night. No one need ever know.

She raised her eyes to find Ben watching her. Something smoldered between them, something hot and intense, something that would not be denied.

Just keep listenin' to your heart.

The entire day had been building toward this moment. She knew it now.

One night. She could have one night. She *needed* one night. Just one.

She leaned toward him. He opened his arms, and she slipped into them.

"Oh, Benjie," she whispered. All of her longing was wrapped up in those two simple words.

He kissed her, sweetly at first, the touch of his mouth upon hers light and gentle. As the kiss lengthened, deepened, Katie drew closer to him. Her fingers delved into his hair. Her heart beat next to his.

When he touched her breast, her lips parted, but her small gasp couldn't escape before his tongue invaded her mouth. Boldly she met his tongue with her own, sparring, exploring, discovering.

His hand gently molded her breast to fit within his palm. Although only the cotton fabric of her bodice and the delicate lace above her corset separated his skin from hers, it seemed too much to Katie. Instinctively she moved closer to him. When his thumb slid lightly over her nipple, she moaned.

"Katie," he whispered, his mouth hovering above hers, "we'd better think what it is we're doing."

But she didn't want to think, and she wasn't going to let him think, either. She glided her tongue along his lower lip and was rewarded with a groan as he claimed her once more in another kiss, hotter, wetter, more passionate than before.

Slowly he laid her down on the blanket, then stretched out beside her. As he drew her close to the length of his body, she felt the hardness of his desire pressing against her. Alarm and reckless wanting warred within her.

One night. Just one night.

With that reminder echoing in her head, she ignored the alarm and gave in to the wanting, taking Ben with her.

He began the slow process of freeing the tiny buttons along the front of her bodice. As he did so, he traced kisses down her throat, following the path of newly exposed skin until it reached the lace above her corset. Katie held her breath as he pulled the bodice free of the skirt waist, then brushed open the fabric.

Cool night air spread along her heated flesh. Her nipples puckered against lace moments before Ben covered one breast with his hand, the other with his mouth. Slowly, gently, he laved one breast, then the other, leaving the delicate lacework damp and clinging to her skin. Involuntarily her body arched. Shivers spiraled down her spine, pooling in the juncture of her thighs.

Time was lost to her, along with reason. There was only the reality of Ben's mouth and hands. She became pliable, malleable, moved by his gentle touch as he removed her skirt, her petticoat, her shoes and stockings, her corset. Like a meal of many courses, he tasted and caressed the uncovered portions of her body—the arch of her foot, her thigh, her stomach, her breasts—until she thought she might go mad.

Finally, in a heated haze, she watched as he shed his own shirt and trousers, too caught up in the passion of the moment to spare a thought for embarrassment or shyness.

Then he was beside her once again, pressing her shoulder with one hand so that she rolled from her side onto her back. With his fingertips he traced a slow and tantalizing trail from her arm, around her breast, and across her abdomen. Her eyes widened in surprise as his hand slipped into place between her legs. A spark of doubt flared but was quickly replaced by a stronger feeling as he began slowly to caress and stroke, at the same time claiming her mouth with his. She closed her eyes and gave herself over to the strange and wonderful sensations his actions provoked.

When at last he covered her body with his own, his knees gently parting her legs, she opened her eyes to stare up at him. Firelight played along his profile, making him look dangerous and dashing. She could feel his taut restraint, knew he was giving her one last opportunity to stop the inevitable.

She wanted him even more because of it.

Lifting her hips against him, she offered him entrance, then gave herself over to loving him, body and soul.

Long after Katie had fallen into slumber, long after the campfire had cooled, Ben lay awake, staring at her profile in the soft moonlight. She lay within the circle of his arm, her head resting upon his shoulder. Beneath bedding made of discarded clothing, he held her close, sharing his body's warmth against the chill of night air.

In sleep she wore a look of innocence, but his memory teased him with the passion she'd displayed just a few hours ago.

He loved her, had wanted her, but he hadn't meant for it to happen this way. He'd much rather have taken her for the first time as his bride. He'd have preferred their first lovemaking to have been in a featherbed rather than on the hard, cold ground. They should have shared a rich supper in an elegant hotel rather than eating cold chicken beside a broken-down flivver. They should have sipped fine wine rather than drinking water from the nearby brook.

His arm tightened, pulling her closer against him. He lowered his head and laid his cheek against her hair. He drew in a deep breath. The musky scent of lovemaking lingered between them, and his body reacted involuntarily, growing hard with renewed desire.

They would marry tomorrow while in Boise City. She wouldn't be able to deny him any longer. Not after tonight. Her love, though yet unspoken, was obvious, and he was certain she would at last see reason.

Of course, she wouldn't want to withdraw from the congressional race. He understood that. But he didn't mind. He believed she would soon realize the futility of a woman serving in Congress. Besides, there was the matter of children.

Suddenly he realized that even now the seed of a baby—*his* baby—might have been planted within her womb. He hadn't planned for things to happen so quickly. But if Katie had conceived, she would be forced to give up her political aspirations.

A warm contentment stole over him as he envisioned their future. Yes, tomorrow they would marry, and when he made love to her tomorrow night, it would be in that elegant hotel with a rich supper, fine wine, candlelight, music, and a soft featherbed.

Closing his eyes, he drifted off to sleep, satisfied with what he knew the morrow would bring.

18

Warmed by her dreams, Katie came slowly awake, aware first of the sounds of nature, then of the closeness of another body next to her own. She opened her eyes to find Ben watching her with a hooded gaze. Her cheeks grew flushed as an unexpected shyness swept over her, along with the knowledge that she hadn't been dreaming after all.

"Good morning, Katie." His voice was low, husky.

She closed her eyes. "Good morning." The words were barely audible.

She felt something hard pulsing against her thigh. Realizing what it was made her grow ever hotter with embarrassment.

Ben kissed her temple, then whispered, "I'll give you some privacy so you can get dressed."

She wished she could thank him for understanding, but she couldn't seem to push the words from her throat.

She felt him toss aside the blanket of clothes, then listened as he walked away from where she lay. When the footsteps blended with the rushing sounds of the river, she drew a deep breath, then opened her eyes a second time. There was no sign of Ben.

She sat up, clutching his jacket to her bare breasts, and looked about. Pink fingers of sunrise spread across a smattering of clouds. Behind the clouds the sky was still pewter but quickly lightening to blue. It was a sunrise like most other sunrises, yet it should have been different. . . .

Because Katie was different.

She rose from the hard earth that had been their bed last night. Her muscles ached, and there was a tenderness between her thighs that only served to remind her of the intimate act they had shared. An intimate act she would gladly—to her shame—share with him again.

Moving carefully, she leaned down to retrieve her undergarments. That was when she noticed the red stains on the blanket that had lain beneath them and on her dress that had served to cover them as they'd slept.

Tears flooded her eyes, hot and unexpected, as she swept the blanket and remainder of clothes into a heap, hiding the bloody evidence from view.

One night. She had wanted only one night. But she had never expected to feel like this. She hadn't known giving her body to Ben would tie her heart all the more closely to him. She hadn't known it would make her irrevocably his, that it would only increase her need to be joined with him again and again.

Dashing away the tears with her fingertips, she moved toward the motorcar, where she retrieved her only other gown from her valise. Then she walked to the small stream that trickled down a ravine on its way to join the river. She knelt beside it and began washing, almost glad for the icy cold of the water against her flesh as she cleansed away the signs of their lovemaking and her lost virginity. Secretly she hoped it would also wash away her desire to have Ben hold her and make love to her all over again.

It didn't.

She donned her undergarments, then sat on a log and began to brush the snarls from her hair. She remembered the way Ben had run his fingers through it last night, whispering how beautiful it was. She closed her eyes and gave herself over to that memory and more. Her body grew hot and languid. Her arm stilled, the tangle of hair forgotten.

Would it always be like this? Would she be doing some normal, everyday task and suddenly be overtaken by a yearning for him?

She envisioned Ben, his naked chest bronzed by the firelight, his biceps flexed and knotted, the muscles in his neck corded and taut, a glitter of perspiration on his forehead. She remembered the feel of him inside her, remembered the rhythmic way she had risen to meet him time after time. She recalled the low, throaty groans, both his and her own.

Her pulse roared in her ears. Then she realized it wasn't only her pulse she heard.

She jumped up from the log and looked down the road. There, rounding the bend, came an automobile. Her glance darted to the riverbank just as Ben climbed into view, wearing his shirt, trousers, and boots.

Quickly she darted behind some underbrush and donned her dress. Her fingers fumbled endlessly with the tiny buttons, but finally she managed to get them all fastened. Hastily she tied her hair at the nape with a ribbon, hoping it looked better than it felt.

She heard the automobile slow, then stop. The engine idled for a moment before dying. All hope that she could remain hidden until they'd driven past died with it.

*   *   *

"Glad to see you're all right, Rafferty." Jeb Hackney stepped out of his Packard. "Uriah said to expect you last night. When you and Miss Jones didn't show up at the hotel, I thought I'd best come looking for you."

Ben pretended a casualness he didn't feel as he watched the reporter from the *Idaho Statesman* move toward the Susan B. "We had some car trouble. Glad you showed up. We were just getting ready to start walking toward Boise." He wondered if Katie had picked up the blanket and the rest of their clothing even as he walked with Jeb in that direction.

"Had to spend the night here, huh?" There was a glitter in his eye. "Too bad. Gets mighty cool up in these parts."

"We managed." He put his hand on Jeb's arm, drawing him to a sudden halt. "But we *are* hungry. You wouldn't happen to have anything to eat in your motorcar, would you?"

Hackney wasn't in the same class of reporters as Uriah Cobbs, but he had a bloodhound's nose for a juicy story. And his eyes told Ben that he was on the scent of a story right now.

The reporter stepped away from Ben's restraining hand, moving with an unerring swiftness around the back of the Susan B. "Slept on the ground, did you?" He glanced over his shoulder. "Wonder what folks will make of this?"

Katie chose that precise moment to make her appearance. Ben swallowed a groan as he watched her walk toward them. Although dressed modestly enough, there was a fullness in her lips and a look in her eyes even a fool would recognize.

And Jeb Hackney was no fool.

The reporter removed his hat and let out a low whistle as Katie drew closer.

One whiff of scandal in the newspaper, and any chance for election Katie might have would be destroyed. She would be held up for ridicule. She would be criticized resoundingly from every public venue. Ben couldn't bear for that to happen. He didn't want Katie to be elected to Congress, but neither did he want her defeat to come this way.

Two long strides carried him to her side. He commanded her with his eyes to remain silent as he took hold of her arm, then turned toward Hackney.

"Mr. Hackney, may I present my wife, Katie Jones Rafferty." He felt Katie stiffen at his words but purposefully kept his eyes on the man before them. It wasn't much of a lie, after all. They would have married today, whether or not the reporter stumbled upon them. Katie had to realize it, just as he had realized it last night.

"Your *wife?*" the man queried as his gaze shifted to Ben. "But I was under the impression it was *Miss* Jones who was declaring for office."

"We were only recently married," Ben answered smoothly, "and haven't announced it yet."

"Hmm." The reporter eyed the jumble of blanket and clothes on the ground near the Susan B. "I'm surprised Uriah didn't ferret out the news."

Katie cleared her throat. "Mr. Hackney, it was my idea to keep our marriage a secret."

Ben glanced at her, surprised by how well she spoke the lie. The words had a ring of honesty that Ben thought just might convince Jeb Hackney.

"You see," she continued, "I was hoping to run for office as an unmarried woman. I would like to win on my own merits, not on those of my husband." She looked at

Ben. "I suppose we should have waited to marry, but Ben was very persuasive."

He caught the flash of anger in her eyes just before she turned her gaze back toward the reporter.

"At any rate, since I would still like to register my candidacy today, I suppose we should get started for Boise." She smiled at Jeb. "I'm most grateful for your thoughtfulness, sir. We are fortunate you came looking for us."

Ben knew what Katie's smile could do to a man, and Jeb Hackney was no exception to the rule. At least for the moment, his suspicions were forgotten. He motioned toward the Packard, saying, "I'll drive you back to the city and then send someone for your automobile."

"Thank you." Without glancing his way again, Katie said, "Ben, dear, would you be good enough to get our things?"

A lesser man would have been quaking in his boots, knowing the fury that lay behind her sweet words, but Ben merely answered, "Of course, darling," just as any besotted husband would have.

Still, as he walked to the Susan B, he wondered what else lay in store for him this day. He was dead certain Katie wasn't going to let his charade go unchallenged.

"Married?" Katie shouted at Ben the moment the door to their hotel room swung closed. "Why did you tell him we were *married?*"

"I did it for you."

"For me? Ha!" She stormed over to the window to stare out at the street below.

"After last night . . ." He left the sentence dangling in thin air, unfinished but saying all.

"Last night didn't change how I feel about marriage, Benjamin Rafferty, and you knew it." She looked over her shoulder. "You knew it," she repeated, his betrayal stinging afresh.

He raked the fingers of his right hand through his hair. "Do you mean to tell me you *weren't* going to marry me after last night?"

"No. No, I was *not* going to marry you."

His expression darkened. "Didn't it mean anything to you, Katie?"

"That's not the point."

"But it *is* the point!" His voice raised a notch.

"It isn't unheard of for people to . . . to do what we did without benefit of marriage. It didn't have to mean anything more than just one night."

He stepped toward her. "It has to mean more for people like us."

"Last night was a mistake." Katie turned back to the window, trying not to give in to despair. "It shouldn't have happened at all." She closed her eyes. "I don't want to marry you, Benjie."

"Hackney guessed the truth. There wasn't any other way to protect you from scandal."

"I'm not afraid of scandal. I've been scandalizing people all my life."

"Not *this* kind of scandal."

She clenched her hands into fists. "I don't care. Besides, maybe all I wanted was just a lover. Did you ever think of that?"

"Katie . . . "

"It's true. And I am *not* going to marry you."

Ben laid his hand on her shoulder, saying tenderly, "I just wanted to protect you. I never meant for what happened last night to happen before we were married. But you know I love you. And you also know that if you don't marry me, all hope of being elected will be destroyed by the gossip. Even the suffrage association probably won't have use for you."

She was defeated, and she finally had to admit it. Still, she whispered, "I wasn't going to marry anyone. Not ever."

"Would it be so terrible to be my wife, Katie?" he asked softly.

No, she thought, it wouldn't be terrible. That was the problem. It would be too easy to be his wife. She feared losing her dream, losing herself.

His fingers tightened, squeezing lightly. "We'll have to go through with it . . . unless you've decided not to enter the race."

She spun around. "Is that what you expect me to do? Just drop out, now that you've tricked me into marrying you?" Anger flared anew. She jabbed her index finger into his chest. "Well, you're greatly mistaken, Mr. Rafferty. I may have to marry you in order to keep my promise to those who want me to run and win, but don't think for one moment I'm going to play the part of your little wife, preparing your meals and ironing your shirts and . . . and . . . " *And warming your bed*, she'd meant to say, but memories of his lovemaking—and her response to it—made finishing the sentence impossible.

He stared at her for the longest time, his eyes searching hers. Finally he took a step backward. "All right, Katie. I understand." He was silent a moment longer, then added, "I'll make the arrangements. There's a judge here who owes me a big favor. I think he'll marry us and keep the matter of the exact date and time confidential." He turned away. "Why don't you run yourself a bath and get spruced up? After the ceremony, you can file for the election. I'll find some way for us to avoid any reporters until then." He headed for the door.

She wanted to call after him, but she didn't know what she could have said to make things better. Deep down, she realized this was as much her fault as his.

She'd wanted his lovemaking without marriage attached. She'd wanted one night, not a lifetime.

But he'd known how she felt about marriage. She'd turned down his proposal, not just once but twice. She couldn't get over the feeling of being ensnared. He claimed he'd done it to protect her reputation, but good intentions or no, the result was the same. Katie was trapped in a marriage she hadn't wanted.

"Sophia, stop that pacing and sit down this instant," Rose Rafferty demanded sharply.

"Something must be wrong," she said as she obeyed her mother, sinking onto a chair beside the kitchen table. "Katie said she would call just as soon as she'd filed. Something must have gone wrong."

"If something was wrong, we'd have heard even more quickly." Rose resumed shelling peas, popping open the pods and, with her index finger, scooping the peas into the bowl on her lap.

Sophia knew she should be helping her mother with their supper preparations, but she couldn't stop fidgeting. Finally she jumped up from the chair again. "I think I'll take a walk over to the newspaper. Maybe Ben has called there."

Her mother merely shook her head and went on with her work.

Outside, the midday sun was blistering the streets and buildings of Homestead. The few horses that were tethered to hitching posts stood with heads hanging low, tails flicking slowly at flies. Dogs slept in the shade of awnings and beneath the boardwalks. The bench outside the hardware store was empty of men, and Sophia suspected the usual bench loungers were inside the billiard saloon, washing away the heat with glasses of beer.

She had just passed the bank and was preparing to cross Barber Street when she saw Geoffrey Rudyard and his sister come out of the newspaper building. When Geoffrey saw her, he waved.

"Have you heard anything?" she asked as she drew closer to the brother and sister.

Penelope answered, "Not a thing. This isn't like Katie."

"Or Ben either." Sophia's glance darted to Geoffrey.

"I think the two of them can handle whatever problems might arise," he reassured the two women in a calm voice. "Even if that automobile of Katie's gave up the ghost, they won't be stranded for long. Mr. Cobbs left on today's train, and he's dogged Katie too long to let her out of his sight for more than a day. I have no doubt that crafty bloodhound will find them in no time."

"But what if they've had an accident?" Sophia persisted, her anxiety increasing with each word. "What if they're lying somewhere, injured?"

Geoffrey placed an arm lightly around her shoulders and smiled down at her as he said, "I think it's far more likely your brother has grabbed the chance to do a bit of spooning with his girl." He put his other arm around his sister. "It's what any red-blooded fellow would do, given the same opportunity."

Penelope poked him in the ribs. "I wish you had tried to 'spoon' Katie, my dear brother, but you never had the good sense to do it. Now you're too late."

Sophia wasn't sure she understood what the two of them were saying. Ben and Katie? "But they're just friends."

"I find that highly unlikely, Sophia my girl," Geoffrey responded with a laugh. His arm slipped easily from Sophia's shoulders, then just as easily he placed her hand in the crook of his elbow. As he offered his other arm to

Penelope, he said, "Allow me to escort you two lovely ladies to Zoe's Restaurant. Perhaps Miss Potter has some cold lemonade to quench our thirst while we wait to hear from Katie and Ben."

Sophia let herself be guided across the street, thoughts churning. Katie and Ben? But how could that be? She'd thought her brother was still mooning over his broken romance with Charlotte.

And Katie? Katie had made it clear she wasn't ever going to marry. She wouldn't be foolish enough to fall in love with her best friend. And she would never be foolish enough to marry him. Would she?

Judge Robert Osgoode was almost finished with the brief civil ceremony. Neither the bride nor the groom smiled, nor did they spare a glance for one another. They simply responded with clipped responses to the questions presented to them.

Ben knew Katie was still angry and hurt. He even understood why. What he wasn't sure of was what to do about it. He loved her. He wanted to make her happy. He wanted to share laughter and joy and pleasure with her. He also wanted to make babies in a large poster bed and then watch those same babies grow up in Homestead.

But before any of that was going to happen, he had to convince Katie that what he'd done, he'd done out of love for her. He had to win her forgiveness and her trust.

". . . and now, by the authority vested in me by the state of Idaho, I pronounce you man and wife." Judge Osgoode paused a moment, staring at the bride and groom. When neither of them moved, he added, "Benjamin, you may kiss your bride."

Ben turned toward Katie. He saw the stiff set of her shoulders, the stubborn tilt of her chin, the thin line of her mouth, and he knew the last thing she wanted was for him to kiss her.

Damn! He loved her even when she was being unreasonable.

Tenderly he took hold of her shoulders and drew her toward him. "I hope someday you'll know how much I love you, Katie," he said softly, for her ears only. "I'll do my best to prove it to you." Then he leaned down and kissed the center of her forehead.

For the first time since they'd walked into the judge's chambers, Katie met his gaze. He saw a flicker of doubt in her dark eyes. But now was not the time to take advantage of it.

He turned toward Judge Osgoode. "Thanks, Robert." They shook hands. "We appreciate this a great deal."

"No trouble at all. Mrs. Rafferty, I wish you well in the elections. I mean that with all sincerity."

"Thank you, Your Honor," she answered.

Ben took hold of her arm and walked her toward the door. "We'll go out the back way and slip over to the secretary of state's office. If our luck holds, no one will ever be the wiser about where we've been."

"If our luck holds?" She cocked an eyebrow, her expression dubious. "Any more luck like we've had already and we're likely to end up in jail."

His heart lightened at the sarcasm in her words. "I suppose it could still happen, Katie. Don't give up yet. Nothing like a jail cell to start a marriage off right."

Despite herself, she smiled at him.

Mentally he renewed his vow. Somehow he would make up for the way this had happened. He would prove he only wanted to make her happy. Even if it took him a lifetime, he would prove it.

And a lifetime was exactly what he wanted with Katie Jones Rafferty.

19

A delegation from the Boise City Chapter of the Woman's Christian Temperance Union, with sashes worn over their shoulders identifying their affiliation, awaited Katie and Ben when they emerged from the secretary of state's office an hour or so later. Behind them was an eager-looking group of reporters, Uriah Cobbs and Jeb Hackney among them.

Ben's grip on her arm tightened slightly. "Looks like someone inside made a few telephone calls while you were filing your papers," he whispered near her ear. "Are you ready for this?"

Katie felt a moment of doubt and fear. She'd had enough upheaval and change for one day. Must she face a crowd of strangers now? But she quickly quashed such thoughts. She was not about to admit defeat because of her own folly. She had an election to win.

Drawing a quick breath for courage, she stiffened her spine and forced a friendly smile onto her lips. Then she moved toward the women.

After a few words of welcome from a Mrs. Walter J. Smith, president of the local WCTU, Katie was introduced to the other members of the delegation. She spoke briefly about her support for issues regarding women's property and guardianship rights while artfully skirting the issue of prohibition without anyone seeming to notice she'd done so.

Looking once again at the formidable Mrs. Smith, Katie said, "I sincerely hope I'll enjoy the support of your members, Mrs. Smith." She offered her hand to the woman.

"I believe you shall, Mrs. Rafferty, judging from what I've just heard." Mrs. Smith's handshake was firm. "I look forward to hearing more from you in the weeks to come."

"Thank you."

Mrs. Smith glanced at the rest of her group. "Come along, ladies. We have our own work to do."

Unable to delay her meeting with the members of the press any longer, Katie turned toward them. She gave each of the men a smile, although the expression was more difficult to maintain when she met Uriah Cobbs's piercing gaze. Again she felt Ben's fingers tighten on her arm, and again she took courage from it.

"Gentlemen, I imagine you have questions for me."

For what seemed ages, she responded to their queries. Most had to do specifically with her candidacy for the United States House of Representatives—why she was running, what she hoped to achieve, her thoughts on the war in Europe. Some delved into her college education and her work with the National American Woman Suffrage Association. One man wondered if her husband shouldn't be the one running for office, given that his father had once been mayor of Homestead.

Uriah Cobbs, however, seemed more interested in her

married status. "Why was your marriage kept a secret, Mrs. Rafferty?" he demanded. "And when exactly did it take place?"

Ignoring the second question, she answered the first with the same excuse she'd used that morning. "My husband is a respected journalist in Idaho, Mr. Cobbs. His pieces are read in many other newspapers besides his own. I didn't want that to influence voters on my behalf." She turned what she hoped was an adoring gaze in Ben's direction. "Frankly, I'm glad the charade ended this early. I don't believe I would have been able to carry it off for long. I'm a poor actress."

"Gentlemen," Ben interjected, "if you don't mind, I'd like to take my wife to dinner. You'll have plenty of opportunities to interview her during the next couple of months before the primaries." With a hand placed firmly in the small of Katie's back, he propelled her away from the reporters.

As soon as they were out of earshot, Katie released a deep sigh. "Thank you."

Her head pounded miserably, and her heart still raced. She'd handled the various newspapermen with ease after the rally in Homestead, but this was different. She didn't like lying. But like it or not, she was stuck with the lie—unless she wanted to withdraw from the election, which she most certainly did not intend to do.

Of course, only the implication they'd been married longer than a few hours was a falsehood. The rest was now true. She *was* a married woman.

Married to Ben. She felt a flutter in her stomach, a skip in her heart. *Married to Ben.*

Would it be so terrible? He loved her, had wanted to marry her. And she loved him. Did their marriage have to be a catastrophe? Couldn't she find some way to be herself and still be his wife?

As they crossed the street, Ben said, "I'll have the hotel send our supper to our room so we can eat in peace."

She was grateful for his thoughtfulness and knew she should tell him she didn't hold him to blame any longer for the circumstances of this day. If they hadn't pretended this morning to be already married, her aspirations for Congress would have come to a sudden and ugly end. Jeb Hackney would have seen to it. And if not him, Uriah Cobbs. She knew Ben had indeed done what he'd done to protect her reputation from scandal, even if it had given him what he'd wanted in the bargain.

She glanced at him as they entered through the wide doors of the hotel. She thought about all the years they were apart, all the times she'd missed him. She could talk to Ben about her deepest secrets. He understood her as no one else ever had, not even her parents, not even Penelope. She'd loved Ben as her dearest friend for as long as she could remember. And since returning to Homestead, she'd fallen in love with the man he'd become.

Need it be so awful, this hasty, unplanned marriage of theirs?

They climbed the stairs, and she became newly aware of the feel of his hand on the small of her back, of the warmth of her skin beneath it. She looked down the hall at the door to their hotel room and realized they would be alone in that room tonight.

Alone as man and wife.

A tingle of desire shot through her, reminding her how easy it was to forget everything except Ben.

The moment he opened the door for her, she moved away from him, crossing the room to stand before the window, just as she had done earlier in the day. She heard the door close softly, heard the click of the lock as it turned.

Alone as man and wife.

"Katie."

She leaned her forehead against the windowpane. The glass was still warm from the touch of the late afternoon sun. In the street below, she saw a man place a "Closed" sign in his shop window. Going home, probably to his wife and children.

"Katie, we need to talk."

"I know."

"Come and sit down," he urged gently.

She turned. He was now standing near the sofa and chairs. He'd removed his hat. His hair was slightly mussed, and she knew he'd raked his fingers through it only moments before. He had a habit of doing so whenever he was troubled.

And now he was worried about her.

She drew a deep breath and let it out before saying, "None of this is your fault, Ben. I have only myself to blame."

"I think we can share the blame."

She shook her head as she stepped toward him. "No. I . . . I chose to"—her face grew hot—"allow last night to happen. And now I must live with the consequences."

"I don't much care to be a consequence." His voice was low, his expression grim.

"Oh, Benjie." She sank onto the sofa and stared at the thick carpet beneath her feet.

He sat on the chair opposite her. "What is it you want from me, Katie?"

She glanced up, wishing she knew how to answer him. "I don't know." Tears pooled in her eyes. "I suppose I want things to be as they've always been."

"It won't happen. They won't ever be the same again. We're different. Last night changed us forever."

"I know," she whispered.

He took hold of her hands, drew her gently from the sofa and onto her knees before him. Then, with a tender touch, he cradled her face with his palms, tilting her head back slightly. He brushed the tears from her cheeks with his thumbs, then kissed the moist tracks left behind.

With his mouth now hovering near hers, he said, "I make you this promise, Katie. I won't ever try to change you. I love the woman you are." He lowered one hand and placed it just above her left breast, near her heart. "I love the woman you are in here." He kissed her lightly, then added, "All I ask is a chance. Just a chance."

Her skin tingled. Her breathing was shallow.

It isn't that I fear you trying to change me, Ben. It's myself I fear.

But for the moment, she didn't care.

With just a slight movement, she brought her lips in contact with his. A languid warmth spread through her veins as she pressed closer to him. His hand slid downward until he was cupping her breast. She felt her nipples harden in response.

With a swiftness and intensity that surprised her, she was filled with wanting. She no longer had to imagine what it would be like to have Ben make love to her. She knew, and the knowing made her desire burn hotter than ever before.

"I think," he whispered as their mouths parted, "I'd better order up our supper."

"I'm not hungry." *Except for you.*

He smiled tenderly. "We'll not rush things tonight, Katie."

She wanted to object. *Let's rush*, she wanted to say. But something in his gaze stopped her, made her feel hot and dizzy and weak all over. Without words he was promising tonight would be special. How, she wondered, could it be more special than last night? Nothing could be better. Nothing.

He stood, bringing her with him. He wrapped her in his arms, kissing her again until she was breathless.

When the kiss ended, he took a short step back from her. His voice almost gruff, he said, "I'll go see about our food."

She nodded, unable to speak.

"I won't be long."

She shook her head.

He touched her cheek with his fingertips. "I love you."

I love you, too.

Ben hesitated, waiting for her to say with her mouth what he could see in her eyes. But she didn't speak, didn't say the words he wanted to hear.

Finally he turned and left the room.

He mustn't be impatient, Ben thought as he strode down the hallway toward the stairs. A lot had happened in the past twenty-four hours. Katie had a right to be confused by it. For all her experiences in Washington, for all her progressive ideas and forward-thinking notions, she was still inexperienced when it came to men.

Or she had been until last night.

Last night.

His footsteps slowed as memories washed over him. He remembered the diamondlike stars in a heaven of black velvet. Black velvet, like her hair. He remembered the fragrance of pine and the song of the river. A song, like the sound of her voice. He remembered the softness of Katie's skin and the sweetness of her mouth. Sweet, like honey. He remembered every last detail of their night on the blanket beside the Susan B.

Suddenly he grinned. He meant to say thanks to that broken-down flivver next time he saw it. If not for the cantankerous automobile, he wouldn't be a married man, looking forward to his wedding night.

He quickened his strides once again, a groom eager to return to his bride.

When she heard the knock on the door some time later, Katie almost decided against answering it. She wasn't in any frame of mind to talk to anyone. If it was Ben, he could use his key. If it was someone with their supper, he could just wait. She'd told Ben she wasn't hungry, and she'd meant it.

But as the caller knocked a second and then a third time, she resigned herself to facing whoever was on the other side of the door. She wasn't expecting who—or, rather, what—she found.

Three men stood in the hallway, all of them nearly totally obscured by enormous bouquets of red roses. Roses and roses and more roses. Large vases filled to overflowing with greenery and long-stemmed, blood-red roses.

"Are you Mrs. Rafferty?" asked a voice from behind the nearest bouquet.

The name stopped her for only a second. "Yes. I'm Mrs. Rafferty."

"Then these are for you, ma'am."

"*All* of them?"

"Yes, ma'am. You mind if we bring them in? They're kind of heavy."

"No." She stepped back, opening the door fully. "Of course. Bring them in."

They paraded by her, setting the vases on a large table near the bedroom doorway. Then one of the men brought her an elegant white envelope. "This here's for you, Miz Rafferty."

She stared down at Ben's familiar handwriting as a cloud of rose perfume filled the room. Forgetting about the delivery men, she slipped her finger beneath the flap and opened the envelope, then removed the note card.

"In the true marriage relation, the independence of the husband and wife is equal, their dependence mutual, and their obligation reciprocal."

—Lucretia Mott

So shall it be. Ben

Her vision blurred as she stared at the card. He knew her so well. Perhaps he understood, after all, what made her afraid to give in to the love she felt for him. And perhaps her fears were unfounded. Perhaps—

"If you'll excuse us, ma'am, we'll be on our way."

She looked up, surprised the men were still there. She blinked away her tears. "Let me get something for your trouble." She glanced around for her purse.

"No need, ma'am. We've been paid." He tipped his hat as he backed through the doorway. "A pleasure, ma'am. And might I say, the mister is a right lucky fellow."

Katie turned her eyes toward the table laden with roses, scarcely aware of the sound of the closing door as the men left. Misty eyed, she crossed the room. With her fingertips she cradled a blossom and lowered her nose to breathe in its heavenly fragrance.

"American Beauties for an American beauty," Ben said from the doorway.

She straightened, turned, and blinked her eyes so she could see him clearly.

"They're your favorites," he added.

"How did you know?"

"You said so in a letter. I think it was after Amelia Christopher's wedding."

"That was years ago. And you remembered all this time?"

He walked toward her. "I remember everything about you, Katie. I always have."

As naturally as if she'd done it for a lifetime, she stepped into his embrace, tilted her head, received his kiss. Her arms lifted to encircle his neck. Her body pressed against his, filled with yearning.

When at last they broke for air, he whispered, "Our supper is on its way up."

Tell them to take it back to the kitchen, she wanted to say. Perhaps her eyes said it for her. Perhaps Ben heard her with his heart. His eyes darkened as he stared down at her. His handsome face grew taut with controlled passion. Katie felt a thrill spiral through her, accompanying a new realization, a sense of power in her womanhood.

A knock on the door announced the arrival of their meal, just as Ben had predicted. With obvious reluctance he released her and went to answer the summons. A moment later two white-coated kitchen servants carried large trays into the room.

"Just put them there," Ben instructed, indicating a pair of parlor tables set on either side of the sofa.

It seemed to Katie the servants moved much too slowly. It seemed forever before they accepted Ben's gratuity and left and she and Ben were once again alone.

He smiled at her—a secret smile, full of promise—and held out his hand. "Come over here."

She went, placing her hand in his, allowing him to draw her to the brocade sofa.

"You may not know this, but the hotel has a fine chef." Ben lifted a cover off a platter. "Lobster à la Newburg." He selected a bite-size piece of meat, picked it up with his fingers, and carried it to her mouth. "Try it," he encouraged softly.

She had only a moment to savor the succulent flavors of cream, Madeira, and lobster before Ben leaned forward and ran his tongue lightly over her lips. The ensuing sensations first surprised her, then stole her breath away.

He continued to feed her, following each bite with another kiss, sometimes on the mouth, sometimes not. Katie had never been more aware of the sensuous textures and odors and flavors of a meal. Her enjoyment in the attention he lavished upon her seemed decadent, but she didn't care. Her nerves tingled. Her blood ran hot. Her loins tightened in a pleasurable ache.

She was scarcely aware of the deepening shadows in the room as day flowed into evening until Ben left her to light a lamp.

When he returned, he knelt on the floor before her. Taking hold of her right calf, he removed her shoe, then kissed her ankle. Katie gasped at the reaction the simple gesture caused within her. He paused a moment, meeting her gaze, holding it with his own. Slowly he slid his palms along her leg, higher and higher and higher, pushing her skirt along with it.

It became nearly impossible for Katie to breathe, watching him as he removed her stocking, feeling the warmth of his hands on her skin, wanting him to move more slowly, wanting him to move faster still. After tossing aside the stocking, he again kissed her ankle. Then he repeated the entire procedure with her left leg.

When he was through he asked huskily, "Guess what's for dessert?"

Heat pooled someplace deep inside, in a secret place Ben had awakened within her, a place she hadn't known existed.

He smiled a wicked smile as he slipped onto the couch beside her. "No, my love. Not yet." Then he lifted a cover from another plate, this one holding strawberries topped with whipped cream. "Try one of these."

A tiny moan escaped her as she opened her mouth to receive the delicacy. She closed her eyes while he traced her lips with a creamy fingertip. When he kissed her, she met his tongue with her own, sharing the sweetness of the sugared cream.

It was his turn to groan.

And suddenly she was in his arms. He carried her into the connecting bedchamber and set her on her feet at the side of the bed. If not for his arms, she would have fallen, so weak were her knees.

"Ah, Katie," he whispered as he began plucking the pins from her hair.

How simple, yet how stirring, the sound of her name on his lips.

The hairpins dropped to the floor, one at a time.

Click.

Click.

Click.

Desire surged within her, hotter than before, almost violent. If he didn't assuage it soon, she feared she would go mad.

Growing impatience emboldened her. She reached for the waistband of his trousers and began pulling the hem of his shirt free. He paused in his attentions to her just long enough to assist her in removing his shirt and undershirt.

Immediately she placed her palms against the hard, muscular plane of his chest, felt his heart racing beneath her hands. She offered her mouth to him for another kiss as her fingers traced a path back to his waistband, then lower. As she attempted to free the first button on his trousers, she brushed against the pulsing hardness of his desire. Brazenly she turned her hand to cup him, felt him tense, heard another groan reverberate up from his chest.

The languorous pace of their love play changed abruptly. Clothing was dispatched with great speed. In his haste to remove her dress, Ben caused several pearl buttons to pop free of Katie's blouse. They bounced and rolled across the floor, the only sounds in the room besides Ben's and Katie's labored breathing.

When they were both naked, he lifted her once again in his arms, this time laying her on the bed. He joined her there and covered her body with his, supporting himself with his arms and legs. With one hand he spread her hair across the pillow.

His breath caressed her face as he whispered, "You're so very beautiful, Katie." He raised above her, sitting back on his heels, trailing his gaze slowly over her body. "So very beautiful."

She allowed her gaze to do the same, following the muscles of his chest to the ridges of his abdomen, then lower still. She let a quick breath escape her as another wave of wanting flooded her.

"So are you," she whispered, a note of awe in her voice. Then she reached for his shoulders and drew him down. "Love me, Benjie."

"Forever," he responded as he entered her body. "Forever and always."

20

Within minutes of each other, telegrams were delivered the next morning by employees of Homestead Telephone and Telegraph to the Rafferty home and the Lazy L Ranch. Both were read by stunned members of the bride's and groom's respective families. The missives were the same: "Katie and I married. Newspapers to announce on Saturday. Katie has filed her candidacy. Will return to Homestead on Sunday evening, following repair of automobile. More information upon our return. Benjamin Rafferty."

Phone lines began to hum as the news spread across Long Bow Valley. Some folks were surprised by the sudden turn of events. Others nodded knowingly, as if they had always assumed the two friends would one day marry. A few were aghast, convinced there was a breath of scandal in the news and disappointed they didn't know the details so they could gossip about it.

Certainly all would eagerly await the return to Homestead of Mr. and Mrs. Benjamin Rafferty.

*   *   *

For an idyllic, sensual thirty-six hours Ben and Katie locked themselves in their hotel room. They touched and explored and discovered. They laughed and teased and tempted. They ate together, bathed together, slept entwined in each other's embrace. Both had a secret wish to hold the morrow at bay, to have this time to savor, knowing instinctively they would need it as a foundation against a still uncertain future.

But they couldn't remain hidden forever, and on Sunday they checked out of that delightful hotel room, still filled with the rich fragrance of roses and musky-scented memories.

Katie stood on the sidewalk as Ben set the levers, then went to the front of the Susan B. She thought she heard him say, "Thanks," as he took hold of the engine crank. It seemed an odd thing for him to say, and she might have asked him about it if she hadn't been suddenly interrupted by the appearance of Uriah Cobbs.

"Good morning to you, Mrs. Rafferty. I see you're about to leave our fair city."

She truly disliked this man, but she tried to hide her feelings as she replied, "Yes. Our automobile is running again, and it's time we returned home."

As if to prove it, Ben turned the crank, and the Susan B roared to life.

"I would have thought you'd make a few more public appearances while in Boise City." He peered at her with a gaze that missed nothing.

Her glance went to Ben as he jumped on the running board and reached into the motorcar to reset the throttle lever. "Another time," she answered absently.

"Are you aware you've captured the interest of the nation with your candidacy for office? The *Statesman*'s received inquiries from nearly every state in the Union. This election promises to make you a sort of celebrity."

Katie didn't want to listen to Uriah. She didn't want to be reminded of the campaign or the election, nor did she want to be a celebrity. She only wanted to think about Ben, about the way he touched her and kissed her and the things he made her feel. A flush rose in her cheeks as she remembered the way he'd looked this morning as he'd loved her atop the rumpled bedclothes.

"You seem distracted, Mrs. Rafferty. Maybe you're having second thoughts about running for office? Maybe now that you're a married woman—"

The pleasant images fled as she turned her gaze upon the reporter a second time. "No, Mr. Cobbs, I have *not* had second thoughts. I am in this race to the finish."

Ben stepped onto the sidewalk just as she made her sharp retort. Taking hold of her arm, he said, "You'll have to excuse us, Uriah. We've a long drive ahead of us."

Uriah Cobbs tipped his hat. "Of course, Benjamin. I understand. I'm sure I'll be seeing you and your lovely wife again soon."

"Yes, I'm sure you will. Good day."

Katie's temper seethed, but Ben's grip on her arm kept her silent as he helped her into the front seat of the motorcar. However, the moment he put the automobile in gear and they pulled away from the curb, she sputtered, "The unmitigated gall of that man! Just because I'm married, he thinks I'll have no more interest in running for political office. It's probably what they all think. Why can't they understand what this is about?"

"I suppose it's natural some folks would assume you'd want to settle down with your husband rather than going off to Washington, D.C."

She looked at Ben, and her anger faded. "That's what you'd like, isn't it?"

He was silent for a long time before he answered, "Yes." He cast a quick glance in her direction, then turned his gaze back to the road. "I can't lie to you, Katie. I wish you wanted the same things I do. But I believe we'll find a way to work it all through. I have to believe it. I love you."

But did he love her enough to let her go on being herself, to let her go on chasing her dreams? She couldn't help wondering when he would start making demands she couldn't fulfill.

Perhaps that was one more reason she had yet to tell him she loved him. So many times during those blissful hours in the hotel room, she'd been tempted to say the words. She'd seen in his eyes the need to hear them. But she hadn't been able to do it. Not then. Not now. The campaign. The fight for suffrage. Those had to come first.

She couldn't risk trusting her heart to him just yet. Perhaps someday, but not yet.

"No, Michael!" Rose Rafferty called to her husband from across the hotel dining room. "Not there. Center the banner above the column." She pointed. "Over there."

"And higher, too," Lark chimed in.

"I'll give him a hand," Geoffrey Rudyard offered, then weaved his way through the tables toward the hapless man on the ladder. "Is there something I can do to help, sir?"

Michael let out a frustrated laugh. "I doubt we'll get it right, no matter what we try." He sat on the top rung of the ladder and looked down at Geoffrey. "Yancy had the right idea. Hightail it into the hills for the afternoon. Between his wife and mine . . ." He let his voice trail off, ending with a shake of his head.

"They are intent on doing it all up brown." Geoffrey grinned.

Michael raised an eyebrow, obviously finding nothing amusing about the turmoil all around him. "Young man," he said dryly, "you're enjoying yourself entirely too much."

Geoffrey tried to contain his laughter but failed. The older man was right. He *was* enjoying himself. He thought it grand that Ben and Katie were married. He thought Ben Rafferty was just what Katie needed. He'd always adored his friend's forthrightness, her ability to focus on an issue and pursue an end with the tenacity of a bulldog. He'd always enjoyed her sense of humor and the pleasure she took from the simple things in life. But secretly he'd also believed she needed to fall in love and discover there was more to life than just her "causes." As important as they were, they were not *everything*.

"As a matter of fact," Michael said, intruding on Geoffrey's thoughts, "there's another ladder out behind the hotel. Why don't you get it, and we'll have a go at this banner together. With any luck, we can hang it to the women's satisfaction before the newlyweds arrive."

"Right away, sir."

"Go through the kitchen. It'll be quicker."

Geoffrey walked to the swinging doors that joined the hotel kitchen to the dining room and pushed one of them open before him. As he passed into the kitchen, he was stopped by the sight of Sophia standing beside a table, an apron tied around her waist, a scarf covering her pretty gold hair. Her mouth was puckered in concentration as she decorated a large single-layer cake.

"Hmm. Looks good."

With a gasp, she jumped back a step. Her hand flew to her scarf, and she tugged it off, then held it behind her.

"Sorry. Didn't mean to startle you."

"I didn't hear you come in." She smoothed her hair away from her face.

He stepped forward, smiling when he saw the smudge of flour on her cheek. It suddenly occurred to him that Sophia Rafferty was a rather beguiling woman. It wasn't simply because she was pretty, although that was certainly true. Nor was it because she believed in woman's suffrage and was working to see it become a reality, although that was important to him, too. No, it was something much simpler, yet more complex, than either of those reasons.

"I must look a sight," she said as he drew closer to her.

"Indeed you do." He stretched out his arm and brushed at the flour on her cheek with his fingertips. "And it's a very lovely sight you make."

She blushed.

Maybe that was it. Too few women of Geoffrey's acquaintance remembered how to blush. They were far too sophisticated—or at least pretended to be. He doubted Sophia would even know how to carry on such a pretense.

"Are you and Penny settled into your rooms here at the hotel?" she asked as she took a step back from him. "Are they to your satisfaction?"

"The rooms are fine."

"You're probably glad to be in town."

"We enjoyed our stay at the Jones ranch, but it was time we stopped imposing on their hospitality. Ben and Katie's wedding gave us a good excuse to leave without offending our hosts."

Sophia glanced down at the worktable. "I hope they like their cake."

"I'm sure they shall."

"And I hope the Susan B doesn't break down again."

"I'm certain they hope so, too."

Odd that he hadn't recognized his attraction to Sophia before today. She was nothing at all like the women he normally took up with. "Tell me, Sophia, have you decided to come back to Washington with us when we leave? Penny is counting on you, you know."

"I'm thinking about it. It's a bit frightening. I'd never planned to live anywhere but right here in Homestead." The color deepened in her cheeks. "All I'd planned to be is a wife and mother."

"There's nothing wrong with that." He wondered if Matthew Jacobs had ever had the nerve to kiss her as she ought to be kissed. From what he'd seen and heard of the gentleman in question, he doubted it. Sanctimonious fool.

For a moment he imagined kissing Sophia. He imagined her mouth would taste like frosting, sweet and creamy. Then he imagined the feel of her heart beating near his chest as he held her close.

"Geoffrey?"

The images vanished.

"I'd like to thank you."

"Thank me. Whatever for?"

She gave a tiny shrug. "It's hard to explain. I think I've been jealous of Katie, the way Ben always listened to her and thought what she had to say was of value." She tipped her head slightly to one side and offered a smile. "Not many men do that, you know. Listen to women, I mean. But you do. You listen to all of us on the committee. I just wanted you to know I appreciate it."

I hope you come to Washington, Miss Rafferty, he thought, and was surprised anew by his unexpected attraction to her. *I think I'd rather like listening to you on a regular basis.*

"Well." He cleared his throat. "I'd best get that ladder for your father. Your brother and his bride will be here before we know it." Then he walked away, pondering his new discovery.

* * *

Ben and Katie picnicked at the river's edge with the hot summer sun directly overhead. Neither of them seemed inclined to leave as soon as they were through eating. So they sat there in silence, each lost in thought.

Katie leaned on one hip, her legs curled at her side. She stared pensively at the river, running wide and slow in this place.

Watching her, Ben thought she looked beautiful. But then he always thought she looked beautiful. "Let's go for a swim," he suggested suddenly.

"Now?"

"It's hot. We've made good time. The Susan B doesn't seem prone to any more trouble this trip."

She looked ready to decline. Then she grinned. "All right. Let's."

"Brave enough to go without your bathing costume, Katie?" It was the sort of dare they'd flung at each other throughout childhood.

"Are you?" she replied with a twinkle in her eye.

"Last one in has to drive the rest of the way to Homestead." He hopped to his feet and began removing his clothes.

With a laugh and a cry of, "No fair," she did the same.

He could have beaten her into the river, of course. Only he stopped midway in his undressing to watch her. He couldn't have done otherwise. He gained too much pleasure from looking at her to miss such an opportunity.

If she suspected she'd been given an advantage, she didn't let on. Skirt and bodice dropped to the ground, followed by various undergarments. She didn't try to hide herself from his gaze, didn't turn her back to him. Perhaps she even took advantage of his spellbound attention. Before he scarcely knew what had happened, she darted into the river, screaming as the cold water enveloped her.

The rest of his clothes were shed in short order, and he raced after her, diving into the water and swimming with long, powerful strokes. She had nearly reached the opposite shore before he caught her. Arms around her waist, he sank with her beneath the surface, then they emerged together, gasping for air and laughing.

He held her close against him, his feet set firmly on the sandy river bottom. With water running from his face onto hers, he kissed her. She wriggled, and his body hardened in response.

Would he ever get enough of her? he wondered as he slipped a hand down her back to her rounded buttock.

She drew her head back and stared into his eyes even as she wrapped her legs around his waist, holding tight against the current. Her mouth parted, and her tongue darted out to moisten already wet lips.

Did she have any idea what she did to him?

Katie smiled, as if she'd read his thoughts, and moved purposefully against him.

"We just might drown," he growled.

Her laugh was throaty, seductive. "We just might."

As he guided her hips to join their bodies together, Ben decided a mountain river could have some advantages over a hotel room and a big featherbed.

And it just might be worth the risk of drowning to find out what those advantages were.

Later, as they lay side by side in the heat of the sun, Katie marveled at the wondrous way Ben made her feel. She hadn't known it was possible to make love in the middle of a river. Truth be told, she hadn't known much of anything about the things men and women did in private. Nor had she suspected she would enjoy the learning as much as she'd enjoyed it over the past few days.

Ben rose on his elbow and stared down at her. "We really could have drowned, you know." His voice was low, his tone once again teasing.

"Worth the risk." She raked her fingers through his still-damp hair. "Honest."

"Ah, Katie." He kissed her forehead. "How I love you." He kissed the tip of her nose. "How very much I love you."

There was a moment's pause, and she knew he was waiting for her to say the words.

He always waited.

She never said them.

She felt the caress of his sigh on her lips an instant before he kissed them. Then he sat up, reaching for his clothes.

"Ben?" She placed her hand on his back.

He glanced at her again.

"Is it like this for everyone? So . . . so *intense?*"

He shook his head. "Only for the lucky ones, Katie."

She sat up beside him. "Will it always be like this for us?"

Before he could answer, the shadow of a cloud darkened Ben's face. Katie shivered, feeling suddenly cold, exposed—and more than a little frightened.

He grabbed her clothes and handed them to her. "Here. You'd better get dressed. It's time we were on our way."

There wasn't a soul in sight when the Susan B arrived in Homestead. The thought crossed Ben's mind that the town looked even quieter than usual—which seemed almost an impossibility, even to him.

He drove the motorcar to the front of the hotel, then turned off the engine. "Well, Katie," he said into the sudden silence, "we're home."

She glanced over at him, and he recognized her surprise. She hadn't thought about this being her home, he realized, about home being anywhere except the Lazy L. He knew she must not have given any thought to Homestead, to what their lives would be like after their return.

Katie looked back at the front of the hotel, saying softly, "I suppose we should have gone out to the ranch first. I'll need to get my things. And I'll have to talk to my parents."

He guessed the reality of their marriage had just hit her and wondered if she were wishing for a reason to avoid going up to his suite.

A glimmer of a smile curved her mouth and dispelled his doubts. "I suppose tomorrow will be soon enough." She touched her hair, tied with a ribbon at the nape after her hairpins had been lost beside the river. "After all, they might wonder why my hair is damp, and I don't think I'm prepared to explain it to my parents."

He grinned. "I don't think I am, either."

He hopped over the side of the car, then went around the front of the automobile and opened the door for Katie. She took his hand, letting him help her out. Then he held her elbow, and they walked into the hotel together.

"That's odd," he said as they entered the lobby. "There's no one behind the desk."

But just before his concerns could deepen, the doors to the dining room flew open and there was a great shout of voices: "Surprise!" And suddenly he and Katie were surrounded by people—half the town, it seemed like— hugging and kissing and all talking at once.

Ben's father slapped him on the back, then shook his hand. "I'm glad for you, son," Michael said. "I suspect the women are upset you didn't get married here, but we're all mighty glad for you both."

"Thanks, Dad."

Rose was the next to hug him, tears running down her cheeks. "I wish you all the happiness your father and I have had, Benjamin."

I hope your wishes come true, Mother, he thought as he returned the hug.

Sophia was next and then his brother Shane.

After that came Geoffrey Rudyard. "About time someone had the good sense to snap Katie up. She's a real find, Ben. But I expect you already know that."

He glanced toward his wife, who was at that moment being kissed by her grandmother. "Yes, I know."

From the dining room doorway, Michael raised his voice above the din. "Everyone come back in here, where there's more room. Give the newlyweds a chance to see what we've done."

Ben reached quickly for Katie's arm before she could be swept away from him. If this party was for Mr. and Mrs. Benjamin Rafferty, he wanted them to go in to it together. For some reason it seemed important they do so.

She looked up at him as they moved forward. Her dark brown eyes were misty, but she was smiling softly.

"Anyone notice your hair?" he whispered teasingly, wanting to make her smile again.

"My mother." She blushed. "I told her we went swimming because we were hot and dusty from the drive."

"Well, that's true."

But he knew she was remembering, just as he was, the interlude that had followed their swim across the river.

"Oh, look!" Katie exclaimed, causing him to turn his gaze away from her and toward the dining room.

Ribbons and streamers hung from the ceiling. Bouquets of bright midsummer flowers—yellow and red and purple—festooned every table. A large white banner hung above the back wall. "Congratulations, Mr. and Mrs. Rafferty!" it proclaimed in bold blue letters.

"Come and cut the cake," Katie's mother instructed, motioning for them to follow her. Lark Jones led them through the crowd, and as they went, they continued to acknowledge all the good wishes and kind words that were being showered upon them.

Katie fought a new onslaught of tears as they moved through a parting sea of friends and neighbors. This was the second party that had been thrown for her this summer, but this one she didn't deserve. They all thought she'd married Ben because he'd swept her off her feet. They thought she'd married him for all the usual reasons, with all the usual hopes and dreams a bride was expected to bring to her wedding. She wished they were right. She wished she wanted nothing more than to be Ben's wife. She wished she could be the wife he wanted her to be, the wife they all thought she would be.

But she wasn't, and she couldn't be, and it nearly broke her heart to acknowledge the truth.

They arrived at the table, set with crystal and china and silver. In the center was a sparkling cut-glass bowl, filled to the brim with red punch, and a huge cake decorated with white and blue frosting, "Ben and Katie" written diagonally across it in flowing letters.

Lark handed her new son-in-law a knife. "Your sister made the cake," she told him.

Katie glanced toward Sophia. She thought of the hours it must have taken her to mix, bake, and decorate the beautiful wedding cake, and again she felt a sting of regret, knowing she wasn't deserving of it all.

Then she shoved the doubts and misgivings from her thoughts. Tonight was a night to enjoy, she told herself, to let herself simply love Ben. And that was precisely what she did. For the next few hours she pretended everything was perfect with her marriage until even she almost believed it. It was easy enough to do, really. It seemed many in Long Bow Valley had expected Ben and Katie to marry, and if there were some folks who suspected that questionable circumstances had led up to the sudden union, they kept those thoughts to themselves. Tonight everyone celebrated the future of Ben and Katie Rafferty.

But the party couldn't last forever. Eventually people had to return to their own homes, and finally only the Raffertys and the Joneses remained.

For the first time that evening, Katie faced her father without a crowd around them. As he looked at her, she wondered what he thought of her sudden marriage.

He took hold of her hand and led her to a corner of the room, where he wrapped her in a tight embrace. Putting his mouth near her ear, he asked, "Are you happy, kitten?"

Once again she found herself fighting tears.

He drew back and looked into her eyes. "It'll be good for you t'have Ben beside you while you're out there fightin' whatever it is you feel you gotta fight." He kissed her forehead. "I won't have cause to worry about you so much."

"You never needed to worry so much anyway, Papa," she managed to say despite the lump in her throat. "I've always been okay on my own."

"Do you love him?"

Strange, how she could keep from saying the words to Ben but not to her father. She nodded as she whispered, "I love him."

Yancy looked as if he would say more, but Lark joined them at that moment, and whatever he might have said was lost to her.

Her mother gave her another tight hug. "We'd best be on our way, Katie. You and Ben must be worn out from your trip and all the excitement of the last few days."

She nodded.

"Your father and I brought some of your things in from the ranch. We put them up in Ben's rooms." She squeezed one of Katie's hands. "Be happy, dearest."

"I will, Mother."

As her parents stepped away from her, Ben moved in to fill the void, placing his arm around her shoulders, holding her close. Together they bade their parents good night, then watched as the Joneses drove away in their carriage and the Raffertys walked down the street toward their home on the edge of town. Finally, with nothing else to delay them, they climbed the stairs to Ben's suite of rooms on the top floor.

Their suite, Katie reminded herself as she entered what served as the parlor.

"I've never done much with it," Ben said with a note of apology as she walked slowly around the room, touching the furniture. "You can change anything you like, do whatever you want to make it feel more like a home."

Home. My new home.

She opened the door to the bedroom. Her best night-gown had been laid across the spread of the large, four-poster bed with its heavy oak headboard and footboard.

Our bed.

She felt a moment of strangeness, knowing this wasn't a temporary stay in a hotel, realizing this really was her home now, that the bed really was her bed. She wouldn't be returning to the Lazy L. She wouldn't be sleeping in her familiar bedroom. Everything was changed now and would never be as it once was.

Then Ben stepped up behind her, putting his hands on her shoulders. He brushed aside the hair at her nape and nuzzled the tender flesh he found there, and she forgot everything else except his touch.

21

The Homestead Weekly Herald, *Homestead, Idaho*
Friday Morning, July 21, 1916
REPUBLICAN RACE FOR CONGRESS HEATS UP:
LOCAL CANDIDATE SCHEDULED TO MAKE
SEVERAL IDAHO APPEARANCES

As of last week, there are now five candidates in the Republican race for the two at-large seats in the U.S. House of Representatives. Congressmen Addison T. Smith and Robert M. McCracken are both running for reelection. The challengers are Burton L. French of Moscow, E. E. Elliott of Sandpoint, and Katherine Jones Rafferty of Homestead.

Mrs. Rafferty, who was married in early July to Benjamin Rafferty, owner and publisher of the Homestead Herald, *has scheduled a comprehensive tour of Idaho, with speaking engagements confirmed for Sandpoint, Moscow, Boise, Twin Falls, and Idaho Falls. Mrs. Rafferty is the first woman candidate for a national office from the state of Idaho. . . .*

It would have been so easy for Katie to give in to the love she felt for Ben. Little by little he chipped away at the protective wall she'd put up between them. There were times she forgot completely the fight for the suffrage amendment and even her own campaign, times when all she thought about was Ben and the love he showered upon her, times she ached to tell him she loved him, too.

She couldn't even blame Ben for her forgetfulness. From the time of their return, he was true to his word. He did everything in his power to help her win the election. He worked tirelessly, masterminding an energetic and innovative campaign. When a delegation of men called upon him at the newspaper, demanding he take his new bride in hand and stop this outrageous and unseemly stunt of hers, he invited them to mind their own business and stay out of his. If he was worried about the effect of her campaign on the newspaper, he didn't tell Katie. In a dozen different ways every day, he showed her how important she was to him. And every night he showed his love again in their big, four-poster bed.

Thus it was easy to forget everything except Ben. Too easy.

They'd been married two weeks when Katie had the nightmare. She dreamed of Ben's lovemaking, and afterward he held her in his arms. Then slowly—ever slowly—she faded away. She simply ceased to exist, evaporating into thin air.

She awakened, heart pounding, her body damp with perspiration. She lifted her hand, staring at it to make sure it was there, that she could see it and prove she existed. Then she sat up and looked at Ben, asleep beside her. It was happening already. He was absorbing her, minute by minute, day by day, just as she'd feared he would.

Then she remembered the way he'd watched her as she'd undressed for bed that night, the way he'd touched her stomach, a tender expression in his eyes. She hadn't understood it then, but suddenly she did.

Ben wanted children. For him it was just another expression of loving each other. Last night he'd been thinking about making a child with her. How could she have been so stupid? How could she have not thought about pregnancy and what it could mean to her?

She sank slowly back onto the bed, rolling onto her side, her back toward Ben. *I won't forget everything I've come here to do,* she promised herself as she closed her eyes. *I can't forget who I am as easily as that.*

The next morning Katie went to see the town doctor, Tom McLeod.

"Have you heard the news?" he asked as she sat on a chair opposite his desk. "I've purchased myself an automobile. I'm expecting delivery in another week."

"No, I hadn't heard. That's wonderful."

"You know, years ago, I told old Doc Varney he and I would one day be making our calls to patients in motorcars. He didn't believe me. I wish he'd lived to see the day." He shook his head, then met her gaze. "Well, that isn't why you came to see me. Nothing serious, I hope."

She fidgeted on the hard wooden chair. Her palms became damp, and she could feel heat rise in her cheeks. "You see, Dr. Tom, I don't . . . That is, I shouldn't . . . What I mean is, with the elections coming and all the traveling I'll be doing, I don't think . . ." She let her voice trail off into silence, still unable to finish a sentence. She'd never before tried to discuss matters of such an intimate nature with a man, not even with Ben, and hadn't known it would be this difficult.

Tom leaned forward, his expression kind and encouraging. "We've known each other a long time, Katie. There's nothing we can't talk about in my office. But I can't help you if you don't tell me what's wrong."

She let out a sigh, then stiffened her spine and squared her shoulders. "I'm not sick, Dr. Tom. I just need to know how to prevent . . . you know . . . getting pregnant." The last words were released in a rush. Her gaze dropped to her hands, folded tightly in her lap.

"Hmm. I see."

"This just wouldn't be a good time for me to have a baby." She glanced up again. "Can you help me?"

"There aren't many reliable means of controlling reproduction, Katie. The only real prevention is complete abstinence from marital relations."

She knew her cheeks must have turned beet red by this time. She had been practicing anything *but* abstinence. Denying herself to Ben would be an impossibility. He had only to touch her cheek or kiss her brow, things as simple as that, and she became helpless to resist his loving.

Tom rose from his chair and walked over to the bookcase against the back wall of his office. "Let me see. . . . Ah, there it is." He pulled a pamphlet off the shelf and brought it to her. "This may be of some help to you. It was written by a woman physician in Holland who has developed some methods of birth control which the wife can employ. One that seems to be quite successful is called a diaphragm. I believe it has merit, and I'd be happy to—"

Katie stood, feeling more embarrassed by the second. "I'll return this as soon as I can."

"No hurry on my account. But if you're serious, I would recommend you come back to see me soon." He gave her a meaningful glance. After a moment's silence he added,

"Not many women are willing to talk to me about the subject, even if they already have more children than they can possibly manage. And, as I said, there are no guarantees. Perhaps one day medical science will think it important enough for in-depth research."

"Perhaps." Feeling awkward, she turned and headed for the door. As she opened it, she said, "Thanks again, Dr. Tom."

"Good luck with your decision, Katie. And give Ben my regards."

"I will." She closed the door behind her, then paused to glance down the street toward the newspaper building. She wouldn't be giving the doctor's regards to Ben, of course. She didn't want him to know about this visit.

She looked at the pamphlet in her hand. No, she couldn't tell him about this. It would hurt him, and she didn't want to hurt him any more than she already had.

Her thoughts agitated, Katie turned and nearly ran smack into Blanche Coleson.

The schoolmarm's glare was as stiff and unyielding as her spine. "Good day, Mrs. Rafferty." She made the name sound offensive, meant as an insult rather than a form of address.

Katie forced herself to be pleasant. "Hello, Blanche. I haven't seen much of you lately. I hope you're doing well."

"Well enough."

"I'm sorry you've been unable to continue helping on the committee." It was a lie, and she suspected Blanche knew it.

If possible, the woman's demeanor became even more censorious than before. "Mrs. Rafferty, I had high hopes when you first returned to this town. I assumed you would be of a serious nature, intent on helping other women be free of the unfair rule of men. I assumed you would help women see they needn't subject themselves to the vile, disgusting impulses of men, that marriage was only for the weak-minded who could not take care of themselves. But when you continued your *friendship*"— the word dripped with sarcasm and suggestion—"with Ben Rafferty, I suspected that you are, instead, a woman who is ruled by her basest nature." She crossed her arms and jutted her chin into the air. "You may have fooled others, Mrs. Rafferty, but you have not fooled me."

Katie was rarely left speechless, but this was one of those times.

"I'll have you know I've been writing letters to the fine leaders of the association. Now they know about you, too. They won't continue to put their faith in you. They'll soon withdraw their support. You'll see."

A tiny warning bell rang in Katie's head. She'd never cared for Blanche much, but she hadn't thought the woman unhinged, either. Now she wasn't so sure.

The schoolmarm pointed down the street toward the newspaper office. "That man has poisoned your thoughts. And he uses his position in this town to make others believe you're something you're not. Well, it won't work. It won't work, I tell you."

"I think I've heard enough," Katie said quietly but firmly.

"You've sold yourself to the enemy. *Harlot!*"

"Good day, Miss Coleson." She turned and immediately crossed the street, wanting as much distance between her and the schoolmarm as possible.

As she hurried along the sidewalk toward the hotel, she told herself she shouldn't be surprised by the venomous words Blanche had spewed. She'd always known the schoolmarm had a hatred for men, that her support of woman's suffrage had more to do with that hate than with truly wanting women to be free to choose their own paths, paths that would naturally take many of them into marriage.

Her footsteps slowed, the schoolmarm already forgotten.

Choices. Wasn't that one of the things she loved most about Ben? His love didn't stifle her, didn't control her. He'd always left her free to make her own choices.

She recalled the words of Miss Mott that her husband had written to her on their wedding day. *Equal. Mutual. Reciprocal.* Ben had been living those words. Had she?

She glanced down at the pamphlet in her hand.

No, she answered her own question. She hadn't been living those words. But she couldn't. Not yet. This was the way things had to be for now.

When Ben opened the door to their suite in midafternoon, he found Katie seated on the sofa, her feet tucked up beside her, reading from a small pamphlet. He strode quickly over to her, leaned down, and gave her a kiss.

"I have a surprise for you."

She gave him a mock frown. "Ben, you really must stop spoiling me." Then she grinned like a schoolgirl. "What is it?"

"Get your hat. We're going for a drive."

"Now?"

"Now."

"But we're expecting Penny and—"

"I've told Geoffrey we'll be late. He'll let the others know." He drew her to her feet, took the pamphlet from her hand, and tossed it onto the sofa.

As usual, he thought about removing all those blasted pins from her hair so it could cascade around her shoulders, the way he liked it best. He thought about removing her blouse and her corset so he could gaze on her ripe, firm breasts, lave them with his tongue, nibble lightly with his teeth. Then he thought about all that would follow and knew it would be a long time before they left these rooms if he followed his inclinations.

"Get your hat," he said again, his voice husky.

Her eyes darkened, as if she knew what he'd been thinking—and had been thinking it, too. "All right," she whispered. "It won't take me but a moment."

She grabbed the pamphlet she'd been reading and took it with her into the bedroom. A few moments later she reappeared, bonnet and scarf in hand.

As she put the hat in place and tied the scarf beneath her chin, she asked, "Do you mind telling me where we're going?"

"I told you. It's a surprise." He took hold of her arm. "You wouldn't want to spoil it, would you?"

She smiled at him, a twinkle in her eye. "No. But if it involves the old water hole, I think we should take some blankets."

"What a delightful thought." He kissed the tip of her nose. "However, the water hole will have to wait for another time." With a flourish of his hand he opened the door and motioned her out of the room.

Within minutes they were in the Susan B, driving west out of town, Ben at the wheel of the automobile. He could feel Katie watching him and knew she was wondering what this was all about. He also knew she would never guess. Not in a hundred years.

For Ben, the last couple of weeks had been almost perfection. Katie was the passionate sort of lover all men wished for but few were lucky enough to find. But beyond that, he simply liked being with her. She had a great sense of humor and loved to tease. She also had a quick temper, but she was just as quick to be sorry for it. Sometimes, when they were meeting with the other members of the election committee, he would listen as she talked and he'd feel a welling up of pride in her intelligence, her dedication, her keen perceptions. Other times he simply sat and considered how lucky he was to be married to her.

"What's going on in that head of yours, Ben Rafferty?" she asked now.

He glanced over at her. "I was thinking about how much I love you."

She smiled—a little sadly, he thought—and he saw the conflict in her eyes, the wish to repeat those same words to him and the fear that stopped her from doing so.

It didn't matter, he told himself. It would happen. He just needed to give her more time.

Looking ahead, he said, "We're almost there." He slowed the Susan B, then turned north off the main road onto a rarely traveled track. "Hang on. It's bumpy."

As if to prove his point, the right front tire dropped into a rut, violently jerking the passengers of the motorcar from side to side. Katie grabbed hold of the door with her right hand and her hat with her left as they followed the track toward the tree-lined banks of Pony Creek, the terrain gently but steadily rising before them.

It took another ten minutes of rough travel before Ben braked to a halt. "We're here."

Katie looked around. "We're *where?*"

"Come on. I'll show you."

They got out of the car, and Ben guided her up a grassy slope. At the top he turned her to face the east. From here they had a fine view of sleepy little Homestead. Katie stared at the town obediently for several moments, then glanced at him in question.

"This is where we're going to build our home." The words filled him with pleasure and warm contentment.

He envisioned a two-story house with porches on two sides and shutters framing the windows. He pictured a tall tree with a rope swing hanging from its thick branches, deep green in summer, stark and gray brown in winter. He imagined children playing in the yard while he and Katie watched them from the porch.

"Our home?" she asked softly.

"I met with Leroy Smith over at the bank this morning. He'll let us have it for a reasonable price. With a bit of effort, we could have the house built before October."

"But why build a house when we hope to be in Washington after the election?"

He'd hoped she would be as excited as he was. She wasn't.

"We won't be there forever, Katie. We'll want a house to come back to." It was as close as he could come to saying he hoped they wouldn't ever be going back east.

"But building a house is an enormous undertaking, Ben. Haven't we already enough to worry about this fall? We'll be traveling so often in the weeks to come, and you're already putting in too many hours at the newspaper and on my campaign. Besides, no matter how much you've tried to keep it from me, I know you've lost more advertisers because of me. How can we afford to build a house?"

Her reasons all made perfect sense, yet they left him feeling angry and out of sorts. His reply was sharp. "We can afford it."

She didn't pay his words any heed. "What's wrong with the rooms we have at the hotel? They're more than adequate for the two of us."

"They won't always be adequate, Katie. A hotel's no place to raise children."

She let out a quick gasp. "We won't be having children yet. Not right away." With a look of regret, she turned away from him. "There'll be time enough to worry about where we're going to live after I've won this election."

It was on the tip of his tongue to remind her she might not win this blasted election, but then he thought better of it. These weeks had been happy ones for them. He wasn't ready for that happiness to be spoiled by an argument. He was certain she would see the wisdom of building a home here. She only needed a little time to think about it.

"Tell you what, Katie." He touched her shoulder. "I'll ask Leroy to let us have until after the primary in September. If you win that election, we'll let the land go. The bank can sell to another buyer when they have one. But if you lose, we'll go ahead with the purchase. Agreed?"

Katie was trapped, and she knew it. Trapped by his logic and by her own dishonest silence. She should have told Ben why they wouldn't be having children any time soon. She should have told him she meant to make certain they didn't, should have told him about her visit to Dr. Tom.

But she'd already disappointed Ben more than he deserved. He'd been so excited about buying this land, and all she'd done was throw excuses in his face. No, she couldn't tell him she wasn't ready to have his baby.

"All right, Ben," she replied softly. "That sounds reasonable enough. We'll wait and see what happens in September."

22

That August was the hottest month on record. Ben sometimes wondered if the heat might account for his mood, but he knew it had much more to do with Katie than weather.

Leaning his forearm against the window encasement, he watched dusk settle over Homestead, but his thoughts weren't on the dusty, deserted street that ran in front of the newspaper office. They were on his bride of seven weeks.

To the folks of Homestead, he thought it must seem he and Katie had a picture-perfect marriage. He knew no one would ever guess his wife had yet to tell him she loved him. And if they had, he was certain no one would know how heavily that omission weighed upon his heart.

In the month since Ben had shown Katie the land where he wanted to build their home, he'd poured himself into the work involved in her political campaign, spending long hours in his office or meeting with other members of the committee. When it seemed he and Katie were too seldom alone, he didn't voice his complaint to her. When it seemed they never talked of anything unrelated to the election, he kept his opinion to himself. When he wondered about their future together, he made love to her and pretended all was well. Occasionally he allowed himself to dream about the house on the western slope, to envision it finished and lived in. Sometimes he closed his eyes and imagined that yard full of children, their children.

And often he prayed his efforts to help Katie win the election would fail.

"Well, it'll be over soon, my friend. At least, the first step."

His troubled thoughts interrupted, Ben glanced over his shoulder. Geoffrey Rudyard's long legs were stretched out in front of him, ankles crossed. His arms were folded over his chest, his head rested on the back of the spindle-backed chair, and his eyes were closed. The two of them had spent the last four hours hammering out plans for Katie's final campaign appearance before the primary, and Geoffrey looked as tired as Ben felt.

Stifling a yawn, Geoffrey added, "I don't believe anything can stop Katie from winning in the primary now."

Sadly, Ben had to agree with him. As Katie had traveled the length and breadth of the state, from the panhandle to the southeasternmost corner, she had gained more confidence, spoken ever more eloquently and effectively about her goals and what she hoped to achieve in Congress, about her vision for the women and men of Idaho and the nation. The gentlemen of the press, at first skeptical and often derogatory, had begun to write some positive articles about her. A few newspapers had even come out in support of her candidacy.

Just as Geoffrey had said, it seemed nothing could stop her, not even the secret prayers of her husband.

"Have you ever thought of going into politics yourself, Ben?"

A crude retort flashed in his head, and if anyone but Geoffrey had asked it, he would have let them feel the heat of his resentment. But he'd grown rather fond of the fellow over the passing weeks, so he kept his thoughts to himself, answering simply, "No, I haven't."

"So, what are you going to do with yourself after Katie's elected?"

That same question had plagued Ben for weeks. "I don't know." Again he looked out at the empty, dusty street.

He'd promised Katie he would help her win this damned election, and that was exactly what he'd been doing. But that didn't mean he didn't hope she would lose. He'd promised he wouldn't try to change her, and he'd kept his word. But secretly he still hoped she would discover their marriage was more important than her blasted causes.

He loved Katie more every day. When he awakened in the morning, he gazed upon her and thought how unhappy he'd be without her. When they were apart, he often stopped whatever he was doing to think about her and wondered if perhaps she was thinking about him, too. Every evening when his work was done, he hurried back to their hotel suite, eager to hold her and kiss her and make love to her.

He smiled. It seemed he would never get enough of Katie, nor she of him. If only all else in their lives were as perfect. If only he could be sure they would one day build that house and spend the rest of their lives there.

He quickly reminded himself that he'd known what Katie wanted when he married her. But, he added silently, in the beginning he'd been certain she would lose. And since that was no longer a certainty, it seemed his dream of that two-story house near Pony Creek was slipping away from him all too quickly.

The idea of living in Washington for the next two years—or more—was a grim one. He'd never liked the hustle and bustle of big cities. He didn't care for the social activities required of those in business and government or the accompanying artificiality he so often found. He liked even less the notoriety he would have as husband of the first woman elected to the nation's legislature.

Geoffrey yawned, then said, "Well, I believe it's time we called it a night. Doesn't seem to be anything more we can do here, and Penny and I are expected for supper at your parents' home."

"Growing tired of hotel fare?" Ben turned around. "Or have I detected some interest in my sister?"

"Whatever do you mean, my good man?" Geoffrey grinned as he rose from the chair and jauntily placed his hat on his head.

"I'm not blind."

Geoffrey's expression sobered. "To be honest, Ben, I do have a certain affection for your sister, but I'm afraid she doesn't return it. Is it possible she's still in love with Mr. Jacobs?"

"With Matthew? I doubt it."

"He's a rather self-righteous fellow, isn't he? I've had the dubious pleasure of a lengthy conversation with him. He implied Sophia is suffering some sort of nervous condition that has altered her judgment. Had the nerve to warn me off her, among other things."

"Oh, did he?"

"I considered showing him what I learned as a pugilist at the university, but Penny saw what I was about and dragged me away before I could strike the first blow."

"Now *that* would have been something for the town

gossips to feast on." Ben chuckled. "I can see it now. 'Geoffrey Rudyard accosted local bookstore owner Matthew Jacobs this last week in Homestead. Mr. Rudyard, an attorney from Washington, D.C., is a member of Katherine Rafferty's election committee.'"

Geoffrey grinned. "That's precisely why my sister had the good sense to stop me. It wouldn't have done Katie any favor to get into a battle of fisticuffs."

Wishing Penelope hadn't stopped her brother, Ben pulled open the door. The two men left the office and started off toward the hotel, walking side by side in silence.

With the coming of evening, electric and gas lamps flickered to life inside homes and the few businesses that stayed open late. Light spilled through windows onto the sidewalk in front of the two men as they headed toward the hotel. For most folks, supper had been eaten, dishes washed and put away. Young children had already been tucked into their beds for the night. Women sat with their baskets of mending, men with their pipes and newspapers.

Quiet, comfortable Homestead.

"Have you thought of getting a job at the *Post* once you're settled in Washington?" Geoffrey asked. "They'd be interested in a man like you."

Ben didn't reply, not certain what his answer should be. He would need something to keep himself occupied while his wife was about the affairs of state. But none of the obvious choices appealed to him.

Geoffrey's hand alighted on Ben's shoulder. "It won't be easy for Katie, being a woman in Congress." He shook his head. "She'll need you more than ever. She's lucky to have your support in all this."

Although he nodded, Ben knew he wasn't supporting Katie the way she needed him to. Did she, or anyone else, ever suspect how heartily he wished for her defeat even while he worked toward her victory?

As if in answer to his silent questions, he remembered Reverend Jacobs's sermon the previous Sunday. "'A house divided against a house falleth,'" the reverend had warned. Ben had squirmed in the pew as he'd listened, feeling as if the minister were speaking directly to him.

A house divided . . .

He raised his eyes toward the hotel, toward the windows of the rooms he shared with Katie. She, Penelope, and Sophia had spent the day over in the neighboring county, drumming up votes, but Katie had called him at the newspaper upon their return an hour ago. She would be waiting for him now.

Would he destroy their house, their future, their happiness, because of his secret hopes?

God forbid!

Katie hadn't felt well for the last couple of weeks. The very thought of food in the mornings had left her queasy and unable to eat. She'd been losing weight, and her dresses didn't fit as they should. She'd told herself it was only because of the demands of her campaign, the visits to strangers' homes, the countless cups of coffee or tea, and an endless supply of cookies and cakes. Besides, she'd been overtired, wanting to sleep longer at night and wishing to take naps in the afternoon. She was certain she would be more herself as soon as all her gadding about was over and done with.

But tonight, within moments after the waiter from the restaurant wheeled in their supper, Katie succumbed to the sickness that had threatened for days, vomiting into the toilet until she was left shaking, too weak to rise.

That was how Ben found her.

"Katie?" He knelt and placed a hand on her back.

She shook her head, unable to speak for the burning in her throat.

Understanding, he handed her a towel.

She wiped her mouth slowly. Another time she might have been embarrassed for him to see her like this. Tonight she was too sick to care.

"I'll get you a glass of water." He rose and left her but was back in less than a minute. "Here. Rinse your mouth."

She obeyed willingly, eager to wash away the bitter taste. "I don't think I care to eat any supper tonight," she whispered feebly.

Ben drew her up from the floor, cradling her in his arms as he carried her to their bed. She let him help her out of her clothes and into a nightgown, neither of them speaking the entire time.

Once she was settled, a pillow at her back, a sheet pulled up over her chest, Ben sat on the edge of the bed and took hold of her hand. "What brought this on?"

"Too many sweets," she suggested, hoping she was right.

"I think I'd better have Tom McLeod over for a look at you."

She tried to smile. "That isn't necessary, Ben. All I need is a bit of sleep, and I'll be fine. It was so hot and dusty on the road today. I'm just tired. Honest."

"Are you sure?" He brushed stray wisps of hair away from her face.

"I'm sure."

He hesitated a moment, a frown furrowing his forehead as he looked down at her. Then he leaned over and turned off the lamp. "I'll leave the door open. Call me if you need anything."

"I will."

He kissed her cheek before getting up from the bed

and going into the connected parlor, leaving the door ajar behind him.

Katie released a sigh as her eyes closed. This was nothing more than indigestion. It seemed every farm wife from here to the Canadian border had felt obliged to offer her something to eat and drink over the past few weeks. Was it any wonder her stomach was unsettled? A good night's rest would do her wonders. She was sure of it.

The next morning Ben paced the parlor of their hotel suite, impatient to learn what was going on in the bedroom where Tom McLeod was examining his patient.

Katie had vomited again that morning. Violently, it had seemed to Ben. There had been circles beneath her eyes, and her face had looked drawn and pale. He couldn't recall ever seeing Katie sick before, and seeing it worried him. She'd told him he was overreacting. She was probably right. But he hadn't let her talk him out of calling Tom to have a look at her.

The door to the bedroom opened and the doctor stepped into the parlor.

"Well?" Ben demanded immediately.

Tom raised his hand, then reached behind him and closed the door.

"What is it? What's wrong?"

The doctor removed his eyeglasses and cleaned them with a towel. "Nothing that won't take care of itself in a matter of months."

"Months?" His heart nearly stopped. "Is it that serious?"

"As the father of four daughters, I can assure you it's quite serious. Bringing a child into this world is an awesome responsibility. But Katie is a healthy, strong young woman, and I don't expect any undue problems with the pregnancy itself."

It took him a moment to assimilate what the doctor had said. "Katie's *pregnant?*"

"It seems to catch us all by surprise the first time," Tom answered as he walked over to where Ben stood. He patted him on the back. "Congratulations."

Katie was pregnant. Katie was going to have his baby. He stared at the closed door to the bedroom. She wasn't sick. She was pregnant.

She would drop out of the race now. They would buy the land west of town and build their house. He'd plant trees around it, lots and lots of fast-growing trees, suitable for climbing up and building tree houses in and swinging from. He'd buy a puppy next summer, and the two—child and dog—could grow up together.

Tom reached for his hat. "I know the two of you wanted to put off children for a while, but some things are better left in nature's hands."

Ben smiled as he looked toward the bedroom door. The doctor couldn't have been more wrong. Ben hadn't wanted to put off having children. This was exactly what he'd hoped would happen. Just exactly.

"It's clear it isn't me you want to talk to." Tom chuckled. "Go on. You can see her. I'll let myself out."

"Thanks," Ben answered absently, already headed for the door.

He heard the doctor laugh again. "Don't thank me."

But Ben ignored him as he turned the doorknob and entered the bedroom, seeking Katie with his eyes.

She was sitting up in bed, several pillows plumped at her back. Her hair flowed loose about her shoulders, the way he liked it best, a dark contrast to the stark whiteness of the bedsheets. She still had circles under her eyes, still looked pale and peaked.

She was pregnant with his baby.

She looked more beautiful than ever before.

"Did he tell you?" she asked as he closed the door.

"Yes." He moved toward her, searching for the words to explain what was in his heart. But there didn't seem to be any words appropriate for the occasion. Anything he thought of seemed inadequate.

"I was too late," she said softly, more to herself than to him, her fingers plucking at the ribbon on her nightgown.

He sat on the edge of the bed, took hold of her hand. "Too late?"

"I was being so careful, and I was already too late."

Suspicion began to gnaw at him. "What do you mean, Katie?"

She looked up, her eyes wide and filled with misery. "This couldn't happen at a worse time."

She isn't happy about the baby. The knowledge caused a hard knot to form in the pit of his stomach. "What did you mean about being careful?"

"I'm sure to win a seat in the primary. Everyone says so. Even you say so. And if I do, then there are all those weeks of campaigning before the November election."

He got up from the bed. "You've been trying to prevent this." It wasn't a question. It was a realization. Her betrayal stung him like nothing else she could have done.

"How could I possibly want a baby now, Ben? By November, my pregnancy will be showing. Voters will think me unable to fulfill my duties. And even if they elect me in spite of it, by the time I'm sworn into office, I'll be big as a cow. How can I—"

"Then drop out of the race."

The room fell silent. They stared at each other, both of them surprised by his suggestion. Or had it been a demand? Even Ben didn't know for sure.

"I can't," she said at last. "You know I can't. You've always known it."

"I think the correct word is won't. You *won't* withdraw from the race." He knew his voice sounded harsh. He *felt* harsh.

"All right," she whispered, "I won't."

He turned on his heel and abruptly walked out, not trusting himself to speak again.

Katie stared at her husband's back as he disappeared through the doorway. Profound regret burned in her chest. Regret for the things she'd said. Regret for the way she'd reacted. She placed her hands on her flat stomach. Ben's baby was growing inside her even now, a result of the love they'd shared.

How could she make him understand what she was feeling when she didn't understand it herself? If being Ben's wife was a threat to all she believed in, how much more of a threat would be this child that was a part of each of them? He would never know how she longed to rejoice over the creation of this new life. But she couldn't. She'd made promises, to herself and to others.

Withdraw from the race, an internal voice urged. *Tell Ben you love him and withdraw from the race.*

I can't, another whispered.

If she dropped out, she would lose an important piece of herself.

If she didn't, she might lose Ben.

Katie sank down in the bed, rolled onto her side, and buried her face in the pillows. Then she wept over the choice she couldn't make.

Ben stood where the living room would have been, looking out where the large picture window would have been. He could see Homestead clearly, even as the shadow of a summer storm fell over the town. Forks of lightning spiked from clouded sky to craggy mountain peaks, accompanied by the distant rumble of thunder.

He'd thought he would spend many an afternoon looking at Homestead from this very spot. He'd pictured Katie standing beside him, their arms around each other. Just a pair of contented married folk. He'd thought their children would grow up in the house they would have built on this site.

But Katie didn't want his children, not even the baby she was already carrying in her womb.

He'd been fooling himself all along, it seemed. He'd thought time would take care of everything. He'd told himself Katie loved him, despite her silence. He'd told himself she would one day understand she could be herself and love him, too. But he'd been wrong. Desperately, foolishly wrong.

Lord, he wished he could hate her. Or at least be indifferent to her. Indifference would have made things much easier. Problem was, he loved her still.

Lightning flashed over the mountains, leading the way for the deluge to come. The cooling air smelled fresh and wet. The wind rose, bringing with it the first drops of rain.

But Ben didn't move. He couldn't. Not yet. Not until the storm was over. Not the storm he could see rushing toward him, but the one he could feel on the inside. The one in his heart. The storm that had come with the shattering of the hopes for his future.

He should have expected this. That day by Pony Creek, she'd told him she wasn't ready to have children. Why hadn't he understood what she'd been saying? Why hadn't he realized Katie would prevent anything from interfering with this election, even if it meant lying to him? Even if it meant not having his child?

What method had she used? he wondered. He'd read

articles about Mrs. Sanger's controversial birth control clinic in New York City. Katie would have known about such things, too, given her involvement with the women leaders of the suffrage movement. Why hadn't he understood what she would do with such knowledge?

Or maybe he *had* understood, and he'd ignored it.

He looked up at the sky just as the rain began to come in earnest. In moments he was soaked. Rivulets of water ran into his face and eyes. His clothes clung to his skin. Around him, long field grass bent beneath the onslaught from heaven. Dirt turned to mud. A thousand tiny streams formed at the top of the hill, racing down the slope toward the banks of the creek.

Standing there in the rain on that isolated hillside, Ben faced the truth. He *had* meant to change Katie. He'd planned to prove to her that the things he wanted were more important than what she wanted, and then she was supposed to have changed. She was supposed to have become the wife and mother he'd envisioned all along.

He cursed as he raked the fingers of both hands through his hair.

He loved Katie, but if she didn't meet him halfway, could he live life her way? He wasn't sure anymore.

He wasn't sure he even wanted to try.

The instant she heard the key turn in the lock, Katie spun from the window where she'd been standing vigil for hours. With her hands clasped in front of her waist and scarcely daring to breathe, she watched the door swing open and Ben enter. He was soaking wet, but it was the resolved expression on his face that caused her heart to nearly stop beating in her chest.

She took a hesitant step forward. "Are you all right? I was worried."

"I'm fine."

"Mr. Trent was looking for you. He called hours ago."

The look in his eyes was as black and stormy as the roiling clouds in the sky.

"I thought you'd gone to the paper from here. I didn't know what to tell Mr. Trent. He said it wasn't like you not to be in the office on Thursdays."

He nodded, but his hard, ungiving expression didn't alter. "I'll change and then head over there. Excuse me." He strode across the parlor and disappeared into the bedroom.

Katie sank onto a nearby chair, feeling chilled. His anger wouldn't last, she told herself. *What's going to happen to us, Benjie?* They'd been happy the way things were. They would be so again. Ben wouldn't remain angry with her. He'd never been able to stay mad at her.

And hadn't her efforts to prevent pregnancy been logical ones, after all? She'd told him she wasn't ready to be a wife and mother. She'd warned him. He should have heeded her warning.

But she found no solace in her silent words of justification.

When Ben reappeared minutes later, dressed in one of his suits, his damp hair slicked back on his head, Katie looked at him hopefully. He was her best and dearest friend. He loved her. He'd never been able to stay mad. Surely he would forgive her this time, too.

"I don't know how late I'll be," he said as he headed toward the door.

"Benjie?"

He glanced over his shoulder.

"Don't you think we should talk?"

"Not yet."

"But—"

He jerked open the door. "Not yet, Katie. We'll talk

about it later." His voice lowered. "When I know what it is I'm going to do."

When I know what it is I'm going to do.

Katie felt icy fingers of fear move along her spine. "What do you mean?"

"Just what I said."

"Ben, I'm sorry I kept it from you. About trying to prevent getting . . . I'm sorry I didn't at least tell you. It was wrong of me. I shouldn't have done it without telling you, but I thought you would understand." That was a lie. She'd known he wouldn't understand or she would have told him. And she could see in his eyes that he knew it, too.

He pushed the door closed again. "You won't withdraw from the race, will you?"

"We've been over that. I can't."

"You won't."

"You're right. I won't."

A few quick strides brought him to her. He grabbed her by the shoulders and yanked her to her feet, the action almost violent. "Damn you, Katie! Is it worth it? Is any of this worth it?"

She was too shocked to form a reply. She'd never seen Ben like this, never felt the heat of his anger in this way.

"Can't you see beyond your blasted *cause?* What about me? What about our baby?"

"Benjie, I—"

He released her and stepped back. "Maybe that's the problem, Katie. You still think I'm Benjie. Well, I'm not. I haven't been Benjie for a long time."

"I don't know what you mean."

He stared at her, the silence thickening between them. Then it seemed the anger drained from him, leaving an icy calm in its wake. "No, I don't suppose you do." He turned and walked back to the door. As he took hold of the doorknob, he said, "I'll stay with you until after the baby's born, Katie. Then I'm taking my child to that house I'm going to build."

"But what about Washington? If I win the election—"

"I'm not going to stay in Washington. I belong here. And so does my child."

Her chest hurt. "What about me?"

"You've already made your choice." He paused. "*Haven't* you, Katie." It was a rhetorical question, not meant to be answered, and he didn't wait for one. He opened the door and left.

"Don't go," she whispered, already too late.

She sat down again, fighting tears, trying to calm herself. It *had* to be all right. She'd always been able to count on Ben. When her father had disapproved of her, Ben had been there to tell her he was proud. When she'd despaired of following her dreams, Ben had urged her on. When most everyone else had said it was crazy for her to run for Congress, Ben had told her she could do it and had promised to help her. He *had* helped her, every step of the way. Ben had always been there to help her. Always.

No, he wouldn't stay angry with her. They would get past this.

They had to.

23

On the eve of her final campaign appearance before the Republican primary, Katie drove the Susan B out to her parents' ranch. She felt a compelling need to be with her mother, to hear Lark's calm voice as she spoke of normal things.

"Katie!" Lark exclaimed as her daughter entered the kitchen. "What a wonderful surprise. I wasn't expecting you today." She wiped her floury hands on her apron before giving her daughter a hug.

The warm, rich fragrance of fresh-baked bread filled the kitchen, bringing with it images of other days when she and her mother had worked together in this same room.

"I thought you'd be too busy getting ready to leave to spare a moment. I'm glad I was wrong. Sit down, and I'll get us something cool to drink."

Trying to sound serene, Katie answered, "My speech is written. Our clothes are packed. We're all ready to go. There's nothing more to be done except catch the train tomorrow." She sat on one of the kitchen chairs. "I wanted to drive down in the Susan B, but Ben said we couldn't take the chance of her breaking down again." *Not in your condition,* had been his exact words.

Lark filled two glasses with iced lemonade, then brought them to the table, setting one in front of Katie. "At least the hot spell has broken. Your trip down to the capital won't be as miserable as it would have been. And it will be nice for you to have Sophia's and the Rudyards' company."

But Katie didn't want to think about her trip or her speech or the election or even her friends. She didn't want to think about anything. For just a few minutes she wanted to pretend she was fifteen again, sitting in her mother's kitchen, carefree and happy.

She took a sip of the lemonade, and when she set the glass back on the table, she touched a deep scar in the surface of the wood. "I remember when this happened."

"So do I. Sam nearly cut Rick's finger off with that knife. I was so scared. Oh, how I wanted to paddle their backsides!"

Katie glanced up. "We weren't any of us model children. Seen and not heard and all that."

Lark laughed. "I should say not."

"Remember how angry I was because Sam wasn't the sister I wanted?"

"You hid in that old line shack near the river. We didn't find you until it was almost dark. That day nearly turned my hair gray."

"I know. And remember the time Ben and I ran Mrs. Percy's drawers up the flagpole after she called us a pair of barbarians?"

Her mother shook her head, still chuckling. "You *were* a pair of barbarians."

"There must have been times you hated being a

mother. I mean, you spent all your time taking care of us, and there wasn't any left just for you."

Her mother's laughter ended abruptly. She leaned forward and covered Katie's hand with her own. "You couldn't be more wrong. I never felt that way."

"Not ever?"

"Not ever."

"But you must have realized there was so much else you might have done if you hadn't married and had children. You could have traveled. You could have gone to Europe or—"

"Things like that can't even compare, Katie. The moment I laid eyes on Yancy, I knew he was my future, my whole life. There wouldn't ever be anyone else for me. I still feel that way. We'd walk through fire for each other. We *have* walked through fire a few times, I guess."

For the first time in her life, Katie was jealous of her mother. She'd never doubted the love her parents shared, but she had underestimated its power. For the first time, she understood fully the joy and strength her mother and father had discovered in each other, the rewards they found in the little things in life.

Was this what Ben had hoped they would share? Could she feel the same satisfaction as her mother if she were to give up her dreams?

Lark's smile was contented and sure. "Sharing my life with my husband and my children has been a blessing, even in the hardest of times. There isn't a day of your childhood I would trade for anything else in the world." She paused, then asked, "What greater thing could I have accomplished than you?"

Katie couldn't think of a reply.

Lark squeezed Katie's fingers. "What is it? What's troubling you?"

Katie shrugged as she pulled her hand free, then rose

and turned to look out the window above the worktable. Beyond the window she could see Drifter, the oldest of the Lazy L cow dogs, lying in a strip of shade. Inside the corral several horses milled around, snorting occasionally, their tails swatting at flies. It was a scene like dozens of others through the years. Just the sort of familiar day Ben liked best, this quiet sameness.

Oh, Ben.

"Katie?"

"I don't know," she finally answered. "I've just been thinking about you and Papa and everything. And me, I suppose. Wondering why I am the way I am."

"What way is that?"

"Different."

"It isn't that you're different, Katie. It's that you're special. You've tried to do what's right for you. And look at all you've accomplished in your short life. The people you've met. The places you've seen."

But Katie didn't feel as if she'd done anything of importance. She felt like a fraud. She felt as though the whole world were crumbling around her, and her confidence, her certainty in her own beliefs, were crumbling with it.

Her mother came to stand beside her, offering silent support by her nearness.

"I was never satisfied to be like other girls in Homestead. I was always going to make my mark on the world."

"And you are. You have."

"I was going to make a real difference. Change things." Her voice fell. "I was going to follow in the footsteps of Susan B. Anthony. Her creed was going to be my creed."

Lark put her arm around Katie's back, and Katie leaned her head on her mother's shoulder.

"But I'm not anything like Miss Anthony. I'm not as strong as she was."

"But you are, Katie. You're very strong. Why would you think you're not?"

"Because I can't do this alone," she whispered.

Her mother tightened her arm. "Needing others doesn't mean you're weak. And you're certainly not alone. Look at everyone who is helping you in your campaign. You have so many friends. Penny and Geoffrey and Sophia. And you have your father and me and your brothers. And, of course, you have your husband. Ben is always there for you."

But she didn't have Ben. She'd lost him days ago. The distance between them was as far and vast as the distance between Washington, D.C., and Homestead, Idaho. They might share those rooms at the Rafferty Hotel, they might work together during the day, but a great distance yawned between them all the same. He never touched her anymore, never tried to hold her hand, never kissed her. He even slept on the sofa in the parlor. The one thing they spoke to each other about was the campaign and then only when others were around. Otherwise they were silent, separate camps, each waiting for the election to be over, each waiting for the months to pass.

Each waiting for the baby to be born.

I'm going to have a baby, Mother. She wished she could say the words aloud. But she couldn't. Not yet. Not when she couldn't say it with the same joy that had been in her mother's voice when she'd talked about her own children.

Lark stared hard at her. "You know you can talk to me about anything, Katie. Anything at all."

"Yes." She nodded. "Yes, I know."

"I think you're just nervous about the elections. You'll feel better after next Tuesday has come and gone." She squeezed Katie again. "I'm very proud of you. Your father and I both are."

"Thanks." Katie forced a smile. "I guess I *am* nervous. And tired."

Her mother gave her one more squeeze, then went to check on the bread in the oven.

"It smells so good in here," Katie said, eager to think of something besides her own worries. "Nothing smells as good as baking bread."

Lark pulled the hot loaves from the oven. "Well, it won't be long before you'll have a kitchen of your own and can bake bread in your own oven. I hear Ben is almost ready to start building on that piece of land he bought."

So, he'd bought the land. He hadn't even waited until the primary was over. But then, last week had changed everything.

"Yancy says Ben's ordered the lumber and hired some men to begin digging the basement next week." Lark turned the pans over one at a time, letting the loaves fall onto a clean cloth on the worktable. "It's a shame you won't get to live in the place long before you go to Washington, but it will be here waiting for you when you get back."

No, she thought, it would be waiting for Ben. For Ben and the baby.

It wouldn't be waiting for her.

"Nothin' more you can do here, boss," Harvey Trent said as he reached for his hat. "You better git yourself a good night's rest. Next few days're gonna be hard ones for you and the missus."

Ben leaned back on his chair, rubbing his eyes with his knuckles. "Yeah, I know."

"I figure next week's edition will be all 'bout your wife's win in the primaries."

"Yeah."

"Don't you go worryin' none about it, neither. I can manage t'put one edition together by myself. You just send me what you want it t'say, an' I'll see that it's done right."

Ben nodded. "I wasn't worried. I've always known I could trust you, Harv."

"Well"—the typesetter pulled open the door—"good night, then, and good luck to the missus. See you tomorrow at the station."

"Good night."

Long after the door had closed behind Harvey Trent, Ben remained on his chair behind the desk. He was reluctant to return to the hotel. Reluctant for this night to pass.

Tomorrow they would be on the train to Boise, he and Katie, Geoffrey, Penelope, and Sophia. Tomorrow night Katie would address the Boise Chapter of the National Council of Women Voters. There would be a great deal of fanfare. All the reporters would be present. Ben would be expected to stand beside his wife and show his support. And on Tuesday the polls would open. On Tuesday Katie would win her place on the Republican ticket. Then would begin the plotting and planning, the making of final strategies for her ultimate win to the U.S. House of Representatives.

Ben didn't think he had the stomach for any of it.

He rose to his feet, dimmed the lights, then left the office, locking the door behind him. He walked slowly toward the hotel, enjoying the cool of the evening, feeling the promise of fall in the night air.

It seemed impossible that summer was already gone. It had still been spring when Katie had driven her flivver into Homestead, bursting into his office with grand schemes for a woman's column. If he'd told her "no" that night, how different things might have been now. If only he'd refused her. But refusing Katie had always been hard for him.

A lot could change in three months.

A lot *had* changed.

His footsteps slowed, and his gaze lifted to the windows of their hotel suite. The lights were on. Katie was there.

It was hell being near her now, wanting to touch her, hold her, kiss her, make love to her. But he couldn't. It was hell seeing the sadness in her eyes and wanting to make her smile again. But he couldn't. A line had been drawn, and he couldn't cross over it.

Spring. The baby would be born in the spring of the year. In April, when the crocuses flowered and the bare tree limbs began to bud. Spring, with its promise of new life, new beginnings. The new house would be furnished by then. There would be a nursery and a room for the housekeeper he would hire, a woman to watch over the baby as well as to cook and to clean.

Not exactly what he'd hoped for when he'd first decided to build the house. He'd wanted Katie to be there with him. But Katie wanted other things.

More than him.

More than their child.

Releasing a sigh, he entered the hotel lobby and headed up the stairs. When he reached the door to their suite, he paused before putting his key in the lock. He drew a slow, deep breath, preparing himself for that first glimpse of her of the day. He tried always to be up and gone before she awakened in the morning. It made things easier. But she was invariably still up when he returned at night. Sometimes he wondered if she did it just to torture him.

Smiling grimly at the thought, he opened the door and stepped inside. A quick glance revealed an empty parlor.

Perhaps he was to be lucky tonight. Perhaps she'd already retired. But the door to the bedchamber was open, the light still on.

Foolishly he moved toward it.

She was standing before the cheval glass in a gauzy white nightgown trimmed with lace and blue satin ribbons. The lamp on the nightstand behind her made the fabric nearly transparent. He could see the ripe swell of her breasts, the narrow dip of her waist, the roundness of her hips. The black waterfall of her hair flowed about her shoulders and down her back.

As if sensing him there, she turned and met his gaze across the room. Desire flared, hot and demanding, in his loins. It would have been so easy to go to her, to carry her to that bed, to divest her of that flimsy nightgown and make love to her. She would have let him. He could see it in her eyes.

Perhaps, if he made love to her throughout the night, she would forget about the train tomorrow. Perhaps he could make her a prisoner in that bed, keep her there with his kisses, his caresses, his body upon hers. She had always responded to him with passion. Perhaps he could make her forget everything else but him.

Katie's gaze fell away, and she stared at a spot on the floor, about halfway between them. "I'm all ready to leave tomorrow," she said softly, as if she'd sensed what he'd been thinking.

Yes, this must surely be hell, he thought. "So am I."

"Mr. Trent will get out the paper?"

"Yes."

"I'll call for your supper."

"Don't bother. I'll do it myself."

She turned her back toward him. "Then I'll go to bed. Tomorrow will be a full day."

"Yes. Good night, Katie."

He knew he should turn and leave, but he couldn't seem to do it. It was as if he wanted to torment himself a little longer, watching as she lifted the blankets and climbed into the four-poster where they'd made love so many times in the weeks since their wedding. In the bed where their child had probably been conceived.

The child Katie didn't want.

He turned and walked away.

From her apartment above the drugstore, Blanche had watched Ben Rafferty walk to the hotel. Now, a short while later, she saw the light dim in what she knew was the bedroom of his suite. *Their* suite. She shuddered at the thought of what could be happening in that room at this very moment.

How she hated and despised them both!

Blanche had tried her best to expose them for what they were. She knew Katie Jones wasn't fit to represent the women of Idaho. She was nothing but a cheap harlot, giving herself to that man rather than remaining true to her calling. And Blanche had told others. She had written letters. But no one paid her any heed.

It was that man's fault. If Ben Rafferty hadn't enticed her, perhaps Katie would have been the woman Blanche had expected her to be. It was his fault. Without him, Blanche might be able to help Katie back on the true path.

She turned from the window, bitterness filling her chest.

"It should have been me," she told the cat. "I tried to tell them, but they wouldn't listen." She sat on the chair and pulled the animal onto her lap. "It's his fault she doesn't listen to me. If she was rid of him, I could help her. Then she'd listen to me. Then I could prove to them all I was right."

Blanche's life seemed more terrible, more unbearable, than ever. School returned to session next week. She would be trapped in that hideous schoolroom with another bunch of unruly heathens.

Trapped. She was trapped. All her life she'd been trapped.

"It's their fault."

It was a merry-looking group on the train station platform the next day. The three young women were all dressed in their finest traveling attire, the two men in suits with vests. Family and friends were there to see them off and wish them well. There was a great deal of backslapping, good-natured joking, and laughter.

Katie hoped the train would leave soon. She feared someone would see through her masquerade and recognize the unhappiness beneath her carefully constructed facade. But no one did. Everyone expected her to be cheerful, and therefore that was what they saw. After all, everything she'd wanted, everything she and others had been working toward, was about to come true. How could she not be excited and happy?

"All aboard," the conductor cried, causing a flurry of activity as one last round of hugs were exchanged.

"We'll be praying for you, darling," Katie's mother promised.

"You've done your best, Katie," her father said, "no matter what happens on Tuesday. In the end, that's all that matters."

She nodded, not trusting herself to speak.

"Come on, Katie," Sophia called from the passenger car steps.

"Take care of her, Ben," Yancy added a bit gruffly.

Ben took hold of her arm. "I will."

Her heart fluttered. It was a simple act, the taking of her arm. The sort of thing husbands did all the time. Yet to Katie it was like a drenching rain after a long drought. She soaked up his touch and wished he might never let go.

But he did. The moment they were on the train and out of sight of their families, he released her.

"I'm going to the smoking car," he said. "Geoffrey, care to join me?"

Geoffrey looked a little surprised at leaving the ladies so soon but agreed to go along.

"Ben's awfully edgy lately," Sophia commented as the two men made their way to the back of the passenger car and through the doorway.

Penelope waved a fan in front of her face. "It's no wonder. He's been burning the candle at both ends. Working on Katie's campaign, writing all those articles, putting out the *Herald* every week, and now starting that new house." Her hand stilled as she looked at Katie. "I was at the paper when he showed the plans to Geoffrey. It's going to be a beautiful house. When you tire of your political life, you'll have such a wonderful place to come back to."

Katie smiled and nodded, unable to confess she hadn't seen the house plans. "Yes, when I tire of it."

A cloud of steam billowed up from the underside of the train, accompanied by a loud *hissss,* then the car jerked as the wheels were set in motion. Katie looked out the window at the people still standing on the platform. Her parents and grandparents. Leslie Blake. Reverend and Mrs. Jacobs. Tom and Fanny McLeod and their daughters. Harvey Trent. So many people to wish her well.

Her parents waved. Her grandmother blew her a kiss. She lifted her hand in return. *Bye,* she mouthed, and saw them all do the same.

"But, Sophia, that's wonderful!" Penelope exclaimed.

Katie turned from the window to see her two friends hugging. "What's wonderful?"

"Sophia has just decided she's definitely coming to Washington with me. Isn't it scrumptious? I was afraid I would have to share our place with a stranger, now that you're married. But now Sophia will be there with me."

"Scrumptious," Katie whispered, only half listening.

She remembered the evening she'd arrived back in Homestead. She remembered how Ben had looked, staring down at those papers on his desk, his brow creased in concentration. She remembered taking him outside to show him the Susan B. "Isn't she scrumptious?" she'd asked him, and he'd raised an eyebrow and replied, "Scrumptious."

It seemed such a very long time ago. Those two people in her memory seemed so young and carefree. Strangers to her now.

Maybe that's the problem, Katie. You still think I'm Benjie.

She looked out the window again. Already Homestead had disappeared from view. In another minute or two the train would carry them out of Long Bow Valley and into the mountain canyons, the tracks following the river on its way south toward the capital. She listened to the *clackity-clackity-clackity* of the turning wheels, wheels that were taking her swiftly away from home.

Swiftly, swiftly away.

In the past two months Katie had become an old hand at campaigning. She knew how to speak to the press. She knew how to smile at leering old gentlemen and how to look austere in the presence of prune-faced women. She knew when to kiss babies and had become adept at avoiding the sticky fingers of toddlers. She was as comfortable talking to a large group as to a single voter. She was used to seeing her photograph in newspapers, grainy reproductions that looked little as she pictured herself.

Thus Katie wasn't nervous when she addressed the assembled hundred or so women—and a few brave men—in downtown Boise's Carnegie Hall that night. She'd written her speech weeks ago and knew the words by heart. No one guessed she wasn't thinking about suffrage or other issues of concern to women. She smiled and pretended an enthusiasm for her topic that she wasn't feeling. Judging by the rousing applause she received at the close of her talk, she had fooled them all, even those who knew her best.

Before other members of the audience could get to her, Penelope was at Katie's side, whispering, "You were wonderful, as always. Congratulations."

"Mrs. Rafferty, you are an inspiration," gushed the president of the local chapter of the National Council of Women Voters as she arrived at the podium. "You're so knowledgeable, so composed."

"Thank you."

"The Republicans couldn't select a better person than you to run for Congress, Mrs. Rafferty," the chapter's secretary proclaimed as she pumped Katie's hand.

"You're very kind."

Her eyes scanned the crowd, but she couldn't find Ben. She'd seen him at the back of the hall when the meeting had begun. He wasn't there now.

Apparently understanding, Penelope leaned forward and told her softly, "He said he had work to do back at the hotel."

From the beginning of her campaign, Ben hadn't missed a single speech or a single meeting with the press. For over two months he'd been beside her, every step of the way, encouraging her with a glance or a smile or a gesture. But he wasn't there now.

Katie forced herself to keep smiling, to keep saying words of thanks when she was complimented, to keep shaking hands and nodding and answering questions. But she felt no joy when others told her she was certain to win in next week's primary, certain to be elected to Congress in November. That was what she'd worked toward all summer. She should have been happy. It was what she'd wanted.

Wasn't it?

An eternity later Geoffrey escorted the three women back to the hotel. Sophia and Penelope, leading the way, carried on a lively conversation about Sophia's impending move to Washington, D.C.

"I do believe Ben's sister may one day run for Congress herself," Geoffrey said to Katie.

"Sophia?"

"You've been an enormous influence on her."

He'd meant it as a compliment, of course, but Katie wasn't sure she was fit to influence anyone. She'd made such a mess of things.

"Have you watched the way she handles the press?" Geoffrey continued. "She's nearly as adept as you are."

Katie cocked her head to one side as she looked at him. "Do I hear a note of affection in your voice?"

He grinned. "You do indeed."

"And Sophia?"

"A bit gun-shy yet, but I think she's coming around."

She squeezed his arm. "I'm glad for you both. Sophia's a lucky girl."

"I'll be the lucky one if she ever returns my feelings."

Sadness washed over Katie, tightening her throat. Not so very long ago she'd heard that same sort of love in Ben's voice. Now he scarcely spoke to her.

Geoffrey's smile faded. "You look tired, Katie."

She shook her head, then shrugged.

"What do you say we forget the campaign completely for a change? We could take the streetcar out to the warm springs tomorrow afternoon. I hear the Natatorium pool is spectacular. And maybe we could take in the theater in the evening."

Katie remembered the last time she and Ben had been for a swim. She remembered the sound of his laughter as he'd chased her into the water, recalled the passion that had flared between them, right there in the middle of the cold-running river.

Would she ever again hear him laugh like that? Would they ever again share that sort of passion?

"Get a good night's sleep tonight, Katie," Geoffrey encouraged as they climbed the steps to the hotel entrance.

"I will," she promised. But she knew she wouldn't. Not with Ben so close to her and yet so far away.

Ben had watched Katie and the others approach the hotel from the window of their third-floor room. Even in the darkness, even from this distance, he'd seen the moonlit sheen in her ebony hair. He'd seen the gentle sway in her walk. He'd seen the way her dress fit her trim figure and wondered how long it would be before her pregnancy showed.

He remained at the window long after the foursome disappeared from view, staring down at the wide street below. He didn't even turn when he heard the door open behind him. "You got a warm reception tonight," he said as Katie entered the bedroom.

"Yes."

"Mr. Elliott is ready to concede before the election

even begins." Unable to refrain any longer, he glanced over his shoulder. "I met him in the bar this evening. Says he'll support the entire Republican ticket, no matter who wins."

"Oh?" She removed her hat and laid it on the bureau.

"I also saw Mr. French. You remember. He's the candidate from Moscow. Good man, but I believe you have a chance of defeating him. So does he, I think."

"Ben?"

"Yes?"

"I"—she seemed to be struggling with words—"I'm sorry it's all turned out the way it has."

It nearly killed him to see her look so sad. He longed to hold and comfort her. But he couldn't. Katie was going to have to decide for herself what she wanted, what meant the most to her. He'd given all he could without her giving some back. If she didn't love him . . .

"I'm sorry I didn't tell you about my visit to Dr. Tom," she added softly. "It was wrong of me to keep it from you."

He turned back to the window. Yes, it had been wrong. Yes, it had hurt him, knowing she hadn't wanted his baby, didn't want the one she was carrying now. The knowledge left a bitter taste in his mouth. But he could have forgiven her even that had she only loved him.

He heard her sigh, heard the creak of the bedsprings.

"I'm sorry," she whispered. "So very sorry."

He knew she was crying by the sound of her voice.

Anger, his only defense against her tears, sprang to life. "What do you want from me, Katie?" He turned, pinioned her with a hard gaze where she sat on the bed. "I'm a man, not some faithful childhood companion you turn to when you need cheering up. I wanted a woman to share my life with. To share *everything* with, the good and the bad. I wanted someone I could talk to, someone who would listen and respond. I never expected you to be some docile homemaker with nothing more on your mind than what to fix for supper. I only wanted you to love me. To think of *us* instead of just *you*."

Tears streaked down her cheeks, but she didn't look away from him.

He took a step toward her. "I did hope you would discover Homestead was where you wanted to be. And I hoped you would welcome a pregnancy with joy instead of thinking it an inconvenience. I even hoped you would lose the election." He cursed as he raked his fingers through his hair. "But we could have overcome all that. We could've found a way to make it work, Katie, if you'd only tried to meet me halfway."

"I'm sorry," she whispered again.

The fight drained from him. "I don't want your apologies." He reached for his hat. "I'm going out." Then he headed for the door before he weakened and tried to kiss away her sorrows.

24

The Idaho Daily Statesman, *Boise, Idaho*
Wednesday Morning, September 6, 1916
SMITH HAS BIG LEAD FOR CONGRESS,
FRENCH AND RAFFERTY IN CLOSE RACE
At 4 o'clock Wednesday morning scattering returns
from 233 of the 742 precincts located in 31 of the 37
counties of the state practically assured the nomination
of the following Republicans for the November election:
For Congress—Representative Addison T. Smith of Twin
Falls and Katherine Jones Rafferty of Homestead.
For governor—D. W. Davis of American Falls.
For lieutenant governor . . .

"By Jove!" Geoffrey exclaimed as he looked up from the newspaper. "You've actually done it, Katie."

She tried to smile, just as she was expected to do. "I only lead Mr. French by seven hundred votes. I could still lose."

"Perish the thought!" Penelope interjected.

Perish the thought? Katie wasn't so sure.

She glanced across the restaurant table at Ben, but his expression was as closed to her as ever. Two weeks of pretending had made them both experts at deception.

"Whoa! Listen to this." Geoffrey cleared his throat as he began reading from the paper again. "Headline: 'Women Make War on President Wilson, National Chairman of Woman's Party Says Western Women Voters Are Opposing Democratic Leaders. Chicago—Miss Anne Martin, national chairman of the Woman's party, issued a statement here Tuesday in which she said: "Feeling against President Wilson for his continued opposition to the national suffrage amendment is steadily growing among women voters. In California, members of the Democratic and Progressive leaders have joined the Woman's party in their fight against the president. The state will be carried by a united Republican and Progressive vote against President Wilson."'" He let out a long, low whistle. "Pity poor Mr. Wilson. All those angry women."

Penelope harrumphed. "Pity him indeed. Perhaps now he'll stop mouthing support and actually do something."

"Katie will see to that once she's sworn into office," Sophia added with confidence.

"I should say she will," Penelope concurred.

Will I? Katie forced another smile and nodded, then rose from her chair. "I think I'd like some air."

"We'll come with you." Geoffrey said, starting to rise, too.

"No. I'd like to be alone for a while."

Penelope frowned. "Are you sure?"

"I'm sure. You stay and enjoy your breakfast. I won't be long."

She left the restaurant, stepping outside into the bright morning sunshine. The streets of Boise were bustling. Wagons, buggies, streetcars, and automobiles vied with each other for space. Men in business suits and farmers in coveralls passed each other on the sidewalks. Women in oversize hats chatted near the doorways of dress shops. Boys in short pants and girls in short skirts chased hoops down a side street. A pack of scroungy mongrels fought over scraps of food in an alley outside a restaurant.

So many people. So much activity. So much noise. Boise City seemed a major metropolis to Katie after a summer in Homestead. But Idaho's capital city was a mere speck on the map in comparison with Washington, D.C., and she knew it. She'd loved the big cities back east once. Would she love them again?

She walked all the way to the front steps of the Capitol building without stopping. Once there, she stared at the imposing stone structure.

I only wanted you to love me. To think of us instead of just you. Ben's words haunted her now, just as they'd haunted her for the past four days. *We could've found a way to make it work, Katie, if you'd only tried to meet me halfway.*

She wanted to meet him halfway. She wanted to love him. But she'd sworn to serve the suffrage cause. Weren't the needs of others more important than her own wants and wishes?

"Spectacular building, isn't it?"

Startled from her reverie, Katie looked at the man who'd spoken to her.

"My apologies, Mrs. Rafferty." He doffed his hat. "Do you remember me? I'm Burton French."

"Of course. My worthy opponent from Moscow."

He smiled. "Yes."

She offered her hand, and he took it. His handshake was firm and honest. "It's a pleasure to see you again, sir."

"I've been following your campaign ever since I attended the rally in Homestead last June. Looks like the voters have been following you, too."

She glanced back at the Capitol. "Have you always been interested in politics, Mr. French?"

"Not always."

"But you knew this was the right time to become involved. You wanted to win this election a great deal?"

"Yes. But no more than you, I suspect."

She glanced at him again. He was a distinguished-looking, middle-aged fellow. He appeared the sort of man who smiled often. She thought she might have liked him, had they the time to get better acquainted.

"Are you married, Mr. French?"

"For twenty years."

"And do you have children?"

"Five. Three daughters and two sons. Our oldest daughter is married. The rest are still at home."

For a moment she thought of that plot of ground near Pony Creek and the house Ben was building there. The *home* Ben was building there.

"They're going to be disappointed," Mr. French continued. "About not moving to Washington, I mean. The entire family's been involved in my campaign from the beginning. Great little team, I'll tell you. I'm proud of them all."

Katie nodded. "I've had a lot of help, too."

"I spoke with your husband the other night. I imagine he's been a great source of support to you."

"Yes." She remembered the countless hours Ben had devoted to her campaign, all because he loved her. Abruptly she changed the subject. "How do you feel about the national suffrage amendment, Mr. French? Do you favor it?"

"I didn't at first," he answered with a note of honesty.

"It took my wife some hard talking to convince me of its merits. But Mrs. French has a way of showing me when I'm in the wrong. It was reminding me what could happen to our daughters that finally made the difference."

"How was that?"

He removed his hat and scratched his head before replying, "The girls are growing up fast. Before I know it, they'll all be married and gone from the nest. What if their husbands aren't from an enfranchised state? If they moved there, my girls would lose the right to vote, a right I've taught them is important. I don't want that to happen. And if it's left up to each state, that's what *could* happen."

"Then you would fight for the national amendment if you were elected?"

"That's what I'm saying."

"I'm glad to hear it."

"Are you afraid there'll be some sort of upset when the last ballots are counted?" He released a soft chuckle. "You needn't worry. My wife's already told me we can pack our bags and go home. She's certain you've won, and Mrs. French is rarely wrong."

Katie offered her hand once again. "Nonetheless, I wish you good luck, Mr. French."

"And the same to you, ma'am."

She bade him good day, then started back toward the hotel, pondering the chance encounter and wondering why she felt as if something were about to change because of it. What could it possibly change? She was almost guaranteed to have won a place in the primaries.

And she and Ben were still estranged.

The Idaho Daily Statesman, *Boise, Idaho*
Thursday Morning, September 7, 1916

FRENCH AND RAFFERTY RACE UNDECIDED AS COUNT DRAGS

With complete returns in from 375 of the most populous precincts in both the northern and southern parts of the state, the results of the Republican primaries confirm the forecasts made in Wednesday morning's Statesman *as to the Republican state ticket. Wednesday night's returns account for about 29,300 votes, which is held to be more than three-fourths of the total ballots.*

One place on the ticket is still in doubt. In the contest for the second of the two at-large congressional seats, Katherine Jones Rafferty has 12,678 votes to her credit, and Burton L. French has 12,084. This close race, with a difference of only 594 votes between the two candidates, will probably have to wait for an official count for a decision.

After six days in Boise City, one thing was undeniably clear to Ben: He would never be able to carry off this farce until the baby was born in the spring. It was too hard to pretend whenever others were around and even harder to be alone with Katie. He would never be able to continue feigning happiness and contentment for the rest of the campaign. He wouldn't be able to go to Washington and make believe there was nothing amiss in their marriage.

Marriage? They didn't have a marriage. They were two miserable people sharing a hotel room. That was all.

He wondered when he would stop loving her. When would the hope die completely? When would he look at her and be able to think fondly on the past without wishing for more?

Ben spared a glance at the others around the breakfast table. They were gathered once again in the hotel dining room, the five of them. As usual, Sophia and Penelope were talking about Sophia's move to Washington, and as usual, Geoffrey was observing Sophia with an affectionate gaze. Katie wasn't participating in the conversation. She was turned toward the window, staring into space, obviously lost in thought, just as Ben had been moments before.

His chest tightened at the sight of her, so lovely in the golden sunlight spilling through the windows. She was wearing a white toque decorated with several osprey feathers. It wasn't a particularly pretty hat, yet on Katie it took on a beauty of its own. Her dress was also white, the simple tubular skirt elaborately swathed in extra fabric around the legs and draped vertically down the back with a black satin scarf.

Katie looked sophisticated, every inch the height of current fashion, a woman suited to be a candidate for Congress. But Ben couldn't help wishing she were wearing bright pink cycling bloomers instead.

He smiled to himself, remembering how shocked Matthew and Sophia had been the day Katie had shown up in such an outfit. They'd thought her outrageous. So had he, for that matter. And he'd loved her for her very outrageousness. Lord, how he missed that lighthearted Katie. She'd become so serious since entering this race for the Congress.

Or maybe—his own smile faded—it was marrying him that had made her so serious, caused her to forget how to laugh. Maybe he was at fault for all her unhappiness. Maybe once they were apart, her sparkle would come back.

Dearest Katie. Wonderful, madcap Katie. What's happened to you? What's happened to us?

"Good Lord!" Geoffrey exclaimed as he jumped up from his chair, drawing all eyes to him. "It's Mother!" Their gazes swung toward the entrance of the dining room as Geoffrey hurried forward. "Mother, we weren't expecting you. How did you get here?"

Eugenia Rudyard was a buxom, imposing woman of uncertain years. Her manner of dress was stylish but understated—except for the enormous hat crowning her head. "I came by train, of course," she said in a deep, rich voice as she approached the table, using her closed parasol like a cane. "And don't look so surprised, my boy. I've traveled many places without you, you know." She winked at him, then looked at each person seated around the table. Finally she dropped a kiss on Penelope's cheek. "Hello, dear one." Then she kissed Katie in the same manner. "You've been busy, my girl."

Katie nodded. "I know."

Eugenia glanced back at her son expectantly.

On cue he began, "Mother, may I introduce Katie's husband, Ben Rafferty?"

Ben had already risen from his chair, and he took Eugenia Rudyard's proffered hand, bowing over it. "How do you do, Mrs. Rudyard?"

"Quite well, thank you." The older woman seemed to look at him with approval. "It's a pleasure to meet you at last, Mr. Rafferty. I've heard your name from Katie often these many years."

"Likewise, madam."

"And this is Ben's sister, Sophia Rafferty," Geoffrey continued, his tone softening almost imperceptibly.

Eugenia smiled. "Geoffrey and Penny have both mentioned you to me, dear girl, and I expect we shall get on together famously."

"Thank you, Mrs. Rudyard. This is an honor."

"Sit down, Mother," Penelope urged, "and tell us why you've come here instead of attending the convention in Atlantic City."

"I'd much rather be here with Katie than listening to

Mr. Wilson spout his support for suffrage while refusing to do anything concrete to bring it about." She settled onto the chair Ben pulled out for her. "And I understand a celebration will soon be in order."

Katie lifted her shoulders. "It's not decided yet. I could still lose." Her glance flicked toward Ben, then away before he could read the thoughts behind them.

And suddenly he longed to be able to read Katie's mind, just as he'd been able to do not so very long ago.

The Idaho Daily Statesman, *Boise, Idaho*
Friday Morning, September 8, 1916
PRIMARY AFTERMATHS
An official count of the vote cast in the recent primary election will be made within the next 10 or 12 days at the secretary of state's office. The vote must be canvassed within 15 days after election, but the board may begin its work within 10 days if it wishes.

As the train rushed north toward Homestead, Katie stared out the window, lost in thought.

She recognized the spot where the Susan B had broken down. She remembered the night she'd spent in Ben's embrace, the way he'd touched her and made her come alive. At the time, she thought she'd only want one night. She'd been wrong.

She recognized the place where they'd gone for a swim and he'd made love to her in the middle of the river. She'd thought the passion between them would be enough. She'd thought she could keep the love she felt for him to herself. She'd been wrong about that, too.

"Katie, my girl, we need to talk."

She turned to look at Eugenia Rudyard, seated across from her in the near empty passenger car. Ben had retreated to the smoking car before they'd pulled out of

Boise. The others in their party had now disappeared, too, and Katie suspected Eugenia had sent them away.

"You aren't happy about this election, are you?" the older woman asked.

She'd managed to keep up the pretense for days, but there was something about the way Eugenia was looking at her that knocked down her defenses. "I don't think I want to win." Ashamed of herself for admitting it, she quickly looked out the window again.

"And why not, pray tell?"

Instead of answering the question, Katie whispered, "I should want to. I know I should want to."

Eugenia took hold of Katie's hand. "But you don't."

She shook her head, keeping her eyes averted. They were nearing Homestead. They would leave the river canyon soon and enter Long Bow Valley. They were almost home.

Home. She longed to be home.

"*Why* should you want to be elected, Katie?"

She blinked away sudden tears. "I owe it to all the people who have supported me. I owe it to other women. I owe it to you and Penny and Geoffrey."

Eugenia's grasp tightened. "And what do you owe to yourself?"

She met the older woman's gentle gaze once again, not knowing how to answer.

"It's no crime to love your husband, my girl. In fact, it's preferable."

"I never meant to marry. I was going to remain single, like Miss Anthony. I was going to serve the cause with everything in me. I was going to be so devoted, so . . ." She shook her head, unable to continue as another wave of tears overtook her.

"Oh, my dear," Eugenia crooned softly as she cupped Katie's chin in her glove-covered fingers. "I know how much you've admired Miss Anthony. I admired her, too. I was privileged to know her for many years, and she was a remarkable woman. But she was the first to recognize not everyone was meant to be like her. We each have to do our part in our own way."

Katie swallowed the hot lump in her throat. "But I was always so sure what I was supposed to do."

Eugenia's hand fell from Katie's chin as she turned her gaze out the window, just as Katie had done before, and she sighed softly. "I have long been a supporter of woman's suffrage. I have always believed in the perfect equality of women. And so did my dear husband." She looked at Katie again. "When Mr. Rudyard was alive, we worked together for the cause of suffrage without ever leaving Massachusetts, and we were no less important than those who traveled far and wide."

Katie felt a flutter of hope, a feeling she hadn't known in weeks. But still she asked, "What about my supporters? They've counted on me. They'll be disappointed."

"Since you respect her so much, Katie, allow me to quote Miss Anthony to you." Eugenia's voice deepened as she continued. "'Every woman in her own home can be a teacher of this great principle of equality. She can instruct her husband and her children in the ways of justice toward all. But for the good and true women in all the homes, but for the loyalty of these home women, who never speak in public, but who in a quiet way are teaching this gospel in season and out of season, we who stand at the front, could never have stood here. We would have had no constituency but for this silent, magnificent army of women in the homes throughout the nation.'" Eugenia drew a deep breath, then asked Katie, "What good is the freedom to choose what is right for ourselves if we fail to exercise that freedom? Isn't it possible your calling is closer to home, my dear? And if it is, that's where you should be."

Katie's heart was racing faster than the wheels on the locomotive. It wasn't merely what Eugenia had just said. It was what all the people who loved her had been saying in various ways for weeks.

What greater thing could I have accomplished than you?

We could've found a way to make it work, Katie, if you'd only tried to meet me halfway.

Sometimes life makes us choose betwixt two things . . . Times like those, kitten, it's most often better t'follow your heart instead of your head.

Maybe that's the problem, Katie. You still think I'm Benjie. Well, I'm not. I haven't been Benjie for a long time.

Do you love him?

I never expected you to be some docile homemaker with nothing more on your mind than what to fix for supper. I only wanted you to love me.

I only wanted you to love me. . . .

At last she understood what her heart had been trying to tell her for so long. Eugenia was right. What good was the freedom to choose if she failed to exercise that freedom? It *was* possible her calling was closer to home. Other women did it. She didn't have to model her life after Miss Anthony. She could make a difference in her own way.

And her home was with Ben. Ben and their baby. She wanted them both.

Katie stood suddenly. Ben. She had to find Ben.

The train whistle blew. From the back of the passenger car, the conductor shouted, "Comin' into Homestead, folks."

She knew what she wanted, knew what she'd always

wanted, if only she hadn't been too stubborn to see. She had to find Ben and tell him she knew what mattered most. She had to tell him she was ready to come home.

She had to tell Ben she loved him.

25

It looked as if there were few doubters left in Homestead. Even Phillip Carson was at the station to congratulate Katie on her apparent win in the primary. The town band played with enthusiasm as the passengers disembarked from the train, and a rousing cheer went up when Katie appeared on the steps of the main passenger car.

From the caboose, Ben watched as his wife was swept into the crowd of celebrants. He knew he should probably make his way to her, stand beside her, return smiles and handshakes along with her. But he couldn't. Let Mrs. Rudyard and the other committee members help her. He couldn't do it anymore. He was through.

Unnoticed, he stepped to the ground and followed the tracks back to Barber Street, then walked toward the newspaper office. He'd caught a glimpse of Harvey Trent on the station platform. He knew he'd have the office to himself, at least for a while.

Homestead looked like a ghost town. Signs were up in

nearly all the shop windows on Main Street: "Closed." The proprietors and their customers were all at the depot, welcoming home a triumphant daughter of the town.

Good for Katie. He was glad for her. She would have all their support during the coming weeks. She wouldn't even miss him. Geoffrey knew as much as he, and probably more, about running a campaign. Penelope and Sophia were tireless workers and full of enthusiasm for the cause. And now Katie would have Eugenia Rudyard, a woman with vast experience in political circles, to help her. No, Katie wouldn't miss him.

He fished in his pocket for the key to the office, then unlocked the door and entered. He hung his hat on the rack before walking to his desk, where he rifled through the stacks of paper awaiting his attention. Nothing urgent. Nothing of interest. Nothing to take his mind off Katie.

"Hell," he muttered as he sank onto the chair.

A separation from her husband might harm Katie's election chances. That would be one way of keeping her in Homestead, he supposed, but it wasn't the way he wanted to keep her there. She had to want to stay—and she didn't. Katie had bigger fish to fry.

No, he would have to go on sleeping on the sofa in the parlor of their hotel suite whenever Katie was in Homestead. But her campaign would keep her on the road often over the next nine weeks. Ben could use the *Herald* as his reason for not accompanying her on the trips. The others on the committee would suspect something was amiss between them, if they didn't already, but it would be up to Katie to explain.

He cursed softly as he got up from the chair. Why didn't he feel better, now the decision was made? Why couldn't he at least feel angry instead of just empty?

He paced to the window and looked out at the deserted street. The days had grown shorter as summer ended and fall began, and afternoon shadows were already long. Out in the valley farmers were busy harvesting their crops. By the end of next month they could conceivably see their first snow of the winter. Before Thanksgiving Katie would leave for Washington. Would her pregnancy be showing by then? Would he be able to look at her and see that their child was growing in her womb?

He cursed again as he headed out the door, not bothering to lock up behind him. Long strides carried him toward Pony Creek, then away from town with the unconscious hope he could walk away from the trouble in his heart, something he'd been trying—and failing—to do for weeks now.

It seemed a lifetime before Katie had the opportunity to escape the crowd of well-wishers. Protesting weariness, she went first to the hotel, but Ben wasn't in their rooms. So she slipped down the back staircase and out through the kitchen door, hoping to avoid seeing anyone else. She had to talk to Ben. It was too urgent to wait. She had to see him and tell him what she'd discovered on the train.

The door to the newspaper was ajar. Katie stepped inside, her heart pounding. "Ben?"

He didn't answer, but he had to be there. His hat was hanging on the rack.

She moved toward the back room. "Ben?"

But he wasn't there, either. The windowless room stood silent and empty except for the printing press, a large table, and stacks of newspapers.

She'd just wondered if he might have gone out back to use the privy when she heard the front door open and

close. She turned and hurried toward the front office
again.

"Ben, I've been looking for—" She stopped when she
saw who was standing there. "Blanche." Disappointment
was evident in her voice. "It's you."

"You must be quite proud of yourself, Katie, now that
you've won." The schoolmarm sounded shrill, her words
echoing in the small office.

"More surprised than anything, I think." Katie glanced
out the window, impatient to find Ben. "Have you seen
my husband? I was just looking for him. We got separated at the station and—"

"They don't know how you betrayed them." Blanche
took a step forward, swinging her small black handbag in
front of her by its purse strings, her movements agitated,
disconnected.

Katie frowned, confused by the comment. "Whom did
I betray?"

"Playing the harlot. That's what you've done. You
pulled the wool over their eyes, but not mine. Not mine, I
tell you."

Katie stiffened. She'd heard this babble from Blanche
Coleson before. She didn't intend to listen to it again.
"Perhaps you should leave now."

"How long will you continue to lie to them, pretending
to be what you're not?" Blanche moved toward her,
shouting now. "Like a bitch in heat! Harlot!" She swung
her handbag, striking Katie on the shoulder before she
could move. "Liar!"

Katie raised her arms to protect herself. "Blanche,
what are you doing? Stop it!"

"I won't let you lie to them. I won't let you. They
didn't believe me when I told them. They ignored me."
She swung her handbag again, this time missing her mark
as Katie ducked. "They ignored me."

A sudden chill gripped Katie as she continued backing away. There was something eerie about the other woman's eyes that struck terror in her heart. She suspected Blanche wouldn't hear anything she said, but she had to try. With a note of calm she didn't feel, she said, "Why don't we go over to Zoe's and talk about it, Blanche? I'm sure we can straighten this out. It's just a misunderstanding." She tried to move toward the door, but Blanche blocked her way.

"I won't let you do this, Katie Jones. And I won't let them ignore me." She raised her handbag again.

Katie was certain she could outrun the schoolmarm if she could just make it to the door. She inched her way toward the press room, thinking the back door might be easiest. Blanche followed, continuing to mutter and mumble and sometimes shout words of accusation and complaint. Katie knew she was trapped in that building with a madwoman, and her fear increased with each step she took.

"I'm going to stop you," Blanche threatened darkly. "I'm going to stop you both."

Suddenly Katie stumbled over a stack of newspapers on the floor. She fell backward, caught herself, twisted around, and started to rise. But before she could get up, something much harder than a woman's handbag cracked against her skull.

Pain exploded.

And then there was nothing but darkness.

Ben slowly made his way back toward town, his thoughts no more settled now than when he'd left the newspaper office. The walk had failed to make his decision about ending his marriage any easier to live with.

If only he didn't love Katie so much. If only he didn't

continue to want to hold her, to hear her laugh, to see the sparkle in her eyes of brown.

He was almost to Main Street when he heard the clanging of the church bell. Startled by the sound, unusual on a weekday, he quickened his pace. Then he saw black smoke billowing out of the roof and windows of the *Homestead Herald*. He broke into a run. He'd nearly reached the building when Blanche Coleson, coughing and choking, stumbled through the doorway.

He heard sounds of the approaching fire wagon but didn't look to see how close it was. He grabbed Blanche by the arm and pulled her off the sidewalk and into the street.

"What happened?" he shouted at her, his glance darting to the building, where he could see orange flames licking at the walls of the front office.

"You did it. You did it. It should have been me they listened to. It's your fault."

His gaze returned to the woman who was struggling to get loose, striking him with her free arm. There was a wild, crazed look in her eyes.

"You should be in there with her!" Blanche shrieked. "Why aren't you in there with her?"

Alarm tightened his belly as he gripped both of her arms in his hands, yanking her toward him. "Who? Is someone inside? Who is it?"

Blanche laughed hysterically.

"Oh, my God," he whispered, suddenly knowing the answer. Then he shoved the schoolmarm away from him and bolted for the burning building. Someone shouted at him to stay back, but he didn't heed the warning. Holding up an arm to protect his face from the heat and smoke, he rushed inside. "Katie!"

Panic made every second agony as he tried to find his wife amid the dense smoke and flickering tongues of fire that filled the front office.

"Katie!"

God, help me. Covering his mouth and nose with his hand, he pushed forward, continuing to pray. *Please, God, don't let me be too late. Help me find her. Help me.*

As if in answer to his prayers, he tripped over Katie's feet. She was lying half-hidden beneath the printing press. He knelt beside her inert form. "Katie." *God, please.* "Katie, I'm here."

He scooped her into his arms and carried her toward the back of the building, moving blindly through the thick smoke. When he found the back door, he didn't waste time trying to unlock it. He simply kicked it with every ounce of strength he had. The sounds of splintering wood could be heard above the crackling of the fire, the shouts of men, and the hiss of steam as water from the fire truck hit the flames.

Once out into the daylight, Ben looked down at Katie. Her eyes remained closed. Her face was blackened by smoke, and there was an ugly matting of blood and hair on the side of her head. She lay as still as death in his arms.

"Don't leave me, Katie. Please don't leave me."

Her lungs hurt. Her throat hurt. Her head hurt. Everything hurt.

"I think she's waking up again," someone said.

She should know that voice, but she couldn't place it.

"Open your eyes, Katie. Look at us."

Her eyelids felt like sandpaper.

"That's it. Open your eyes."

Everything appeared fuzzy, and the lamplight hurt. She blinked. Once. Then twice more. Her vision began to clear, and she made out Tom McLeod's face hovering above her. Beside him stood his wife, Fanny.

He smiled. "Welcome back. Think you'll stay with us this time?"

"Dr. Tom, what—" She was overtaken by a fit of coughing. Her throat felt raw, as if she'd swallowed lye soap. When she tried to sit up, pain exploded behind her eyes.

The doctor put his hand on her shoulder to keep her down. "Easy now. That's what happened last time. Give yourself a minute or two."

"Last time?" She closed her eyes again, then took a deep breath and let it out.

"You've had a nasty blow to the head, Katie. You woke up once before but passed out again. Do you remember what happened to you?"

Her mind remained blank. She couldn't recall anything beyond a moment ago. It was a terrifying feeling to have no memory.

"Relax, Katie. Give it time."

They'd been in Boise. She remembered that. The election. It looked as though she'd won the election. They'd come back on the train. When? When had they come back? Today? Was it still today? She'd been looking for someone. Ben. She'd been looking for Ben. She'd gone to the newspaper office to talk to Ben.

And then she remembered. "Blanche." She looked at the doctor. "It was Blanche."

He nodded. "Sheriff's got her over at the jail. She won't hurt anyone again."

"She tried to kill me?" Katie whispered the question, as if doing so would keep the words from being true.

"Looks that way."

She remembered the crazed way the schoolmarm had been talking. She remembered Blanche saying she was going to stop them. Stop them both. Fresh panic ignited as she grabbed the doctor's arm. "Where's Ben?"

"It's all right, Katie. He's the one who saved you. He didn't move from your side until after you came to last time. Sat here for hours."

Her throat tightened as she fought hot tears.

"I finally told him he had to get some air and some rest or I was going to lock him out of my clinic."

"I need to see Ben, Dr. Tom." She tried to rise a second time.

He eased her back on the bed. "He'll be back before long, I'm sure. You just rest easy. You're going to have a terrible headache as it is for quite some spell."

"What about the baby?" She covered her stomach with both hands. "Was the baby harmed?"

His expression grew serious. "I can't say for certain, Katie. Your body suffered a serious shock. You don't seem to be in danger of miscarrying. I'd say chances are good everything will be all right." He patted her shoulder. "I've done what I can. We'll have to leave the rest in God's hands."

She closed her eyes. *Don't let me lose Ben's baby. Please.*

"You rest now, Katie. Someone will be here if you need anything."

"I need Ben," she whispered, too softly for the doctor to hear.

A full moon shed a silvery white illumination over the land. Lamplight twinkled from the windows of houses in town and from farmhouses sprinkled across the valley.

Ben looked down at the picture-perfect setting, then turned his back on it and stared at the building site. The workmen had already erected the frame. With a little imagination he could see each room of the house he'd planned to build there.

But it meant nothing without Katie. In one horrible moment that afternoon, he'd discovered—almost too late—that what he wanted was meaningless without Katie. He didn't know what he would have to do. He didn't care what he would have to sacrifice. He loved her too much to risk losing her.

Those long hours, sitting beside her in Dr. Tom's clinic, had been the worst hours of his life. She'd looked so pale, so small and helpless. She hadn't moved, had barely breathed. He guessed the good Lord hadn't heard as much from Ben in the whole rest of his life as He'd heard from him in the last few hours.

Ben would never forget that terrifyingly wonderful moment when Katie's eyes had fluttered open, when she'd looked at him, her eyes glazed. She'd tried to sit up, then had slumped back on the bed. Dr. Tom had thrown Ben out of the clinic not long after that, telling him Katie was going to be fine. She wasn't in a coma. She was just sleeping.

He'd started to go to the hotel but had ended up here instead. And he knew why. He was going to tear it down. This wouldn't be a home if Katie wasn't in it. He'd promised God a lot of things during those hours beside Katie's bed. Now he was going to keep one of them.

He picked up a shovel and placed it over his shoulder. An ax would have done the job faster, but he wasn't going back to town for one. The shovel would have to do. He chose a stud, then readied for his first swing. But he was stopped by the sound of an approaching horse and buggy. With a soft curse he turned around and watched the buggy climb the gentle slope, unable to tell who had sought him out here in the middle of the night.

Nothing could have surprised him more than seeing Katie, the white bandage on her head gleaming in the moonlight, step out of the buggy once it was stopped.

The shovel dropped with a clatter as he took off toward her. Seconds later he was cradling her in his arms.

"This is crazy," he whispered near her ear. "What are you doing here?"

"I made Sophia bring me."

He tossed a censuring look in his sister's direction without relaxing his hold on Katie.

"Don't be angry with her. If she hadn't brought me, I'd have come by myself. She knew I meant it."

He tightened his arms, drawing her even closer. "I can't believe Dr. Tom let you do this."

"He didn't." She pulled her head back from his chest and looked up at him. "He wasn't there. I snuck out."

"Well, I'm taking you right back to the clinic," Ben said gruffly.

Katie shook her head. "Not yet. Please." She touched his forehead with her fingertips. "Soot," she whispered. "Sophia told me about the fire. The newspaper. Everything you've worked for. I'm so sorry."

Funny, he hadn't thought about the paper. He didn't even know if anything had been saved or if it had all burned to the ground. It hadn't mattered to him while he was sitting beside Katie's bed, praying for her to survive.

"Katie, there's something you need to know. I'm going with you to—"

She placed her index finger over his mouth. "Shh. Don't say anything. Not yet." She glanced toward the skeleton of the house. "Take me over there, Ben."

Why was it always so difficult for him to say "no" to Katie?

Gently he lifted her in his arms. She locked her hands behind his neck as he strode toward the house site. He carried her through what would have been the front door and over to the wooden staircase leading to what would have been the second floor. Then he sat down on a step, still holding her in his arms. If he had his way, he would never let go of her again.

And Katie didn't want him to let go. It was a miracle he still wanted to hold her, a miracle he still loved her. She was the luckiest woman alive, and she knew it.

She drew back slightly so she could see his face, bathed in moonlight. "I was looking for you on the train."

"I was in the caboose."

"I needed to tell you something."

He touched her bandage. "I could've lost you."

"Listen to me, Ben. I've been so wrong. So selfish."

"No, I should have understood."

This time she covered his mouth with the flat of her hand. "Don't interrupt. Please." She frowned, her head aching. It was so hard to think, so hard to find the right words to say. "I've realized something over the past week. I've looked at everything so idealistically. I've never had to test any of my beliefs. It's all come so easily to me. Even my father's disapproval has been tempered in love."

He kissed the palm of her hand, and she had to fight to ignore the sensations it caused.

"I've never had to risk losing anything, Ben. I've never taken into account any costs. But life is about risks and costs." She moved her hand to his cheek. "I was so busy fighting for freedom for women that I forgot what that freedom meant. I thought the only way to make things happen was to live like someone else."

"Like Susan B. Anthony," he said.

"Yes. Only her life isn't the right one for me. I want my own." She drew a shaky breath. "I want a life with you, Ben. I love you."

Silence seemed to blanket the valley. Crickets and hoot owls hushed. The creek stopped its gurgling. The night breeze quieted. All she could hear was the beating of her heart in tempo with Ben's.

"Katie—"

"No, I'm not finished." Her voice softened. "Let me finish."

He agreed with a nod.

"You've done all the giving in our marriage. I know you'll stand beside me, no matter what." She drew closer to him. "But, Ben, I want to give, too. Remember when you told me marriage was about compromise? I want us to compromise. I want us to find what's best for both of us. I think we can. Don't you?"

His smile was tender, loving. "Yes, I do."

"And, Ben, I want this baby more than anything." She took his right hand and placed it on her belly. "If it's a boy, I want him to grow up like his father. I want him to judge people by who they are on the inside. I want him to have the courage to go after what he wants, no matter how hard it is. I want him to be patient and gentle and stubborn, just like you. I want him to love, to laugh, and to be strong in his own beliefs. And if it's a girl—"she grinned—"I still want her to be just like her father."

"Are you finished?" he asked after a moment's silence.

She shook her head, ignoring the throbbing it caused. "I want you to know how sorry I am. I hope you can forgive me."

He waited a heartbeat. "*Now* are you finished?"

She nodded.

He drew her closer against him, staring down into her eyes. "That's a lot of thinking for a head that took such a hard blow. Now it's my turn. I came out here to tear down this house. It wouldn't mean anything to me without you. I've been stubborn and angry. I wanted you to want what I want."

"I do, Ben. That's what I've been trying to tell you."

"I tried to take away your dreams and ambitions."

She cradled his head between her hands. "I'm going

to withdraw. If the final count shows I've won, I'm going to refuse to continue. Mr. French is a better candidate, and he'll support the amendment. He told me so."

"You don't have to do that, Katie. I'll never make you choose again."

Was it possible to love him more with each passing moment?

Katie blinked away sudden tears. "Papa told me we always have to make choices in life, Ben. And I want to make the right choice this time."

"Ah, Katie," he whispered, brushing her hair back from her face.

She loved the sound of her name when he said it like that. It made her blood run hot and her knees go weak.

He rested his forehead against hers, still holding her gaze. "I think there'll be plenty of time to sort things through, find out what's best for all of us, you, me, and the baby. Right now, there're just two things I want you to do before I take you back to the clinic, where you belong."

Her heart began to hammer in double time.

"First, tell me again that you love me."

She tried to smile, despite the tears she was still fighting. "That's easy. I love you, Benjamin Rafferty. I'll love you the rest of my life and then some." She swallowed the hot lump in her throat. "What's the second thing?"

She could feel the warmth of his breath on her skin. She could smell his wonderfully masculine scent, a hint of sweat and bay rum mixed with smoke and soot. She could see the love in his eyes, blue eyes turned black in the night. And she felt heaven in his arms.

"The second's easy, too," he whispered. "Just kiss me, Katie."

And so she did.

The Homestead Tri-Weekly Herald, *Homestead, Idaho*
Wednesday Morning, November 3, 1926
KATHERINE JONES RAFFERTY WINS
DISTRICT SEAT IN IDAHO
HOUSE OF REPRESENTATIVES;
OPPONENT MATTHEW JACOBS CONCEDES

*The landslide victory of Katherine Jones Rafferty of
Homestead was apparent within hours of the polls closing yesterday. An active leader in the Idaho Chapter,
National Council of Women Voters, and an advocate of
women's rights on state and national levels, Mrs.
Rafferty has pledged to fight for better schools for Idaho's
children; fairer labor laws, particularly in regard to
women; an improved North-South highway to better
handle increased automobile traffic; and support for
Idaho farming and lumber industries.*

*When the State Legislature is not in session in Boise,
Mrs. Rafferty will return to Homestead, where she resides
with her husband, Benjamin Rafferty, owner and editor
of the* Homestead Tri-Weekly Herald, *and their three
children, Anna Kate (9), Lawrence Michael (7), and
Norma Sue (5).*

*Here to help celebrate Mrs. Rafferty's victory are
Justice and Mrs. Geoffrey Rudyard of Washington, D.C.
Mrs. Rudyard, the former Sophia Rafferty, is well-known
as the second woman elected to the U.S. House of
Representatives and is now completing her third and
final term of office. The Rudyards have one son,
Benjamin, three months of age.*

Dear Reader:

Researching the American "woman's suffrage" movement during the early part of this century was a fascinating and enlightening experience. When I was in school, women's history was not a part of the general curriculum. I hope that's no longer true, for it's an important part of our past as a nation and especially so to women.

Attempting to be true to historical dates and events while still writing an entertaining novel can have its challenges. There were so many admirable and interesting individuals who fought for the enfranchisement of all American women during the second decade of the twentieth century, and there were several interrelated organizations that took different roads to the same end. If I have erred in regard to any of these individuals or organizations, I beg the reader's indulgence. The fault is solely my own.

Please note that I have taken creative license in having Katie Jones Rafferty declare her candidacy for the United States House of Representatives. No woman ran for Congress on the Republican ticket in Idaho in 1916 (Burton French won the Republican primary and was then elected to office). However, a woman *was* elected to the U.S. House in 1916: Jeanette Rankin from Montana (Montana was one of the twelve enfranchised states at the time). Also note that my portrayal of Mr. French is entirely from my own imagination.

Robin Lee Hatcher

BIBLIOGRAPHY

American Women's History: An A to Z of People, Organizations, Issues, and Events by Doris Weatherford, Prentice Hall

Born for Liberty, A History of Women in America by Sara M. Evans, The Free Press

Failure Is Impossible, Susan B. Anthony in Her Own Words by Lynn Sherr, Times Books

History of Idaho by Leonard J. Arrington, University of Idaho Press

Jailed for Freedom, American Women Win The Vote by Doris Stevens, NewSage Press

Two Paths to Women's Equality by Janet Zollinger Giele, Twayne Publishers

Let HarperMonogram
Sweep You Away

SECOND CHANCES by Sharon Sala
Romantic Times Award-winning Author
Matt Holt had disappeared out of Billie Jean Walker's life once before, but fate has brought them together again. Now Matt is determined to grab a second chance at love—especially the kind that comes once in lifetime.

FOREVER AND ALWAYS by Donna Grove
Emily Winters must enlist the help of handsome reporter Ross Gallagher to rebuild her father's Pennsylvania printing business after the Civil War. But will working closely with the man she's always loved distract her from her goals?

Special Holiday Trade Paperback

CHRISTMAS ANGELS: THREE HEAVENLY ROMANCES by Debbie Macomber
Over Twelve Million Copies of Macomber's Books in Print
The angelic antics of Shirley, Goodness, and Mercy are featured in this collection that promises plenty of romance and dreams that come true.